ROBBED BLIND

A JACK MCMORROW MYSTERY

Other books by Gerry Boyle

ROBBED BLIND

A JACK MCMORROW MYSTERY

GERRY BOYLE

ISLANDPORT PRESS

ISLANDPORT PRESS

Islandport Press
P.O. Box 10
Yarmouth, Maine 04096
www.islandportpress.com
info@islandportpress.com

First Edition: December 2022
This Printing: May 2023
Printed in the United States of America.

ISBN: 978-1-952143-49-6
Ebook ISBN: 978-1-952143-62-5
Library of Congress Control Number: 2022932039

Dean L. Lunt | Editor-in-Chief, Publisher
Genevieve A. Morgan | Editor
Piper K. Wilber | Assistant Editor
Emily A. Lunt | Book Designer
Trevor Roberson | Cover Designer

For my growing family, with love, and for Vic, as always.

PROLOGUE

He stayed at the back of the aisle, read the labels on the vodka and whiskey, waited while some lady in a giganto puffy jacket handpicked a bunch of scratch tickets.

Like it made jackshit of difference. Loser.

Then he stepped up, coffee in hand, slid a $5 bill under the Plexiglas screen. The cashier girl put the snowmobile lady's bills in the drawer, shifted back, picked the fiver off the counter.

The other cashiers, even if they looked okay from a distance, turned out to be old or ugly or both when he put the gun on them. But this one was different. Dark eye makeup, made him think of the blonde replicant chick in the first Blade Runner. *He felt a stirring just looking at her through the glass necks of the bottles. Her nails were olive green, like the color of an army uniform. Cool piercings. He wondered if there was metal in her tongue. Nice body, like she worked out, but maybe not. Vape in the pocket of her red QuikStop shirt. Maybe just skinny. Cute bordering on hot, even in the dorky store uniform.*

Another worker came from the back room and asked her for something. Cheery guy who sounded African. No surprise; they were taking over the town.

She moved to her right, bent down, allowing him a good look at her butt. Nice. She stood, gave the Black guy one of those clicker things that spits out price tags. The guy walked away, which left just the two of them. He concentrated, waiting for eye contact.

She asked him if he was in the QuikStop Coffee Club. He smiled and shook his head. She caught it peripherally, didn't ask him to join. Just pawed his change out of the drawer. His smile was locked in. Ready. He held out his hand, under the hole in the glass, hoping she'd brush his palm with her fingers when she gave him the bill and coins.

She didn't. Just slapped the change on the counter and pushed it across, ignoring his outstretched hand.

He lowered his hand and picked up the money.

Bitch.

"Have a good night," she said, but she didn't care if he did or didn't, just like the others.

The stirring was replaced by a blank, familiar feeling.

ONE WEEK LATER, 4:15 A.M.

He watched for a ten-count from the parking lot (his max). No customers, no African guy, just the Blade Runner *chick behind the counter.*

He moved quickly, pulling on the zombie mask as he walked in. Stopped to the left of the register and the plastic screen and pulled the gun from inside his jacket, pointed it right at her stupid face.

"All the money. The safe, too."

This was the moment he had waited all week for. The sudden realization of what was about to happen. Now he had her full attention. Nothing like a nine-millimeter in the face to make somebody snap to.

She just shook her head and sighed. Like she'd had a bad night and this was just one more thing.

Surprising. Most started blubbering.

"Now," he said. "Move your ass, bitch."

She did move, but slowly, like little kids do to piss off their parents. Shoved a carton of chewing tobacco out of the way, a bunch of tins.

"Hurry up," he said again, teeth clenched.

"Yessir, Mr. Zombie," she said.

Attitude. This chick was pissing him off.

She keyed the drawer and it slid out. She took out the bills, stacking them neatly in her hand like she was counting the till. Then she shoved the money under the Plexiglas so he had to take two steps to retrieve it.

"Cute," he said. He gestured with the gun. "The safe."

She started in with some bullshit about it being locked until the next shift showed up, and he was fed up. He moved around the counter fast, pressed the gun hard against her temple, the muzzle sinking into the soft skin at the point where her cheekbone met her temple.

"Now," he said.

He was so close he could smell her shampoo, her gum, the vape on her breath.

She looked at him sideways, over the gun barrel, like she wasn't afraid, like he was nothing, even with his gun against her head. Just like that girl in his old homeroom he'd sort of asked out, getting his nerve up for weeks, finally saying in the hallway, maybe she'd like to come to his house, play Warcraft. The same look, her smart-ass answer replaying in his head right there in the store. "Know when I'd want to do that? Like never."

His finger on the trigger started to itch.

He shook the feeling off, remembered the objective. The safe right there, the store's weekend's worth of cash.

What to do with the girl.

Using his other hand and a swift kick behind her knees, he shoved her hard to the floor, forcing her to kneel, and pressed the gun to the back of her neck.

She complied. About time.

"Unlock it," he said, "or I swear to God, I'll blow your fucking bitch-head right off."

A tap at the keypad on the door of the safe. She pulled the door open, took out two plastic zipper cases. Held them out and up, and he snatched them with his free hand.

She stood up, without asking, making him shift the gun from her neck to her forehead. And then she just stood there with a sort of smirky look, like she thought it was some stupid game, and he was stupid, too.

He had to go, had stayed way too long. Didn't she know he could kill her? One squeeze of his finger and she'd be dead, brains on the wall, blood draining out on the floor. Take that, you friggin' slut. He could picture it, just like the movies.

She stared straight at him, and then she let out this long sigh and slouched. Like she was bored. She put one hand on her slim little hip, crossed her legs, and pressed one black boot against the other. Like she knew he thought she was hot. Like she was saying, "You can go now, you dipshit. I'm working the overnight shift in this dumpy store full of crap, and still, I'm so out of your league." Like he'd been dismissed.

Goddamn tease. They all were.

He scowled under the mask, pulled back the gun, and swung it hard. The barrel raked her forehead. She fell backward, knocking the box of tobacco off the counter on the way down. Tins spilled out and rolled away as she writhed, hands on her head, blood flowing through her fingers.

He turned and walked deliberately out the door, facing away from the surveillance camera on the canopy above the gas pumps. As he crossed the parking lot, he stayed in the shadow of the building, his boots crunching in the snow.

Around the corner, he heard a car pulling in.

He quickly pulled the zombie mask off, stuffed it into his jacket pocket. Kept walking.

"Who's the dipshit now?" he said.

1

Lights shone over the parking lot, at 4:45 a.m., the brightest thing for a mile in the darkened downtown, probably visible from space. A single car in the lot, an old Nissan covered with a shift's worth of snow.

I parked, grabbed my notebook and phone off the truck seat. Research questions running through my head, anticipating what Carlisle at the *Times* would want to see in this story I'd been working on. What's it like to be a store clerk on the overnight shift with Zombie out there? Every time the door opens, do you think it's him? Have you thought about what you'd do? Are you afraid? Have you thought of getting a different job? Is your husband/wife/partner worried about you when you're at work? Do you have a gun?

Across the lot and under the gas pumps, past the display of windshield washer fluid, the propane locker. I opened the door, stepped in, and looked left. Nobody at the counter. Looked around for a moment, two. Nothing. Where were the workers? Then a guy coming from out in the back, red QuikStop shirt, moving fast, looking concerned.

"You here?" he called.

African accent.

He passed me, went around the corner of the counter, said "Oh, my God."

I followed.

A woman on her back on the floor. Blood on her face, a dark stain on the neck of her red uniform shirt. The guy had his phone out, said, "We need an ambulance. QuikStop, Porto Street. She's hurt, her face all blood."

The woman groaned and he handed me the phone, and bent to hold her head. The victim was young, blue-streaked hair. Black bloody blotches. I grabbed napkins from the dispenser on the counter, handed the guy a bunch. The woman put a hand up—blue fingerless gloves—and touched her forehead just into her hairline. She winced, the guy kneeling beside her. He dabbed at her face where blood had run into her eyebrows, all around a black stud.

"He hit me," she said. Angry, not afraid.

"You don't talk," the guy said. He took her hand. "Help is coming."

"With his gun," she said. "Asshole. He has the money."

"Just lie back," the guy said.

"He got the safe, too," she said.

"Who?" I said.

"Zombie," she said.

A little before six, still dark. I waited on a bench outside the emergency entrance, an eye on both possible exits. A spitty snow fell as people came and went; a young couple with a crying baby, a guy in a mechanic's jacket, his hand wrapped in a towel. An older woman sobbing as she came out of the ER doors, a young guy holding her up, saying as they passed, "I know, Mom, but he had a good life."

Nobody who looked like they'd been pistol-whipped.

A Clarkston police SUV was parked in the circle, a detective's Malibu close behind it. Another police SUV pulled in, a young cop at the wheel, an older one riding. They slowed, looked at the ER door, and continued along the circle and out. An ambulance rolled up—lights, no siren—and backed up to the ER.

I got up and walked around the corner toward the outpatient entrance, turned back to my bench—and there she was.

The young woman from the store, head bandaged now, uniformed police on both sides of her, a detective just behind. The woman scanned the drive as a white van drove in, eased up to the curb in front of me and stopped. It was a beat-up Dodge Caravan, white with blacked-out windows and rust at the edges of the doors and fenders, as if someone had squeezed it and brown stuff had run out. Music coming from inside, a droning sort of chant. The driver was an older guy wearing a red plaid winter hat, the kind with the flaps that cover your ears.

I glanced back, saw the woman talking to the police. I moved closer, heard her say "No, really—I'll be fine."

The police started for their cars, and the woman came toward me, standing between her and the white van. I waited, smiled as she approached.

With the blood cleaned up, I got a better look. Under the bandage, her hair was cropped short, and streaked with an iridescent blue. She was twenty, maybe, and her face and build were narrow. High cheekbones and a pointed, upturned nose. I held the smile as she looked past me at the van. When she was ten feet away, I slipped the notebook from my back pocket.

"Hey," I said.

She slowed.

"Jack McMorrow. I'm a reporter. *New York Times.* I was at the store. Talk to you for a minute?"

She stopped, glanced beyond me at the van. I could hear the motor idling, the music playing. The police pulled out, eyed the van as they passed, and were gone.

"Can I smoke here?" she said.

"I have no idea," I said.

"Screw it," she said. "What are they gonna do? Arrest me?"

She took a vape from the pocket of her jeans, raised it to her lips, and inhaled. Held it for a few seconds, then exhaled a cloud of fruit-smelling steam that wafted into the cold air and floated away. She took a couple of more deep draws, puffed like she was sending smoke signals.

Her face was cleaned up. There was a bar through her right eyebrow with black beads at each end, a black stud in her nostril, another below her lower lip. Her dark eyes were etched all around with a band of black mascara.

"Are you okay?" I said.

"Nine stitches and a wicked headache. Cops said it could have been worse. I mean, like, no shit. Thanks for pointing out the obvious, right?"

I smiled. Took a pen from my pocket and said, "So, would you mind telling me what happened?"

Another cloud of fruity mist. A shrug like it was no big deal—at least, the retelling.

She was standing behind the counter, unpacking tins of Skoal, she said. When she looked up, he was right there, the Zombie robber, his gun pointed at her face.

"It was weird. For a second I see the mask and I think COVID. We still get some masked people. But they don't have guns."

"What did he say?"

"He goes, 'Give me all the fucking money or I swear to God I'll kill you.' "

"So what did you do?"

"I kinda froze. I was looking at the gun."

"What did it look like?"

"Like a Glock or something."

"Do you know a lot about guns?"

"No. Maybe it was just what I'd guess a Glock looks like. Black and sort of square."

"Who else was in the store? Just the guy I saw?"

"Just me and Mo. But he was in the bathroom. He has IBS."

I looked up from my notebook.

"Irritable bowel syndrome," she said. "Sorry. TMI."

"It's okay," I said. "So, did you say anything?"

"Yeah. I gave him the money from the register, but I told him I couldn't open the safe. I said I'd just signed out and the next shift manager had to open it. And she wasn't in yet."

"Was that true?"

"No," she said.

"Why did you say it?"

"I didn't want to give him all the money."

"Why not?"

"I don't know. Me and Mo had worked all night. It was wicked busy, from, like, eleven to two. A couple of drunks gave Mo a hard time, go back to your own country, all this shit. I told them I was calling the cops and they gave me a bunch of crap, too. After all that it just didn't seem fair that this asshole could just walk in and take, like, twice as much we make in a week."

She looked across the parking lot, her face illuminated in yellow light.

"I see. What did he say then?"

"He started screaming at me—'I could kill you, bitch.' There's no mouth hole in the mask but I could see his lips and his teeth through the fabric. It was kind of meshy. All wet there from his spit. Very angry."

"So then—"

"I gave him the money."

"So when did he hit you?"

"After that. I thought we were done, he was gonna run out the door, you know? And he just reached back and smacked me with the gun."

"Huh," I said. "But he had the money. You weren't resisting."

She shook her head.

"No. I mean, it makes no sense, except that he was really pissed off."

"At you."

"At me. At the world, maybe."

"Were you worried that he might shoot you, after he got the money?"

"Not really. I mean, he might've shot me. But mostly I was worried that Mo would come out of the bathroom and just walk right into it. Mo's Somali. He's got, like, five kids, works two jobs. Really great guy. If he'd've shot Mo, that would have totally sucked."

"Yes," I said. "It would have."

We stood there on the pavement. Another ambulance arrived and another left. I scrawled the last of her comments in my notebook and then looked up at her.

"One last thing," I said. "I didn't get your name."

"Sparrow," she said.

"Like the bird."

"Right."

"Were your parents into birds?"

"No, it was just because I was small. I was premature."

"Huh," I said. "Last name?"

"Will this go online?"

"If you don't mind."

She looked at my notebook.

"What paper did you say?"

"*New York Times.*"

I slipped a card from my pocket and handed it to her. She looked at it.

"It just says 'Jack McMorrow.' "

"I'm a freelancer. I work for other places, but this story is for the *Times.*"

She turned the card over, then back.

"Looks like something old guys use to try to pick up girls," Sparrow said.

"No," I said. "Just stories."

She examined the card for a moment more and then stared hard at me, like she was daring me to lie to her face. "You're legit, right? Not some friggin' weirdo creeper?"

"You can google me. I have a *Times* ID I can dig out if you want to see it. It's old, so I look a lot younger." I smiled.

She eyed me for a moment more.

"Okay. Sparrow Aldo. A-L-D-O. Like 'Where's Waldo?' without the W."

I wrote that down, said, "Could I have your number? In case I need to clarify anything?"

She hesitated, then recited the number, which I wrote down, too. I nodded toward the van.

"Your dad?"

"My dad doesn't drive," she said. "Raymond's a friend of mine."

She moved to the van and stood on the curb, one hand on the door handle. The same Clarkston PD SUV rolled up. It stopped in the middle of the drive and the spotlights came on.

"They don't want you talking?" I said.

"Nah," Sparrow said. "That's just Blake. He looks out for me, too. Him and Ray. On the street they call him Shooter."

I made the connection.

"The fatal shooting in Portland. The kid with the paintball gun."

"Right."

"Huh," I said, the story coming back. Kid with a gun, but it wasn't real. Shooting ruled as justified, but a lot of protests and marching. So this was where that young cop had landed.

She opened the door. The music blared. Gregorian chants, like the truck was some sort of rolling chapel.

"One more question, Sparrow," I said.

"Yeah?"

"Do you feel lucky to be alive?"

She looked away. When she turned back, her eyes were moist. A crack in the tough facade.

"Sometimes. Other times I don't give a shit either way."

2

The van drove off.

I started walking toward my truck, away from the SUV. I was in the parking lot when a siren whooped and I stopped and turned, squinted into the spotlight glare. The SUV reversed toward me, slid to a stop in the snow. The cop in the passenger seat got out, then his partner a split second behind him.

I shoved my notebook in my pocket, looked at the first cop—gloves, watch cap, a hard face for his age.

"Hands," he said. "Where we can see 'em."

"I'm a reporter," I said. "Covering the robberies."

"Just do it, sir," he said.

I slid my hands out of my jacket pockets, slowly. Raised them up in front of me. The other cop—older, heavier, red-cheeked and silver at the temples—circled behind. He clamped a hard hand onto my left shoulder, patted me down—chest, waist, inner thighs, tops of my boots. I felt him nod.

The young cop relaxed.

"ID," he said.

"Left front jacket pocket."

The cop behind me came around, reached in, and pulled out my wallet. He flipped through it, pulled out some cards.

"*New York Times*," he said. "What the hell are you doing here?"

"Working," I said. "I was at the store."

"When the Somali guy found her," the older cop said. Like the worker's African heritage was somehow pertinent.

"Right," I said. "But he could have been Scottish. Would have found her just the same."

The young cop stepped closer. His partner moved in front of me, to the left, handed the wallet over for further inspection.

"You're—" the young cop said as he started to open the wallet.

"McMorrow. I'm a reporter."

His eyes narrowed, the warning bell ringing.

"There's no story here, bub," the older cop said. "So shove off."

I shrugged.

"I don't know about that. Five armed robberies in nine days. All the store clerks are women. Robber in a zombie mask, which means he wants notoriety, make a name for himself. Likes giving the police the finger. This time he pistol-whips the clerk even though she's already given him the money. Appears that he's escalating, right? A violent dangerous criminal, and the whole state is asking why he hasn't been caught."

A beat.

"I think there might be a story here, Officer."

He moved in fast, hand on his taser, in my face. "Don't get snarky with me, asshole. Be the last thing you do today standing up."

"Then there would definitely be a story"—I looked at his name plate—"Officer Salley."

He leaned closer. I could smell his coffee breath, see where he'd missed a spot shaving, under his left nostril. "You want to go downtown and talk about this? 'Cause you're about this far from —"

"Sal," the younger cop said.

Their radios spat something, numbers and call signs. They listened, turned away, Salley saying, "Three-nine en route."

"Stay out of our way," Salley called over his shoulder as he hurried to the car.

The young cop stayed back, handed me my wallet, said, "I've read some of your stories."

I glanced at his name plate. BRANDON BLAKE. "I've read a couple of stories about you."

"I'm just one of many on this one," he said.

I slipped my license and *Times* ID back in their slot, tucked my wallet back in my pocket.

"The girl Sparrow said you look out for her," I said.

"Nothing we don't do for a lot of people."

"Still good of you."

Another beat.

"You ever ride solo, or always with your partner?"

"We mix it up. Trying to cover more ground these days."

"Then how 'bout a ride-along? Story has to include the search for the Zombie robber from a patrol-car view. I think you'd be good."

"Nah. Me and the press . . ." He took another step back.

"I've heard about you—that you go pretty rogue."

"I like to think I'm just thorough."

Blake glanced back at the cruiser. Salley was on his phone.

"Lieutenant Pushard. She handles media."

I took out my phone. Looked at him. After a moment, he recited the number, then waited, feet spread in the at-ease position, black boots against the snow.

I got the dispatcher, asked for the lieutenant. He said he'd take a message. I said, "They'll want to know the *New York Times* is in town." He said, "Hold on."

I waited, maybe ten seconds. The phone clicked and rang again.

"Lieutenant Pushard."

A woman's voice. All business.

"Jack McMorrow."

"Huh. Right."

I told her what I wanted, the hunt for the Zombie robber from the POV of the cruiser, ride-along with Officer Blake.

Another pause, this one longer.

"I met him at the hospital."

Silence, Pushard thinking.

"I'll have to talk to Blake, see if he's on board."

"He's right here."

I handed Blake my phone. He said, "Yup . . . right." Listened, probably to his marching orders. This is the *New York Times*, so make the department look good. Don't screw this up.

Blake said "Got it," handed the phone back over.

"Okay," she said to me, "but we don't want anything in there that this perpetrator can use to his advantage."

"Of course."

"And it would be good for you to have the department's perspective from a higher level. So we'll need to talk."

"Right," I said.

I thanked her and said good-bye, rang off.

"It's a go," I said.

"Keep your friends close and your enemies closer," Blake said.

"Michael Corleone."

"Machiavelli, actually," Blake said. "Six a.m. tomorrow. The department, back entrance."

As he turned and started for the cruiser, a question was already forming in my head.

After one fatal shooting, are you ready to do it again, Officer Blake? Point your gun at Zombie and pull the trigger?

I'd pitched it this way to Carlisle at the *Times*—a beleaguered Maine mill town under siege, police frustrated, store employees, especially women, fearful and tense, some people wanting Zombie shot, others rooting for him as he robbed convenience store chains that were, in their view, ripping people off anyway.

The pitch got me one more contract—no small thing, since I didn't do multimedia. Ten years ago, my calls to editors were returned in hours. Now it was days. Sometimes never. One magazine editor had asked me if my stories were data-driven. I said no, they were driven by the human experience.

Which was how the Zombie robbery story already was playing out.

I was parked in the street back at the store, watching a kid do a TV report from the scene. He'd set up a tripod with a phone, was standing in front of it. A selfie from the front lines.

Sitting in the truck, I jotted it down: the world of overnight shifts, where people work for minimum wage in stores open all night. Beaming neon light into the darkness, attracting a whole group of people that move in the shadows, emerging to hunt and scavenge, scrounge a meal, use the bathroom, get a warm drink if they have the coin. Sometimes, with the snow spattering the windows, a clerk offers a free coffee. After all, in the early-morning hours, they are all creatures of the night.

I looked up as the van passed.

Raymond was at the wheel, no sign of Sparrow. He slowed as he drove past the store, which was closed, police tape stretched from the gas pumps to the side of the building. Raymond continued on. I pulled out, did a U-turn and followed.

He drove out Porto Street, the main drag heading north. We passed a few drab houses, some dark, some with lights on. Businesses had sprung up on the street and they clung like stubborn weeds: a bottle-redemption place, a tire shop, a discount supermarket, a Dunkin' where cops were parked.

Raymond took a left and I followed. He was driving slowly, taillights flickering when the van hit a bump. I hung back as we passed small ranch houses, an occasional double-wide squeezed onto a treeless lot. It was a well-kept neighborhood, the kind where people were proud to have a house, had worked hard in the mill way back when to pay for the place. There was a tow-behind camper in one driveway, a small boat on a trailer in the next. Kids grown, a little money for modest toys, beer on the table, dinner on Friday at Applebee's.

In this block of Clarkston, Maine, life was okay. And okay was all you could ask for.

Raymond took a right at the end of the street, then another right on the third side street, then pulled into the driveway halfway up the block. I pulled to the curb.

It was a low-slung bungalow, the entrance on the driveway side. There was torn plastic sheeting tacked across the front in a failed attempt at insulation. Trash barrels and cartons barricaded some sort of cellar entrance. The driveway hadn't been cleared and the van skittered and hopped along two wheel ruts in the snow before Raymond parked somewhere beyond a porch wrapped in broken lattice.

There were lights showing but only dimly, the windows throwing an orange cast onto the snow. I backed up, followed the driveway. The van was parked there, out of sight of the street. I left the motor running as I looked around.

The porch was filled with junk: pallets, plywood, plastic crates, folding tables, a stack of ratty firewood, like twenty years ago somebody had cut up a tree that had blown down in the yard. There was a door behind the piles of stuff, a narrow path to it. Lights were on inside, showing the same dim orange glow.

I turned the motor off, grabbed my notebook, walked up to the door. There was a rusty metal plaque that said THE JANDREAU'S in script.

I knocked.

Waited.

Listened.

Heard the chants again. Monks. Latin, muffled. Then the clomp of approaching boots. The door opened.

Raymond, older up close, maybe mid-sixties but still baby-faced, smallish deep-set eyes and a russet tinge to his chubby cheeks. His parka was medium blue, clashing with the red plaid of the hat. The earflaps stuck straight out like wings.

"Hi there," I said. "Jack McMorrow, the reporter who was talking to Sparrow."

"I know," Raymond said. Like he'd been expecting me.

The chanting continued.

"Sorry to barge in, but could I talk to you for a minute?"

He stepped out and shut the door behind him. The monks were more muffled still.

"Gregorian chants," I said.

Raymond brightened.

"Are you Catholic?" he said.

"Born and raised."

"How old are you?"

"Forty-two."

"Then you missed out on the real church."

I waited.

"Your whole life," he said. "After Vatican Two. No Latin, Pope John turned the solemn Mass into a hootenanny. Guitars and tambourines, everybody in a circle. Two thousand years. Gone."

I smiled.

"We had a monsignor in New York City when I was a kid," I said. "St. Jean Baptiste Church on Seventy-Sixth Street. He did Latin Mass every Sunday, seven a.m."

"*Dominus vobiscum,*" Raymond said, in this chanting sort of voice.

It came back to me, stored in some dusty part of my brain. "*In nomine Patris, et Filii, et Spiritus Sancti,*" I said. He beamed. I knew the secret handshake.

"I was an altar boy, carried my bag up Third Avenue. My cassock, the white thing that went over it, the—"

"Surplice."

"Right."

"I can still smell the incense," I said.

"Did you do the censer? Father Paul—this was at St. Ann's—he always picked me. You'd swing it, three touches to the chain. Chink, chink, chink. The puff of smoke. After Mass, we put the ashes down a special grate in the parking lot. It was consecrated. St. Ann's is closed now, but I still go."

"To a closed church?"

"I used to help out. I saved a key."

I pictured him, kneeling alone in the gloom.

"I'd love to see it," I said.

He gave me a closer look.

"I don't know. Do you still go to Mass?"

"St. Francis of Assisi," I said. "In Belfast." I'd only been there once, for a story about a ninety-year-old nun on a hunger strike protesting the war in Iraq. A white lie. I'd tell it in Confession.

Raymond shifted his weight. The floorboards creaked in the cold.

"He kissed the leper's cheek."

I delved into my past.

"And gave sermons to birds," I said.

"Yes. Francis saw God in all of creation."

"Even rocks."

A pause, and then he said, "Do they do the Latin there?"

I had no idea.

"I think it's on Saturdays," I said.

"Some Catholics are keeping the true church alive."

"There's a name for it, right?"

"Traditionalist Catholics, some people say. Real Catholics, I say. You know what Pope Leo said."

I didn't.

"Christians are born for combat."

My mind went to Mel Gibson. A fringe group in Kansas or Missouri or someplace that elected its own pope. It was in the *Times*.

"Are you part of that militant thing?" I said.

"I don't believe in violence. During his time with us, Jesus was totally against it. I just collect statues and other sacred items. Some of them go to home chapels, where Catholics gather to pray in Latin. I suppose some of them are what you'd call militant."

"Really. How do they find you, Raymond?"

"We tend to find each other, people who know the Vatican can't stamp out the true miracle of the Mass. I mean, some people say Satan took over Pope John's soul for that time."

Sounds unlikely, I thought.

"You think Satan could really do that, with a Pope?"

"Sure. Just like he does with molester priests. When you get weak, Satan senses an opening. Holy people are more at risk, because they're a greater conquest. That's why a lot of us think Pope John can't teach until he recants. Some of us think all the popes since him are fake, too. I mean, how could you give up the Latin?" he said. "Turn the host and wine into the flesh and blood of our Lord Jesus Christ and then, 'Hey, time for the tambourines!' "

He was out of breath. I waited. He looked at me for a moment, and then his lips started to move, but silently. He was praying. And then he stopped, said, "The Lord sent you. I'll be right out."

There was a word for it. I stood on the porch, searched on my phone. Sedevacantists. Conservative Catholics who think the Pope's seat has been vacant since Vatican II.

Footsteps. I put the phone in my pocket, took a step back.

Raymond opened the door and I moved to my right to peek inside—and saw, literally, Jesus.

He was hanging on a cross, six feet high. There was red-painted blood coming from the spikes in his hands and feet and more on his forehead under the crown of thorns. Smaller statues—Mary, and Jesus, in various shapes and sizes—were lined up along the wall like it was the Catacombs. I felt a claustrophobic chill, then a wave of déjà vu.

Me in the church, eight years old, staring up at the statues with a combination of fascination and terror. Their expressions, frozen in pain or sadness. For the row of Marys in the hallway, it was an odd wistfulness, like they were wondering how they'd ended up here.

Raymond was surrounded by the characters of his faith.

He glanced back.

"That Jesus on the Cross," he said. "The artist was Polish, 1860s. He did an amazing job. You know, the thorns are so sharp that if you touch them, you can draw blood?"

I looked at Jesus, the rivulets of blood running down his temples. Saw Sparrow on the floor, blood running down her forehead, too.

"Do you hope they catch whoever it was that hurt Sparrow?" I said.

"Oh, there will be a judgment of the unrighteous," Raymond said.

"When?"

"When God says the time is right."

"Some of us can't wait that long, Raymond. Show me your church."

The former St. Ann's was a block down, a sign out front for a Portland commercial real estate outfit that said PRIME INVESTMENT OPPORTUNITY!! The church was tan brick, its stained-glass windows dark and dirty, the steps covered with snow. There was a real estate lockbox on the front doors, which made it look like the parish had been closed by some official edict.

Raymond parked the van in front of a nail salon, and I pulled in behind him.

We walked past the church and into the parking lot for a dentist's office. Raymond led the way to the back of the lot, then crossed to a metal gate in a steel fence that marked the boundary of the church property. There were footprints—presumably his—and he followed them through the gate and up a short set of steps to a side door. He pulled a set of keys from his parka, fitted them in the lock. Then he pulled the door open and led the way inside.

He took off his hat. There was the smell of mildew, the feel of damp carpet underfoot.

We walked along a wall and out into the darkened church, Raymond navigating the darkness like a blind person at home. Halfway across the sanctuary, he turned right and led the way to the second pew from the front. He sidled in, blessed himself, and knelt. I did the same.

Raymond lowered his forehead to his hands. I looked around, my eyes adjusting to the half-light. The colors of the stained glass barely showed, like a flickering candle. The altar was covered by a blue tarp. There were blank spaces in the walls where statues had been. The pew was dirty, the kneeler covered in grit. When I knelt, I felt something under my feet. I looked down to see a dead pigeon, kicked it aside.

Raising his head, Raymond said, "It's still a sacred place."

"For sure," I said.

He stayed kneeling, hands folded in front of him, stared at what had been the altar. There was the faint noise of traffic, a truck downshifting. We knelt for five minutes, Raymond lost in prayer, me waiting. He looked up beatifically at the shrouded altar, blessed himself again, sat back on the pew. I did the same.

"How often do you pray here?" I whispered.

"Three times a week," Raymond said, whispering back. "And holy days of obligation."

"Do you go to a church that's actually open?"

"Sunday. The Basilica, for Communion. The Latin Mass, six a.m."

"Huh."

"This was my pew when I was a kid, if I wasn't serving."

"With your parents?"

"No. They slept late on Sundays because Saturday night was a big drinking time, which is why I don't drink. I came to church by myself. They were glad to get rid of me."

We stared straight ahead. There was a flutter somewhere in the darkness above us, a faint patter of something dropping from the ceiling.

"How do you know Sparrow, Raymond?"

"The store. We get out of work at the same time. She doesn't have a car, so I give her a ride. She brings me a coffee."

I looked at him for a hint of lecher, maybe an old-man infatuation. Didn't see it.

"What do you do for work?"

"At night? I stock shelves. Walmart."

"What, like ten to six?"

"Six-thirty. We get a dinner break at two a.m."

A picture began to form. Stacking stuff all night under the garish box-store light. Surrounded by statues all day, the monks droning on. Pricking his finger to share blood with Jesus. Maybe reading militant Catholic stuff.

How did this young woman fit into his life, with her piercings and blue hair?

"Think Sparrow will be okay? Sometimes people hold up in the moment. It's afterward that they collapse."

Raymond shook his head.

"She can't let herself."

"Why not?" I said.

"Her father. He's really sick."

"She takes care of him?"

"Yeah. It's just the two of them. Her mother's dead. Dad's name is Riff. His liver's shot."

"Riff?"

"He played guitar. In rock bands," Raymond said. He whispered like the music stuff wasn't appropriate for a church. "Her mom was a singer. Sparrow showed me on her phone. YouTube."

"He can't work," I said.

"No," Raymond said. "He gets a check."

I understood. Sparrow had no choice but to go back to the QuikStop after having been robbed and smacked with a gun. She was supporting her dad.

"Back to work like nothing happened?" I said.

"That's what she said. She told me she gets a bonus for being robbed. Fifty dollars, if she doesn't quit, or call in sick."

"Which she doesn't plan to do."

"She won't. She's tough. I mean, she only sleeps for a few hours in the afternoon. In the morning, after work, she gets Riff ready for the day. Makes sure he has his meds. A good breakfast."

We sat. The church was cold, a numbing chill that seeped through everything. My foot hit the dead pigeon again. It was frozen.

I asked where Sparrow lived, sticking to my reporter's mantra: One source must lead to another.

Raymond hesitated, then told me. First floor of a triple decker on a street off Fatima, one of the main drags north of downtown. Next to a tavern called the Red Hen.

He slid forward and knelt. More praying. I said I had to go, would find my way out.

"Nice of you to help her," I said.

Raymond shrugged. There was a drip on the end of his nose. He wiped it with the back of his hand.

"What Jesus would do," I said.

"If Jesus had a car," Raymond said, and he folded his hands in front of him and closed his eyes.

3

The Red Hen was a low-slung cinder-block building with an awning over the door and an ice-blue Bud Light sign glowing in the front window. I turned right, passed the empty parking lot, rolled slowly by Sparrow's apartment house.

It was a tenement, brown with peeling beige trim, a small gable-roofed porch at the front door, three mailboxes on the wall facing the driveway. There was a folding chair on the porch. A light was on in the front room on the first floor, the shades down.

I drove to the end of the block, turned around. On the second pass I looked up the driveway. A sagging garage, an old box truck, paint bleached out and the right rear tire flat.

As I passed, another light came on, a couple of windows toward the rear. I pictured the routine Raymond described: Sparrow coming home, Riff getting up. Sparrow making him breakfast, making sure he'd taken his meds, chatting a bit, doing the dishes and laundry, then heading to her room. Sitting on the bed, texting her friends. "You're not gonna believe what happened. I'm just working, you know, behind the counter and I look up and . . ."

Instead, the front door opened, and Sparrow stepped out.

She was wearing the same parka, the hood up, bandage showing. Closing the door behind her, she stepped over to the chair, brushed snow off the seat, and sat. I drove on, pulled into the tavern parking lot, parked and looked back. She was sitting in the chair, a cloud of steam around her head. As I watched, she raised the vape to her mouth.

I turned the truck, circled back, and pulled up. Buzzed the passenger window down and turned the scanner up. It hissed and scratched. I got out and Sparrow looked at me, kept vaping. I walked to the bottom of the steps and stopped. She was holding her phone, wearing the blue fingerless gloves.

"Hey, Sparrow. Raymond told me where I could find you," I said. "May I come up?"

She blew out a billow of steam, said, "Suit yourself."

I climbed the steps and stood by the railing, which looked rickety.

"I saw Raymond driving back by the store. After he dropped you off, I guess. We talked."

Sparrow took another puff, blew it out and said, "Raymond's a good shit."

"Yeah. Told me about his religion stuff. We were both altar boys. Compared notes on incense."

"Ha. He must've loved that. He's trying to save me. I tell him it's too late."

She smoked under the hood, the bandage and piercings making her look like a pirate. For a moment I could picture Sparrow the little girl. Putting her parka on, her mittens, her mom telling her to stay in the yard.

"How you feeling?"

She shrugged.

"Headache. May have a scar, but it'll be under my hair."

"You could shave your head and really own it," I said.

"Did that when I was fourteen. First anniversary of my mom dying."

"I'm sorry."

"A fentanyl casualty when there was, like, this wave of them. Way too strong a dose, junkies dropping like flies. At least my dad's more of an alcoholic. You kill yourself slowly, but in the meantime, you're around."

There was a pause in the conversation, both of us looking out at the street, the dirty snowbanks.

I glanced over at the truck, the back door covered with stickers: RIFF CALDERONE BAND . . . THE MIGHTY MIGHTY BOSSTONES . . . I BRAKE FOR WILLIE.

"I feel like maybe my story is changing a little," I said.

She tucked her phone up her sleeve, turned her vape in her hands. It was metallic blue like her hair.

"At first it was going to be about a city living in fear."

"Terrorized by the Zombie robber?" Sparrow said. "I've got other crap to deal with."

"Raymond told me. I mean, a little of it. Your dad being sick. Just the two of you."

Sparrow's eyes narrowed. She raised the pen, inhaled and blew off the steam, looked away.

"So what if he'd pulled the trigger?"

"You mean, who'd look out for Riff?"

"Is that his real name?"

"Yeah. He had it legally changed."

"One name? Like Madonna?"

"No. Riff Calderone. Except that's made up, too. He thought it sounded like Johnny Ramone."

"Right. And that wasn't his name, either," I said. "It was John Cummings."

Sparrow looked at me.

"I'm from New York City. What was his name before?"

"Ronald Hunsler. He always hated Ronald."

"Huh. But you're Sparrow Aldo?"

"My mom's name."

I paused.

"I should go. I can hear him walking around. Riff really needs his coffee first thing. Gotta have him caffeinated when I tell him about this."

She tapped the bandage as she stood to go, without answering my question. Who would take care of Riff if she died?

"I'd like to meet him. If you think that would be okay."

"You kidding? Riff and the *New York Times?* Better block out some time. And hire a few more fact-checkers."

She turned to the door, then stopped.

"So what did your story turn into?"

I slipped my notebook into my pocket.

"The world of the city at night as this is going on. People looking out for each other. Like Raymond picking you up at the hospital, you not wanting your co-worker to come out of the bathroom during the robbery."

"So, a feel-good robbery story?"

"Something like that."

Sparrow looked pensive.

"You don't like it," I said. "Hey, that's fine. You're the one who got smashed in the head."

"It's fine. It's, like, 'Hey, Zombie, eff you.' I gotta say, he's a scary dude. 'Cause I don't think it's about him taking the cash and going to get cranked. He's seriously pissed off, in general. I could tell when he was talking to me, the gun out, almost like he didn't care about the money. Just wanted to get some kind of revenge."

She pushed the door open and music spilled from inside the apartment, pounding guitar chords behind someone singing like Elvis. Sparrow turned to me.

"And you could tell this by —"

"The zombie mask had eye holes, and his eyes were full of hate. I mean, I don't think I even know this person, and it was like he hated my freakin' guts."

I sat in the truck, went over my notes, underlining, circling, pondering this person who had become the central character in my story. Thought of a possible lead, the rest of the story coming together in my head:

A pistol-whipping didn't scare Sparrow Aldo.
Aldo is 20 with a bunch of onyx piercings and a streak
of blue in her hair. She works the overnight shift at the

QuikStop, a convenience store in Clarkston, Maine, a brick-walled mill town on the Androscoggin River. On Thursday, a person wearing a zombie mask stuck a handgun in her face and demanded money. It was her first armed robbery. It was the robber's ninth in two months. Aldo gave him the money. Then Zombie, as he's known here, split her head open with the barrel of his gun.

Sparrow Aldo likes the idea of this story, though—how the robber is actually making the community of cops and clerks and night-shift shelf stockers closer. "It's like, 'Hey, Zombie, eff you,' " she said.

I sat back, looked up at the house, and saw a man cross in front of the window to the left of the porch. Stooped. Long hair. A halting gate that suggested he was using a cane. Riff paying the price for sex, drugs, and rock and roll, but the bigger price was being paid by his daughter.

It was 8:15 a.m., the sky dirty gray to the east, strip-mall lights dimming in the morning light.

I put my notebook down on the seat, drove to the end of the block, and turned around. When I passed the house again I slowed, but couldn't see anyone. They were probably in the kitchen, Sparrow making coffee.

I headed back into the center of the city, past closed storefronts, tenements with a few lights showing, an old woman in a purple parka, draped over a porch railing with a cigarette in her hand.

Clarkston had been a mill city, French-Canadian immigrants leaving their farms in Quebec to take jobs at sprawling brick mills filled with a maelstrom of clacking, whirring looms that churned out endless miles of cloth. A clock in the mill tower told the whole city the time, whether you were early or late. And then one by one the mills closed, work shifting to the south, then overseas. The mills went silent as tombs and despite efforts to use them as office space, storage, industrial-hip homes for start-ups, the city still felt abandoned, disused, a massive brick ruin.

Now we sell each other stuff from the Dollar Store. Work in hospitals and nursing homes to keep the old-timers going a little longer. Patronize the local weed shops, make another night in front of the TV seem not so bad. Look with suspicion at the Somali immigrants.

I drove down Porto Street, could see why Zombie had passed on the weed stores. Too much security, too much risk. I drove past a couple of Somali convenience stores, wondered why they hadn't been targeted. Maybe they closed too early. Maybe they didn't generate enough cash, selling hijabs and phone cards and halal meat. Maybe the robber was Somali and wouldn't prey on his own people. Or maybe he was white? Did he wear gloves? If Sparrow could see his eyes, could she see the lids?

For our next conversation . . .

I drove into the downtown, mostly dark, the drinkers crashed, addicts sleeping it off, workers still getting ready for the day. The courthouse and law offices were closed but soon would be getting to the business of making some sort of order out of the chaos. Consequences for breaking the rules. Rules applied to the consequences. Who's next on the docket?

There was a police SUV idling by the library, another coming up behind me. The robbery task force at work, waiting for Zombie to strike again. The public clamoring for an arrest; police infuriated that the twerp was getting away with it. I needed Zombie to keep it up until my story was done and published.

"City Relieved by Robber's Arrest" wasn't going to cut it.

I swung east and saw the steeple of the Basilica, the massive stone church where Raymond got his Latin fix. Was that enough? Did he hang out with other ultra-orthodox Catholics? I'd read somewhere that some of them were preparing for war with Rome. Raymond didn't seem like a warmonger, but maybe it wasn't something he wore on his sleeve. I drove on.

The road east passed houses with yards, restaurants offering Thai, Mexican, Chinese. Used-car lots and car washes, gun shops and bottle redemptions. And then city gave way to tired country: overgrown pastures, groves of sumac and poplar, dead-end subdivisions sliced out of the undergrowth.

The fastest route home to Waldo County was to hop on the turnpike, jump off at Augusta, and continue northeast. I took the slow way:

Sabattus, Wales, a crossroads that someone had named Purgatory. The winters there must have been long.

I drove east—Litchfield, West Gardiner—over frozen streams with muskrat houses showing like snow-covered tents. I jumped on the interstate, continued all the way to the Kennebec River, followed it north. It was mostly frozen, too, dark streaks where the current ran over shallows and left open water. Through Hallowell, antique buildings stuffed with antique stuff that nobody wanted. Past the State House, the gold dome putting a patina on the rough-and-tumble that went on inside. Over the river, took my usual look at the old psych hospital, twenty-first-century offices covering up nineteenth-century horrors.

The outskirts of the city were punctuated by pastures marked with fading signs advertising subdivisions that would never happen. Barns bulldozed by neglect, double-wides rolled in next to houses that were collapsing in the slowest of motion.

And then it was the hills of Waldo County, stubbly woods ringing snow-flattened fields. I drove north mostly alone, slowed to look at Lake St. George, ice-fishing shacks lined up like Bedouin tents on a snow-white desert. At Liberty, I turned north, the black-strip road weaving between hilltops. This was the way into my sleepy hollow, and I felt myself ease into the calm that this last stretch always brought on.

A right past shadow-dappled Frye Mountain, onto a single lane through woods and pastures, past the occasional empty metal chicken barn, farmers storing junk since the chickens had gone the way of the Clarkston Mills.

And then I was in Prosperity, winding my way to the Dump Road, where old-timers were getting older and homesteaders were digging in. And then there was us.

Clair's big Ford pickup was parked by his barn. Roxanne's car was in the driveway. Snowshoes were propped against the shed. Somebody had been out and now they were back. I parked, gathered up notebooks and pens, a cardboard cup of now-cold tea. Went inside, kicking the snow off my boots on the way, scraping them on the mat.

The kitchen was warm, the fire going. Roxanne was at the counter, sleeves of her sweatshirt rolled up as she mixed bread dough with a wooden spoon.

"Hey," she said.

"You were out?"

"Yeah. Saw two white rabbits."

"Snowshoe hares for a snowshoer," I said. I leaned in, gave her a kiss. "Nothing sexier than an outdoorswoman."

Roxanne smiled, leaned back. "Should I start wearing down underwear?"

"As long as it doesn't have too many buttons. Where's Sophie?"

"Upstairs. Tara's here."

"Did they tend to the pony?"

"Yes. Said Pokey was all good, then they retreated to their girls' cave."

"What are they up to?"

"Being twelve going on sixteen. I tried to get them outside but they resisted mightily."

"Their loss, missing the hares in their winter coats."

"Tara can find pictures on her phone," Roxanne said.

"Ah. That debate still going?"

Roxanne stirred the dough. She was strong and muscles showed on her forearms.

"Oh, yeah. I think we should maybe do it. I mean, we don't want her to be the only non-Amish teenager in town who doesn't have a phone."

"It seems like Pandora's box. A portal to misery, this place where everything's fake and shallow and meaningless."

"She's going out into the world, Jack. You can't stop it."

She scraped the dough into a bread pan.

"How was your morning?"

"Productive," I said. "Good stuff."

I went through it. The robbery, seeing Sparrow bloody on the floor, Sparrow at the hospital, her supporting her father. Raymond and the thorns, the empty church. Blake the shooter.

"You were there? Right after this armed robber?" Roxanne said. "Jesus, Jack."

"He was long gone."

"Yeah, but what if you'd walked in on it? My god, you could have—"

"I'm fine," I said.

"Still."

I shrugged. Roxanne shook her head.

"It was great. Absolutely real. And this clerk woman, she's tough as nails."

"On the outside, maybe," Roxanne said. "Emotional scarring can hide some serious trauma, keep someone from really healing."

There was the shudder of a door opening upstairs, the thumping of the girls coming down. They were in shorts and tank tops, Tara—six inches taller, twenty pounds heavier—squeezing out of Sophie's clothes.

"What are you—" Roxanne said.

"We need snowshoes," Sophie said, as they ran by. "Yo, Dad."

And then they were in the shed, then back, carrying snowshoes.

"TikTok," Sophie said.

"So what is this supposed to—?" I said.

"We're gonna do a snowshoe dance," Sophie said.

"And it goes online?" I said.

"Miranda and Carla in our class did a snow angel dance," Sophie said.

"Like, eleven thousand likes," Tara said. "They did it in their bathing suits."

"No way," I said.

"Relax, Dad. We're gonna wear shorts. It's supposed to be like we put snowshoes on here even in the summer. We're gonna say it's Fourth of July in Maine. Get it?"

"I want to see it first," Roxanne said, but the girls were gone, headed outside.

"God almighty," I said.

"It's what kids do now. These synchronized dance moves like backup singers."

"For pedophiles."

"There's way worse things for them to search for than two kids clomping around in snowshoes."

"Two pretty young girls."

"Jack."

"I don't like it. Are their names on there?"

"No."

"So people see this and—"

"They can like the video. Or follow them."

"Follow them home," I said. "This is nuts. Don't you read about these teenage girls who meet some loser online and he takes a bus to their town and rents a motel room and—"

"Jack, I know. But that almost never happens. This is the way the world is."

"Not our world."

"No, but we can't sequester her here forever. It's like trying to stop the sun from rising. We just teach her what's right and what's wrong and—"

"In a world where there doesn't seem to be any idea of either?" I said. "Good luck with that."

Roxanne paused, looked at me.

"Are you okay? What happened this morning?"

I thought for a moment, said, "This Raymond—he's a weird guy, but I can see his point. When I was a kid, we had lists of things that were wrong. Lying. Fighting. Disrespecting your parents. You went to Confession and listed your sins."

"To a priest who may have been the biggest sinner of all," Roxanne said.

"But at least you knew what wrong was. I'm just saying there's something screwed up about a world that has no rules at all. Anything goes. Steal, just don't get caught. Lie, if it's convenient. Hurt people and walk away. Twerk on TikTok, or whatever the hell it is they do."

"Jack."

"What?"

"Relax. It's all going to be okay."

"I know. It's just that sometimes I feel like I'm witnessing the decline of civilization."

"But not now. The story is work. You can leave it behind. Sophie is a great kid. She'll navigate all of these things, with our help."

She kissed me again. Once, twice, then for a long time. When she leaned back, she said, "They're shooting a scene at school tomorrow with Mr. Ziggy. Nine to noon."

"On a Saturday?"

"You know Mr. Ziggy."

"Doesn't he have a life?" I said. "Young guy, a Saturday? He ought to be out on a snow machine or ice-fishing or something."

"He's all about this movie. Kids are totally into it. Sophie said he told Tara she was really good and could be in the movies."

"Way to raise hopes to be crushed. She's probably had enough of that already."

"It's not her hopes I'm worried about at this minute," Roxanne said.

She moved close, said, "Relax, Jack McMorrow." Closer and we kissed. Softer, slower, in anticipation.

"You're pushing yourself pretty hard these days. What time did you leave this morning?"

"Four. A little after."

"What? Like, five hours' sleep?"

"That extra effort is the difference between an okay story and an important one," I said.

"I get it," Roxanne said. "But don't drive yourself into the ground."

"I have to," I said. "I mean, my stories have to have meaning. This is my one shot."

"At what?" Roxanne said.

I looked at her, surprised she had to ask.

"At life. At accomplishing something real."

"You've accomplished a lot, Jack. Your stories have helped a lot of people. You've captured all these things that would have slipped away otherwise. And you've got our family."

I took a deep breath, exhaled slowly. Roxanne put her hand on my shoulder.

"Sometimes I worry about you. It's always been like this, sort of, but lately, I feel like whatever you're looking for, it's always just out of reach. It's like you just finish one story and you're off chasing the next, even harder. It's like you're trying to find the perfect story, this Holy Grail that's out there somewhere."

"I am. Stories that are true. That sum up human existence."

"You know what sums up human existence? Us, being together."

She put her arms around me.

"Hitting this girl when he didn't have to, robbing all these stores in a row—this Zombie guy sounds like a psycho nut job," Roxanne said.

"You learned that stuff in graduate school."

"I don't want anything to happen to you, Jack."

"I'm fine. It's a story."

"I have a bad feeling. Like maybe what we have is too good to be true. Too perfect to last."

"I'm not going anywhere." I paused. "Except back down there. See this girl Sparrow again. Maybe her dad. The cops."

"When?"

"Tomorrow. Early. It's when it's all happening. He usually hits places between three-thirty and four-thirty a.m."

"So go later. I'm serious, Jack," Roxanne said.

"You don't cover a battle after it's over," I said.

"No," she said. "You don't. But how many of them don't make it home?"

The girls were outside in the yard beside the shed. Tara's phone was on a tripod set on the woodpile, music playing. They were singing along as they danced in their shorts and tank tops, snowshoeing left, then right, then doing a shuffling pirouette. As they turned, they swiveled their hips, hands on their buttocks.

What the hell?

"Hey, guys," I said. "When you're done, do you want to take the big toboggan over to Cemetery Hill?"

"We have to do the edits," Sophie said. "You add the audio on TikTok. So it looks like we're singing, but it's the real song."

Sophie turned to Tara, said, "I messed up the turn. We need to do the whole thing again."

"Let's add the booty shake," Tara said.

She shuffled in her snowshoes to the tripod, hit the phone button, shuffled back.

The music began and the dance resumed, the girls mouthing some sort of poppy hip-hop.

I cringed, bit my tongue.

A glimpse of Clair coming out of the path from his barn, headed for the deck. I watched the next take, the girls indeed shaking their butts after the hip-swivel thing. Who the hell was this for?

I shook my head inwardly, went inside, met Clair at the sliding door.

He stepped in and kicked off his boots.

We moved to the kitchen, and Clair walked over and gave Roxanne's shoulder a squeeze.

"How's my favorite baker?" Clair said.

"Busy," Roxanne said. "The bread was supposed to be a project for Sophie and her friend, but they didn't make it past the flour."

"TikTok," I said. "They're sure the snowshoe dance will go viral." I sighed.

"How kids roll," Clair said. "My parents thought Little Richard meant the world was going literally to Hell."

"There was a whole lot of shaking going on."

"The Devil's music for sure."

"Still, this is some weird alternate reality," I said. "What's wrong with the real one? A snowy day in the Maine countryside. Tracking deer. There was a snowy owl at the dump."

"Gratification doesn't come instantly out there," Clair said, smiling. "Rabbit hunting, it can take all day."

"Rabbit hunting? My God, listen to you two old codgers," Roxanne said, wrapping loaves of bread in foil.

"Hey, I FaceTime with my grandkids," Clair said. "Scheduled to talk to Louis at ten-thirty on WhatsApp."

There was a beat. He looked at his watch. Roxanne stopped smiling, ripped a length of tin foil from the roll.

"Louis," I said. "He's back?"

"Still in Canada."

"It's been two years. You heard from him out of the blue?"

"Texted me. Said he was bringing Marta back to Maine."

"Jesus," Roxanne said. She wrapped the first loaf, tore foil for the second.

"When?" I said.

"This week."

Roxanne thumped the bread onto the counter, turned to us.

"I'm sorry, but let Louis be her knight in shining armor, or whatever it is he's doing. It's not your fight, Clair. And you, Jack. Don't even think about it. She's not worth it. She's a manipulative, lying nut-case."

She shook her head, rammed the foil back in the drawer, slammed it shut. With an exhale of exasperation, she left the kitchen, went down the hall and up the stairs.

I looked to Clair, nodded to the door to the shed. He followed me outside and down the driveway. We climbed in to the truck and I turned on the motor and the heat.

"Roxanne isn't a fan of Marta."

"Nor Mary," Clair said. "Wants me to have nothing to do with it, or her."

"But Louis is a Marine."

"And he still needs help."

"And you've got the skills."

"A step slower," Clair said, "but I know the drill."

We sat. Clair held his phone in front of him and waited.

The screen read 10:30. Then 10:31, 10:32.

"He's usually right on the dot," Clair said.

"After more than two years of being incommunicado? What's he been doing?"

"I don't know. He just said he'd call."

The motor idled softly. Another two minutes went by. I shut it off. The two minutes became five.

"This isn't right," Clair said.

"A lot can happen in a week," I said.

"All he has to do is text."

"Maybe he lost his phone. Maybe it ran out of juice. Maybe he's talking to somebody and can't get off. There's all kinds of—"

The phone rang, a faint pulsing beep like a sound from a hospital room. Clair put it on speaker.

"Hey," Clair said. "We were getting worried."

"Guy from next door knocked," Louis said.

"What did he want?" Clair said.

"Money for drugs," Louis said. "He knows better than to try to steal something from me."

"Nice neighborhood," I said.

"Morning, McMorrow."

"Good morning to you," I said. "How you doing? Been a while."

"Fine," Louis said.

"Fine, as in no news, or fine, as in something to report?" Clair said.

There was a military tone in his voice, like Louis was in the jungle with a radio.

"Fine, as in she's ready to be extricated," Louis said.

4

There was a pause, that news sinking in.

"Against her will?" Clair said.

"No."

"You talk to her?" I said.

"Yeah."

"Is she okay?" Clair said.

"More or less," Louis said.

We waited.

"She's with a guy named Bill Lambert. Goes by Snake. He's the president."

"What do you mean, with him?" I said.

"Like, living in his house. Riding around with him. In the winter, he drives a decked-out pickup. An officer rides shotgun. She's in the backseat."

"Is she there voluntarily?" Clair said.

Another pause.

"I don't know," Louis said. "She seems pretty out of it."

"How did you find her?" I said.

"Long story. Started with a phone. She left one behind."

"She'd called this guy Snake?" Clair said.

"He'd called her. A few times. Burner, but police grabbed this one in a raid. Numbers matched. Guy I knew in Canadian army in Iraq is a cop now. He helped me out."

There was a blur of static, the connection frozen. Then Louis was back, mid-sentence.

"—no different from any other personnel recovery," Louis said. "Operation is set for next week."

"She wasn't captured by the Taliban," Clair said. "And you're not Seal Team Six."

"Some of the same training," Louis said. "I knew a couple of those guys."

The call broke up. A couple of chickadees landed in the cedar at the end of the shed. Then a couple more. And the call broke off.

Clair said, "What if you're recovering somebody who doesn't want to be recovered?"

He tried calling back. Nothing.

I googled Bill "Snake" Lambert. Most of the hits were stories from the *Montreal Gazette*.

"President of the Montreal chapter of the Wild Ones."

Clair didn't answer, the implications settling in.

"Racketeering, drug trafficking. He got off. That was in 2017. Weapons charges, 2011. Sentenced to two and a half years. They're like the mob. I'll bet her ex was hiding money for them, all those offshore accounts."

"And skimming," Clair said.

"Until they killed him and Marta took off with her million dollars."

"Their million."

"So they get some of their money back and the thief's girlfriend."

"Win-win," Clair said.

We sat. The chickadees had moved on. The truck cab was cooling.

"Two years? That's a long time," I said.

"Thinking with his heart," Clair said.

"Which isn't thinking at all."

A few seconds of quiet, the two of us sitting like a long-married couple, comfortable with the silence. And then Clair said, "I saw it a few times, especially when the unit was really tight. Somebody's buddy would get killed, emotions would take over. Gonna even things up and maybe they do, for a moment, or a minute. Things go wrong when process breaks down. Good way to end up dead."

The cooling motor ticked. More chickadees flew into the cedar, or maybe they were the same ones. I glanced over. Clair had his phone in both hands, held it in front of him like a book. In that moment, he looked old and weary and worried.

"He's very capable," I said. "And he brought enough firepower for a platoon."

Clair was looking straight ahead, seeing only what was in his head.

"I know," he said, and I could hear his breathing, the faintest of sighs. "He survived Fallujah, Diwaniya, all those months kicking in doors. But I don't want to lose another one. Too many of them."

A beat.

"You know I'm starting to dream about them again."

"Nightmares?" I said.

"No. In my dreams they're alive, young and brave, trying to do the right thing, parents proud of them. And then I wake up. That's the nightmare part."

We were silent again, for a longer time. Chickadees came and went. It was impossible to know if they were the same ones. So much I didn't know after all these years.

"You can't control him," I said.

"But I can't abandon him," Clair said.

"You're headed north?"

He turned to me and mustered the smile that usually meant he had everything under control.

"It's a Marine Corps thing. You wouldn't understand, being a lifelong civilian and a professional scribbler to boot."

He popped the door open. The girls came around the corner in their shorts and sneakers, carrying their snowshoes.

"See what I mean?" I said.

"Yeah," Clair said. "I loved Little Richard. But some guy from TikTok shows up, we'll kick his butt right down the road."

I worked on my notes from Clarkson until after three. Roxanne worked on a paper for school, the girls did their editing in Sophie's room.

The song played over and over as they dubbed it in. When it wasn't playing, they were on the phone to someone, talking and laughing, occasionally shrieking.

And then it was time for Tara to go home. They climbed into the back of the cab of the truck, whispered as I drove out to Knox Corner, took a left, and headed north on the ridge. There were stubbly fields with cornstalks bristling from the snow, smoke coming from the chimneys of the houses. It was like everyone had gone underground, dug into their snow caves, hoping the provisions lasted until spring.

I turned off at Tara's dead-end road, the corner marked by a trailer surrounded by junked cars and trucks, a pit bull tethered to the bumper of a rusted-out F-150. The girls were laughing, looking at Tara's phone.

"Maine princesses?" Tara said, and they sputtered.

A quarter-mile in, there was a painted sign nailed to a tree. It said PRIVATE—TRESPASS AT OWN RISK. The road got rougher, the cleared path narrowing like the plow guy hadn't finished. I concentrated, banging over the frozen wheel ruts, snow and rocks spraying the wheel wells when I went astray.

After a mile or so, the woods cleared on one side and Tara's house showed, her mom's Jeep parked by the door. It was an old, brown-shingled Cape with a porch built on the front. There was a barn connected to the house, tattered cedar shingles clinging like seaweed on a rock. Stuff propped against the walls. Pieces of plywood, an upside-down sign that said RAW MILK, another that said NO TRESSPASSIN in hand-painted lettering. Rough draft of the one down the road.

I pulled in, heard Tara say, "Oh, good, Jason's gone."

"Why's that good?" Sophie said.

I looked at my phone.

"Him and my mom were fighting."

I held my phone up to my ear, pretended not to listen.

"Jason's friends were here, shooting guns in the back field. They had this big bonfire after they got done, and one of them came to the house and he wanted to use the bathroom. My mom said no, she doesn't want him in her house, and then Jason got all mad."

I switched the phone to the window side.

"He says it's his house, too, and my mom says, no, it was her grampa's land and he left it to her mom and her mom left it to my mom. He says he's half-owner now, 'cause he's her boyfriend, and some law thing says he can own the farm, too. And these are his friends. So he can have them over when he wants."

"Huh," Sophie said.

"My mom says they're scary bad people and they aren't friends, they're like an army with all their guns and trucks. Sometimes Jason, he just, like, goes back in the woods after they fight—there's an old camp back there—but this time he was, like, drunk, so they were screaming, and Jason said it doesn't matter what my mom thinks because he has his rights."

"How many of them are there?" Sophie said.

"Like, a lot. Maybe twenty?"

"And they all bring guns?"

"Lots of guns. Different ones. And they have these uniform things, just the shirts. They have regular pants. They have PL on the back. That's for Patriot Legion. Jason says they're a—"

She paused.

"—a sortium."

"What?" Sophie said.

"A sortium. That means they're the bosses of all these different group things but they come here to be, like, part of Jason's one. My mom says they're little boys playing soldier."

Sophie laughed. "It must be loud, all the shooting."

"We have like a million acres. There's this gravel pit way far in, with all these old rusty trucks and stuff. It's creepy. That's where they practice."

Tara looked at her phone, said, "I should probably go in."

"Where do they come from?" Sophie said. Her father's daughter.

"Like, all over. Last week there were two new guys from Portland. One of them came to the house. They had guns that were really big. One was like a cannon. My mom said it was because they have small—"

She looked at me.

"Never mind."

I lowered the phone. "So, Tara," I said. "What are these guys practicing for?"

She hesitated, then said, "Jason says Maine isn't a real state 'cause of the Constitution or something, and Augusta takes people's kids and all their stuff."

I could feel's Sophie's eyes widen.

"Interesting," I said. "What do you think they're planning to do?"

"I don't know exactly. Jason let me come to the campfire once. They were all drinking beers and saying they don't like Augusta. Which I think is like the offices and stuff. The two new guys, they don't like Muslim people, they have to fight back for Jesus. I don't know. It was pretty boring, and they kept talking and talking. I just put my headphones on. Jason said that was disrespectful, so I couldn't come anymore."

She looked to Sophie, said, "Bye, Soph. I'll watch the likes."

Tara opened the truck door and slid out, started up the path trampled in the snow.

Her mom came to the door of the porch, opened it as Tara ran up, turned and waved. Tara went inside and her mom—purple parka, leggings and boots, streaky blonde hair tied back—stepped off the porch, went to a picnic table that was covered with a blue tarp. She pulled the tarp back from the bench as Sophie got out, waved, and climbed into the front seat. Tara's mom bent to light a cigarette. I said to Sophie, "Be right back."

I got out, walked up the path, and then crunched over the snow to the table, said, "Hey, Tiffanee."

She blew out smoke, smiled, and said, "Hey, Jack. Thanks for having her."

"No thanks necessary," I said. "They get along great."

"Tara loves Sophie. All she talks about is how smart she is in school."

A husky, engaging voice, but she sounded weary.

"Long day?" I said.

"They're all long, working at a call center. Had a guy today say I was lying when I said I wasn't in India. I sounded too American so I had to be faking."

I smiled. "Damned if you do."

She took another drag. "Sit," she said, patting the bench beside her.

"Can't stay," I said, still standing. "Just want to let you know they made a video. For TikTok."

"Oh, jeez. Tara's, like, totally addicted."

"They do a dance on snowshoes."

"Cute. That'll bring in the likes."

"With shorts on and tank tops."

"Jeez. Must've froze their little—"

She caught herself.

"—butts off."

"Their enthusiasm kept them warm."

I looked away at the woods.

"Just wanted you to know. I mean, there are a lot of older guys looking at this stuff, I imagine."

She flicked the ash off. "Oh, the guys have lots of other crap to look at. Women flashing their cleavage, shaking their butts. It gets more serious from there."

"So you don't think that—"

"Not to worry. It's totally harmless."

"I don't know," I said. "A lot of weirdos out there."

"Just kids' stuff for kids," Tiffanee said. "They all do it."

She inhaled, blew the smoke away from me. It hung in the cold air. I hesitated, then said, "Tara was telling Sophie about the shooting practice."

Her expression hardened, showing creases around her eyes and mouth. She dropped the cigarette onto the snow and stepped on it with her boot.

"You know, boys and their toys," Tiffanee said. A forced half-smile.

"Sounds like some serious weaponry. Fighting against the State? Going to war for Jesus?"

"Oh, God, mostly it's just talk. Jason and his buddies invite these other guys up. I think they just want a place to play soldier."

She dug out a pack, pulled out another cigarette. Held it.

"I was thinking, though—and maybe you would know about this, with your news writing and all. Could I get in trouble? Even if I don't have anything to do with it? I woke up in the night thinking, can they take the farm?"

No smile now. Just a weary woman who looked like she was burdened by something. Or everything.

"It depends," I said. "I covered a case once where a guy drove to meet up with a prostitute and they busted him and seized the family car he was driving even though his wife had no idea. Years later, the law was changed to say they can't do that if the owner doesn't know anything about the crime."

"But what if I do know? I mean, sort of. They go out there and shoot up old cars, crawl around in the woods."

"So it's not laser tag," I said. "If the purpose is to commit a crime, like storming the Capitol or taking the governor hostage or shooting up a mosque, and you knew about it—"

Tiffanee lit the cigarette, took a deep drag.

"Jason has been totally pissed at everybody in Augusta since they wouldn't let him see his son because his girlfriend said he beat her up, but he says he never touched her. Gus is nine now. His mom—she married some dude, moved to Florida. Jason sees him, like, once a year."

"That's too bad," I said.

"Doesn't help his case, the crazy e-mails he sends. He's always saying he's gonna take her to court for kidnapping, she'll see Gus in twenty years. Of course, he could see him more if he moved to Florida."

"More fun to rage and shoot at stuff," I said.

Tiffanee didn't answer, put the pack and lighter back in her pocket.

"So you think I could get in trouble?" she said.

"Like, what if someone got shot out there or something. It's your property, just like if they slipped on the ice on your stairs."

"But I don't have anything to do with their crap."

"I'm sure. But even if the cops don't come after you for aiding and abetting, providing the training ground or whatever, there could be a civil suit. Somebody gets killed and the family comes after you for providing a place for it to happen, you being the owner."

Tiffanee shook her head, took a long draw on the cigarette.

"He knows I don't like it and he does it anyway," she said. "Not to whine, but I wish I'd meet one guy who didn't turn out to be an asshole. I've had a drunk, Timmy. That was Tara's dad. Sweet as pie when he was sober—which was almost never. And then there was Roy. He was okay, but come to find out he was banging my best friend. Guy before that, Lucas, he was cool, but he got hooked on oxy, ended up trying to rob a freakin' bank. Got as far as the parking lot. And now Jason, who thinks he's Rambo."

She took a last quick puff on the cigarette, tossed the butt onto the snow with the others. She stood, a big woman, tall as me. Broad-shouldered, which was good, considering the weight that was on them.

"Do you think this is something that might really happen?" I said. "This trying to overthrow the government or make war on Muslims or whatever they're saying?"

"I don't know. I do know there are more of them every time. This time, some of them were pretty scary. The religious guys, I mean, they're not joking around. And the guns, they get bigger. Now they have those night-vision things, crawling around in the dark."

We walked, side by side on the snowy path.

"Where's Jason today?"

"We had a wicked go-round last night. He stayed in the camp out back. They all leave today. They have jobs, I guess. Have to pay for all their toys. They do this on weekends."

We walked. At the driveway, she stopped, turned and held my arm.

"Can I ask you a favor, Jack?"

After a moment's hesitation, I said, "Sure."

"Would you not tell anyone about all this? I mean, Jason would be pissed if he knew Tara was talking about it. He made her swear. And the people at the call center. Not sure what they'd think if it made the paper for some reason."

"Just Roxanne," I said. "I tell her everything."

Tiffanee smiled. "Must be nice."

We were turning around to head back down the road when the first truck emerged from the woods. I pulled over, like it was a dictator's entourage.

The first pickup was a big black Chevy, black wheels, too. Two guys in front, two in back. A tonneau cover over the bed. Massachusetts plates.

"Play date's over," I said.

"Are those the Patriots?" Sophie asked.

A convoy followed, all jacked-up pickups, grim-looking guys in camo baseball caps. We sat in the road in front of the house and watched. I counted twelve trucks in all. Most had three or four guys. The second-to-last one had two, the passenger hatless, a big guy with a pale bald head. He looked over at us, a cold, hard stare, before the truck pulled away. The last truck, a primer-black Dodge, stopped at the road entrance and the driver got out. He was short and stocky, gray-and-black camo, pants tucked inside black boots. A sidearm in a holster.

He walked back, pulled a steel cable out of the trees, and drew it across the road. Hooking the cable to some sort of hasp, he snapped a padlock in place.

The clubhouse was private. No girls allowed.

"Jason, I presume," I said.

He got back in his truck, pulled out into the road like he was going to follow the convoy. Looked in our direction, and stopped. He wheeled the truck around and roared toward us, the pickup sliding to a stop, the driver's window buzzing down. I opened mine. Jason looked down at me. A chubby-chinned guy with a scruff of beard, like lichens on a rock. Even in the truck cab, he seemed short.

"Hey," I said. "Just dropped Tara off."

He nodded, barely.

"I don't think we've formally met," I said. "I'm Jack. This is my daughter, Sophie."

Another nod. I waited.

"Yup," Jason said. "The reporter."

"Right. When I'm not a dad."

"Friggin' media. You people screwed me over big-time. My kid's mother called the cops, said I hit her. Sure, she had bruises, but that was because she was a falling-down drunk. Arrested me for domestic violence assault, and you all put it in the paper. Freakin' mug shot, like I was a goddamn serial killer."

He took a breath. His truck throbbed like it was impatient with all the talk.

"Sorry to hear that," I said.

"Tried to fight it, but you know it's all rigged. Human Services, the DA, the cops, the media. You all have your agenda."

I didn't reply, but he didn't seem to expect it.

"Hey, I learned the hard way. Their rules, you lose. My name in the paper for something I never done, and it all went right to shit. Business went under, customers canceling, nobody even calling me back. Vehicles repo'd."

Sophie was looking over at him, taking it all in.

"Point is," Jason said, "she can hang out with Tara, but I don't want you hanging around. You can meet one of us at the end of the road."

"Suit yourself."

"Tara can call."

"Will do."

"I mean, it ain't like we're gonna be buddy-buddy, you know what I'm saying? 'Hey, how you doin'? Have a nice day.' "

"My loss, no doubt," I said.

He looked at me closely, not sure if that was a joke.

"Just so we understand each other."

"Oh, I think we do," I said.

"Good," Jason said. "Lamestream media. Just one more branch of an oppressive government, sucking up to the power people, aiding and abetting the rape of this country."

He gave the truck a rev, like a challenge. Looked at me and our stares locked. Mano a mano.

I decided to let it roll off, with Sophie there.

"See you at the end of the road," I said.

I saluted, drove away. Looked over at Sophie and smiled. Said, "Oversharer or what?"

5

We were a hundred yards down the road when a bird flashed in front of the truck, dipped and skimmed the field to our right.

"Sharp-shinned hawk," I said. "They stay here all winter."

"Huh," Sophie said, as the bird disappeared into the tree line.

Another pause, Sophie thinking.

"So what's Jason so mad about?" she said.

"Sometimes people feel like their whole world is falling apart. They work in a factory that closes or they get laid off. A lot of people are getting rich and they're not even making it, and they think the world is against them."

Sophie considered it, quiet in that wheels-spinning way she had. The intersection was coming up, the cluster of junk cars on the right.

"You think he was telling the truth?"

"I think probably he believes he was."

"Then that wasn't fair, what happened to him."

"No," I said. "But violence or trying to overthrow the government or whatever it is they're talking about—that's not fair, either. Your mom did that job. She saved a lot of kids from very bad situations."

"What about the reporter part? Did you hurt innocent people?"

"Not intentionally. Fact is, he was arrested. You report that because you can't have the government going around disappearing people. It holds the police accountable when you make it public. In Providence, when I started out, they used to try to get me to leave stuff out of the police reports."

"What did you say?"

"No."

"What if those people were like Jason—had their businesses ruined, and maybe they were innocent?"

"If that was decided in court, we reported that, too."

"What if it was too late?" Sophie said.

"Nothing's perfect," I said. "Some people get hurt."

"Like what?" Sophie said. "Collateral damage?"

"Where did you learn that?" I said.

"School," she said. "We were talking about the Iraq War. Drones shooting missiles and hitting the wrong house. Killing little kids."

"Huh," I said. "Louis fought there."

"Was he in charge of drones?"

"No," I said. "He fought house to house."

Sophie went quiet, more processing.

We were a couple of miles down the road. It was almost three o'clock, and ahead of us, the sky already was darkening to the east. Over the fields to the north, a flock of crows flew against the backdrop of a dark gray cloud bank, heading for their roost.

We turned to the west off of Knox Ridge, the pastures white on the spruce-streaked ridges in the distance. Prosperity was on the far side of the closest crest, my sanctuary, a refuge from the mayhem that was all around us. But today it felt like I was under siege, by Jason and his crazy militia, by TikTok and booty dances, Tara and her phone.

I glanced over at Sophie.

"The world is messed up, Dad."

"Sometimes," I said.

"Will those guys shoot people?"

"I don't know. Sometimes marching around is enough. Sometimes people just want to be part of something."

"What about the other times?"

"Then you can have a problem."

"Will they try to shoot you and Mom? She took people's kids away."

"No, honey," I said. "We'll be fine."

On the steering wheel, my fingers were crossed.

A moment of quiet and then Sophie said, "Our video has over eight hundred likes already."

I thought the crows were way more interesting, but only said, "Really. Is that a lot?"

"For us. Some people have thousands and thousands. But we just started posting."

She paused.

"I really need my own phone."

"We'll talk about it."

"I'm twelve, Dad. This is ridiculous. I'm the last one in my class."

"So we'll talk about it."

Another long pause. We passed farm equipment rusting in a field, like burned-out tanks on a battlefield.

"Why do you think these guys come all the way to Tara's house to shoot guns off?" Sophie said.

"Because where they live, you shoot guns and the police come and arrest you."

"They must really like shooting guns to come all the way from Massachusetts."

"Yes," I said. "They must."

"And they have uniforms."

"Some guys like playing that they're in the army. Most of them never were for real."

"Not like Clair and Louis."

"Right."

"Tara said they shoot at targets shaped like people."

"Huh. Interesting."

We rode, quiet for a minute. The fields passed. The main road was up ahead.

"Why would Tara's mom be with Jason then?" Sophie said.

"I don't know. Maybe he has a good side. Maybe he's better than being alone."

"That's kind of sad."

"Yup," I said.

And then we were home. She got out of the truck and trudged up to the house and went inside. I sat for a minute, feeling like pulling up the drawbridge, locking the door and turning off the Internet. No TikTok, no Twitter, no perverts watching my daughter dance in snowshoes. No phone to suck you into a world of crass, vulgar crap.

I followed Sophie into the house. And then my phone buzzed.

I took it out, read the text.

Sparrow.

—HEY JACK. SOMETHING I WANT TO TALK TO YOU ABOUT. MAYBE NOT FOR THE STORY. WILL YOU BE BACK IN CLARKSTON TODAY?

I glanced at Roxanne watching me. Tapped my reply:

WASN'T PLANNING ON TODAY. CAN WE TALK ON PHONE?

I took off my jacket.

—KIND OF IMPORTANT. I'D RATHER TALK FACE-TO-FACE.

An emoji. It was frowning.

I hung up my jacket, picked up Sophie's boots and set them against the wall. The phone again. Roxanne was frowning, too.

I'M WORKING TONIGHT. LATE IN THE SHIFT PRETTY SLOW. CAN TAKE A BREAK.

—WHAT WAS THAT? FIVE A.M.?

I made a quick decision.

SEE YOU THEN.

Roxanne glanced at me, said nothing.

It was a quiet afternoon. I went out to the woodshed, split firewood with a maul, picked up a hatchet to slice up kindling from a pile of scrap boards. Tools that hadn't changed since medieval times, except they were less frequently used as weapons.

I brought in a load of wood, stacked it by the stove. Sophie was on the couch, reading something on her iPad, taking notes. Roxanne was in her chair, working on her laptop.

"You have to be quiet, Dad," Sophie said. "Mom's at a hard part of her paper."

Dinner was turkey hot dogs, homemade beans, kale salad. Sophie talked about school, the play *Annie*, Mr. Z picking Tara for the lead. "We're thinking we could do 'Hard-Knock Life' on TikTok," she said.

"It kind of is for her," I said.

"Her mom's nice," Roxanne said.

"Not Jason," Sophie said, started to say something, but stopped, and started eating salad, looking down at her plate. I waited, then told them more about Raymond and his statues, the Jesuses and Marys lined up like it was an audition.

"That's kinda creepy, but sort of cool, too," Sophie said. "Like he's doing his thing, doesn't care what anybody thinks."

That was very true. Raymond answered to a higher power.

And then we did dishes and went to our respective corners. Roxanne was typing furiously in front of the wood stove. Sophie went up to her room to read for school—a book called *How to Change Everything* by Naomi Klein. I hoped Sophie changed something, at least.

I read a few chapters of a bio of Benjamin Franklin, getting to the part where he finally gave up on being a Brit and went all in on the Revolution. Was that what Jason was doing? Getting ready to shoot redcoats from behind stone walls?

After a couple of hours, I put the book down, went outside. The wind had picked up from the northwest. I stood outside the shed door and looked at the stars, emerging as the clouds raced east. I remembered my father's one lament about us living in New York City: that the lights were pushing out the stars. Now it was more than lights crowding me in Prosperity, Maine.

I listened to the oak and beech leaves rattle in the wind, then went inside and took a Ballantine ale from the refrigerator. I opened it as Roxanne shut her laptop, got up from her chair. She came to the kitchen, poured a glass of Cabernet, took a sip. I sidled up to her at the counter and kissed her on the cheek.

"Is that first base?" I said. "I can never get those bases straight."

"I think that's the on-deck circle," she said.

"Maybe we'll go extra innings," I said.

She leaned over, kissed me back. My cheek. I turned, kissed her on the lips. Once, twice, three times, like a butterfly tentatively landing on a flower. The last kiss lingered. Her lips were soft, her mouth warm. She smelled like wine.

"Isn't spring training pretty soon?" Roxanne said.

"I think this could be an extended at-bat."

She laughed.

"What? You were listening to sports talk radio and got all worked up?"

"No. I think I just need to be close to you."

She held me tighter.

"I feel the same way. We need to check in with what started this whole thing."

Before the Internet, I thought. Before the walls started closing in. Before the world turned crude and crass and started spinning out of control.

But I didn't say that, just moved closer, murmured, "What was it that started it?"

"Us," Roxanne said.

"I think I heard Sophie click her light off," I said.

"We could be extra quiet," she said. "Just in case."

"That would be a first."

"Exploring new frontiers."

Another kiss, this one longer, the momentum building like we were rolling downhill into each other. Roxanne drew me to her for the many-thousandth time.

"I need you," I said.

Another kiss, a breathless break.

"I could do a booty dance for my one follower," Roxanne said.

"I'll click through. Or swipe left. Or whatever it is you're supposed to do."

"My influencer," Roxanne said. She picked up her wine, handed me my beer. Took my hand and led me to the stairs.

We were quiet enough. Long breaths, the creaking of the bed. A simmering sort of buildup as we moved together with a resolve that said each touch was important, each shift of our bodies was inevitable, that there was no stopping, not then, not ever. Our mouths melded, our chests pressed together until our heartbeats were one. And then a slow, determined dance, legs sometimes intertwined, sometimes apart. The dance we'd done so many times before but still, the improv startling as we darted in, seized the other, held each other still until we couldn't be still anymore.

And then I was looking up at Roxanne, her eyes closed, lost in me as I lost myself in her. Her open mouth, breath coming quickly, and then a beautiful smile, and I suddenly thought of the statues, the rapture, the moment when we leave this world for another.

Which we did. And then, after a moment that couldn't be measured in time, she shuddered once more, then eased back down. Kissed me and laid down, her breasts on my chest.

"And that," Roxanne said, "is how it all started."

"The stars were aligned."

"Among other things. Like I thought you were hot as hell."

"Likewise," I said. "Still do."

After a few minutes, us feeling the beating of our hearts, the slow up and down of our breaths, she lay down beside me, pulled the covers over us. She reached her wine from the bedside table and took a sip, and then we were quiet for a long minute. Maybe two. Then Roxanne said, "Who was that?"

"Who was who?"

"Texting earlier."

"Sparrow. The store clerk in Clarkston."

She sipped again.

"What did she want?"

"To tell me something."

"About the robbery?" Roxanne said.

"I assume so."

"What was it?"

"She didn't want to tell me on the phone."

"Like, how early?"

"When I wake up."

She turned to me.

"What if you're all worn out?" Roxanne said.

I turned to her, kissed her. Softly, this time.

"I'll cross that bridge."

We both lay back down.

"Jason," I said.

"Uh-huh."

"He hates the DHHS."

"Him and a lot of other people. What, did we pull his kids?"

I told her the story.

"Was he convicted?"

"I don't know. Even if the charges were dropped, according to him, it was too late. Damage was done."

"Alternative is to leave women with batterers even more often than they are now," Roxanne said.

"I know. I get it. But Sophie was trying to wrap her head around it."

"Does he know what I did for a job?"

"I don't think so."

"It's like we're both the enemy."

"Cops are probably in there, too."

"Huh," Roxanne said, and then she was mulling. "Sophie can't go over there. I'm sorry."

"No. The Patriot Legion has maneuvers next weekend. Somewhere in the back forty."

"Should we tell somebody?" Roxanne said. "What if they actually do something for real?"

"I think they're still practicing."

"For how long?"

"I don't know. Tara said they call it the consortium. Leaders of other groups coming here for hands-on training."

"Maybe we need Clair and Louis," she said. "When is Louis back?"

"I was going to tell you. He found Marta."

I felt her mood shift. As I recounted the conversation, her grip on my hand loosened. She pulled the blanket up under her chin.

"Don't tell me you're going up there, Jack."

"No. Just Clair. He said he and Louis had it under control. I think Clair feels responsible for him somehow."

"For Louis? He made his own bed. She's poison with a capital P. Her ex laundering money for criminal gangs, or whatever he was doing. They kill him and she ends up with the head criminal? And they're bringing her back here? What, like Jack in the Beanstalk stealing the goose?"

"That seems to be the plan."

"The giant comes after him, you know."

"Yes," I said.

"Jesus," Roxanne said. "And you're worried about TikTok?"

6

My watch vibrated me awake at 2:45 a.m. I listened to Roxanne's soft breathing for a moment, then rolled out of bed. By 3:10 I was headed down the road, a mug of tea in the cup holder. It was a gray-blue night, a bright three-quarter moon pale at the edge of encroaching clouds creeping in from the south. I didn't see another car until nearly Augusta. On the highway south, I was alone, just me and my addiction, driving to Clarkston to score.

There was one car in the QuikStop parking lot, a dented Nissan with racer wheels and blacked-out windows. I presumed it belonged to Mo.

He was behind the counter when I walked in, gave me a booming "Hello, sir," the employees' way of making initial contact to gauge whether the customer was friend or foe. I said hi, asked if Sparrow was working.

"The beautiful Miss Sparrow is always working," Mo said, and he leaned down and pressed a button and said into a microphone I couldn't see, "Your friend is here."

She came from the back room with her parka on, hood up and the bandage peeking out. I said hello and she said, "Hey. Let's talk outside."

I followed her out of a side door, which she propped open with the cardboard from a six-pack of Budweiser. She tossed the cartons into a recycling bin, turned to me, and took out her vape. She held it up to her mouth and inhaled.

"Thanks for coming down," she said.

"No problem," I said.

She hesitated, finally spat it out.

"I have this thing I'm wondering about," Sparrow said, looking away. "I mean, I don't want to bother my dad. He's got enough, being sick. Raymond, he's got opinions, but he mostly knows about saints and shit. I figure you seem like a good guy, and you're sort of in between a cop and a regular person."

I shrugged.

"The Zombie thing," Sparrow said.

I waited for her to do two drags on the pen.

"When he was here," she said.

"Robbing you."

"Right."

"I mean, I'm looking at the gun."

"Yeah."

"You know how I said I just kept looking at the gun the whole time. That wasn't true."

"What were you looking at?"

"I was looking at him. There's this light in the ceiling that's crooked. I don't know, somebody replaced it and couldn't get it to fit, so they just left it."

"Uh-huh."

"So it shines, like, right into the customer's face. And there's this second, or maybe more, where it's like I can almost see through the mask. Like when you can see through a girl's skirt sometimes, you know? When the light kinda comes from the back? Except this was from the side."

"So you could see him?"

"It was like I could see what he looked like, even with the mask on."

"And you didn't tell the police that."

"No," Sparrow said.

"Why not?"

Another puff, a scowling exhale.

"I don't know. I mean, I got my dad. He needs me, you know what I'm saying?"

"So what does that have to do with ID'ing the robber?"

"Well, think about it, Mr. McMorrow."

"Jack."

"Okay, Mr. Jack. I'm the witness and I'm looking through the photos, like they do on TV, and maybe he's not in there. But word gets out on the street—except for Blake, I don't trust these cops for shit—the girl from the QuikStop, she saw the robber. So what do they do? Go start rounding up more suspects or whatever, and Zombie, he knows I can ID him. Hey, ten armed robberies? That's serious prison, right?"

"I'd guess six to ten years, depending on priors, whether he has a good lawyer," I said.

"Right, so he's got a gun. He's sticking it in people's faces who can't do anything to him. What if he could save himself ten years in prison just by getting rid of a witness?"

We stood in the cold by the dumpsters. Sparrow turned off the pen and dug in her parka pocket, came out with a pack of Marlboros. "I save 'em for emergencies," she said. A lighter came from the other pocket. She lit up, blew real smoke into the night. Her eyes and piercings glittered in the parking lot lights.

"I think it's a stretch," I said.

"You didn't see him. His hand was shaking, he was so pissed."

"But if you can ID him, maybe you'd stop him from shooting somebody in the next robbery," I said.

"You think I should tell the cops?"

I considered it for a second. She tossed the cigarette onto the ice, and it sparked and went out.

"Here's a problem," I said. "An ID through a mask won't stand up in court. His lawyer will shoot it right down. Give you a lineup of guys in zombie masks, say, 'Pick out my client.' But it could be probable cause to get a warrant, pick the guy up, maybe get a confession. Search his place and find the gun, anything traceable to a robbery."

"But without that he might get off anyway," Sparrow said.

"Yeah."

"And then it was all for nothing."

"I don't know. It gives them a prime suspect. That might stop him, even if he isn't arrested. Hard to pull off robberies with cops on you day and night."

She dug out another cigarette, put it back, and shoved the pack back in her pocket.

"My dad will smell it," she said. "He hates it when I smoke."

We stood.

"I have to get back. Working three hours' OT."

"Okay," I said.

"Thanks for talking."

I was thinking that I'd have to use this new wrinkle in my story. I decided to hold off telling her that until I was in deeper, but I did say, "Sparrow."

"Yeah."

"I thought you didn't care if you died. That night, you were mostly thinking about Mo."

She tucked her hands in her pockets, hunched her narrow shoulders under the jacket. Her eyeliner was heavier on her right eye than on the left. I wondered if that was deliberate. I waited.

"I thought about it," Sparrow said. "The doctors say my dad's got two years left, max, unless we get the miracle drugs. So I have to hang around that long. After that, it's like, whatever."

I replayed that quote in my mind. Sparrow took a couple of steps toward the door. Stopped and turned.

"Can I tell you one more thing? Like, off the record?"

"Yes," I said.

"He might know I know."

"Know what?"

"What he looks like. I was looking at him, over the gun. He said, 'What?' Then he looked up at the light, back at me."

Sparrow paused.

"And then what?" I said.

"That's all," she said.

I smiled. "Sparrow, like you said, I'm somewhere between a cop and a regular person. We know when someone isn't telling the whole truth."

She looked away.

"I gotta give Mo a break," Sparrow said, and she went to the propped door, stepped inside, pulled the beer carton inside. The door locked behind her.

I met Blake at the back door of the PD, a brick building that could have been an old school, except for the police vehicles behind the chain-link fence topped with razor wire. He pulled the SUV out, stopped by my truck on the adjacent street. I got in, and Blake swiveled the computer monitor out of my way, then handed me a release.

It said if I got hurt or killed, it was my problem. I signed it and handed it back and Blake tucked it into the console.

"Coffee?" Blake said.

We drove through the darkened downtown, took a right up the hill toward the hospital. The lights of the Dunkin' showed up ahead, cars lined up for the drive-through. He parked out front next to a cleaning-service van. When we stepped inside there were two other guys waiting in line, uniform jackets with the cleaning company logo. One, a skinny teenager, blond hair tied back, was buying.

"One of these days, dude," the younger one said to the other, "somebody gonna start shooting. It'll happen. Guns, they're made to be shot."

The kid glanced back and saw Blake, said, "Officer."

Blake nodded.

I smiled. "You talking about Zombie?" I said. "You think someone's going to get hurt?"

He looked at us warily, the cop and the guy asking questions. The older guy had his back turned.

"I'm a newspaper reporter," I said. "*New York Times.* Here to do a story on the robberies."

I eased my notebook out. No quick moves.

"It's just, like, a gun's made for one thing, that's shooting," the kid said. "You know what I'm saying? Somebody goes for the alarm, tries to be a freakin' hero, and bam. You got dead people on the floor."

The older guy looked at him with cold disapproval.

"You know he can put that in the paper, right?" he said, glancing back at me. He was big and broad-shouldered, shaved head. The guy from the second-to-last truck in the convoy at Tiffanee's place.

I looked at him and our eyes locked for a moment.

"You look familiar," I said. "Have we met?"

The same cold stare, faintly condescending, like he was on a mission I wouldn't understand.

"No," he said, looked away. Chitchat was over.

I took a pen from my other pocket, started to write before the moment passed.

"So people are worried about that?"

The young guy hesitated. "Just a fact of life. Guns don't kill people. People kill people."

The line moved. We followed.

"May I ask your name?"

"I'm Snow," he said.

"Right. And you, sir?" I looked at the other guy and smiled.

"This dude's Mumbo," Snow said.

"That's your name?" I said.

"Close enough. And don't put me in your story," Mumbo said.

The line moved. They stepped up and Snow ordered. Large iced coffee, extra sugar, extra cream. Mumbo got a large hot black. He hurried Snow to the pickup counter, where they kept their backs turned. When the coffees came, they turned, Mumbo hustling Snow outside. As I watched, Mumbo got behind the wheel. He snapped at Snow, who turned away. Mumbo backed the truck out.

"Post-release," Blake said. "New program. They get jobs subsidized by the State, live in a halfway house. Nobody can afford rents anymore, much less somebody just out of prison. Supposed to keep them from returning to a life of crime."

"I think I've seen the bald guy," I said. "One of a bunch of guys doing paramilitary training out in the woods in Waldo County."

"Guns?"

"You don't do it with broomsticks," I said.

"You sure? He's a felon. That could put him back inside."

I ordered a medium tea, skim milk. Blake ordered two large coffees, one iced vanilla, one hot, cream and sugar. We moved to the pickup counter together.

"So what'd these guys do?"

"Snow—that's his street name. Burglary, mostly. Stole anything wasn't nailed down. Not a bad kid at all once he got off drugs. I've talked to him quite a bit."

"Driver?"

"Mumbo."

"Huh. What's that for?'

"According to Snow, it's short for Mumbo Jumbo. Inside he was always praying in some foreign language. Cell mate thought it was Romanian. He'd done federal time and there are a lot of Romanians in prison. Big cyber criminals, scam artists. Turns out Mumbo was praying in Latin."

"Catholic."

"Strange one. Came up from Mass., moved some drugs—meth and fentanyl. Used the cash to buy guns. Had a trunk load when they took him down. Somebody he bought from ratted him out to save their butt from something. So Maine DEA goes to try to flip him, move up the chain. ATF, too. Won't give them anything."

"Unusual. Most of them sell their mothers in a proffer meeting."

"Story is he sat down in the room with the prosecutor, detectives, his lawyer. His reply to every question was the same, 'Only the Lord can judge me.' Or something like that."

"A higher power."

"Or he knew what would happen to him in prison if he talked. So no deal. Did a couple of years, kept his mouth shut, except maybe when he was praying. And here he is."

"When he isn't crawling around the woods in camo," I said.

"You sure it's the same one? Guys with shaved heads all look kind of the same."

"It was the eyes," I said. "The way he looks right past you."

"I know. Like you're a bug."

"Or maybe a sinner," I said. "And both deserve to be stepped on."

Blake's eyes darted across the restaurant, the parking lot—a cop thing.

The tea and coffee came, the woman behind the counter looking at me like I'd ordered lemonade in a barroom. We went back to the cruiser, settled in, drove back onto the street.

"You still live on a boat?" I said.

He gave me a quick glance, then looked away.

"I read the stories," I said. "*Bay Witch*. A wooden Chris Craft cruiser. Still keep it on Chandler's Wharf?"

Blake smiled. "Thing about the internet. There are no secrets."

"No," I said.

There was a long pause. I waited, then said, "How's Clarkston compared to Portland?" I said.

"Nobody in Portland lived there more than five minutes. Every traffic stop was a crapshoot. This is small-town in a lot of ways. Pull somebody over, good chance they look familiar. And except for the drug dealers from away, the dirtbags tend to be natives."

Eager to talk about that, not about himself.

"Crime less random?"

"Clarkston, they mostly kill people they know," Blake said.

He smiled, barely, as someone who had killed someone he didn't know at all.

We drank. The tea was weak.

"You think the Zombie robber is from here? Off the record."

"Yeah. That's what makes it so threatening to people. Somebody's son or nephew or cousin. Somebody you see every day."

And Sparrow saw right through his mask.

"Think he'll shoot somebody?" I said.

"Anytime you bring a gun to a crime . . ."

The words hung there amid the coffee smell, the radio chatter.

Blake knew what could happen. You could shoot someone. You could get shot by a cop.

We were off Porto, winding our way up the hill between tenements. I changed the subject, working my way closer. "Raymond," I said. "What's his deal, you think?"

"Gentle guy. Very quiet, unless he likes you. I mean, he decides right away. He likes you, he might let you into the chapel there."

"The chapel?"

"His house."

"He took me to the empty church with him."

"Oh, you're in."

"And I got a glimpse of the giant crucifix."

"And statues. And paintings. And candlesticks from altars. And cups and tabernacles and missals and rosary beads. The place is packed, every single room. He was showing me this box that people kept in their houses so a priest would have what he needed to give a dying person the Last Rites. Late nineteenth century, they were very common. It had a little tableau sort of thing behind a window."

A tableau sort of thing. Blake was no dope.

"Where's he get this stuff?"

"When a church is deconsecrated, they call Raymond, let him have first dibs. He works with dealers out of state, too."

"This is a guy who stocks shelves at night."

"In the world of old religious stuff, I guess he's a player," Blake said.

"Some of these ultra-orthodox Catholics are militant. What about him?"

Blake thought. "Too much of a loner," he said. "But he may know people like that, supplies them with statues or something."

I considered it, sipped my tea. We were driving alongside a park, benches along the perimeter, basketball courts empty in the icy street-light. There were random lights on in the triple-deckers, like the other windows had been shot out. I put the tea in the console, picked up my pen and notebook.

"So why Sparrow and Raymond? Is it that they're outsiders and police are, too?"

He reached for his coffee, sipped. I waited.

"I can't talk about Sparrow. She's part of our investigation."

"Raymond, then. Why him?"

Blake considered it as we circled the park.

"For your story?" he said.

"Right."

"Okay. He's smart, interesting, and a good reminder not to judge people by their cover."

I wrote that down.

"He's also one of those people with one foot in a different time. I mean, who believes in saints? For most people, it's just a fairy tale. Back then there was God, who was good, and the Devil, who was evil. No fifty shades of gray in between."

He said it with longing. I wrote in the notebook, looked over at him. He was watching the street, but still, there was a feeling that he was looking inside himself, too, carrying some sort of burden. It was a look I saw in Clair and Louis. I was thinking, killing people in the line of duty will do that. And then the radio barked.

"What's that?" I said.

"Natives getting restless," he said. "Right around the corner. We're first man in."

We saw them from the end of the block, a cluster of people, something going on in the middle.

They were in front of a dirty storefront—no sign, blacked-out windows. Closer, we could hear shouting, hooting, whooping.

"Social club," Blake said as he pulled up. "BYOB to get around the liquor laws, so they can drink all night. End up out here."

He got out, started toward them. I circled the cruiser and followed. There were a dozen people, in a circle, mostly men. Blake said, "Move aside—move it," and a couple of them did. At the center were a man and a woman. Forties, weathered drinkers' faces. They were circling like boxers, the woman bigger by four inches and fifty pounds. No jackets, shirts torn. The guy's hairy chest bared, the woman's breasts spilling out of a red bra. Their faces were scratched. The guy's nose was bleeding down to his chin.

"Go ahead, take the skanky clapped-out bitch," the woman shouted. "Deserve each other, you lying piece of shit."

And then she launched, grabbed his arm and pulled him in, both of them spinning. She got him in a headlock and started punching his face, the crowd hollering "Pound him!" And then Blake was in the middle, pulling the woman off, the guy staggering backwards.

"Enough," Blake shouted, shoved the woman to the edge of the crowd. The guy darted in, tried to get a last shot. Blake, all alone, said, "Stop now," and pushed him away with one hand. The guy stumbled into me, started to jump back in. I grabbed him from behind. The woman saw her opening, tried to run past Blake, and he pulled her back, said, "Last warning. Both of you."

The guy kicked at my shins, tried to stomp my feet. I spun him around, flung him to the pavement. He made his way to his hands and knees, blood dripping onto the sidewalk.

And then someone shouted, "What are you gonna do, Blake? Shoot 'em?"

Others joined in.

"He has a squirt gun, Blake. Blast him."

"It's a cell phone, Shooter. Blow his head off."

"Shoot me, Blake. I'm unarmed."

And then they started chanting, "Shooter, shooter," the guy on his feet now, laughing and coughing. A lull and the woman yelled, "Drunk Lives Matter," and they took that up, were still chanting when the second cruiser pulled in.

"Tired of chasing Zombie?" a guy yelled, as two more cops waded in.

"You'll never catch him, you morons," a woman said, and then, "Go, Zombie, go."

That chant started, but then the woman fighter took a swing at one of the new cops, and the female officer put her to the ground, started cuffing her hands as she squirmed and kicked.

Blake held her legs still until the cuffs were on and the other cop yanked her to her feet.

"You can shoot her now," someone shouted. "She's handcuffed."

More shouting as a cop bulled the woman to a cruiser. Blake waded into the crowd and grabbed the guy, twisted his arm behind his back, and other cops surrounded him and led him away.

The crowd started separating into twos and threes and sauntering down the sidewalk, a couple of them stumbling over the snowbanks into the street.

I stood and watched as the cops conferred, nodded, broke ranks. Cruisers pulled away, the drunk woman kicking the seat in front of her.

We went back to the cruiser, got in. I looked at Blake, saw a scratch on his neck, a smear of mucus on his jacket. He reached into the console, took out a package of disinfecting wipes. Dabbed his neck, then wiped his jacket.

"Thanks," he said.

"Another day at the office?" I said.

"Order restored," he said.

"Hard to take?"

"What I signed up for," Blake said. "How 'bout you?"

"Documenting the human condition."

"And it ain't pretty."

"No," I said.

We drove on, winding through the bumbling mass that is humanity. Traffic stops and tickets, a kid racing on the main drag. A mom who couldn't control her nine-year-old. A guy whose ex wouldn't let him into his former apartment to get his PlayStation. An old man vomiting on his shoes in the park. A woman who said the kid across the street was looking at her with a telescope.

Cold streets, dirty snowbanks. No Zombie.

It was just after nine when I got out of the cruiser in the PD lot, turned back, the door still open.

"One last thing," I said. "Mumbo. What's his real name?"

Blake tapped at the screen above the console.

"Joseph Loyola, aka Hugh Payns." He spelled it out. "Bo Taranto. Lots of aliases."

I wrote them down.

"Doesn't sound like your typical drug dealer," I said.

Blake put the cruiser in gear.

"I'd say that's one thing this guy isn't," he said.

7

The white minivan rolled up at 9:30 a.m. sharp, Sparrow working OT. Raymond parked in the lot across from the side door of the store, left the motor running. Two minutes later, Sparrow stepped out, walked to the front passenger door, and climbed in.

Raymond pulled out. I followed.

He drove directly to Sparrow's house. They sat in the van for five minutes, then Sparrow got out and went inside. There was one light on.

As I followed Raymond home, I wondered what they talked about. The drunks who rolled in? Which aisles he restocked? The gas pump that broke. His latest statue?

He pulled in the driveway, parked in the same spot. This time I pulled in along the street, walked up the driveway. He was getting out of the van, reached back in and came out with a paper grocery bag. He saw me, crumpled the top shut, put it back on the seat. Day-old doughnuts from the supermarket?

"Morning, Raymond," I said.

"Mr. McMorrow."

We both smiled.

"Hope you don't think I'm stalking you. I just had a few more questions. And I thought just maybe I might impose on you to see your collection."

Raymond hesitated and looked away, like he was consulting somebody. The man upstairs? Then he turned back, smiled, and said, "I thought you might be interested in that. Being a Catholic."

"And a former altar boy," I said.

"I prayed on it," Raymond said. "I think this is God's plan."

Before I could comment, he walked to the door, pulling out a ring of keys like a janitor would carry. He started unlocking the locks. I counted. There were four, including two deadbolts. I guessed he didn't want anyone stealing Jesus.

Raymond bent to the last lock, turned the key, and pushed the door open. There were dim lights on inside, and I could hear the monks chanting, left on all night. He led the way and I followed.

The place was full, even more than my earlier glimpse had prepared me for. The big Jesus on the Cross. Statues lining the hall, many of them life-sized, like a Madame Tussauds for saints. And Jesus. And Mary. Many Marys, all doe-eyed, lined up like entrants in an Elvis impersonator contest.

I followed Raymond into the first room. It was lit with a yellow-bulbed chandelier and electric candles in red vases. There was an altar rail, pictures hung on all the walls. Crucifixes, dozens of them, bearded Jesuses, legs crossed, spikes through their feet. A six-foot tapestry, a shawled woman with hands clasping a cloth.

"Is that Mary too?" I said.

"Veronica," Raymond said. "She wiped Jesus's face."

We kept walking, the statues staring as we passed.

"St. Barbara," Raymond said. "St. Dominic, with the book. St. Anthony, that's him with the baby there. And you've got your St. Francis, with the bird on his shoulder. The one with the lamb, too. You know he's the patron saint of animals."

"Right," I said.

We passed into another room, more crammed than the first. A display case of chalices, glittering in the candlelight. Another bearded Jesus, his chest cleaved open.

"The Sacred Heart," I said, pulling from my childhood.

"That came from a church in South Boston," Raymond said. "And you see that one there, the emperor with the dark skin. That's a Black Madonna. It's made of wood. From Poland."

Black Madonna had a drapey crown sort of thing on her head and was holding a black Jesus, who was wearing the same outfit.

"Interesting," I said.

"Yes. You know I just found a nineteenth-century St. Apollonius. He was drowned by the emperor Maximillian. That one's coming from a dealer in Pennsylvania. I'd been looking for a good Apollonius for years."

He picked up a metal chalice, held it up with two hands like he was saying Mass.

"They're turning churches into old-age housing. Can you believe that? They say attendance is down. Sure it is. Who wants to go and hear a priest read from Hallmark cards?"

He put the chalice down and kept walking.

"A lot of this, people grabbed it because they couldn't stand to see it thrown away. Then they pass away, and their next of kin, they don't want it. The other day I heard from a lady; she owns storage units in town here. Guy didn't pay his bill; she opens it up goes through it and there's a statue of Mary. She'd heard I collected."

"So it comes here," I said. "Like stray cats."

Raymond smiled.

"Sometimes, but I'm fussy now. That one was a bad reproduction. I still found a place for it. You see those archangels?"

I did. Three of them, five feet high, wings unfurled.

"That's Michael with the spear. High-quality, hand-carved in Germany From this shop—everyone wants their stuff."

"Interesting," I said.

Wild, I thought.

I glanced around the room; the saints assembled like that army of statues of Chinese soldiers they found in a tomb. Everyone staring blankly, frozen mid-faith.

"That Blessed Virgin, I had five just like it. Pretty common, late nineteenth century. But I found it a home. I mean, you can't let these holy things go to the dump. That would be sacrilege. Thankfully, the true church is coming back. Home chapels. I sell some to those folks. Sometimes, if there's no priest, they just gather at home to pray."

"In Latin," I said.

"Yes. *Pater noster, qui es in caelis, sanctificetur nomen tuum.*"

Our Father . . .

He put the chalice back in the case, setting it down precisely, cycing it, moving it a half-inch to the left.

"So there's a network of collectors like you?"

"Oh, yeah—and dealers. One near Philadelphia. They're very careful who they sell to, 'cause there's a lot of weird people out there. They know that I'm going to honor these things. I might even open a chapel, sort of a museum, you know?"

His eyes had gone a bit glassy. I nodded.

"There's a big dealer in Belgium, although the shipping will kill you. I keep my eye out, but it has to be special. I just got King David with the harp there."

Another statue, bearded King David with his hand on the strings. Hovering over it was a winged cherub hung from the ceiling by wires, like Peter Pan on Broadway. A religion funhouse, their gazes inescapable. I felt myself thinking of the way out, how long it would take to make it to the door.

"Amazing," I said.

Raymond smiled, led the way down a narrow path between statues and paintings, into the next room, like a passage in an Egyptian tomb. He stepped in and I followed. Dim yellow light, more statues, ornately framed paintings covering the walls, tapestries hung over the windows. There was a six-foot wooden cross screwed to the ceiling over a double bed, like something from an S&M club. The bed was covered with a blanket printed with a woman saint.

"Our Lady of Guadalupe," Raymond said. "She appeared in Mexico in 1531. To a poor Indian named Juan Diego. I love it because she chose him. It says God accepts all people."

He looked at me and smiled, like just maybe I'd also make the cut.

We backed out of the bedroom.

"How long have you lived here, Raymond?" I said, walking down the hallway.

"My whole life," he said. "I grew up in this house."

"So were your parents devout Catholics, as well?"

"Ha! No. They were devoted to their booze. And fighting with each other. The church, St. Ann's—that's where I went when they were screaming and swearing and throwing things and I couldn't stand it anymore. Jesus found me sitting there, this little kid, all alone."

I pictured it, him wearing the same hat.

"And the priests? How were they with you?"

Raymond turned to me, the first time I'd seen anger.

"All this pedophile stuff, it's totally exaggerated. A few bad apples."

A barrel full, I thought.

"I mean, Father Paul, he was great. I could talk to him."

"About your parents' fighting?"

"About everything. I didn't have friends, not my age, but he was my friend. We talked about all kinds of stuff, God and Christ. He gave me my first book about the lives of the saints. Then he gave me a scholarship to go to St. Ann's School. It's turned into offices now."

Raymond waved a hand over the bedroom like it was proof of something.

"So when I hear this stuff about all priests being perverts or whatever, I know it's a lie. And to lie is a sin."

"And sinners go to—"

"Hell, or Purgatory," Raymond said.

I thought of the crossroads of the same name on my way home.

"Depending on . . ."

"On the severity. Most people are offered a chance for expiatory purification."

"Like Dante," I said.

He glanced at me blankly. Father Paul hadn't given him *The Inferno*.

I turned back toward the door, started to retrace my steps. On the second pass, the collection seemed to have multiplied.

"What does Sparrow think of your collection?"

"She thinks it's cool. Her dad used to collect guitars, but then they sold them to pay for his meds. She gets it."

I kept walking, Raymond right behind me. From every direction, statues were watching, lamenting my lost soul. And then we were back at the door. I breathed an inward sigh of relief, thanked Raymond. He said I could come back anytime.

I walked out the door, across the porch, and down the driveway. He walked with me, our footsteps crunching in the grit and ice. At the truck he held out his hand awkwardly and we shook, like we'd made some sort of pact.

I got in the truck, started the motor. The police scanner on the dash scratched to life. He still was standing there so I lowered the window.

"One more question, Raymond. Why do you think you and Sparrow are such good friends?"

He looked at the ground, then at the soot-gray sky.

"I don't know. I guess because we're both outsiders," Raymond said. "We don't quite fit. But we fit with each other."

"Some people might find it an odd combo. I mean, the hair, her age, all the piercings."

Raymond smiled, looked at me calmly, like nothing I said could surprise him.

"It's not about appearances," he said.

"True," I said. "Do you worry about her? With the robbery and Zombie still loose and all?"

"Of course. I pray for her every day."

I pictured it, Raymond kneeling, Jesus, Mary, and the saints looking on silently.

And then the scanner chatter from the truck changed pitch, the tone suddenly urgent. I heard, "Pay-Day Check Cash. Three-two en route." Then another chiming in. Someone saying, "Has the suspect left the premises?"

"Where's Pay-Day Check Cash?" I said.

"Porto Street. Cut through here, take the first right after the high school."

I put the truck in gear.

"Check-cashers are the money changers in the temple," Raymond said. "They rip off the Somalis. If they got robbed, it's God's will."

Pay-Day Check Cash was another cement-block building, neon sign in the front window, bars over the glass. I parked beside a detective's unmarked sedan, lights flashing in its front grill, and walked toward the shop. There was an ambulance amid the police vehicles, backed up to the door, lights flashing.

A patrol cop, his back to me, saw me and turned back.

Blake. I walked up and stood beside him, figuring he'd been assigned to guard the perimeter. We watched as an EMT came out, put her bag back in the truck.

"Either very minor or the person's beyond saving," I said.

Another EMT emerged. He paused to talk to a detective, then went to the passenger side of the ambulance and got in.

"Minor," I said.

This time Blake sighed, a long, nearly silent exhalation of breath.

"Where's your partner?" I said.

"Salley? He got off," Blake said. "I stayed."

Overtime.

"He seemed a little stressed," I said.

"Yeah, well, we're all straight out. He does some private security work. For marijuana stores. Trying to fit that in."

"You think it would be all hands on deck with the PD."

"Seniority," Blake said.

"What if Zombie does shoot someone?" I said.

"Then all the OT is mandatory."

Blake stared as cops came out. Crime-scene crew arrived in an SUV, got out, and started suiting up.

We stood at arm's length. Blake was in military stance, legs spread, boots planted in the snow, both hands on his belt.

"Stopped and saw Raymond," I said.

He glanced over, seemed surprised.

"And I went to Sparrow's house yesterday."

"You always go to people's houses for stories?"

"Wanted to see how she was doing."

"She's tough. Can't fall apart, even if she wanted to. You know about her dad, right?"

"Yeah. What's the matter with him?"

Blake paused.

"Killed his liver with drugs and alcohol. Rest of him with cigarettes."

"So she's his nurse?"

"Only child," Blake said.

"Huh. Stinks to be her."

He looked away, like he'd said too much. We didn't speak for a three-count, then he said, "This trooper I know, I talked to her last night. She said you're not a bad guy, as reporters go."

"I hate it when people get all gushy."

Blake watched the other cops. "I don't like the press, the crap on social media."

"The internet, it's the wild west. People look for what they want to be true."

"What about you, McMorrow?"

"I write what I know to the best of my ability to be the truth. Which is different from just being accurate."

"And they publish it?"

"So far," I said.

He seemed about to ask another question when he turned, and I did, too. A woman was approaching with a recorder in one hand, a microphone in the other.

"Shit," Blake said.

He turned away and I watched as the woman kept coming. She was fortyish, a hard, angular face, dark hair pulled back and sunglasses on top of her head. Lace-up boots and jeans, a black down vest over a black sweater, black leather gloves.

She swept past me, circled around beside Blake, and said, "What's happening, Blake?"

He ignored her as she sidled closer, stared straight ahead.

"It's amazing, don't you think," she said. "How one guy in a Halloween mask can outsmart an entire police department. I mean, cops all over the place, detectives, the armed-robbery task force, dogs and night-vision and DNA and who knows what else. And still, Zombie makes you all look so—"

She paused, looked upward as if the right word were floating around in the cold morning air.

"Inept," she said.

Blake's jaw clamped tighter. His right hand was on his belt, just in front of his gun.

She smiled at him, then looked at me like she'd just noticed there were three of us, not two.

"Hey," she said.

I nodded. She circled around to my side, the microphone still in her hand, fixed me with her gaze. It seemed to be intended to be disarming.

"Stephanie Dunne," she said. "With a U and two Ns."

She had a radio voice, like she was performing.

"Is that thing on?" I said.

She kept her eyes fixed to mine.

"No. Should it be?"

I shrugged.

"Are you a detective?" she said.

"No," I said.

She waited, gave me a flirty smile, and said, "Are you going to make me guess?"

"Reporter," I said. "Newspaper."

"Ah, last of the Mohicans. Haven't you heard newspapers are dying?"

I nodded.

"So they say."

"I got out five years ago. Who are you hanging on with?"

"*New York Times*," I said.

Her microphone hand twitched. She moved closer.

"Cool. I do a podcast," she said. "It's called Who Dunne It?"

"Clever."

"Perhaps you've heard it?"

"Missed it somehow," I said. "Mostly I read books. On paper."

She smiled, said, "Ouch. But you know, this is the way people get their stories today. Think of it as being read to."

"Nothing against podcasts," I said.

"They break down the wall between content and consumer, that's all. I'm a storyteller," Dunne said, "Mr.—"

"McMorrow," I said.

I looked away, watched the cops hurrying back and forth.

"Jack McMorrow," she said. "No freakin' kidding. We must have a very big story to bring you to our fair city."

I watched the cops some more. She edged closer.

"I do crime."

"Likewise."

"We should talk. Can I buy you a coffee?"

I glanced over her shoulder, saw Blake looking at me, shaking his head. I looked back to Dunne.

"Kind of busy today."

"But you'll consider it," she said. "Great. I think your voice would add a lot to my reporting."

She fished a card out of her left vest pocket and held it out. I took it and looked. Her name, a phone number, @WhoDunneIt on Instagram.

I put it in my pocket.

She switched the microphone to her left hand, held out her right. I clasped it and she gave me a long-gloved squeeze.

She turned to Blake and said, "Brandon, what's the plan? If Zombie comes back and tries to rob a cop, you're ready?"

She gave a little snort of a laugh, then moved away, looking at her phone. Blake shook his head.

"Seems pleased with herself."

"Smile to your face and stick you in the back," Blake said.

"How so?" I said.

"Month after I got hired here, she did a podcast on me. Without me in it. I said no comment."

"Dragged it all up?"

"Oh, yeah. Talked to the blogger in Portland. Brought up my dead mother, my drunk grandmother raising me. Got it out of my ex-girlfriend."

"I see."

"My ex tried to defend me but Dunne twisted it all around, made it sound like I was a psycho. Then she has this hired-gun shrink weigh in. Said cops are acting out their deep-seated fears and unresolved anger when they shoot a suspect."

"Huh. You afraid of anything?"

"Not much."

"Angry?"

"I don't get mad anymore."

"You just get even?" I said.

Blake didn't answer. We watched the detectives and some ranking uniforms who were standing by a big SUV, talking to a guy in a teal puffy parka and a white baseball hat. Another guy was standing next to the first guy. His parka was bright orange. He had his hand on the other guy's shoulder. The first guy was rubbing his wrists.

"Owners?" I said.

"Yeah. Reginald and Dan. Reginald's the one with the hat. Good guys. They're a couple."

"First time the victim wasn't a woman."

No reply.

"Most criminals really stick to the playbook."

Still nothing.

"Looks like Zombie tied Reginald's wrists."

Blake neither confirmed nor denied. Reginald was telling his story. Detectives listened. One took notes.

"So he was the only one working?" I said.

For a moment Blake didn't reply, then finally he broke, said, "You're thinking it just happened. But you didn't hear that from me."

It took me a second. The owners and detectives moved to the shop entrance. Reginald was going through the motions of closing the door, turning the key in the lock.

"So that's it," I said. "He got him when he was leaving, not when he arrived for the day."

Blake didn't say anything.

"That means it happened last night, but the report just came in. The husband must have arrived."

We watched as the guy reached under his parka. They'd asked where the victim carried his gun.

"Zombie beat him to the draw," I said. "Forced him inside, probably with a gun pressed against his neck."

A beat, and then Blake said, "That trooper, she said you were a pain in the ass sometimes, but you always kept your word."

"Good to have one firm rule to go by."

"So anything I say to you about this case is off the record. Totally."

"Yes."

"Your word."

"You got it."

Blake glanced at me, then back at the shop, the detectives following the guy in the jacket as he led them deeper into the shop and out of sight.

"Safe is in the back room. Room is locked up. Where they keep the cash."

"Made him open the safe and then tied him up?"

No reply.

"They find the victim's weapon in there?"

A beat, and Blake murmured, "No."

"Serious escalation," I said, "from a point-and-run."

We watched as the check-cashing guy led the cops back inside and the door swung closed. A couple of plainclothes—baseball hats, badges on their belts—started toward us. Blake stepped between me and the building and the other cops, put up both hands, and said, "No press past the sidewalk. You're gonna have to back off, sir."

I did, and he followed, herding me away.

I slowed, let him move beside me.

"Local press won't have these details, I'm thinking," I said.

He looked away from me, pointed to the sidewalk beyond the parking lot, like he was shooing me away.

"Payback," Blake said. "Like they say, it's a bitch."

Five minutes later Pushard came out of the knot of milling cops and made a beeline for my truck. She was in plainclothes—jeans, knee-high brown leather boots, and a black parka. She looked tough and smart. I wondered how she tolerated the Who Dunne It?

I got out, circled the truck, jumped the snowbank. When she got close, I could see that she was not happy. I smiled. She nodded grimly, said, "Mr. McMorrow."

"Lieutenant."

"How was your ride-along?"

"Good. Blake's a thoughtful officer."

"Very."

She glanced away.

"Listen, I'm familiar with your work."

"Another loyal *Times* subscriber," I said.

"My boyfriend works for Bangor PD, off the record."

"The homicides last year."

"Yes," she said.

"Tough town," I said. "But not as tough as this one."

"I wouldn't advise playing those kinds of games here."

"I don't remember any games in Bangor. Just people getting killed."

"Right. Just be straight with me, and I'll do the same for you."

"Fair enough."

"I do have to say, I don't know why the *New York Times* would care about a robbery in Clarkston, Maine."

"Nine robberies," I said. "But it's more about the community and how it's reacting."

"If you think that's a story," she said.

"I do."

"But you can't publish the unconfirmed details."

"The robber getting the drop on the armed victim," I said. "Locked in the back room overnight."

"We're not releasing anything. Nada."

I slipped my notebook from my right pocket, a pen from my left. Wrote that down. Pushard stiffened. I was going to be a problem.

"I'm not confirming anything, other than to say there was a reported robbery and this is an active investigation."

I looked over her shoulder at the throng of cops.

"Got it," I said.

"You understand that releasing any details at this stage can jeopardize the investigation," Pushard said.

"I get that that's your position."

"Look, I have a very good relationship with the news content creators here," she said, as though reading my mind.

"What about the reporters?" I said.

She started to give back, thought better. She was a pro.

"If you give me your number, I'll make sure you're informed of any major developments in the investigation."

"How 'bout the minor ones?"

She took off her left glove and, as I recited, typed my number into her phone.

"This is a serious escalation from the other robberies," I said. "No little point-and-run."

Pushard looked up from the phone. She was tired. It was exhausting, saying nothing.

"Like I said, we're not releasing any details."

"Okay. Then speaking generally, as someone in law enforcement, isn't it true that when you start tying people up, the potential for harm to a victim or the perpetrator goes up exponentially."

"I don't do hypotheticals," she said.

"Check-cashers are usually armed. Did the robber disarm this victim?"

"No comment."

"I see surveillance cameras. You're looking at footage, right?"

"The investigation is ongoing," she said.

"And one more question. You can confirm that this was another Zombie robbery? The mask?"

This time she just stared.

8

I wrote it sitting in my truck. Three hundred forty-eight words for the New England roundup online. I even offered a headline that the copy desk would no doubt reject: "Latest 'Zombie' Robbery Raises Stakes in Maine Mill Town."

I e-mailed the story in, texted Carlisle to tell her it was waiting, that this was just a small preview for the bigger story to come. I didn't say that the point was to get the story out there fast and cement the deal with Brandon Blake—that I needed a crack in the wall that was the Clarkston PD, and Blake appeared to be it. If he wanted to stick it to the local press, I was ready and willing. Nothing like a source with a chip on their shoulder.

I googled Blake, and keeping an eye on the quieting crime scene, waited for the phone to load.

It did, news stories piling on. Everything Brandon Blake touched turned to mayhem. I knew the feeling.

Outside the check-cashing place, the police ranks had thinned. Pushard, a couple of detectives, two high-ranking uniforms, probably directing the robbery investigation. Pushard was talking on camera to a TV reporter, a tall guy in a bright red parka with the station's logo on the front. The guy was very handsome, with thick brown hair that stood up in the front. The on-camera interview lasted about a minute. When they were done, Pushard gave the TV guy a tap on the shoulder.

No zip ties in that report.

I was sitting in the truck when they pulled out, the brass in a big unmarked SUV, Pushard in an Impala. She saw me as she drove past and her head swiveled. I watched her in the mirror as she braked, probably weighing whether to come back and keep an eye on me. Then she kept going, more press to muzzle.

I waited for two minutes, got out of the truck, walked to the front of the shop and flipped up the police tape. Knocked on the door.

From inside, the guy in the teal parka looked up from behind a counter with a Plexiglas shield, like a bank drive-through. I held up my *Times* ID, which he couldn't see from that distance but would look official.

The door buzzed. I pushed it open and stepped in. Walked to the counter and spoke into a microphone. Who I was, where I was from. "I just talked to Lieutenant Pushard with the PD."

I made it sounded like this was her idea, slipped my notebook out. He watched me through the glass as I opened the notebook, flipped the pages like I was a cop taking the report. I looked up, all business.

He had a tan that looked darker under the white cap. The cap said MYRTLE BEACH in green cursive with a golfer in the background. There was a handgun on the counter to his right. It was what Sparrow had imagined a Glock looked like.

"And your name, sir?"

"Reginald."

"Last name?"

"LaPlante."

"I have a couple of questions for you, Reginald, as the victim "

He waited, both hands on the counter above what I figured was an empty money drawer.

"How did you get loose?" I said.

"I didn't," he said, his voice muffled through the speaker. "My husband woke up and I wasn't there so he called the cops and came down with the keys."

"They came in and found you."

LaPlante nodded.

"And this was Zombie."

Another nod.

"I'm told he bound you with zip ties."

He hesitated, embarrassed.

"Yeah."

"Do you think he'd cased the place? I mean, to know there was a secure room out back?"

"Wouldn't take much casing. Come in to cash a check, stand in line. We go back and forth to the room sometimes."

"You and your workers?"

"Just the two of us. We run the business together."

"Got it," I said. "How much did he get?"

"I'd rather not have that in the paper."

"How 'bout an approximation. Just to give the readers a sense of the seriousness of the crime. Four figures?"

"Oh, yeah."

"Did he say anything?"

"Nothing. Not a word. Just put the gun on the back of my neck."

"You couldn't get yours out?"

"Came up behind me when I was friggin' with the key. It sticks."

"Late last night, around ten, right?"

"Just before eleven. We close at ten."

"And your husband went home early."

"We overlap. He opens. I close."

"And that always worked for you before, being alone here at night."

"Never a problem. But it won't happen again."

"What won't?" I said.

"Getting robbed. We'll have one of us closing the door, the other one ready."

"As in—"

"Locked and loaded."

I wrote that down, every word.

"Would you have shot Zombie if you'd had a chance?"

"You shitting me? I'd shoot him right now."

"You sound angry, Reginald."

"All these robberies, this Zombie crap," he said. "Well, maybe this is a freakin' game for him, but it's not a game for us. We work our butts off for our money. I'm talking twelve-hour days for the last five years, hauling ourselves outta bed in the dark and the cold. Now it's gonna take us weeks to make that money back. For him to come in and just take it—"

I remembered what Sparrow told me, Zombie calling her a bitch, angry at her—at the world. What was it that Zombie hated in Reginald? Misogyny morphed into homophobia?

"I'll tell you what. He got the drop on me once. Won't happen again. I'll put a round right through that mask, keep on shooting."

> *After the chick at the QuikStop, all the others before seemed like a bunch of talk. Gimme the money! Now! Hurry up! Like a bad movie, some crap you never heard of with a bunch of no-name actors you pulled up on Netflix.*
>
> *He didn't know if he could do it that way anymore, not after he hit the chick, saw the blood running down her forehead and into her eyes. That was real. Got right to the heart of the matter. You give me the money, I just hurt you, didn't shoot you right there. Consider yourself lucky I spared you. Because you didn't deserve it.*
>
> *He was home, his mother at work at the nursing home, wiping up poop like the people with the dogs. She'd say, "They're hiring. It would get you out of the house." He'd say, "Are you kidding me? I'd rather poke myself in the eye with a stick." Then he'd go to his room, apply for a job to shut her up. Never reply if he heard back.*
>
> *He put his hands on the radiator, knowing what they meant by "chilled to the bone." That was the hardest part of this Zombie gig—not the actual robbing, but the staying still afterwards. Nothing colder than a parked car. Nothing colder than the floor of the backseat, even with his new rechargeable heated socks. Nothing harder than counting the*

seconds and minutes for the whole hour. One-thousand-one, one-thousand-two, one-thousand-three, like kids did when they played hide-and-go-seek. The time he counted, face against the bark of a tree in Shane's backyard, but they didn't hide, they just left. He was searching and searching, not finding anybody, not knowing they all went over to Vanna's house and had Doritos and Mountain Dew, him wandering around the backyards, looking behind garages, down on his hands and knees to look under cars. Finally realizing they were gone—the joke was on him. Finding out Vanna set it up, the little bitch she was even then, him never doing anything to her, ever. Because he was the youngest. The smallest. Because everybody else thought it was funny.

So now he counted, shivered, feet warm, the rest of him frozen, knowing an hour got him to after five a.m., just as people started showing up on the streets, headed for work. Him picking a car that had been parked in the same place for days, figuring odds were it was someone working at home, like everybody did during COVID.

At first he got nervous when somebody walked by, stopped near the car. One time it was someone walking fast, headed right for him. He dug the mask out, put it back on, slipped the gun from his jacket. But that one kept going, probably a chick doing the walk of shame. Not that anyone ever walked home from his place. Not like he dreamed, picturing some girl he'd just seen at Starbucks, them going at it for hours, her gathering up her clothes from the floor because she had a boyfriend but the boyfriend wasn't that good in bed. Kiss him on the forehead on the way out, him waking up later, finding her bra in the bathroom, some lacy black thing, bringing it with him to Starbucks next time, walk up to her. Say, in a cool sort of way, "You forgot something," and hand it to her, all rolled up in a little gift bag. She'd open it, then blush and smile and close the bag up quick, say, "Thanks. It was amazing."

Not that it would happen. He'd given up on all of them, the bitches.

9

It was after almost 12:30 when I pulled up in front of Sparrow's house, shut off the motor. There were lights on in the front room and a guy came to the window and looked out. Long hair, a flat wool cap on backwards. Very '90s.

He moved away from the window.

I picked up my phone, opened YouTube. Searched for Riff Calderone Band. A few videos. I opened the top one. "Live at Geno's, Aug. 3, 2011."

And there he was. Riff stepping up to the mic. It was blurry, shot from the audience.

He was lanky, leather vest and no shirt, jeans and cowboy boots. Tattoo on his right arm. Long stringy hair tucked behind his ears. Whistles from the crowd. The band—guitar, bass, drums, pedal steel, a background singer. Sparrow's mother? She was thin, hollow-eyed, pretty in a gaunt sort of way. A tunic with designs of flowers. She held onto the mic stand like it was holding her up.

The band tuned up. A pause. Riff counting down from four. Flat picking. "Gentle on My Mind," the Glen Campbell song. Riff sang, raspy and low. The woman singer doing harmony up high, still hanging on to the mic stand. End of the first verse, the other guitar starting up. Solo, pretty mellow, then building, notes bending, distorting, like Jimi Hendrix had stepped in.

And then Riff, screaming the second verse, the band slashing into the song, view blocked by the crowd bouncing. Tempo building, all chords now, Riff running across the stage with the mic, the singer extending phrases, gripping the mic in a stranglehold. Riff sliding on his knees to a stop as the song ended in a crescendo of feedback. Silence. Two bars of Riff picking softly. And end, still kneeling, head bowed over the guitar.

The crowd screamed and cheered and clapped. Riff hauled himself to his feet. Went over and gave the singer a kiss. Sparrow's mom, for sure.

"Huh," I said. "This guy was the real deal."

I texted Sparrow:

ANY CHANCE I COULD CHAT WITH YOUR DAD? I'M IN TOWN. IN FACT, I'M OUT FRONT.

I waited. A couple of guys pulled into the parking lot in a beater pickup, went into the Red Hen. I looked back at the house. Nothing. I waited some more, still nothing. I was reaching to start the motor and leave when my phone buzzed.

Sparrow.

—I'M GOING TO BED. HE'S HERE. HOPE YOU HAVE SOME TIME. HE'S A TALKER.

I thought of Roxanne at home. Hesitated, then slid out of the truck. Walked up the steps to the door. It opened and Riff Calderone looked out at me and smiled.

He was gaunt, face gray, faded brown hair tucked behind his ears under the cap. Jeans and a frayed T-shirt, Iggy Pop's faded image on his sunken chest. He said, "Hey, man. Coffee's on."

Riff turned and shuffled off, slippers scuffing on the wooden floor. I followed, down a short hallway. The walls were lined with posters: the Riff Calderone Band, mostly Portland bars, a couple in Boston. A doorway to the left. The living room, a glimpse on the way by. More posters. An electric guitar covered with stickers on a saggy plaid couch.

And then we were in the kitchen. A round metal patio table with two chairs. Rows of pill bottles lined up on the counter like toy soldiers. The smell of coffee and disinfectant.

Riff pulled a chair out, turned it toward me.

"Sit," he said. "Milk? Sugar?"

"Black's fine," I said.

He took a mug off a shelf, poured it full. Topped off another mug, his own. Put them both on the table. Moved his chair out and sat, then slid my mug toward me. I picked it up. He held his mug out and we touched them and sipped.

In the fluorescent light his face was more yellow than gray. His eyes were yellowed, too, behind a hooked nose, sunken cheeks etched with broken blood vessels, a crust of salt-and-pepper beard. I took out my notebook and pen.

"Been in the *New York Times* already," Riff said. "Maybe you saw it."

"No," I said. "Must have missed it."

"Really? Oh, you need this for your story, for sure."

He waited until my pen was poised.

"So we were at CBGB, Patti Smith was playing. 'Because the Night' had just broke and she has everybody in the club up and shakin'. And then she gives 'em some patter. She goes, 'There's this dude named Riff Calderone here all the way from Maine'—somebody tipped her off—and she invites me up. Didn't see that coming, dude. I go up front, roadie hands me a guitar, an old Strat, and plugs me in. I step up to the mic. The room is like freakin' packed, the way they did sometimes at CBGB. I wait, just standing there. Finally it's all quiet, them thinking, 'Who the fuck is this guy? Does he have stage fright or what?' And then I start in."

He looked at me. Paused.

"You know 'Jambalaya'? Hank Williams?"

"Sure."

"Right. So, nice easy a cappella at first, then add a little finger picking. 'Son of a gun, we'll have big fun on the bayou.' "

He had a nice voice, a smoker's rasp. I smiled.

"And then I stop. I give it this wicked long pause. Like eight beats. My eyes are closed. They're thinking, 'What the hell? Is that it?' And then I open my eyes and look around at the band. I go, 'One, two, three, four.' And then I launch, man. I mean it's all Riff, just rippin' the shit out of that song. Band jumps right in. I mean this is Patti's crew, right? They get it. I mean, we just crank the ever-loving piss out of old Hank and the place goes fucking nuts. They're dancing on the tables, diving into each other, a coupla chicks are up on the stage, one rips off her shirt."

He stopped for breath.

"Freakin' scene, man."

Another sip. Riff swallowed and took another deep breath.

Dramatic tension.

"So, come to find out there's a music writer there from your very own paper. Next morning—you see where this is going, right?—it's in the *New York* fucking *Times*. The writer, she goes, 'Patti Smith put on her usual sublime and poetically caustic set. But the surprise of the night was Riff Calderone, who is from Maine, and sat in to deliver a scalding tribute to Hank Williams that tore the roof off."

He smiled.

"A scalding tribute."

"Nice," I said.

"Know how she ended it?"

"No."

Riff held up his hands like he was framing a marquee.

" 'Punkabilly is born.' "

"Wow," I said.

"Yeah."

He sat back in his chair.

"So I coulda stayed in New York. Patti said I should bring the band down, open some shows, go with her on the road. But the old lady had flunked out of rehab, the rug rat was up here with my mom. I decided to head home."

"I see."

"Right. I mean, we'd play Boston once in a while. Opened for the Pixies and Iggy at the Channel, hooked up with the BossTones a coupla times before it all went to shit. So, lotsa things coulda happened but, you know, family and all."

I nodded.

"Responsibilities," I said.

"Right. Then C.J., that's the old lady, she ODs, and my mom gets friggin' Alzheimer's, and just like that, I'm a single dad. Played Portland—Mathew's, Geno's—could fill those places seven days a week. Patti, she keeps calling. 'Calderone! Get your punkabilly ass down here.' I say, 'Patti, girl, I'd love to. But I got obligations.' "

He sipped again.

"Iggy, he rings me up. 'Riff, dude. Totally dig your stuff. You gotta get outta the boonies.' I'm like, 'Love to, Iggy, but duty calls.' "

"Taking care of Sparrow," I said.

"Right," Riff said. He laughed. "Now she's takin' care of Riff." He shook his head.

"You're sick," I said.

"End-stage liver disease."

"Sorry."

"It sucks, Jack. It's Jack, right?"

I nodded.

"Drugs and booze, man. The road takes a serious freakin' toll. I literally gave my life to my music."

He glanced at my notebook, waited for me to get that line down. I did.

"Right."

"Took the old lady quick, but it's killing me the slow way, you know what I'm sayin'? Belly all bloated, can't breathe with all the fluid pushing up against my lungs. I go in and have that drained, needle like a friggin' garden hose. Feel better for a coupla weeks, fills back up."

I frowned.

"Need a fucking Excel spreadsheet to keep track of the meds. Diuretics, shit to dissolve my gallstones. Another one to treat bile acid, but that makes me itch like a bastard. Meds for that, too."

He turned toward the pill bottles on the counter.

"I'm on Medicaid, but it don't cover half of this shit. There's this one med, it'll give me five more years."

"Great," I said.

"Sovaldi. Doesn't that sound like a composer or something? It costs like eighty grand for three months. That's a thousand bucks for each pill."

"Wow."

"State won't cover it. I mean, my life ain't worth eighty grand? After all I done for people, bringing them joy with my music? Gonna put me out to die?'"

"What about a GoFundMe thing?"

"Tried it. Raised like twenty-two hundred. I said, what am I? A goddamn beggar?"

"Huh."

"Hey, I gave up arguing. Life's too short. Especially mine. But Sparrow, she's like a freakin' bulldog. When the girl isn't working, she's on the phone with the State, the insurance people, explaining the situation, my condition. You gotta be, like, on death's fucking door to get their attention. This country's health-care system sucks, let me tell you."

"Sparrow really works it," I said.

"Oh, yeah. All to keep her old man alive a few more years. I say, 'Bird.' Sometimes I call her Bird. I say, 'Screw it, Bird. You don't need me. Let me go. I had my time onstage,' but she won't do it. Raised her right, even by myself, working as a full-time musician."

"She seems like a good person," I said.

"Oh, yeah. Like I said, I tried to give her some good family values, especially after her mother left us. Freakin' fentanyl, dude. Bad stuff. Me, I was sensible. Booze and blow, baby. You just gotta pace yourself. I mean, I could go for days, just like Keith."

"Right. So now it's just the two of you. Does she have relationships? Friends?"

"Nah. There was a guy in high school. Mr. Hipster. Had the look, but inside he was a dope. Never had a fucking original thought. Then this chick she met in Portland, they hooked up for a while. She was wicked cool. Thought that might stick, but the chick moved to Boston to learn tattooing and it faded out. Now there's this cop, he gave her a ride home a coupla times, but who knows. A cop? Probably his way of serving the public."

"She has Raymond, right?" I said.

Riff took a long drink. His fingernails were yellow, too, long on his pick hand. He lowered the mug and swallowed.

"Church Man? You know, at first I thought he must be a perv. You know these TV preachers are total goddamn leches."

He sipped. I waited.

"You heard about his house, right."

"Yes."

"Hey, you want to live with a bunch of saint statues—whatever floats your boat, dude. I used to have, like, forty guitars."

"But you don't think he has bad intentions?"

"Ray-Ray? Nah, he's just weird. But we all are, right? He gives her rides, but it's just 'cause he's looking out for her, some Christian charity thing. Hey, we can't afford a car. I can't drive, anyway, because of the seizures. Fuckin' insurance for her would be a fortune. Her being under twenty-five, had an illegal transportation, a DWI, a couple of accidents. So it's good thing she isn't walking all winter."

"I see."

He brightened. "Hey, you know that music Church Man listens to?" I nodded.

"All these monks chanting, like, twenty-nine-part harmony. Shit's pumpin' in that van when he pulls in."

"I've heard it," I said.

"Okay, listen close here, Jackie."

I leaned in.

"You start with the chanting, right? Aaaaoooommmm. *Kyrie eleison.* You just let it float, you know? And then in comes the drums, just the floor tom, nice and slow. Boom, boom, boom. Then a kinda subtle bass line, off beat on the drums, laying down the vibe. You let that get into a groove—the chanting, the rhythm behind it. And then—wham. Ripping power chords, reverb cranked up, distorted to friggin' hell, let the fucking feedback ride, baby."

He jumped out of his chair, skinny arm whirling around an air guitar. And then he coughed, stopped playing and leaned toward me. I could see the yellows of his eyes.

"You know what I'd call it?" Riff said.

He waited for me to guess.

"I don't know," I said.

"Punk monks."

I grinned. He slapped his bony knee.

"Dude, what'd I tell ya? He may be dyin', but ole Riff Calderone still got it going on."

I drank the coffee, which was no longer hot. Looked around the kitchen. It was neat and clean, the towels folded, dishes put away. Sparrow's chore before she went to sleep?

He got out of his chair and winced. He stayed stooped, felt his lower back.

"Listen, Jack, I gotta hit the can. Goes with the territory with all these meds I got inside me."

I said it was good meeting him.

"We'll talk again, bro. I got a million stories. Sid Vicious, now there was a man on a mission. Met him in this dive bar on Bleeker Street. Sid goes, 'Hey, you're that wanker from the woods. Love your stuff.' I say, 'Sid, the pleasure's all mine.' He's like—"

"A last question, Riff," I said, interrupting.

He paused.

"Do you worry about Sparrow?"

Hesitation, as he returned to the present.

"With the Zombie robber?" Riff said.

"Yeah. Most people don't get pistol-whipped at work."

"I know. I told her, 'Just give him everything, Bird. It ain't your money.' "

"But she did. And she still got hit. Did you hear he did another one last night. A check-cashing shop."

"Busy bastard. But that's okay. He'll make a mistake. They'll bust his sorry ass."

"As long as he doesn't shoot someone first," I said.

"Hey, I'm surprised somebody hasn't blown him away already. This being Maine, all the guns out there."

"Check-cashing guy said Zombie got the drop on him."

"Hey, Zombie got balls, gotta give him that," Riff said, shuffling from the room. "Somehow he stays one step ahead."

10

That's what the newspaper said. I read the story in a print copy I picked up at the QuikStop, a middle-aged guy with a goatee behind the counter. I watched as a guy with a hammer holster on his belt and droopy jeans mulled over the cigarette selection.

The goatee guy unlocked the case, took out a carton of Newports. Hammer Holster paid with a hundred-dollar bill, stuffed the change in his pocket. The goatee guy called out, "Destiny, need you up front."

A redheaded woman trudged around the counter and took the guy's place at the register. He walked off with a swagger of authority. I was second to the front when he came out of the back room with a messenger bag over his shoulder.

I cut the line, left two dollars on the counter, followed him out the door.

He was getting into a black Tahoe, like the Secret Service uses to haul presidents around. I walked up to the driver's door and he reached for the bag. When I got close, I could see the gun pointed at the window. I put up my hands.

"Just a reporter," I said. "Jack McMorrow. *New York Times*."

After a long moment, he lowered the gun to his lap, still pointed in my general direction.

"Gotta be careful these days," he said.

I said, "Right. But I'm going to take a notebook out of my jacket pocket, okay?"

He nodded. The gun was a Sig with a fancy night sight, like Louis's. Preferred weapon of Navy Seals and store owners in Clarkston, Maine.

"Now a pen," I said, and I slipped it from my pocket, opened the notebook. He zipped the window down and said, "Get in. It's cold."

I did, waiting as he slipped the gun into a holster that was fastened to the driver's side of the center console. I sat, notebook on my lap. The inside of the truck smelled of his cologne and the leather seats. He was maybe forty, and his jacket was Patagonia, quality, like the gun. He was carefully shaved, with a precise haircut, the sides cut short and longer on top. A guy who cared about his appearance and spent money to keep it just so.

"Who are you again?"

I told him again.

"Slow news day down there or what?"

"I cover Maine for them," I said. "And you are?"

"Bob," he said.

"Bob who."

"Just Bob."

"You're the owner?"

"This store and two others."

"This your first robbery?""

"Yeah. Been lucky until now."

"Sparrow got a pretty good cut."

"And we lost a chunk of change. That hurts."

"I'm sure," I said. "But Sparrow could have been shot."

He patted his side.

"I'm in the store, be the last place he ever robs."

"You'd shoot him."

"You bet your ass."

"You think you'll lose workers because of this?"

"The robberies? Nah. No, what I lose 'em to is welfare. Government handing out money. That's my competition."

"But not Sparrow?"

"She's a good one. Smart. Hard worker. Accurate with the money. Keeps the machines clean."

"Machines?"

"Coffee, slushies, the swirly shakes. They gotta be spotless inside and out or you're asking for trouble."

I nodded.

"Got a work ethic, that kid. Doesn't call in sick every time she's hung over like some of 'em. Want to lay around, have everything handed to them."

Bob's phone buzzed in its holder on the dash. He looked, pulled it out, started texting, finished. He looked up, ready to go.

"You know her backstory?" I said.

Bob shook his head, shrugged.

"Just her dad's sick or something. You get involved in their personal lives, it's like a black hole."

A word to the wise.

I watched the snow sifting through the yellow glow of the parking lot lights like falling ashes. It was around one p.m., the sky a pale gray. I reread my notes from my conversation with Bob, noted his description of Sparrow's work habits, that she didn't fake sick when she called in. And beyond that, her life, like the lives of all the night-shifters, was a black hole.

I circled that quote, sat back. Thought that I should have confirmed the model Sig that Bob was carrying. Details. I wondered if he would be coming back to the store.

The wipers had opened a widening porthole in the snow-covered windshield, and I looked out at the street, headlights on in the cars. An unmarked brown SUV passed, one of the top cops from the check-cashing scene at the wheel. He slowed, glanced over at my truck, kept driving. I sat, the pain-in-the-ass reporter who wouldn't go away.

I had Sparrow, Raymond, Riff, two robbery scenes, police saying very little. The general climate was represented by the cleaners in the Dunkin' talking about Zombie, the fact that they were part of a post-release program a nice touch. I needed another store employee, thought of Mo from Somalia, supporting his family and maybe having a gun stuck in his face.

Zombie pulls the trigger and Mo's wife and kids are out of luck.

I was thinking that the counter clerks and the cops were both at risk with armed robbers on the loose, that maybe Zombie would want to go out in a blaze of gunfire. I looked around the lot for the blacked-out Nissan but it was gone, presumably Mo with it.

Getting out of the truck, I was headed into the store to check when Blake pulled in, Salley riding shotgun in the police SUV.

Blake parked out front by the propane tanks. Salley got out, walked by me and said, "No news in New York?"

I smiled.

He proceeded into the store, holding the door for a woman coming out with a pile of blonde hair and a black leather jacket. Salley watched her backside all the way to her car, grinned to himself, and went in.

I walked to the driver's side of the SUV. Blake buzzed the window down.

"Hey," he said.

"How goes it?" I said.

"It goes."

"Any news since we spoke?"

"Like an arrest? No."

"Like a suspect?" I said.

Blake didn't answer. The radio blurted and he turned it down.

"So what do you do now?"

He looked back at the store.

"Off the record."

He took a deep breath and frowned.

"You hit your snitches, see if they're hearing anything. Task force— that's not us—looks for patterns. Time of day, part of the city. If he has a job, he's doing this when he's off. Maybe going to or from. Checking surveillance footage before and after the robberies, in the stores, near the stores. Did same person come in day before, scope the place out? Did he park on a side street? Do we see the same vehicle? What's the common denominator? The task force has a plan."

He glanced back at the store.

"Still in there chitchatting," I said.

"He's having a thing with a woman who works days," Blake said. "One-track mind. Like a dog that should have been fixed."

"Yeah. But listen, how does he get away so fast? The robber, I mean."

"Between us?"

I nodded.

"Hard to say. Get into a vacant house maybe."

"Dogs can't track him?"

"It's not that easy. They can lose him in the street. Puddles, cars driving over the track. Had him for a couple of blocks one of the early ones, then lost it."

I looked back at the store, saw Salley walk past the Slurpee aisle with the red-haired woman. They were headed for the back. A whisper from the radio. "Gimme fifteen, working on information."

Blake sighed, said into his shoulder mic, "Ten-four. I'll make a swing around."

To me he said, "It'll be a half-hour."

"Let me guess," I said. "His wife doesn't understand him. He's thinking of leaving her."

He shrugged. "Sometimes vulnerable women are attracted to power."

"And some cops get off on having somebody they can control. Something tells me he's not hitting on the attorneys at court."

"They like his money, too," Blake said.

"Weed security pays well?"

He smiled.

"Quick coffee?" he said.

"Sure."

He put the SUV in gear.

"Dunkin' drive-through. How do you take it?"

In the form of tea, I thought.

"Black. No sugar."

"Follow me. There's a place we can stop."

The place was behind one of the mills off Canal Street.

I followed him across a short bridge and down a brick-lined alley. The alley led to an enclosure lined on three sides by brick walls with plywood-covered windows. The plywood was shredding at the edges, the graffiti faded. A broken fire escape dangled twenty feet above the pavement. A dead pigeon lay on the ground beneath it, clawed feet up, feathers strewn.

We parked, window to window. Blake handed my coffee over, and we opened the plastic tabs on the lids. He lifted his cup and said "*Salud.*" We sipped, lowered the cups. The two vehicles idled, shrouding us in a steam cloud of exhaust.

I waited. Good reporters can sense when silence is their best friend.

Blake shifted in his seat. Took another sip, watched the snow hit his windshield and melt.

"The kid I shot," he said, finally. "He was getting back at his parents. 'Hey, Mom. Watch me get myself killed. Maybe you should have loved me while you had the chance.' "

Suicide by cop.

"You were merely a tool."

"Yeah. Put this uniform on, for some people you're just a prop."

He seemed to be heading for something. I waited again.

"Thing is, I get that kid, totally. My mom was pretty wild, died running drugs on a sailboat. I was three. She always left me with my drunk grandmother, like I was a dog you drop at the kennel. Never told me or anybody else who my dad was, so I was on my own."

The radio blurted and Blake turned away to listen. A resident reported an unlocked parked car a block from the check-cashing shop with a blanket on the backseat. A K-9 unit was dispatched. "If he holed up . . . ," Blake said.

He continued.

"After she died, my grandmother homeschooled me, which meant all day by myself watching the History Channel while my grandmother was passed out. Ask me about the Bataan Death March. Boer War. Texas when it was part of Mexico. Pancho Villa. The Black Plague."

"Great preparation for Jeopardy," I said.

"For knowing how the world works," Blake said. "I wasn't mad at her then, but I was when I got older. Like, it took years for it to sink in, what she'd done. How irresponsible she was. So I get it. Thing is, I could have talked to that kid if we'd had the chance. Instead, all I got to say was 'Drop your weapon—drop your weapon.' "

"Not much of a conversation," I said.

"No."

I sipped. I didn't know why Blake was choosing this moment to give me his backstory, but it seemed right to me, too. Maybe it was the snow or the warmth in the cars with the motors idling. I turned the motor off. Blake left the cruiser running.

"I had no rules growing up," he said.

"Makes sense you would choose a job enforcing them."

"Everything can't just be anarchy. If it is, the weak get crushed. The powerful, the violent predators—they take everything."

"Rob stores and pistol-whip the woman behind the counter."

"Exactly."

We both sat for a minute with that.

"You have a family?" Blake said.

I nodded. "Wife and daughter."

"Could be your wife. She runs in to get a gallon of milk. Zombie panics and bam, your wife is dead and you're a single dad."

His phone beeped. He picked it up from the console and read a text. Put it down and shook his head.

"I gotta go," he said. "Salley's all done."

"Hey," I said. "Can I text you if I have questions?"

Blake hesitated, then recited the numbers. I shot him a text and his phone beeped again. He put the truck in gear, then looked down at the computer screen in the SUV.

"Blanket in the car was for a dog," he said.

I pulled out slowly, then drove out and over the bridge. The canal was frozen over, coffee cups and beer cans embedded in the ice like bugs in amber. On the brick canyon wall of the mill, windows were boarded or broken, the pigeons flying in and out. I thought of the hundreds of workers who had sat at looms, hour after hour, day after day, year after year. Joints worn through, backs permanently bent, but families fed and educated.

Now some made their money at gunpoint.

And people like Brandon Blake tried to stop them.

There was something pure about his motivations, ascetic about his life. Working patrol in this tattered tenement town on the night shift, living alone on a boat in a frozen harbor. Driven by a sense of duty to uphold the rule of law, protect people like Sparrow and Raymond from predators, catch the bad guys and put them in jail.

Sparrow. A crush? A love interest?

As I pulled away from the mill, I pictured the scene. Sparrow shot behind the counter, the death penalty for working hard so she could take care of her sick dad. Raymond, deciding to see what was keeping her, takes a round in the chest as he comes through the door. A dutiful daughter and a good samaritan; this time they end up on the floor in pools of blood. I knew I was catastrophizing, but it seemed possible. Like Blake said, not this time. Who knew what might happen tonight, or any other night, for that matter.

I registered that I was on the main drag headed for the turnpike, saw the street that led to Raymond's house. The truck practically turned itself.

A block in, I pulled over. Texted Roxanne:

STILL IN CLARKSTON. A LAST STOP FOR THE STORY, THEN I'LL HEAD HOME. SEE YOU IN AN HOUR AND A HALF. LOVE YOU.

But as I put the phone down and wended my way through the side streets, I knew it wasn't only for the story that I wanted to see Raymond again. It was about my faith, or lack of it—why I felt a pang of longing when I told him about my days as an altar boy, when I'd taken part in rituals a thousand years old. Life was simpler then. Good and evil. Sins, listed by type and seriousness. The faithful and the heathens. Black and white. Heaven above. Hell below. A comforting sort of fiction. Or not.

I pulled up, saw the van in the driveway. I parked behind it, got out and headed for the door. I had my notebook in hand but I wasn't even sure what I was going to ask him. Maybe I didn't want an interview. Maybe I just wanted to talk.

Crossing to the door, I could hear the monks chanting loudly, like Riff had cranked up the volume. For a second I thought maybe Riff had come over, was telling Raymond about his punk-monks idea. But how would Riff get here? Had Raymond picked him up? Had Sparrow come, too? Were the three of them hanging out?

On the porch, the chanting was louder, coming through the walls and the door, which was open a crack. I knocked and it opened an inch wider. I called, "Raymond. It's Jack McMorrow." He wouldn't hear me with the monks, so I pushed the door and it swung inward. I took two steps, stopped short.

I backtracked out to the truck. Opened the door and unlocked the glove box. Took out the Glock, reached under the passenger seat and found the magazine. Snapped it in, chambered a round. With the gun at my side, I walked back to the house, crossed the porch, and pushed the door open. Walked slowly down the hallway. The monks were still chanting at the top of their lungs.

There was a statue smashed on the floor by the door, Joseph holding Baby Jesus, but Joseph's head was gone. I took another step, felt plaster crunch under my boot. Looked down, and saw an angel's wing. Just one, dismembered.

Mary was on the floor, too, one of the many, this one with her face scraped off. A painting of Jesus, glass shattered in the frame, one hand held up in front of him as if to protect himself. A crucifix on the floor, a dent in the wall above it, like it had been thrown like a tomahawk. A dirty footprint coming from the kitchen.

I kept going. Slowly.

Everything had been pulled from the shelves and the refrigerator, tossed onto the floor. A mound of food—boxes of noodles and cereal, mustard and ketchup. Smashed dishes and emptied jars. A loaf of bread scattered like someone had been feeding ducks. Everything in a pool of milk.

I kept walking, my boots sticking to the floor as the smell grew stronger. Food and urine and maybe blood. I stopped at the bedroom door, which was nearly closed. With the barrel of the gun, I pushed it open.

Froze.

Swallowed hard. Focused.

I stepped in, gun raised. Looked right, left, took three quick steps. I listened but the monks were too loud. I yanked the closet door open.

Shirts on hangers, shoes on the floor.

I turned back. Took a step through the rubble of broken plaster and glass and dropped to my knees. A plaster scene under my hand, a station of the cross. I dropped close to the frame, the painted title: JESUS FALLS FOR THE FIRST TIME.

I stood up, no one in the room except me and Raymond.

He was on the bed, wrists taped together above his head, another loop around the carved headboard. His head was in a clear plastic bag and he'd been beaten, his left eye swollen, dried blood running from his nose and mouth down his neck.

His jeans were pulled down to his knees, his boxers down to his thighs. There was a condom on the bed, still in its torn wrapper.

Gun in my right hand, I slipped my phone from my pocket, unlocked it, and dialed 911 with my left thumb.

I told the dispatcher who I was, where I was. I said there'd been a murder. He asked if I'd done it. I said no.

11

We were standing beside a police SUV, me and two detectives, one on each side of me. I'd seen them at the check-cashing shop, from a distance. Now they had names.

Sanitas, a big guy with a chest-protector belly, and Jolie, short-haired and angular, the skin around her eyes smoked like sausage skin by cigarettes. They were likely younger than they looked.

"So again, this is police business. At this time you're a witness, not a reporter," Jolie said. "So this is off the record, okay?"

"Got it."

"You didn't touch anything?" she said.

"Just where I stepped."

"You should have turned right around and walked back out," she said.

"I thought Raymond might need help."

"That's what we're here for," Sanitas put in.

I looked at him. "Better late than never?"

"Listen, wise-ass," he said.

"That's what I'm doing."

"So you found him—" Jolie said.

"Just like you did."

"What did you see?"

"He was tied to the bed. A plastic bag over his head. He was dead."

"Why did you want to see him?" she said.

"I told you. He's in a story I'm writing. He's good friends with Sparrow, the QuikStop clerk who was robbed."

"You always bring a gun to your interviews?" Sanitas again. "They won't talk, you shoot 'em in the foot?"

"I told you. It was in the truck. I got it when I saw what the place looked like. In case somebody was still inside."

"Be the hero?" he said.

"Not get killed," I said.

They looked at me, not totally buying it.

We all took a breath.

"Okay, okay," Jolie said. "How long had you known Mr. Jandreau?"

"A couple of days."

"So you just dropped by?"

"It's what reporters do—at least the good ones."

"You sure you weren't after something else?"

I looked at her.

"Like what? A hundred statues of Jesus and Mary?"

"Like an intimate interaction," Jolie said.

"What?"

"Let's cut to the chase," Sanitas said, taking over. "You saw the condom. All that kinky shit. Freakin' cross over the bed, bloody crucifixes."

"They're supposed to be bloody. Jesus was nailed to a cross and the crown was made of thorns."

"Looked like a goddamn S-and-M club."

"No way. Raymond was more like a priest."

"Like they're lily white?" he said. "I could tell you some stories."

Jolie interrupted. "What about this? Jandreau puts something out there online, guy responds, things go wrong. Maybe he doesn't put out the way his date wants. Maybe says something to insult the other guy's manhood."

"Right. The bag over the head. That's a sexual enhancement," Sanitas said. "Suffocation. It's supposed to make—" He caught himself.

I shook my head. "You saw the place. It's like a church."

"You can turn anything into some sort of perversion," Jolie said.

"Hey, they have fake nuns in porn," Sanitas said. "It's a whole category."

She looked at him and he stopped talking. I took it that she was senior.

"He say anything about relationships? A boyfriend?" Jolie said.

"I told you, no."

"Girlfriend then?"

"No. He was a total bachelor from what I could tell."

"Drugs?"

"Not that I could see. He didn't drink, either. Parents were alcoholics."

"Anything about enemies?" Jolie said. "You think any of these religious items are worth much?"

I shook my head again.

"The paintings aren't exactly Botticelli," I said. "There was a chalice, but I'm sure it wasn't gold. Besides, it's supply and demand. Way more of this stuff than people who want it."

"Where'd he get all this crap?" Sanitas said.

I turned to her, away from him.

"Raymond said he'd get a call when they were going to shut a church down in Maine. There's a term. Decommission, or deconsecrate. He'd go and look for what he needed for his collection. He specialized in Mary and martyrs."

"Jesus Christ," Sanitas said.

"So the diocese, or whatever, would give him first dibs," Jolie said.

"Right. And pickers around here, they know he's into this, they'd call if they saw something, like in a yard sale. He also had some dealers he worked with. He said there are places out of state and in Europe that sell the higher-end things. He told me he'd just located a statue of St. Apollonius."

"Who's that?" Jolie said.

"A saint who wouldn't recant to a Roman emperor so they drowned him."

"This whole thing is pretty whacked."

"He was a quiet, nice guy. Worked nights stocking shelves. Very old-school religious. He didn't deserve this." I was having a hard time imagining Raymond soliciting sex from a stranger. It just didn't fit.

We watched more crime-scene people arrive, leaning on their cars as they stooped to booty up.

"Whatever," Sanitas said. "All I know is, we needed this like a hole in the head. These guys couldn't do us a favor and hook up in Portland."

"It wasn't a hookup," I said. "I'm telling you." Everything in my experience was telling me this was a setup.

"Whatever it was," he said, "they coulda gone to a Super 8 in Westbrook. We got an armed robber to deal with."

"They were looking for something," I said. "The house was ransacked."

"Or somebody got upset. Trashed the place in a rage. It happens," Jolie said.

"Maybe a kinky love triangle," Sanitas said. "These people are known to be wicked jealous."

"What people?" I said. "Murderers and victims?"

He got the look from Jolie again.

"Let's get in the car, Mr. McMorrow," she said. "I'll take your statement."

I said it all again. Jolie recorded it on her phone and took notes. Then she gave me back my gun, told me I was free to go.

I stood by the curb, between the police tape and the bystanders, who had emerged from their houses and were standing in a clump. Sanitas was pulling them aside one by one, no doubt asking if they'd seen or heard anything out of the ordinary. A guy in a Celtics jacket was shaking his head.

I walked a few steps away and took out my phone, called home.

"Hey," I said.

"Hi," Roxanne said.

"I'm in Clarkston."

"Uh-huh."

I could hear dishes clinking.

"What are you doing?" I said.

"Making an afternoon snack. Tara is over."

"Oh, good. What are they doing?"

"Practicing their dance moves. Sophie's, like, this budding chore-ographer."

More clinking.

"What are you making?"

"Nachos. Tara may stay for dinner—I'm not sure. She's going to call her mom."

"Okay."

"Yup."

She called away from the phone. "Girls, nachos are ready." I waited, finally said, "Something has happened here."

No reply, chairs scuffing the floor.

"Raymond, the man I told you about with all the church stuff."

I paused. Roxanne said, "Do you want sour cream?"

"Am I on speaker?" I said.

"No."

"Good, because Raymond—"

"It's in the back, behind the ketchup," Roxanne said.

I watched Sanitas, who was talking to a woman in a purple parka. She seemed to be last in line. In the background, I could hear the girls guffawing, then Sophie saying, "Oh, my God, Tara. You have cheese all over your face. Gross."

"I should go," I said.

"Yes, I should go, too."

"I'll be home later. I should be there by—"

I hesitated, considering a realistic ETA.

"Whatever you can do, Jack," Roxanne said. "We'll see you when we see you."

"Love you."

"Love you, too."

Away from the phone, Sophie said, "Where's Dad, anyway?"

Jolie had come out of the house and waved to Sanitas, who was walking up the driveway. I hurried over to the neighbors, before they scattered. They were mostly older, gray-haired and stooped, huddled in their jackets in the cold. I told them who I was and what I did.

"He was a nice man," a gray-haired woman began, like the neighbors of victims always say on the TV news. "He always waved and smiled."

"Religious," a guy in a Celtics jacket said. "He was saving all the stuff they take out of the churches."

"You can't just bring it to the dump," the woman in the purple parka said. "It's been blessed."

"By a priest," said her husband, shorter than her by a head.

They all nodded seriously, clearly Catholics in practice or upbringing.

"Have you been inside his house?" I asked.

They shook their heads.

"Just saw him unloading," the gray-haired woman said.

"I offered to help him carry stuff one time," the small guy said. "He said he could handle it. He was stronger than he looked."

"He had a dolly," Celtics Jacket said. "And these boards he put over the steps."

"So no friends coming by?" I said. "Family?"

"Only child," the gray-haired woman said. "The mom was still alive when we moved here. It was the two of them, but she never came outside."

"She drank, didn't she?" the woman in the purple parka said.

"Mrs. Jandreau?" the small guy said. "Like a fish."

"And then she died," the gray-haired woman said. "We bought the house in '83, she didn't last a year after that."

They nodded and there was a moment of silence.

"So you didn't see much of him?"

Celtics Jacket: "Only one he opened the door to was the mailman or UPS."

And me. Maybe Sparrow had given him the high sign, a signal that I was okay.

"Nobody last night?" I said.

More shaking heads. It was like interviewing a flock of sheep.

"Would you have noticed if somebody had come by here?"

"Depends on the time," Purple Parka said. "We were watching TV."

"The music contest," her husband said. "They sing and somebody gets voted off. I'd rather watch police shows, but the wife, it's her thing."

"It was the finals," his wife said.

"Didn't hear anything? Banging or yelling?"

"We have to turn it up loud," she said, and nodded to her husband. "He won't wear his hearing aids."

"The mill," Celtics Jacket said. "Twenty years in there and you're deaf as a stone."

Like the sound of statues being thrown against a wall. Or shouting. Or screaming, which there might have been. Unless they'd taped Raymond's mouth, taken it off at the end.

I closed my notebook, thanked the neighbors. As I started to turn away, the woman in the purple parka said after me, "I never worked in the mill. I was in retail."

I turned back.

"My hearing's fine," she said. "That's why I could hear it."

"Hear what?" I said.

"Like I told the police detective, we live across the street and down two."

She turned and pointed to a small blue-sided ranch house with an attached single-car garage and a fake well on the front lawn. She stuck her hand back in the warmth of her pocket.

"The show had just ended and this girl whose mom died, she won. She's like sixteen and she has a beautiful voice. And she's sweet. I was rooting for her. Her dad was there, and he was so proud."

I waited.

"I was going to bed and he was in the bathroom. I heard somebody walk by. You could hear the crunching on the ice in the street."

"What time was this?"

"A little after eleven."

"Which way was the person going?"

"Out to Montcalm, out of the neighborhood."

"Were they walking quickly?"

"No, just walking. Like somebody taking a stroll. Not like somebody walking to get someplace."

I was writing now.

"Did you think that was unusual?"

"A little. Most of the street is older folks. We turn in early, don't tend to walk after dark, especially in the winter. You could slip and fall."

"Did you look out to see the person?" I asked.

"No. Like I said, I was ready for bed. I did call to Harry—he was in the bathroom—and reminded him to make sure the doors were locked."

She paused and moved a step closer. Harry did, too. The rest of them followed.

"You do know we have a robber on the loose," she said.

"Dressed like a zombie," Harry said.

"You have to be extra careful," she said.

"Do you think it could have been Zombie who killed Raymond?" I said.

"You never know," she said.

"Heard he paid for his statues with cash," Harry said. "Guy lives alone with a stash of money, word gets out, Zombie gets wind of it."

He raised his eyebrows.

"Hell of a lot easier than sticking up a store for a hundred bucks," he said. "Alarms going off, surveillance cameras, cops coming from all directions."

"Are you in law enforcement?"

"No, I just watch the shows."

I was writing. I stopped and looked up.

"Then why would they kill him?" I said. "That would seem a lot harder than just pointing a gun at somebody and walking out the door."

"Witnesses," Harry said. "Gotta tie up loose ends. It's business."

Having not seen the carnage in Raymond's house, the group nodded in agreement.

12

I took notes. The older couple, Harry and Crystal Lemieux, had a lot to say. Harry wanted to stay longer and talk cop stuff, having watched a lot of TV, but Crystal took him by the arm and led him away. The rest of the neighbors went home, too, so they all missed the taxi that pulled up a little after three thirty.

The back door opened, and Sparrow sprang out.

She ran toward me, saying, "Who could do this?" She was sobbing, saying, "He never hurt anybody, never."

I turned toward her, reached out with one arm to console her, maybe take her by the shoulder, but she swerved and ducked under the police tape and ran up the driveway, still sobbing.

"Sparrow, no," I called, and bolted after her, caught her just as Sanitas came out of the door onto the porch. I took Sparrow by both shoulders, thin under her sweatshirt, turned her around, hustled her down the driveway to the street. She thrashed for a moment, tried to dodge by me to go back to the house, but I held tight, and she sagged. I'd started to guide her toward my truck when Sanitas caught up.

"Miss Aldo," he said. "We need to talk to you."

"Where's Blake?" Sparrow said, hardening. "I want to talk to him."

"No, you need to talk to me."

We'd stopped, turned. Sparrow was disheveled under her hoodie, the bandage gone now, a jagged brown line showing through her shorn hair, her fingers and hands gray-white. She had on black sneakers, no laces, and no socks, revealing a tattoo on her pale ankle, just below her leggings. Initials and a date. Her mother's death?

She straightened, said to Sanitas, "Who killed him?"

"We don't know. That's what we're here to try to figure out."

"Try to figure out? You think you won't be able to? Well, start figuring, for fuck's sake. This man, in his own house—somebody just comes in and kills him? I mean, what the fuck?"

She started to cry again, wiping her eyes with the back of her hand like the child she'd once been.

It all rolled off Sanitas's barrel chest. He leaned down and toward her, the fringe of blue hair showing from under her hoodie, and said, "Sweetie. You want to help us catch the dirtbag did this to your friend? You come with me."

He put a big arm behind her, shepherded her toward the cop cars.

Jolie was coming down the driveway and the three of them got into an SUV, Sparrow and Jolie in the back, Sanitas in the front. He turned toward Sparrow and Jolie leaned closer, began to talk.

I walked along the street, looked up at the house. Lights were on, figures passing by the windows. A crime-scene tech walked to Raymond's van, parked in front of my truck. More company than this house had seen in decades; maybe ever.

In that moment, I pictured it again: the crinkled bag, the pale skin, the rivulet of red-black blood running from one nostril to his lip. His eyes open, mouth frozen in a half-smile. Maybe he'd been praying. I hoped so.

My lead. I started writing the story in my head.

CLARKSTON, MAINE—*Raymond Jandreau, a solitary and deeply religious man who filled his modest house with items collected from decommissioned churches, was murdered here in his home Thursday.*

Jandreau, 41, was found tied to his bed [I knew they wouldn't want this detail released], his collection of statues smashed and strewn around the house. In this former mill city, unnerved in recent weeks by a string of late-night armed

*robberies committed by a gun-wielding robber in a zombie
mask, it was one more affront.*

The quote:

> *"Guy lives alone with a stash of money, word gets out,"
> said neighbor Harry Lemieux, who speculated that the
> "Zombie robber" may have heard about Jandreau's habit
> of paying cash for statues and decided it was easier to rob
> him than convenience stores.*

The sex part had to be included.

> *Police are also investigating whether the killing was
> the result of a sexual tryst gone wrong.*
> *But if the murder was connected to the rash of robberies,
> still unsolved despite the efforts of a police task force, it would
> be a serious escalation in a crime spree that has left one store
> employee injured and a city feeling besieged.*

I'd need a police quote there. Lieutenant Pushard?

> *The investigation is just getting under way. There is
> no indication at this time that Jandreau's murder and the
> robberies are connected [???].*

I looked up at the house again, scanned the scene for details. The
packing crates stacked on the porch. The tattered plastic wrapped along
the foundation. The dirty ruts that led up the driveway.

I took my phone out, left Carlisle a voicemail at the *Times*. The
basics of the story, that I saw it as on the section front for the New
England edition.

"But remember," I said. "This isn't the story—the bigger story about the robberies, this fraternity of night people, how they're connected. This changes that one, but it's still coming."

I looked over, saw Sanitas getting out of the car. They were winding up.

"Gotta go," I said.

I hung up.

Police had set up a security perimeter three houses down. There were a couple of TV crews there, a reporter and a newspaper photographer with a very long lens. He was focused on the SUV, Jolie leaning close to Sparrow in the backseat. If she got out now, she'd be on the front page.

I headed for the SUV, thinking I'd turn her away from the camera, but then heard another siren, a quick *whoop*.

It was a pickup, a blue strobe on the dash. The press and the patrol officer moved aside and it drove through. Parked with the rest of the cops. Blake got out.

He was in jeans and a black parka, baseball cap. He strode up to Sanitas and they huddled for a few seconds. Then he walked to the SUV as Jolie and Sparrow got out. Sparrow hurried to him and collapsed into his arms. He said something to her, patted her on the back. Then he saw me, led her over.

"I don't want to go home," she said, wiping her eyes. "I need to stay here. For Raymond."

"I'm here," Blake said. "McMorrow's here."

"I don't care," she said.

"Sit in the truck," he said, handed me the keys, and started over to the huddle of cops.

We sat in the front seat. Sparrow had to move a coil of rope from her side and put it in the back. I started the motor and turned up the heat. Sparrow pulled her hood tight and pressed her legs together for warmth.

It had started to snow again, small flakes that plummeted to the ground like tiny meteorites. The fan whirred, still blowing cold air.

"How you doing?" I said.

"Shitty," she said.

"I know."

"They said you found him."

I nodded.

"How bad was it?"

"Bad enough."

"Do you think he was scared?"

"No," I said. "He looked kind of calm, like he might have been praying."

"Did they cut him?"

"Not that I could tell. Maybe a couple of punches."

"He wouldn't care what they did," Sparrow said. "He would've known he was going to Heaven."

I turned and looked at her. The piercings and the jagged cut reminded me again of the big Jesus, the blood from the crown of thorns.

"Do you believe in that?"

"For Raymond I do," she said.

We sat and watched. Blake had left the detectives and walked up to the house. The heat began to come on.

"It's wrong, what they're saying," Sparrow said. "He didn't care about sex."

"So the theory that he hooked up with somebody online—"

"Total bullshit," Sparrow said. "I would've known."

"He never talked about anything like that?"

She shook her head. "Not women. Not men. Not anybody."

A small shock of blue hair fell across her forehead.

"A secret life?" I said.

"We had no secrets," she said. "We talked about everything. His fucked-up parents, always fighting like he wasn't even there. I told him I was lonely sometimes, and he said he was never lonely. He was always with Jesus."

"And Mary and Joseph and all those saints."

"It was crowded in there," Sparrow said.

"Yes."

A tech backed his way out of my truck, looking for blood? Evidence my story didn't add up? She turned and walked to the porch, then inside.

"There were a couple of things that led them to the sex theory," I said.

Sparrow turned to me, ready to argue.

"Sex? Raymond? Are you frigging kidding me? Like what?"

"I'm not supposed to share details."

"I won't tell anyone,"

I hesitated.

"A plastic bag over his head," I said. "A condom on the bed."

"Used?"

"It didn't appear so. Maybe they didn't get that far before whatever happened, happened."

Sparrow shook her head. "No freakin' way."

Blake came out of the house, walked down the driveway, stopped to talk to Jolie and Sanitas and a couple of uniforms. He scowled and shook his head, left them, and walked to the truck. I got out and he stood beside me, the door still open. He got in, closed the door, and buzzed the window down.

"It's an easy out," Blake said. "One-night stand gone wrong."

"No way," Sparrow said.

"The way the place was smashed up," I said.

"That's not sex," Blake said. "And the bag. That's how you get somebody to talk."

"Enhanced interrogation technique," I said.

"Poor Raymond," Sparrow said.

"You think he had a lot of cash?" I said.

"He always had money. They cashed his check at the store. He paid cash for all of his statues and crap."

There was a pause. I was thinking of Raymond, the bag coming off, him gasping for air. Where's the money? The bag going back on.

Blake hit the wipers. They brushed snow off the windshield and onto my boots.

"They made Sanitas lead," he said.

"Which means?" I said.

"He's third string. Not a high priority."

"The robberies," Sparrow said.

"That's where they'll focus their resources," Blake said.

"He was one of the nicest people in the world," Sparrow said. "And somebody killed him. That's a big deal."

"Very big," Blake said.

She reached over and took his hand. Squeezed for a beat longer than only a friend would, and let it go.

13

Once it was cleared, I backed my truck down the driveway. Two houses down there was a cruiser parked in the middle of the street, a cop standing beside it with her arms folded across her chest. Behind her were a couple of television cars, reporters and camera crews unpacking equipment. I pulled up, still distracted. Blake and Sparrow?

The cop waved me through but a guy with a camera on his shoulder stepped out and started shooting. His reporter, a better-looking guy, hustled from their car, a notebook in his hand. He got beside the truck said, "Channel 9, WJHG. Can I talk to you, sir?" I kept driving, left them standing in the middle of the street. Pulled up to the corner and stopped.

A car was parked at the intersection and the driver door popped open.

Black leather jacket. Sunglasses on top of her head.

Stephanie Dunne jumped out, stepped in front of my truck, put a gloved hand out and smiled. Moved around to the driver's side, keeping her hand on the hood as though holding the truck in place.

I lowered the window. She leaned close. She had a lot of hair and I could smell shampoo.

"Jack," she said. "We have to talk."

"Says who?"

"Says the story."

"What story is that?" I said.

"Raymond Jandreau."

"You doing spot news now, Ms. Dunne?"

"Steph," she said. "And no."

I didn't reply but I left the window down. For Dunne, an opening.

"Raymond was a complicated person," she said. "I want to tell his story."

"So tell it," I said.

"I'd like you to be part of the new podcast series."

"It's a series?"

"Don't you think he deserves one? You've been in the house."

I didn't answer.

"It's incredible," she said. "All the statues, the cross over the bed."

"You've been there?"

She hesitated.

"No, but I've talked to people who have."

A source in the PD.

"Put them in your podcast then."

"They aren't storytellers," Dunne said. "You are."

I shrugged. The motor idled. She kept her hands clamped to the door.

"Can we just talk? Off the record?"

She smiled.

"Five minutes? Come on, Jack, it's cold out here."

I nodded to the passenger side and she walked around the front. I pushed the Glock further under the driver's seat and moved my notebooks, and she climbed in. She was tall and her black boots had heels, so it took a few seconds for her to get situated. Then she turned to me and smiled.

I pulled out and through the intersection and she leaned toward me as she maneuvered to put her seat belt on. Perfume fragrance mixed with the shampoo. She was very made-up, which seemed odd for a podcaster.

"I'll buy you a coffee," she said.

I was cold and tired so I drove up to the main drag, took a right. It was the opposite direction from home. As we approached the Dunkin', Dunne said, "God, no. Keep going."

I did, and when we were downtown, she motioned toward the town's fancy coffee shop, a place called Sit. I passed it and pulled up to the curb.

"We can stay in the truck," I said. "Keep this truly off the record."

"Sounds good. Kind of cozy in here."

She leaned close as she fumbled with the seat belt again. Turned to me and said, "How do you like it?" like it was some sort of double entendre.

"Black," I said.

"Dark roast? Medium roast?"

"Whatever," I said.

"Tough guy," she said, and she smiled, lifted her long legs up, and pivoted and slid out of the truck.

I waited.

Police drove by on robbery patrol, two in each SUV. It seemed ineffectual, driving around waiting for somebody to call 911. I wondered if the detectives were having any luck, hitting up the snitches. Then I wondered how long Sparrow and Blake had been seeing each other and how she kept it hidden from Riff. Maybe Salley wasn't the only one showing up at the QuikStop for romance. Then I realized I was thinking about all of this to keep from thinking about Raymond—a kind, private man killed in a most horrible way.

And then Dunne was back. She got the door open, climbed back in, put the coffees in the console. Hers was small. Espresso.

I'd left the motor running, the heat on, and she took off her gloves. She reached for her coffee and said, "All these podcasts that follow a crime—you know what they have in common?"

"No."

"The crime is over. It's all rehash."

"Okay."

"I want to do real-time crime. Who killed Raymond Jandreau? We don't know, but that person is out there and may kill again at any moment. That's the tension that drives the story."

I shrugged. Dunne sipped, paused, like I'd conceded the point.

"So Raymond was gay."

"I have no idea." I thought about what Sparrow had said—not anybody. "Asexual" was a better fit, but I wasn't about to tell Dunne that at this point.

"I heard they found a condom."

"Easy way to make a murder look like a sex crime."

"Or easy way to make a sex crime look like a sex crime," she said.

We both sipped. Traffic passed in the salty slush, making a sloshy sound like waves on a beach.

"How did you come to find him?"

I hesitated.

"This is off the record," I said.

"Yes. My word as a fellow journalist."

A stretch, I thought. "I was just stopping by. I had questions for him."

"For your story."

"Right."

"Which is about?"

She was starting to feel pushy.

"The people affected by the robberies."

"How was he one of them?" Dunne said.

"He was a regular at the QuikStop. Friend of one of the employees. She was the one who was robbed. He always drove her home."

"Was he screwing her?"

I looked at her and frowned.

"No. She's twenty."

"Hitting on her?"

"No."

"Then he was gay."

"No, he was a bachelor. Very Catholic."

"I rest my case," Dunne said, and sipped. "So the crosses and the candles, you think that really was a religion thing?"

"I know it was," I said.

"How?"

"My gut and fifteen years of listening to people. You get a sense when people have secrets."

We drank coffee. A couple of young guys sauntered by, hoodies up, trying to look like predators. Like in Clarkston, Maine, it was eat or be eaten.

"My sources say it was a sexual tryst gone wrong," Dunne said. "Some online hookup."

"Your sources are jumping to conclusions. If they're investigators, they don't know what they're doing."

"I have to go with the story as it presents itself."

"You don't have to do anything."

She looked exasperated. Recovered.

"Okay. Jack. I'll cut to the chase. I'm new to this. I've been self-publishing, have a couple of local guys doing audio as a favor. I pitched this idea to somebody I know at Apple, just informally, and she liked it. Know what she really liked?"

"No."

"You. And the *New York Times*."

"Huh."

"I could get a real production deal. With Apple, it could totally take off. I mean, I have, like, two thousand subscribers, four K on Instagram."

I must have looked unimpressed.

"I know that isn't much compared to the *New York Times*," Dunne said.

"It isn't," I said.

"I need ten thousand per week to get serious advertiser attention. Right now, I have a hot-tub company and this coffee shop."

I nodded.

"But some of the subscribers are journalists, in Maine and elsewhere."

"Good for you."

"So I kick things off, they run with it. Before you know it, the story is out there, takes on a life of its own."

"True or not," I said.

She sipped again. The hot coffee had begun to melt her lipstick, made it look like blood.

"So here's what's true," Dunne said. "Local man, collector of statues from Catholic churches, is found dead, tied to his bed under a six-foot cross. The murder is reported by rogue freelance *New York Times* reporter Jack McMorrow."

"Rogue?"

"You definitely push the boundaries, Jack."

"Look up the definition," I said.

I swallowed some coffee.

"McMorrow had come to know the dead man when he was alive, of course. Sources said he told police he walked into the house, saw the smashed statues and general wreckage and went back to his truck to get his gun, before returning to the premises only to find Jandreau dead on the bed. Only then did he call 911."

I thought of Carlisle hearing this, the conversation with various higher-ups. He went to get his gun? Freakin' McMorrow. Here we go again.

"Sources say there was evidence of sexual activity on the bed."

"Not true," I said. "There was just the condom."

"Used?"

I drank more coffee, didn't answer. A dump truck went by and flung slush on the side of my door.

"What's the question you're trying to answer?" I said.

"Why the *New York Times* is at the scene of a sex murder before the cops."

"I just told you."

"But it raises other questions," Dunne said.

"Like what?"

"Who killed Jandreau? Was it connected to the Catholic Church? Is there a sex cult thing going on here? What does the Church know, and when did it know it?"

"You've got to be kidding."

"I'm just asking the questions, Jack. The public has a right to know."

She looked at me, her eyes wide with righteousness.

"That's bullshit and you know it."

"Hey, don't shoot the messenger, Jack. I don't mean that literally. I'm assuming that gun is in here somewhere."

She looked down at the floor. I put my coffee down, shoved the truck in gear. Did a U-turn and started back toward Raymond's house and Dunne's car. Dunne sat and sipped her coffee, a half-smile showing behind the cup.

"Gotta get out of this backwater, Ms. Dunne?" I said.

"Please call me Steph, Jack."

"So you invent a bunch of sensational nonsense that will spread your name on Instagram."

"You say it's nonsense. But we know the Church has secrets that it wants to keep hidden. I mean, thousands of child abusers. All those billions of dollars in gold in the Vatican. All these powerful people are in it together. They control everything."

"And Raymond is your way to cash in on the conspiracy theory."

"What if he's a symptom of a bigger problem?"

"He's not. He was a quiet, gentle man in Clarkston, Maine, who just wanted to be left alone."

"What if he found Church secrets along with those statues? Names from a pedophile ring. I mean, they came from all over, right? Maybe the Church needed to silence him. You're the one who said the sex thing might be cover for a regular murder."

I didn't answer.

"The Church finds out what he knows. They send a hitman, set it up to look sexual."

She said the word slowly like it was seductive.

"I thought you said it was a sex crime," I said.

"I said it might be," Dunne said. "That's the great thing about the new journalism. I just raise questions. I don't have to have the answers."

I turned off the main drag, drove down the block, and pulled up beside Dunne's SUV. Dunne reached for the door handle, moved over and got out. Before she closed the door, she leaned back in, looking at her phone.

"Your photo at the crime scene is doing great on Twitter. 'New York Times writer Jack McMorrow first to discover religious statue collector's grisly murder.' "

"I'm a stringer. You know, not staff."

"Whatever. Hashtag murder scene, churchsex. I had just under four thousand followers on Instagram—I'm up to over five thousand since this went out. Ninety-six retweets. No, over a hundred now. Doesn't hurt that you're not hard on the eyes."

She looked away from the phone and at me.

"Raymond doesn't deserve this," I said.

"Well, he won't know now, will he?"

"I will."

She leaned closer.

"Is that some sort of threat?" Dunne said it huskily, like we were flirting.

"I'm just reporting a story," I said.

"And like it or not, you're in this one, Jack. You're in deep."

14

I called Roxanne twenty minutes from Clarkston, then again as I passed Purgatory. The speed limit at the crossroads was thirty-five and I blew through at sixty, following the two bare tracks in the snow-covered highway. I wasn't seeing the road, just a whirl of faces and places, voices in my head.

Raymond on the bed, his wrists abraded by the cord. Raymond telling me about the saints, the martyrs, him at peace in his house full of Jesuses. Cops at Dunkin', the guy named Snow. Cops at the check-cashing place, Bob with the Sig. Raymond's gray-white face, red-skinned necklace. The statues smashed. Sparrow distraught, Blake angry, them holding hands. Dunne and the photo on Twitter, me at the end of the driveway, the house in the background. Jack McMorrow at the scene of the sex murder, looking furtive. What did he know? And when did he know it?

Gritting my teeth, I held it in and then the scream erupted. "God-damn it all to hell!" The words reverberated in the truck cab. I punched the steering wheel, then the dash. Took a deep breath. Calmed myself. Drove. Ten minutes later I called Roxanne a third time, said, "Be there in an hour."

And I was, rolling into the driveway, skidding in the snow and stopping just short of the shed. Roxanne's car was parked off by the cedars, snow-covered. The toboggan was leaning against the shed door. I snapped the magazine out of the Glock and put it in the glove box and locked it. The gun went under the seat.

They were all in the kitchen, rolling up strips of dough. Sophie was doing video with Tara's phone: Tara with the rolling pin, wearing the apron we'd given Sophie for Christmas when she was six. Tara was saying, "Now I'm going to tell you how to roll your buns."

She turned her back to camera and swiveled her hips.

TikTok.

Tara put the phone down and they started cutting the strips.

"Hey, Dad. They're hot cross buns," Sophie said. "We found the recipe online."

A blast from my past. Easter, the buns served with brunch, my mother taking them from the oven, me squeezing the icing from a plastic bag with a hole. The cross on the buns representing Jesus's cross. Something about the spices and the stuff they put on his body after they took his body down, dressed it for the tomb. I kept it to myself. Once again.

"Smells good," I said.

"We're doing a video," Sophie said. "Tara is taking some home."

I'd been gone fifteen hours, hadn't eaten. There were cookies on a plate on the counter and I grabbed one, chomped it down in two bites, reached for another.

"My mom has a cross on a necklace. Maybe I could wear that for the video," Tara said. "We used to go to church when I was, like, four, but then the minister was hitting on my mom even though he was married, so we stopped."

Roxanne and I exchanged glances. She shook her head, put a cookie sheet with the first batch of buns in the oven. I moved toward her, leaned in to kiss her as she closed the oven door. I got a brush of her cheekbone.

"Hey, stranger," Roxanne said.

"Sorry to be gone so long. Things kept happening."

"I figured."

I turned and Tara was watching us sideways, shy-eyed and half smiling. Sophie was cutting out more strips of dough, lining them up in a row. She said, "We're ready for more buns."

They started rolling the dough, Tara making her raw buns carefully, Sophie spinning them up and dropping them on the plate. Roxanne said, "Girls, I'll be right back," and folded the towel and left the kitchen, started up the stairs. I followed, heard Tara say to Sophie, "Is your dad always nice to your mom?"

Roxanne was in the laundry room, pulling clothes out of the washer and loading them into the dryer. I stood behind her and said, "Tara asked Sophie if I'm always nice to you."

"My guess is that isn't the case at her house," Roxanne said.

"If her mom isn't into tactical weapons, I imagine there'd be some conflict."

"I was thinking how we used to pull kids if there were unsecured guns in the home."

"It's not your job anymore."

"No," Roxanne said.

She flung the last handful of clothes into the dryer and slammed the door shut. I reached out and touched her back as she said, "Clair stopped by. He said he needs to talk to you."

"About what?"

"He didn't say. The girls were right there."

"I'll stop over," I said, and hesitated. "Raymond, the man with the statues . . ."

She squeezed by me and stepped into Sophie's room with an armload of dry clothes. I followed.

". . . Somebody killed him."

She stopped folding. Turned.

"What? When?"

"Sometime during the night."

"Why?"

"I don't know. But also, I was the one who found him."

"My God."

I described the scene, the short version.

"That's awful," Roxanne said. "Are you okay?"

"Yeah. I mean, I'm not hurt."

"Who would have done that? Why would they kill him?"

"Cops say it was a sex thing. There was a condom, but I think it was a plant. I think they were looking for something. A neighbor said he paid for his church stuff with cash. Maybe word got out that he had a stash of money, then he didn't want to give it up. He was tied up, like he'd been interrogated."

"Oh, the poor man," Roxanne said.

"He was eccentric as hell but a good person. Helped Sparrow out, even though they couldn't have been more different."

Roxanne put a hand on my shoulder. It was way short of a hug.

"Cops are going to seize on the condom thing, write him off as some sort of pervert."

She took her hand off my shoulder, stood there with her arms across her chest.

"You don't know that."

"I do. Or at least, I think I do. I won't settle for their version unless it's the whole truth."

"So we'll see you in a week," Roxanne said.

She turned back to the folding.

"I don't know," I said. "The story has a hook now. The murder. I can't drag it out too long. And other people are going to be reporting it, at least the official version. I'll want to get in there while it's relatively fresh. They'll be putting their stories out in the next couple of days. There's this podcaster who wants to talk about Catholic sex cults."

Roxanne had her back to me, was rolling up Sophie's socks, putting them in a pile. She turned back.

"I'm sorry. I know you liked him."

"He was like a ghost from my past or something."

"And I think it's a past you yearn for."

"Sometimes," I said.

A beat.

"You know, this isn't a guy waving a gun around a store."

"No. Serious upgrade."

"Please be careful. I have a bad vibe about this place, all these people."

"I will be. As always."

She looked at me.

"More careful than that."

She put her arms around my neck, faced me, her face somber.

"I just have a weird vibe. I want you around, Jack. For a long time."

"You'll get sick of me," I said, and then Sophie called up the stairs, said Roxanne's phone was buzzing. Roxanne said she'd be right there. She put the socks in the bureau drawer, then underwear and shirts and pants.

"Where's Tara's dad?"

"He lives in Texas. She said he visits once a year, in the summer, when it's too hot in Galveston, or someplace near there. This guy Jason is the latest live-in. Before that there was one named Roy."

"This one. I mean, kind of crazy, what's going on out there."

"I could report it," Roxanne said. "And Sophie would lose her friend."

"And Tara wouldn't see what normal looks like."

"If that's what this is, Jack," she said. "Maybe everybody else is normal and we're the ones on the fringe."

She moved past me to the stairs.

"Good luck with the bird girl," Roxanne said. "We're going to the school, meeting up again with Mr. Ziggy about the video."

"Really? Is he working? At six-thirty at night?"

"He's one of those people, their job is their whole life."

"Seems odd," I said.

"He loves the kids, the theater. This one has wizards in the woods, like the Hobbit"

I didn't answer.

"Somebody in this world has to have good intentions," Roxanne said.

"I used to think so," I said.

The lights were on in Clair's barn. I went up the driveway and saw his big Ford parked behind the house. There was smoke coming from the barn chimney, and I looked up and watched it swirl upward into the snow and then I let myself in. Inside, classical music drifted up through the rafters, something that sounded familiar.

I walked into the workshop, saw Clair at the bench, a chainsaw bar locked in the vise. He was hunched over, running a file over the chain.

"Beethoven?" I said.

"Handel. Water Music. It's like mixing up the Beatles and the Rolling Stones."

"Your generation, not mine."

"Keep forgetting you're just a pup."

I smiled. He kept the file moving, eyes trained on the tooth of the saw chain.

"Hate to put a tool away without giving it once-over," Clair said.

"Put it away?"

"I'm headed north."

"Canada."

"Louis."

"Operation Marta."

He nodded, pulled the chain to expose the next set of teeth.

"Never leave a Marine behind?"

"You could say that," Clair said.

He started in again, the file making a smooth rasp against the music.

"When are you leaving?"

"Tomorrow, early."

"Last year you would have had to sneak in."

"Now I can go in the front door," he said.

I looked over at the other bench, the one that had a different purpose. There were guns laid out: a shotgun, a rifle, two handguns. An assembly of plywood painted black. It was cut in the shape of the floor of a truck.

"Custom packaging," Clair said.

"Don't get caught. Border guards have seen it all."

"I'll have my friendly demeanor."

"What's the story, for when they ask?"

"Going to visit a couple of guys I served with."

"Canadians in Force Recon?"

"Yeah. A hundred and thirty Canadians died in Vietnam, other places we fought. Crossed the border and enlisted. They put their names on a wall in Ontario."

"These guys expecting you?"

"Yes. If the border people call."

He moved the chain again.

"How long will you be gone, you think?"

"Back next week, I'd guess. We're not hanging around."

"What can I do for you?"

"Keep an eye on Mary. Don't forget to feed and water the pony."

"Sophie will be on it," I said. "She brings her buddy from school."

The music shifted, grew quieter.

"Pianissimo," I said.

"Very good. Hope for you yet."

"Marta know she's being extricated?"

"Oh, yeah. Louis talked to her. Sounds like she's basically being held captive, like house arrest. Keeping her high."

"Huh. So you and Louis against a bunch of outlaw bikers."

"I know," Clair said. "Doesn't seem quite fair. Maybe we'll shoot blanks."

I smiled. He filed. I watched. The music played.

"Roxanne says you're working in Clarkston."

"Yes."

I gave him the download. When I was done, he kept filing. Moved the chain again. I waited.

"So you're gonna do the investigation the police won't."

"Something like that."

There was another long pause.

"Assuming you're right, who else did this Raymond interact with? I mean, if he was kind of a loner."

"I don't know. People he worked with, maybe. The collector crowd. This woman Sparrow. Neighbors said he kept to himself."

Clair put the file down, unclamped the saw from the vise.

"So likely you'll be talking to the person who did it."

"Possible," I said.

"Watch yourself. You won't have me to save your butt."

"And vice versa."

"Yes."

He moved another saw, his biggest Stihl, into the vise and clamped the bar in place.

"Sophie has a friend, lives other side of Knox Ridge. Mom's boyfriend and his buddies are playing army in the woods."

"Huh. Army's kinda fun when nobody shoots back and you get to go home at night."

He filed. It made a scritching sound. The music picked up. Allegro.

"Boyfriend is not a fan of government. Or reporters."

"Understandable, I suppose. But problem with those folks," Clair said, "is they never seem to have an endgame. Kind of like the Taliban. Way easier to blow things up than to run a power grid."

"Maybe they just like shooting guns and drinking beer around the campfire."

"Nothing wrong with that. Unless they start shooting up Augusta."

"Hard to say," I said. "I just met the guy. He said we could never be buddies."

"You are an acquired taste."

He turned the chain, stroked it with the file. I listened to Handel for a moment, a log popping in the stove.

"You ever think it would be nice to be able to just look away?" I said. "Not be the one to have to jump in?"

"Like normal people?"

"Uh-huh."

"We're not normal people," Clair said. "Never will be. It's what we signed up for."

"Roxanne says she's worried about me, something going wrong."

"The reality of aging. One step too slow, you can compensate with experience. Two steps, that can be trouble."

"But you're still going."

"No choice," Clair said.

"No," I said. "That's the problem."

He bent over the bench, stroked the saw tooth with the file.

"That's it, Jack," Clair said. "In a nutshell."

He'd watched the video of himself on YouTube a thousand times, at least. Knew it by heart.

Posted by some store worker. All grainy and gray, him coming through the door, zombie mask on, gun down low. Walks right up to the register, points the gun at the lady, some old hogosaurus that looks like a man. She puts her hands up, takes a step back. There's no audio, but he adds it in his head, him saying, "Just get the fucking money and you won't get hurt." She starts to cry, says she has a grandson and he's three—like, what did that have to do with anything? Then it clicks. This is her way of saying, "Don't kill me," which he had no plan to do anyway. He says, "Shut up and get the money." So she goes to the register, still crying, wiping her eyes, taking forever. He goes around the counter, shoves her out of the way, and she stands there, boo-hooing, him thinking, I'll give you something to cry about, you stupid cow.

Cleans the register out, stuffs the bills in his pocket. Turns back to the crying lady and tells her to lie on the floor. She looks at him and doesn't move, so he points the gun at her face again, says, "Get down." Shoves her down, and she really starts to go nuts, talking about her grandson, how his name is Harley and she loves him so much. Jesus, like he needed that crap. He says, "You stay down and shut up." Then he turns and looks up at the ceiling, smiling under the mask, gives the camera the finger. And walks out, all calm.

This was the third robbery, early days. Somebody had snagged the video, posted it to YouTube. It went viral: two hundred thousand views in a couple of days, a link in the newspaper, tweeted all over the place. The mask looked very cool on camera.

The comments weren't all negative. You go, Zombie . . . Nobody can touch the Zombie robber . . . OMG, who is this guy? . . . I think he hangs out with Spiderman . . . F—— you, Clarkston PD . . .

Watching it, he was thinking how he could use it to get laid, or at least a date. Maybe hinting to some chick that he knew who Zombie was, like when Bruce Wayne says he can get in touch with Batman.

Anyway, guy who owned the store, some Indian from India or something—don't regular Americans own anything anymore?—he tweets that it wasn't his people put the video out there, must have been the cops. The PD said it wasn't them, the lady cop who always did the talking on the news saying Zombie shouldn't be turned into a celebrity because he was a dangerous criminal, and besides, that could spark copycats all over the place, turn Zombie into a franchise.

What? Screw that, somebody else getting credit for his robberies? No way. It was his idea, and it wasn't fair somebody could just steal it. He'd bought the mask online (there were hundreds, stupid Walking Dead), and he'd bought the gun at a sporting goods chain store in South Portland.

He watched the video again, paused at the frame where he flipped off the camera. He was the one risking his life, jail, cops ready to blow him away. Hell, Clarkston PD had that cop who'd shot the kid in Portland, the kid pretending to rob a bar. That cop had gotten away with it, so why would any of them think twice about putting a bullet in Zombie's head?

So maybe he'd stop, let somebody else take the hit.

But damn, that sexy little replicant chick, he wanted to see her again. He wanted her on her knees in front of him. He wanted to make her beg.

15

Sophie had left me a note next to a plate with a hot-cross bun on it.

FOR DAD, WHEN YOU GET HOME

Jacket still on, I took a Ballantine from the refrigerator, opened the can, and, in recognition of Sophie's presentation, poured it into a pint glass. I walked to the sliding doors. There was a jar of peanut butter on the table on the deck, a knife, and a bag of bird seed. The TikTok video?

I went back to the kitchen, drank some of the ale, finished the bun. Checked my phone and saw a text from Dunne:

—HI JACK . . . HOPE WE DIDN'T GET OFF ON THE WRONG FOOT
. . . REALLY LOOKING FORWARD TO WORKING WITH YOU . . .
PEOPLE ARE HOOKED ON THIS ONE ALREADY.

I drank more beer. Checked out the *Who Dunne It?* Instagram and there I was, outside Raymond's house behind the police tape. The blurb said: "First on the scene, *New York Times* reporter Jack McMorrow, after conferring with police about the brutal murder of a religious statue collector in Clarkston, Maine. McMorrow, armed with a handgun, reportedly found the body amid dozens of broken statues of Jesus. More to come." #newyorktimes #truecrime #jackmcmorrow #mainecrime

"God almighty," I said. Checked my e-mail. Sure enough, one from Carlisle at the *Times*. Two words in the subject line: Call me.

I put the phone down, ate and drank. Heard steps on the deck and then the door sliding open, Roxanne and the girls walking over to join me.

"We got some chickadees in the video," Sophie said. "They ate out of Tara's hand. It's for the video project."

"Very cool," I said. "That's part of the story?"

"Tara is Gloria. She came from the planet Nature and all animals love her. Mr. Ziggy says she's really talented."

Tara smiled shyly at the praise.

"Great," I said. "Mr. Ziggy sounds pretty hip."

"He's cool. We need binoculars next time. Can I bring yours?"

"Sure," I said.

"Tara has to go home. Her mom called."

Tara looked at the floor. Sophie said, "You can come back tomorrow."

"We'll see, honey," Roxanne said.

"I can take you home, Tara," I said. "Let's go."

The three of us climbed into the truck, the girls in the small seats in the back. Tara balanced a plate of buns on her lap.

They chatted about birdfeeders, Tara saying she put bread out for birds in her yard once and crows came. "Jason shot one," she said. "He said crows are dirty and can give you diseases."

We drove up to the top of the ridge, took a left at the tractor dealer, then headed west. There were farms, rolls of hay wrapped in plastic and nestled in the snow. Houses with rusty plow trucks parked, one with the town's name, PROSPERITY, spray-painted on the doors. Next place was the low-slung house surrounded by junked cars and trucks, parts of lawn mowers and bicycles strewn like the place had been strafed.

I pulled over. Texted Tiffanee.

YOU WANT TO MEET US AT THE END OF THE ROAD? JASON SAID THAT WOULD BE BEST.

We waited. No response. Tara whispered to Sophie, who said, "Tara has to pee."

"Roger that," I said.

I took the right, followed two ruts in the middle of the snow-covered road, slowed at Tara's and pulled in. Jason's pickup was parked in the dooryard next to Tiffanee's Jeep.

I stopped behind the truck, parked with the motor running. I got out and opened the back door. Tara slid out, the plate of buns held in front of her. She started for the door on the trampled path. We waited as she climbed to the landing, pulled on the storm door. It was locked. She pressed the doorbell and waited. Then she hammered on the glass. After a minute, I saw movement in a window to my right.

A glimpse of Tiffanee peering out, and then she was gone.

I looked to Tara as the door rattled and she pulled it open, waved to Sophie, and stepped inside. The door closed behind her. I put the truck in gear. Saw Jason come out of the door, holding the plate of buns. Out of his truck, he was short, like he'd stepped off his stilts. He had a pot belly under a black T-shirt, a strip of hairy gut showing. Gray sweatpants, unlaced work boots.

I got out of the truck, thinking for a fleeting moment he was going to thank me. He approached, the spotlight beside the door shining into my face. Stopped ten feet away, and threw the plate like a Frisbee. It hit me in the chest and dropped at my feet, the buns scattering on the snow.

"We don't need your fucking charity," Jason said.

I looked at him, counted to three.

"Watch your mouth," I said. "My daughter's in the truck."

I turned, walked to the truck, and closed the doors. When I turned back, he was closer, standing with his hands on his hips, his belly extended in front of him.

"I ain't watching nothin'," he said.

In the glow of the taillights, I could see he was drunk, eyes unfocused, swaying slightly on his feet. The plate was five feet in front of him, sticking up from the snow. I walked to it, bent down, and picked it up. As I did, he kicked snow in my face.

Remembering that Sophie was watching, I took a second to stand up, wiped the snow off, said, "Tara thought you'd enjoy them because she made them. No charity there."

"I told you not to come here," he said.

"I texted. Nobody replied. Tara had to go to the bathroom."

"Don't want you snooping around here. I heard what your old lady does. Kidnaps people's kids, locks 'em up."

I smiled, anger starting to boil like water in a kettle.

"If you mean Child Protective Services, she did use to work there," I said.

"Lamestream media and the Gestapo. In one friggin' house."

I took a breath. Set my feet.

"You know you're kind of a caricature, Jason," I said. "The drunken loser, right out of central casting."

"What did you call me?"

"A caricature. It's when certain characteristics are exaggerated to create a comic effect."

I turned back to the truck.

He followed. "Where you goin', smart-ass?"

I could see Sophie, wide-eyed in the backseat. He cursed me again.

"How 'bout we continue this conversation when there aren't kids around," I said.

He moved closer, shoved my shoulder. The movement caused him to waver slightly.

"How 'bout we continue this now."

"Will I have to keep explaining all the big words?" I said.

As I said it, I put the plate on the hood, moved toward the rear of the truck and away, out of Sophie's line of sight, I hoped. He followed, gave me another shove from behind.

I turned back to him, noted that the sweatpants wouldn't hold up a gun, probably not a knife. He gave me one more shove, and I took a step back.

"Come on, pussy," he said. "Where's your big words now?"

I thought of what Clair always said. In hand-to-hand, it's all about balance and anticipation.

Then again, maybe Clair would have gotten into the truck and driven away.

Probably not.

He stepped in, threw a wild roundhouse right.

I turned and ducked and it glanced off my shoulder. He stumbled as he recovered from the follow-through, then swung again, this time with the left.

It bounced off my other shoulder and I almost smiled to myself, knowing he was drunk, knowing he had nothing, even sober—knowing I wanted someone to take it out on. Raymond dead on the bed. Sparrow sobbing. Dunne cornering me, putting my name out there. All of it a big sour mess, and he was about to bear the brunt.

"Wrong place, wrong time, bub," I said.

He rushed in, tried to get me in a bear hug, fling me down. He smelled of alcohol, bad breath, body odor, cigarettes. I spun him away. He staggered, then righted himself, came at me again. Another wild right, and this time I blocked it with my forearm, stepped inside. He was wide open and I was turned, feet set, my right arm up and cocked, ready to drive him with all my weight, put my fist through his face.

And it came to me.

That maybe this guy is taking something out on me, just like I was about to take something out on him. There would be no winners. Just blood and broken teeth, maybe a jaw—all his—and me trying to explain it to Sophie on the way back home. The cops later.

The math didn't add up.

I dropped my arm, fended off another punch, a left, way weaker. Took him by both shoulders, spun him once, and bulled him backwards. Put a leg out and tripped him and he fell hard on his back in the snow, grunted as he landed. I dropped on top of him, a knee on his chest, clamped my hand on his throat and squeezed. He tried to spit in my face but the phlegm dribbled onto his beard, his chin.

I counted to ten in my head, kept going. Thirteen, fourteen, fifteen…

He was gasping for breath. I let him struggle, felt him panicking under me, legs starting to flail. I eased my grip and he took a short wheezing breath, then another and another.

"Next time you'll get hurt," I said.

"Fuck you," he said, teeth clenched.

I got off him, walked to the truck, and slid in. Deliberately buckled my seat belt, put the truck in gear. Jason was on his hands and knees, coughing and spitting onto the snow. I wheeled out to the road and drove, pulled over a quarter-mile down the road, and turned to Sophie.

She looked at me with big dark eyes wide, lips pursed.

"Why was he so mad?" she said.

"I don't know. I think he was having a very bad day."

"Was he drunk?"

From the mouths of babes.

"He had been drinking, for sure."

"Did you beat him up?"

"No, I just tried to calm him down."

She looked out the window and was silent for a few seconds, then said, "I think our buns are ruined."

"I'm sorry about that."

Sophie took a deep breath like she was gathering herself up. She turned back to me.

"I hope he doesn't blame Tara and her mom."

"For what?"

"Him trying to punch you and you pushing him down and kneeling on him."

And choking him until his eyes bulged out.

"I hope so, too, honey," I said. "I really do."

16

Sophie was quiet the rest of the way home. I prattled on, told her about Sparrow and Riff, that Riff was a musician. She picked up my phone, searched. Riff's voice filled the cab, the slashing guitar.

"Cool," Sophie said. "It's not what you think it's going to be."

I smiled.

"But he should be on TikTok. I could chop this YouTube stuff up, get it out there."

"He could have a whole new following," I said.

She watched Riff for a few miles, said, "Who's Patti Smith?"

We pulled into the drive, parked by the shed. I got out and came around and took her hand for the walk to the house, our boots crunching on the crusty show. I told her some people's lives are hard, that we just got lucky. Sophie gave my hand a squeeze and led the way inside.

Roxanne was making a very late dinner, which Sophie said was "civilized like Europe." She kicked off her boots as Roxanne chopped carrots and celery at the counter, chicken sautéing on the stove.

"Pot pie," I said. "Yum."

She turned to Sophie, who pulled off her jacket.

"How was Tara's?"

"Not good," Sophie said.

Roxanne took a step over, knife in hand.

"Why, honey?"

"Jason was drunk and he threw the buns at Dad. Then he tried to punch Dad, and Dad had to calm him down."

I looked at Roxanne.

"What happened?" she said.

"That about sums it up," I said.

Sophie said she was cold and wanted her sweatshirt. While she was upstairs, I gave Roxanne the extended version.

"We could call the police," she said.

I shrugged. "Somebody got hit with a plate of muffins. Somebody else was drunk. Big deal."

"I know. But it's not a healthy environment for a child."

"Nope."

"But if I call DHHS, it will probably go in a file somewhere. No injury, no evident threat to the family."

"One of those buns could have put my eye out," I said.

"Or they do send somebody out, and that gets very awkward." She was lost in thought for a few moments, then said, "Did you hurt him?"

"Just his pride," I said.

"I hope he doesn't take it out on—"

"I know," I said. "That's what Sophie said."

Dinner was somber. Sophie ate her chicken pie, all but the celery, and a bun for dessert. I asked about the school video and Sophie said it was fun—but like it wasn't anymore.

"Must be cool to be a wizard," I said. "Were you filming out in the woods?"

"Yeah. Mr. Ziggy got a new camera," Sophie mustered. "But I got snow in my wizard boots and my feet got cold."

Roxanne looked at me, eyebrows giving a flick. Sophie put her plate by the sink, then took her iPad and headphones off the counter, left the kitchen, and went up to her room.

We did the dishes quietly, and then Roxanne went to the easy chair by the fire and opened her laptop. I laid a log in the stove, then put my jacket on and went out to the truck.

The clouds had blown through and a rising half-moon was showing above the tree line to the east. I stood for a moment in the shadow of the shed and watched and listened. Dry beech leaves rattled in the wind in the trees beyond the driveway. Clouds scudded across the face of the moon. There was no other sound.

I walked to the truck, went to the driver's door, and unlocked it. I leaned in and took the Glock from under the seat, then reached over and unlocked the glove box, took out the magazine. I snapped it into the gun and slipped the gun into my jacket pocket, started down the road.

There were lights on in Clair's house, but the barn was dark and his truck was gone. I crossed myself for him, then stopped and stood still. Where had that come from? Raymond? If there had been a Catholic church nearby, would I have gone in, knelt at the altar rail, and prayed?

I kept walking, my footsteps crunching in the brittle snow at the roadside. A small flock of winter robins flushed from a blackberry bramble and fell away in the darkness. I hadn't gone twenty steps when my phone rang. I reached into my right pocket, found the Glock, fished in my left. Took the phone out and looked at it and answered.

"Hey," I said.

"McMorrow," Carlisle said. "We have to talk. Is this a good time?"

"As any," I said.

I could hear horns, a siren, a bus door hissing open or closed.

"How are things in the big city?"

"The usual bliss," Carlisle said.

"You should move up here. It's idyllic."

"I can tell. This latest thing—"

The siren got louder and we waited for it to pass.

"Raymond," I said.

"Yes."

"Pretty dark, even for your stories."

"Life is like that sometimes."

"As you never fail to remind us, McMorrow," Carlisle said.

Her footsteps paused, then resumed. Crossing a street.

"You headed for the subway?"

"Norikoh. That sushi place on Twenty-Fourth. We had lunch there."

"Right," I said.

I remembered. One of my stories, about a homeless girl who was murdered in Bangor, had caught the eye of the new Metro editor. She had asked Carlisle to ask me if I would consider coming back full-time. They flew me down and we had a nice lunch. I said no.

"Listen," Carlisle said. "You know I'm your biggest fan. But the social media folks saw this blogger's tweet, the one where she tagged us. You finding the body. Carrying a gun."

"Not in that order," I said. "And she's actually a podcaster."

"Whatever. The point is, it went from there up to Vanessa."

"Uh-huh."

"And from there it went to Legal."

"Okay."

"Not really."

"They don't like stringers finding bodies?"

"I suppose sometimes that can't be helped," Carlisle said.

"Stuff happens," I said. "I mean, conflict reporters find bodies all the time."

"I know. But what they really don't like is contracted writers carrying guns on *Times* business."

"I wasn't carrying it in the concealed sense. It was in my truck," I said, feeling the weight of the Glock in my pocket.

"I know, but then you were carrying it. What if you'd shot somebody?"

"Way better than them shooting me."

"They see the newspaper as being liable."

"If I get shot while reporting a story, you're liable for that, too."

"Maybe. But they just get very fidgety about guns these days. I mean, the school shootings. Texas, Buffalo. That guy in the subway in Brooklyn. Gun control and Washington. It's just so fraught."

"I know."

"So I'm arguing back that in this case, you had to have it for protection in a crime scene, and in Maine the police can be very far away. And you carry a gun in your truck because you live in the country and work cutting down trees sometimes, and there are bears in the woods."

"Black bears. The University of Maine mascot."

"I'll mention that. It speaks to how common they are."

"They keep Maine's human population in check," I said.

Her footsteps paused. She was at the restaurant.

"So what's the bottom line?" I said.

"I'm still working it. But if I don't prevail, we may have to take a break."

I took a long breath, exhaled a puff of steam in the cold night air.

"What about this story?" I said.

"I'd say right now it's forty-sixty."

"So I'm writing it on spec."

"You'll get a kill fee."

"Not exactly a motivator."

"Come on, Jack. You're writing this one for the same reason you write all your stories," Carlisle said. "Because something inside you drives you to do it. That you get paid is almost incidental."

"Easy for you to say. Ammo isn't cheap."

"We'll talk."

"Maybe," I said, and hung up.

I stood in the road. Clouds passed over the moon and it got darker. I turned back, started for home. A partridge flushed in the woods to my right, a fox or a fisher coming up empty. A frozen moment, looking at the fluttering bird, then back to work, snout in the snow, snuffling for the next scent.

That was me. Back to work, sniffing for clues, looking for a track. I kept walking, was turning into the driveway when my phone buzzed. I looked. The name "Blake" lit up the screen.

"Hey, sorry to bother you."

I heard the crunch of tires on ice.

"You working?"

"Yeah," he said. "Headed in. Picked up half a shift."

"Raymond?"

"Zombie. Word is Raymond can wait."

"What's a life compared to fifty bucks and some gift cards?"

"Between us, it's like they think he had it coming. Should have known the risk when he hooked up with some guy on Grindr."

"That's wrong in several ways."

"Yup," Blake said.

I stopped outside the shed door. I could see Roxanne and Sophie, just their heads over the back of the couch. Roxanne was having a heart-to-heart about Tara and Jason. I should be there.

"So what are we going to do?" I said.

"I get off at nine tomorrow morning."

"Nine-fifteen at Dunkin'," I said.

"We'll be there," Blake said.

"We?"

"Me and Sparrow."

Right. Sparrow. Officially Blake's new flame.

I went inside, walked to the front room. Too late.

Sophie was on the couch now, watching something on her iPad, earbuds in. Roxanne was in the easy chair, typing on her laptop. Schoolwork.

"Hey," I said.

Roxanne looked up. Sophie didn't. I went to Roxanne, gave her shoulder a squeeze.

"Everything good?" I said.

"It's okay." Her voice was just above a whisper.

"You talked?"

"Yes. We worked our way through it."

"Sorry I wasn't there. Should I talk to her now?"

Roxanne gave a little head shake.

"I'd leave it alone now. She'll have questions, maybe tomorrow. It's the way she processes."

A beat.

"I'm sorry it happened. That guy's a powder keg."

"Seething with anger and resentment."

"On the plus side, he can't fight," I said. "Becoming a lost art. Like tying a good knot."

Roxanne looked at me over the laptop.

"I'm trying to teach her that we don't settle our disagreements with anger or violence."

I bristled. An undercurrent of anger and resentment and frustration boiled up.

"Some people," I said, "don't even need a disagreement. I didn't disagree with this Jason guy. I doubt Raymond disagreed with whoever killed him. Sparrow didn't disagree with Zombie, but she still got cracked in the head. It's a violent world, like it or not. Now more than ever."

Roxanne put a finger to her lips to quiet me, glanced at Sophie. She looked engrossed in whatever it was she was watching. Roxanne looked back at her laptop screen and started typing. Conversation over.

"I didn't even hit him," I said.

She kept typing, then spoke without looking up.

"I'm worried about Tara and her mom."

"Sophie shouldn't go over there," I said. "Even if he's gone."

"No."

More typing. She reached for a legal pad and started flipping pages.

I waited, then said, "I'm leaving early tomorrow morning. I have to meet Blake in Clarkston."

More typing.

"Clarkston cops are putting Raymond's murder on the back burner."

No reply.

"We're going to talk to a couple of people who are flashing a lot of cash."

Nothing.

"And then I'm going to start with the church down there, see what they can tell me about the value of the statues, what they know about Raymond's collecting, about this St. Apollonius."

I paused.

"I'll be home by mid-afternoon," I said.

Roxanne paused her typing.

"I won't count on you for dinner," she said. "Be careful."

I was on my own.

17

I woke up at five, no alarm needed. Eased clothes from the drawers, padded out of the room to the sound of Roxanne's soft breathing. I paused at the door to Sophie's room and listened. Heard nothing, so I eased it open, walked in, stood by her bed. Her hair was dark against the pillow and there were stuffed animals strewn about the bed like there had been a wild party. Twelve going on sixteen, but sometimes twelve going on eight. I leaned over her and gave her an air kiss, told myself I'd leave Clarkston by twelve thirty, be home before two. I thought of leaving her a note, but then she'd be disappointed if I were late.

I took a shower, dressed in the bathroom. Went downstairs and restarted the fire in the kitchen stove, ate four slices of peanut-butter toast and drank a cup of tea as I watched it catch. I put another log in, damped the draft. Went to my desk, picked up the laptop. My notebook. Flipped the pages back.

Joseph Loyola, Bo Taranto, Hugh Payns.

It didn't seem like a variation on the spelling of the Canadian city.

I searched for Loyola, got the latest score for the university basketball team. Was Mumbo a fan? I tried Ignatius and got the saint and my old church. Taranto pulled up the city in Italy. Bo Taranto pulled up lighting fixtures. Hugh Payns hit pay dirt.

Hugues de Payens lived in France in the eleventh century. Among other things, he rounded up some buddies and founded the Knights Templar to protect Christian pilgrims to the Holy Land. The Templar part came from the place they first laid out their bedrolls: a temple to

Solomon in the palace of Baldwin II in Jerusalem. Like Mumbo, the famous crusader had different names. Hugo de Paganis, Hugh Payns.

Another search: Bohemond of Taranto was a leader of the First Crusade. My old friend Ignatius Loyola came around four hundred years later. The one-time soldier went on to found the Order of the Jesuits.

Mumbo, recently released from the custody of the State of Maine, knew his history. Maybe a modern-day crusader had found a training ground in the backwoods of Prosperity, Maine.

I was still mulling it over as I went out the door at quarter past six, tires crunching on the frozen gravel. Could the consortium of antigovernment militants include far-right Catholics? What battle did Mumbo have in mind? A war with leftist priests? What did this have to do with anything, other than that both Mumbo and Raymond were old-school Catholics?

My focus shifted back to Raymond. I drove east to the turnoff at Freedom Road, pulled over. Picked up my phone and went to Spotify, searched for Gregorian chants. Selected Gregorian Requiem, Chants of the Requiem Mass, and the Latin came over the speakers in the dark, cold, and deserted morning like Raymond's ghost.

"*Vade in pace*, Raymond," I said aloud.

I sat there for a moment, startled at the words. Another fragment of my Catholic past, risen to the surface like a buried bone heaved up by the frost. I found myself wondering: What if Raymond had been right? What if he was sitting up in Heaven, instead of statues around him, the real thing. Raymond strolling through the gates, all those saints and martyrs giving him high-fives. Raymond thinking, I told you so.

It was just before eight when I pulled up in front of Raymond's house, shut off the motor and the lights, leaving the yard in the dark shadows of the winter morning. The street was quiet and the house lay in darkness. Crime-scene tape fluttered in the dim wash of the streetlights. I pictured the shattered statues, broken and beheaded like bandits had ridden through the halls on horseback, swords swinging. The bed indented in the shape of Raymond's bound body.

If criminals sometimes returned to the scene of the crime, would someone return here? Had they found what they were looking for? Had Raymond, in the last bouts of suffocation, sucking the plastic into his mouth in desperate gasps, given it up? If not, what would their next step be?

I got out of the truck and walked up the driveway to the tape. I took out my phone and started taking photos: details for the story I wasn't giving up on, whether I was paid for my time or not. Raymond's car, now abandoned. The dolly on the porch. The stack of dismantled wooden crates.

My eye caught a piece of wood where there appeared to be a label. Looking up and down the street, I stepped over the tape and went up and onto the porch. The label was partly torn off, half obscured. I looked around again, then lifted boards off the pile, stacked them until I reached the label. It had folded where it had come off the wood and I folded it back.

It was addressed to Raymond. The return was Vintage Church, the address in Ardmore, Pennsylvania. I took a picture, then put the boards back on the pile as they were.

Once I'd finished, I heard a dog bark, a small one. I turned and saw Mrs. Lemieux walking down the street toward me, a small white dog pulling on a leash in front of her. The dog was wearing a blue jacket. She had a plastic bag in her other gloved hand.

I slipped under the tape, walked down the driveway. I waved and smiled and Mrs. Lemieux smiled back. The dog continued to bark and she told it to shush and it did, wagging its tail and straining to get closer. She clicked the leash handle and the cable went loose and the dog scrambled toward me, jumped up and scratched at my jeans. I scratched it behind the ears and it settled, still leaning on my legs.

"He likes you, Mr. McMorrow," she said.

"Yes. Good taste in strangers."

She beamed at the dog.

"He doesn't like everybody. We've had the same mailman for twelve years and Roger practically goes through the door to try to get at him."

She crouched and patted the dog's back.

"Isn't that right, Roger. You'd like to eat that mailman."

"I think it's the uniform," she said. "Same with the man who delivers the oil. Another man came last week looking for Raymond's house. One of his deliveries. I said Raymond was across and down two, and he said okay. The number was missing from the slip."

"I see. So he went over?"

"He asked me if it looked like Raymond was home and I said no, because his van wasn't there. He said he'd come back now that he knew where it was because Raymond had to sign for whatever it was. A statue or a picture, I'm sure. But Roger—I had to lock the storm door and hold it closed. I was afraid he was going to go right through the glass."

"I'm sure," I said. "So that guy had a uniform on?"

"Yes, with the name of the company."

"Did you catch what it was?"

"No," Mrs. Lemieux said. "I was more worried about Roger. He was going ballistic."

Roger fell back to four legs, walked over to the snowbank, sniffed and peed.

"Did you tell the police about this?"

"No," she said. "That detective, he just kept asking if Raymond had any man friends. Men coming and going. I said, 'Raymond didn't have any friends—male, female, or indifferent.' "

"You told the detective that."

"Right. And he says right back to me, 'You sure there weren't men coming by? Men who maybe were younger?' It was like he wasn't even listening."

Sanitas had it solved. Now he just needed evidence.

Roger sniffed my boots.

"So the delivery guy with the statue or whatever—he wasn't FedEx or UPS?"

"Oh, no. Roger knows them. He hears the truck pull up, he goes crazy."

"Big truck, small truck?"

"Medium. Just one of those delivery vans. It was white, I think."

"Would you recognize the driver?"

"No, because he had one of those neck things pulled up. Like Lucille at church, she still comes to Mass all wrapped up like a mummy. I say, 'Get over it, Lucille. We all got the shots.' She says it could be just dormant, could come springing back up."

"Right," I said.

Roger was bored with the conversation and started pulling Mrs. Lemicux away.

I walked to the truck, got in behind the wheel, and wrote it out. Ended with, Was St. Apollonius in the van? Is that what they wanted? Was Raymond unable to hand it over because it had never arrived?

Blake's truck was idling outside the Dunkin' when I pulled in a little after nine, shutting off the motor and silencing the monks. Sparrow was sitting close to him, and as I watched, she leaned over and kissed him on the cheek. Then the lips. Then the lips again, their heads darting in and out like hummingbirds on a flower. Reminder kisses, as in, Don't forget how hot it was, will be.

They saw me and Blake slid out. He was in plainclothes: jeans and a black Carhartt jacket and black tactical boots. He looked younger out of uniform, but still there was a hardness to him, a man always on a mission. Sparrow had her hood up, leggings and hiker boots. Her work gloves, black with no fingers. Very '80s punk, like her dad.

I walked over. Blake nodded and Sparrow said, "Hey." They led the way inside, and Blake bought coffees for them, this time tea for me. We sat in a booth that faced the window, a cop thing since before Wyatt Earp. I was on one side, they were on the other.

"How was your night?" I said.

Blake went first. "Unproductive. Task force had a tip that Zombie was gonna hit a Cumberland Farms on Sabattus Street. Detectives sat on it and we all waited. Nothing."

I looked to Sparrow. She frowned and dabbed at her scab with her forefinger.

"Same. Bob came in at midnight, stayed until five. He was all jacked up on Red Bull, had his gun in a holster, reached for it every time the door opened. I was afraid he'd go and shoot some random customer."

Blake said to me, "I guess our tip got leaked."

We drank through the gaps in the plastic lids.

"That won't keep you awake?" I said.

"I haven't slept since he hit me," Sparrow said. A crack in the armor.

The conversation paused as a guy shuffled past, orange hunting hat for deer season protruding from the hood of his sweatshirt.

"Listen," Blake said. "I asked around. People who are usually reliable."

"Uh-huh."

"Looking for somebody showing up suddenly with a lot of cash."

"Like they won the lottery?" I said.

"More like a good scratch ticket," he said.

"They buy a round at a bar?"

"Or score some meth, throw a party," Sparrow said. "Or maybe they're smarter than that, turn the drugs into more cash. I mean, maybe this isn't your average tweaker."

"I still think the place was more ransacked than trashed. Tying Raymond down. Interrogating him."

Sparrow winced, sipped. Her fingernails were painted dark blue and they tapped the cup.

"The condom, in plain view," Blake said.

"Exactly," I said. "And?"

"One strong possibility."

"There were people in the store when Raymond picked me up," Sparrow said. "Like, multiple days, the same ones. I didn't think anything of it then, but what if they followed Raymond home? That's how they knew where he lived."

"We see if there's overlap," Blake said, calling it in on his radio. "Guys with sudden cash also in the store."

I drank my tea and we waited for a response. Customers came through the door, each one accompanied by a blast of cold air. Sparrow started brainstorming.

"Maybe I go to their door," she said. "Say I'm looking for somebody supposed to be living in another apartment."

"Why?"

"I don't know. It's a friend of mine."

"What if they recognize you from the store? You end up making the connection, they figure out you're working with the police."

"We lose business?" Sparrow said.

"You're there late, Mo in the men's room. Shoot you through the window? I don't know."

We pictured it, the car pulling up, the shot fired, Sparrow down and the car pulling out.

"I'll go," I said. "Say I'm from the *New York Times*, looking for another tenant, do they still live in the building."

They looked at me over their cups.

"Sparrow stays back, close enough to see the door. Who answers. Who we flush out."

The next partridge in the snow.

"But will they be up?" I said.

"If it's meth, they'll be up for days," Sparrow said.

I hesitated, picturing some psychopath murderer with a head full of methamphetamine. Then I thought of Raymond, heard the Gregorian chants. The statue man with the stash of cash. Easy pickings.

We drank some more. There was a steady stream of cars inching by outside, lined up for the drive-through. Some people coming in and out, tracking salt and gravel across the tile floor. Regulars, familiar faces. A couple of high school kids getting their sugar high. Contractors, their trucks idling in the lot. Then, a flash of familiar, at least vaguely: Mumbo and Snow. Regulars. I wondered if he'd been back to the boot camp, or if the consortium had taken a break.

Blake put his head down, like he didn't want to get into a conversation. They picked up their coffees and left. A woman in a short black jacket and high-heeled boots glanced at Blake, sorting where she'd seen him, then nodded. He nodded back and smiled.

"Knows Salley," he said. "She runs one of the dispensaries he works for."

"How's the cash-hauling business?" I said.

"Lucrative," Blake said. "With the robber out there, they decided to send out a decoy van with two security guys. Salley makes the run alone in his wife's Altima."

"Where does he go?"

"Industrial park by the interstate."

"Guy spends years busting people for weed, now he makes money on it," Sparrow said.

"That's his good side," Blake said.

We drank a bit more, then looked at each other.

"Time?" I said.

"Now or never," Blake said.

"Before we go, one question," I said.

They waited.

"So, you two are a thing."

They looked at each other.

"Yes," Sparrow said.

"Just confirming. Because you never mentioned it. Riff didn't seem to know about it when we spoke."

"It just sort of happened," Blake said. He shrugged, maybe a little embarrassed.

"Good for you," I said. "You have a lot in common. Raymond. And Zombie. You saw him face-to-face. Brandon would like to."

"With a mask," Sparrow said.

No more talk about her knowing those eyes anywhere. I guessed they didn't share everything. Or maybe they did. Let somebody else come forward? She had Riff to take care of. But then, she was game for hunting a real killer, not a potential one. And so was I. With family to support, wife and daughter I loved, Glock in my parka pocket.

"There's a chance it could go sideways," Blake said. "A guy knocking at the door is either a cop or there to buy drugs."

I reached back and pulled out my notebook, held it up.

"I come in peace," I said.

We stood. Drank like someone was about to make a toast.

"You think we're crazy?" Sparrow said.

"No, I think it might work."

"I mean, the cop and the store clerk hooking up."

"You mean, for this, or in general?"

"In life," she said.

"No," I said. "You have a lot in common. You always want to do the right thing."

"Like putting this dirtbag away," Blake said.

"Like nailing his sorry ass," Sparrow said.

"Yes," I said. "Just like that."

Blake's radio crackled.

The address was on Pine Street, where there were no pines. The couple was known officially as Shayne Zola and Gayle Dupuis, Blake said. Shayne was also known as Jug, for drinking straight from half-gallons of Smirnoff, and Gayle as Twinsey, for formerly being one. Her twin brother had died in a car crash during a police chase. Both had criminal records—theft, drug possession, assault, criminal trespass.

"Long on quantity, short on quality," Blake said.

Number 39 was a triple-decker overlooking a small rectangular park. The park had cannons and a gazebo, both scrawled with graffiti. There were clusters of young guys at three of the park's four corners, the groups mostly differentiated by race. They were hooded up, doing that stationary shuffle, checking their phones.

We parked on the street down the block from the house. I got out with Sparrow. We walked to the tenement while Blake circled the park and parked with a clean view of the front of the building. The guy with the cash was supposed to be on the first floor. There was a stairway to the upper floors inside the front porch.

I went up the steps to the porch, Sparrow behind me. The first-floor apartment had two windows, curtained by bedsheets. We could hear shouting and laughter and music, country-and-western. Chris Stapleton. A woman singing along.

We kept going up the stairs. The second floor was quiet, the windows dark. There were bags of trash on the floor by the door. Cats or rats had torn them open and there was frozen garbage scattered. Coffee cups from a convenience store. A gnawed rotisserie chicken. A plastic whiskey bottle with cigarette butts inside. Dirty diapers.

I stepped to the door and put my face up and peered in. Saw plastic chairs, a plaid couch, a shopping cart someone had dragged inside. I knocked.

We waited. I knocked again, louder, said, "Anybody home?"

There was no reply and we went to the third floor and repeated the process. There was less garbage there, just a rusty bicycle with flat tires and no seat. The apartment was empty.

We walked down the stairs, past the garbage, down again to the first floor. The music was hip-hop now, the same woman rapping the lyrics. Sparrow behind me, I took out my notebook, opened the metal storm door. I gave her a last nod, then knocked.

The voice went silent. The music was turned down. The sheet in the window to our right was pulled aside a few inches. I saw a bearded white guy, the rest of his head shaved close. Sores around his mouth.

Meth it was.

I smiled at the guy and the sheet fell closed. We waited.

The sheet opened again, this time a woman. Gaunt. A ring in her upper lip. The same sores. I smiled again.

"Yeah?"

A man's voice said something on the other side of the door.

"Hi there. I'm Jack McMorrow. I'm from the *New York Times*. Could I talk to you for a minute?"

No reply. A moment to process that one.

"I'm a reporter. Doing a story on the Zombie robberies. I was looking for the people upstairs."

A beat, then the same voice. "They moved."

"Do you know where they went?"

"He's in jail. I don't know where she went."

"Could I talk to you for a minute? As long as I'm here?"

Another long pause.

"Just for a minute. Background. I don't even need to know your name."

We heard chains rattling, locks turning. The door swung halfway open.

The guy with the beard, gaunt and sunken, his head shaved and starting to grow out. A black T-shirt, neck tattoo of flames. Dirty jeans and a big commando knife in a sheath on his belt. He scratched at the sores around his mouth.

"What do you want?" he said.

I repeated my pitch. I turned to Sparrow.

"This is a friend of mine. She's from here and she's driving me around. I flew up from New York."

Sparrow was looking out at the street. She glanced at him, nodded from under the hood.

"I'm talking to people in town about the robberies. I was told the people upstairs actually witnessed one."

"Maybe. I don't know."

Beyond him was a wooden spool, the kind used for big reels of cable, that served as a table. There were cigarettes in dishes, beers and hard iced tea. The drugs had been whisked away.

"Close the door. It's fucking freezing." The woman who'd been singing.

"Listen—"

"Hey, could I just talk for a minute? Just what it's like to be in this town with Zombie hitting all these stores."

"No, I probably ain't interested."

"Your wife, maybe?"

"She's not my wife."

"Shut the door, I told you," the woman said. "I'm practically naked and you're making it friggin' freezing in here."

He shuffled in place, started to swing the door shut. I put my hand out and stopped it and he took his hand off the door to scratch his face again. There were footsteps and the woman appeared, also gaunt, eyes bloodshot, thin blonde hair pulled back. Yoga pants and a stained white tank top, her breasts barely covered, a tattoo of a rose showing in her bony cleavage, stem to blossom. A necklace of dark beads.

I started in with my pitch.

"Dude," she said. "Like I give a shit."

Her eyes were dilated and there were scratches on her neck.

"It wouldn't take long, just to talk about how it feels—"

"Fuck off," she said. "And take your bitch with you."

She looked at Sparrow, jarred into reality.

"Hey, you're the chick from the store," the woman said. "The one that got robbed."

"Right," I said. "I know her dad from New York. He's a musician and we met when he was playing in the Village. Have you heard of CBGB? Back in the day it was—"

She pulled the guy back, reached to slam the door shut. The necklace fell out of her shirt. It was made with wooden beads, dark and light brown, and a cross that dangled. Made to pray the rosary.

18

We drove the length of the park and took a right, out of sight of the house, and parked. Blake's pickup pulled up in front of us. We got out and walked to his truck, where Sparrow got in. I stood at the open window.

"The rosary beads. She was wearing them."

"I thought it was just a chain," she said.

"No, it was a rosary. Did they look like devout Catholics?"

"Addiction doesn't care what religion you are," Sparrow said.

"It's a Catholic town," Blake said. "At least it used to be. Could have been something handed down."

"Everybody wears crosses," Sparrow said. "It's a style thing."

"She didn't look like she was worried much about style," I said. "When were they in the store?"

"Mornings," Sparrow said. "They bought Twisted Tea and cigarettes and candy bars. Addicts who are in withdrawal really crave sugar. My mom had coffee with five sugars, then she'd be on the phone looking for somebody to hook her up."

"When in the morning?" I said. "Like, three?"

"Six," Sparrow said. "Always showed up just when I was cashing out. If they were late, sometimes they'd wait while Mo logged in."

"So when you left with Raymond?" Blake said.

"They'd be done and gone."

"And since Raymond was killed?" he said.

"Haven't seen them, but it's only been one day."

"I guess we know where they've been," Blake said.

We mulled it over. I said, "Could they pull this off?"

"Killing someone?" Sparrow said.

"Getting away with it," Blake said. "Not being caught in the house, whole thing blowing up."

"They seem pretty out of control," I said.

"Now they do," Sparrow said. "They've been bingeing. Could have gotten the cash, gone right out and copped an ounce. Been high ever since. But I've seen addicts and how they can get it together if that's what it takes for them to keep drugs coming. My mom, she could seem like a Girl Scout leader if that's what it took to get money for heroin. But only for a day or two. Then she'd get cash from her new friend or the temp job or whatever, and score."

There was a respectful pause.

"So they might be able to get it together to plan this," I said.

"Hear the rumors on the street," Blake said. "Guy's got cash. Lives alone. Stops at the store every morning."

"So they follow him home, come up with a plan to come back," Sparrow said.

"How do they get him to open the door?" Blake said.

It came to me. An epiphany.

"She starts saying the rosary," I said. "For Raymond, it would be irresistible. A siren call."

They left—Sparrow to check on Riff, Blake dropping her and heading for the boat and a nap and a fresh uniform for the night shift. He said he'd swing by Pine Street with Salley, see if the party was still on. And he'd hit the snitches again and see if he could shake out any more on Jug and Twinsey. Sparrow would watch for them at the store, ask Mo if he'd noticed them hanging out in the parking lot. Meanwhile, I'd go looking for statues.

I zigzagged three blocks up to the top of the hill, where the Basilica was perched overlooking the city like a medieval castle. It had once been a beacon for Franco-American millworkers, but they were gone with the mills. Now the church drew a shrinking contingent of white-haired worshippers, catered to the poor and downtrodden, and made sure a priest was available for the local hospital, inmates at the county jail, and the continuous stream of funerals. Including Raymond's, I assumed, after the medical examiner was through with his earthly remains.

The rectory was behind the Basilica, on the other side of the hill. It was made of stone, too, and there was a new Volvo SUV parked in the slot designated as "reserved."

I parked next to it and went to the door and pushed the buzzer. Waited. Pushed again and waited, then swung the storm door open and knocked.

Just like on Pine Street, there were footsteps, then the sound of locks opening. The door opened a crack and a white-haired woman peered out.

"Yes," she said.

I told her who I was and where I worked. The door didn't open wider.

"I'm also here as a friend of Raymond Jandreau," I said.

A stretch, but in Raymond's social circle, maybe a bit of truth.

"Oh, well then," she said, and opened the door wider, invited me in.

The hallway was carpeted and hushed. She didn't introduce herself, just motioned for me to follow her. She walked with the forward lean of a supplicant, a hint of self-doubt but eager to please. I followed her as she went through a doorway to the left, into what looked like a reception room. She motioned to a chair and exited. I remained standing.

There were framed pictures of some gray-haired priests and bishops, with a side table against the wall and a porcelain vase on the table. The vase was filled with flowers. I leaned down and sniffed. They had no scent.

There was a painting of Jesus with his robe open and beams emanating from his sacred heart. It was like he was a superhero and the heart was his power, which was true to many, including Raymond. Jesus was handsome, fair-skinned, blue-eyed, brown hair long and flowing like he could have been at Woodstock. It was the same look as found in the paintings at Raymond's house, and I wondered if there had been an original model, the progenitor of centuries of Jesus likenesses.

"Mr. McMorrow. How can I help you?"

I turned and there was a priest there who did not look like that Jesus. He was dark-skinned, short and on the plump side, and his accent said South Asia.

He smiled and came to me, held out his hand. I took it and it was soft to my squeeze.

"I'm Father Aneesh," he said. "And you're a friend of our dear Raymond. So terribly sad."

"It is."

"Raymond was a good man and a good Catholic."

"Yes," I said. "And an interesting version of both."

He looked at me, surprised, then recovered. Motioned to two armchairs, half-facing. He went to one and sat and I took the other. He sat back and I leaned forward, like someone having an audience with the Pope.

"Raymond's collection," I said.

"You've seen it?"

He said it like it was a rare privilege.

"Yes," I said. "Have you?"

"No, I never visited Raymond's home. He told me about it, though. We donated some pieces from St. Ann's, after it closed."

A parishioner at arm's length.

"His boyhood church," I said.

"Yes," Father Aneesh said. "I understand the church was a great solace to Raymond when he was a child."

"His sanctuary, he said."

"It makes it doubly sad, that his life started with such difficulty and ended in this way."

"It does," I said. "But I suppose you could say the same of a lot of murder victims. Being killed often ends a life filled with struggle."

"The world can be a cruel place," he said.

"Often," I said.

He didn't reply.

It was time for my pitch, so I gave it—that I'd come to town to do a story on the robberies, met Raymond, among others, and that the story had grown to include the relationship between the two.

And then Raymond was killed.

"So that is your story now," Aneesh said.

"Right. Part of it. Raymond, his collection. How he acquired the pieces. One of them, he told me, had first been offered to the church here."

"It happens, but we can't accept that sort of thing. St. Ann's still has some in the basement."

"Raymond didn't want them?"

"They didn't add to his collection," Father Aneesh said. "He was quite a curator, actually. He knew what he wanted."

"But the one offered to this church," I said.

"Yes."

"He took it, even though he had something like it."

"It was like someone offering a stray cat to an animal lover. He said he'd find it a home."

"Where did this stray turn up?"

A hesitation, like this might be confidential. "A parishioner owns some of those garages where people put their leftover things," the priest said.

"Storage units."

"Yes. The person who rented the unit didn't pay the bill and didn't communicate, so she had to remove the items."

"Including the statue."

"Yes. She's a good Catholic and felt it wasn't right to just dispose of it."

"I'm sure," I said. "Did she offer it to you, and you put her in touch with Raymond?"

"Exactly. I felt he'd try to find it a home."

"And did he?"

"I don't know. I do know he took it from her. She told me what a nice man he was."

"They knew each other."

He hesitated.

"Yes. They were regulars. She sits in the front, though. There's a little group, five or six women. They've known each other since they were children. That would be a good story for you. They're mostly widows, I think. They attended Mass religiously before the pandemic, and when we opened back up, they were first to return. Germaine wasn't there on Sunday. It's hard in the snow."

"How 'bout Raymond?"

"He was a regular, too. Seven a.m. on Sundays and Wednesdays. He always sat in the rear pew to the far right as I faced him. We'd have the first four rows with worshippers, and then Raymond in the far distance. I think he felt most comfortable worshipping alone. For some people, church is a social occasion, but that wasn't the case for him. People connect with God in different ways."

He smiled.

"Yes. And he was from another time."

"There is a place for that. But as Pope Francis says, the church must change with the times."

I glanced around the room. It could have been 1950. I was guessing the median age of that first four rows was eighty-five.

"The parishioner with the storage units. Do you think she'd talk to me?"

"I don't know. If you're a friend of Raymond's, perhaps. Theresa may have her number."

"Great," I said.

"But Theresa may be busy."

Doing what? Washing his vestments?

"It must be a lot of work, keeping this place up," I said.

"Oh, we have a cleaning crew. They just got out of jail. The Church is all about redemption. They're good men who society has treated very roughly."

"I'm sure," I said.

We sat and looked at each other. He was very carefully groomed, eyebrows sculpted. The room was still. I heard him inhale, exhale softly. Somewhere deeper in the rectory a clock chimed.

"Mr. McMorrow. By your name, I guess that you may be Catholic."

I nodded. "Growing up. St. Ignatius Loyola, New York City."

"So you'll be respectful writing about Raymond and his religion."

"Very," I said. "Raymond and I shared stories about being altar boys."

"We call them servers now," Father Aneesh said.

"Right."

We eyed each other a bit more. He smiled benevolently like just maybe he'd consider making me part of his flock. I smiled back.

"Where are you from originally, Father?" I said.

"India. Kerala, in the southwest."

"Interesting. What brought you to Maine?"

"There was a pastoral need and I was called."

With a shortage of homegrown priests, the diocese went recruiting.

"I see," I said. He smiled. I smiled back.

"Do you know how Raymond was killed?" I said.

"Not really. Just that it was something unfortunately—how to put it?—sexual in nature."

"That isn't necessarily true."

"You've been told that?"

"I know that. I found his body," I said.

He put a hand over his heart, which was underneath his black shirt. "I'm sorry. I will pray for both of you."

The priest went quiet in that way priests do, waiting until the other person is ready to confess. I held out for a good thirty seconds, but something was on my mind. Had been since I'd left Raymond's house.

"Do you believe Raymond's in Heaven?" I said.

"That's not for me to judge," Father Aneesh said humbly. "The Lord makes that call."

"But you knew him. What's your gut?"

He seemed flattered to be asked.

"He was a devout man. The circumstances of his death notwith-standing."

"The alleged sex part, you mean."

He shrugged.

"If it were true, you think it would keep him out of Heaven?"

"We condemn the sin, not the sinner."

"Raymond wasn't much of a sinner, from what I could tell," I said.

"All of us are sinners. But we are all worthy of redemption."

"Good to know," I said. I was getting weary of his certainty, like he had it all figured out.

"Theresa."

"Oh, yes. Let me check."

He took out a phone and texted. I was surprised he didn't pull a velvet cord.

We waited, still smiling, and Theresa came back. He asked her if she had the number of the woman who called about the statue. She said, "Yes, Father." He asked if she could get it for me. "Of course, Father," Theresa said. She didn't curtsy on the way out.

In a minute, she was back, an index card in her hand. She gave it to Father Aneesh, who handed it to me. I looked at it. It had the name Germaine Babineaux, an address in Clarkston, and a phone number. I copied the information into my notebook.

"We'll forgo the usual process," he said. "For Raymond, the collector of saints."

He smiled, benevolence shaded with beneficence.

"Sitting alone in the back of the church," I said.

"Oh, but he wasn't always alone. The back of the church is where people dip a toe in, and sometimes those people haven't been close to God. Last week there was another man back there."

"This man came to Mass with Raymond?"

"No," Father Aneesh said. "He sat behind him. I noticed because Raymond always stayed to pray privately after Mass ended. This man did the same. It was encouraging."

"He prayed?"

"Apparently. Perhaps following Raymond's example. And when I looked out of the sacristy, after I took off my vestments, they were still there. Raymond got up and left, and this man did, too."

"They left together?"

"No, Raymond left and the second man followed. He blessed himself awkwardly, like someone who hasn't been in church for a very long time."

Or ever.

"What did he look like, this second man?" I said.

"Oh, it was hard to tell. They were far away and the church is dark. But you know how Raymond looked young for his age?"

"Yes."

"I may be mistaken, but I think this man may have looked young, too. A round face. I thought maybe they were related. Of course, if that were the case they would have sat together, one would think."

But not if the man had followed Raymond in, then followed Raymond out.

"Anything else about him that struck you?" I said.

"Just that he seemed like a worker. Sometimes we have strangers at Mass who are homeless, come in to get warm, find some peace in their stressful lives."

"Right."

"But in this case, I thought they probably both had gotten off work. You know Raymond worked overnights. Mass ended his day, which was why he could linger in prayer. This man stayed, too. Like his work was done, and now it was time to be closer to God."

Maybe, I thought. Or maybe it wasn't time for that at all.

The address was a side street behind the hospital, a half mile from the church. It was a square, two-story house with a single-car garage to the rear, the kind of place built after World War II for returning veterans. There were window boxes under the first-floor windows. Plastic red geraniums that poked miraculously from the snow.

I parked out front, walked up the driveway to the side door. Neither had been cleared and there were no footprints; no one had come in or out in a couple of days. I hoped Germaine was still in there.

There was a bell switch and I pushed it. Waited. There was no sound from inside, and the curtain over the window in the door didn't move. I pushed it again. Still nothing. I looked to the backyard, saw an empty birdfeeder on a pole, a pair of mourning doves pecking in the snow beneath it.

I pressed again and held it. Counted to ten. The curtain parted. A woman peered out.

"Germaine?" I said. "They sent me from the church."

She was older, seventies, a long nose and eyebrows penciled on. Her right eye was bruised, yellow and purple. Her upper lip was scabbed, like it had been split. There were gray-blue fingermark bruises on both sides of her jaw, like somebody had taken her face in their hands and squeezed.

"Germaine," I said. "I was just with Father Aneesh."

No reply.

"Are you okay? Theresa gave me your address."

The curtain parted and she looked at me, said, "Who are you?"

Her voice was muffled through the glass.

"I'm Jack McMorrow. I'm a friend of Raymond's."

"Tell them I'm fine," she said.

"I can't lie, Germaine," I said. "That would be a sin."

She frowned and the curtain closed. A chain rattled and a lock turned. Déjà vu.

Germaine opened the door, then pushed the outer door open six inches.

"There," she said. "You've seen me. I say I'm fine."

"But your face?"

"I fell," Germaine said. "Getting out of the bathtub."

"And landed on your face?"

"Yes. It was clumsy of me. I should have put a towel down to step onto."

"I'm sorry to hear that. May I come in?"

She hesitated. "You know Father Aneesh?"

"Yes. I was just chatting with him. Theresa was there. Your name came up."

A car drove by slowly, a white-haired woman at the wheel. Germaine turned, took a step back into the house.

"Come in, then," she said. She moved into the room, and I followed, and she closed the door behind me. There was a small entryway, shoes lined up on plastic trays. A plastic container of sidewalk salt. She continued through another door to a sitting room with two cloth armchairs with antimacassars on the arms and a fireplace with framed photos on the mantel. Kids and a grandson, smiling at the camera. A black-and-white of a middle-aged man, heavyset, with hair slicked back.

Germaine motioned me toward one of the chairs, said, "I don't drink coffee. I'm sorry."

"That's okay. I just had some."

"It makes my heart race. The doctor said no caffeine, not even tea."

"You're wise to give it up, then," I said.

I sat. She did, too. She was short and slight, in jeans and a jersey turtleneck pulled up under her chin. Her feet, in white sneakers, barely touched the floor.

"How is Father?"

"He's good. He says hello."

"He's a nice man. He's from India, you know. The priests aren't French anymore."

Her Franco accent added to the nostalgia.

"No," I said.

"We had one who was Filipino, Father William. We all liked him, but he was transferred."

"I see. Father Aneesh said you have a group of friends you come to Mass with."

She nodded, her bruised face like a victim photo at an assault trial. There were fingermarks on her forehead as well.

"Yeah, us girls go to Mass and then we have coffee at McDonald's. It was hard during the COVID. We had to watch Mass on TV and have our chats on the Zoom. My grandson would send us the thing to click on."

She glanced at the boy in the photo on the wall.

"That's good."

"He's twelve. He knows all about computers."

The conversation paused. Time to dial in.

"I understand you have storage units," I said.

She looked surprised that I knew.

"Yes, my husband Ludger started it. He said you just build them and then rent them out. No more putting money into it, just money coming in. But then it wasn't even a year, and he had a heart attack and I had to take it over."

She pronounced it Lou-gee.

"Ludger can't help you at all?"

"Oh, no. He passed away. Boom. Right there."

She pointed to the couch.

"I'm sorry."

"I talk to him anyway. Why not? He can't talk back now. I tell him, 'Ludger, building the units, that's not the half of it.' "

"I can imagine. People coming and going. Not paying their bill."

"Oh, goodness, yes. And you're stuck with their stuff. People save the most worthless junk. But hey, complaining never did any good, right? Some of it, I've taken to the dump. Some of it, I sell it on the Facebook."

She smiled, winced as she stretched the split lip.

"That was quite a fall," I said.

"Yes. But I'm lucky I didn't break a hip. My friend Lucille, she broke her hip and went to the hospital and never came out."

A tough old bird who seemed to have met her match.

"Another reason I stopped, Germaine," I said.

She waited.

"I knew Raymond."

A new wariness in her blackened eyes.

"You're a friend of Raymond's?" she said.

"Yes. Sort of. I'm a reporter. I'm writing a story on the Zombie robberies, and I met Raymond through that. He showed me his collection."

She stiffened, seemed to draw back in her chair.

"He told me you gave him a statue that was left in a unit. Like him, you don't believe religious things like statues from churches should be thrown away."

"I gave it to Raymond," she said, hurrying the words. "I don't know what he did with it."

She slid off the chair, made for the door.

"I've got things to do."

I got up, trailed after her. She was holding the door open when I caught up. There were bruises on her forearms, but no abrasions on her wrist. It would appear she hadn't been bound.

"Germaine, what really happened to your face?"

"Nothing. I fell."

"I've seen a lot of beating victims," I said. "You're one of them."

"The floor was wet. You should go now."

"And I think if you weren't wearing that turtleneck, I'd see marks where somebody squeezed your throat. Did you call the police?"

"You can go now, sir."

"Are you afraid they'll come back?"

She took me by the arm and guided me to the door. Her grip was hard, her fingertips like sharp points.

"Germaine," I said. "Do you know what happened to Raymond?"

"I don't know anything. You have to go."

I considered whether to say it, and did.

"Somebody killed him, Germaine," I said. "They killed Raymond in his house."

She didn't swoon. Didn't collapse. Didn't even flinch. She just opened the door, her bruised face close, eyes ringed with yellow and purple like some garish makeup.

"I don't know nothin' about that," Germaine said, and she gave me a push out onto the landing.

The chain rattled. The lock snapped. I stood for a moment. The curtain opened and then closed.

19

I drove down the street to the main drag, pulled into the parking lot at a Burger King, where the cars in the drive-through spewed clouds of exhaust and the air smelled of French fries even through the truck windows. I opened my notebook and started scrawling.

My visit with Germaine, her battered face, her Franco accent—the fear that bled through as she attempted to make it all seem normal.

I don't know anything. You have to go.

Someone had beaten her, threatened to come back if she called the police. Maybe said they'd kill her grandson. If they were smart, they'd know where he lived. Where he went to school. What time he walked to the bus stop.

I wondered if they'd had to get out the plastic bag. I thought not. She probably was speechless after the first slap, babbled after a couple of punches.

About what?

Raymond killed during some sort of interrogation; the house ransacked. Germaine beaten, frightened into silence. The common denominator: the statue of Mary. Left in a storage unit—but by whom?

I wondered if she could stonewall the police like she'd stonewalled me. I wondered who would care enough to leave their Zombie patrol to investigate a crime that hadn't even been reported.

Blake.

I was reaching for the phone to call him when it buzzed on the seat. I didn't recognize the number, connected, and said, "This is Jack."

"Yo, newsman. Got a minute?"

Riff.

"Sure," I said. "What's up?"

"Like to talk but don't like phones. If you're in town, take a spin by."

"Be there in five," I said.

"Meet you at the Hen. I'll walk over."

I pulled into the lot in front of the Red Hen, and Riff was waiting by the door. He was wearing his wool cap backwards and a worn black leather jacket over gray sweatpants. The coat was two sizes too big now and the sweatpants were tucked into black motorcycle boots.

I got out, walked over. "Didn't know you were a biker."

"Dude," Riff said, "there's a million things you don't know about old Riff. I got more stories than the Bible."

He opened the door to the bar and held it for me, making a flourish with his arm to invite me in.

I went in and it was dark, the Celtics on the TV over the bar, a few guys in baseball caps hunched over Budweiser longnecks. They turned in unison, and one of them said, "Riff, they let you out."

"Went over the wire," Riff called over. "Take more than a few egghead docs to keep me penned up."

But he shuffled to a table in the back, was breathing heavily when he scuffed the chair out. He fell into the chair. "Don't get sick," he said. "Sucks the life right outta ya."

I sat, too, and he said, "Whatcha having? I can't drink, but don't let that slow you down. It's on me."

"Coffee's fine," I said. You ordered tea here at your own risk. "If I have beer now, I'll fall asleep at the wheel."

"I have a beer now, I'll fall asleep forever," he said, and he laughed and coughed, turned to the bartender and called, "*Garçon! Deux cafés au lait, s'il vous plaît.*"

The guys at the bar, still watching him, smiled and muttered something between themselves.

Riff took a couple of long breaths, drummed on the tabletop with his yellowed fingernails.

"My daughter likes your music. She found you on YouTube. She's twelve."

"Hey, no shit? Love it when music jumps generations."

"She says you should be on TikTok."

"Cool. Let's do it."

The bartender, a burly guy with a shaved head and a goatee, brought the mugs of coffee and creamer and sugar in a metal bowl, like you'd use to feed your dog. Riff was digging in his coat for money, but the bartender said, "On the house, Riff, my man. Good to see you," and they bumped fists.

After he left, Riff ripped up three sugars and dumped them in his coffee. Stirred, said, "What's your daughter's name?"

"Sophie."

"Nice. There was a groupie named Sophie back in the day. Weren't she a hoot."

He caught himself.

"No offense."

"None taken."

He stirred the coffee, tasted it. Grimaced. Put the shaking mug down.

"Haven't told Bird, but the numbers are going south."

"Sorry to hear that, Riff."

"Yeah, well."

He sipped the coffee, his hand shaking.

"Look at that. Ain't finger-pickin' with that. Old Riff's headed for the last power chord in the sky."

I sipped my coffee. He put his mug down with a thump. Coffee spilled onto the table and he wiped it with a paper napkin.

"What'd the doctor say?"

"What can she say? They'll adjust the meds, see if a new combination works better. I'm not stupid. I can read the writing on the wall."

"And that stuff, the expensive miracle drug?"

Riff shook his head.

I hesitated, almost said it. That putting his story out to a couple of million people—somebody might come forward. A fund manager spent more on wine for a dinner party. I wondered if Carlisle would go for that. Dying Rocker Needs New Fans. The subhead: In Maine mill town, inventor of punkabilly pays price for sex, drugs, and rock and roll. Or something like that.

"But I didn't call you to whine," Riff said.

"I'd definitely need a beer for that."

I smiled. He sipped again, the coffee spilling. He wiped it up.

"Don't usually snoop," Riff said. "Bad enough Bird has to live with me, without having me in her business."

I waited. The guys at the bar hooted at the basketball game. A big dunk that got a replay.

"But she's been kinda quiet. I figure it's Church Man getting killed. She liked that guy a lot."

"I know they were close."

"But now she's hooking up with that cop. The one killed the kid, got exiled to our fair city."

He sipped the coffee, the trembling causing ripples on the surface.

"You've met Blake?" I said.

"Once. I was on the porch. He dropped her off in the police car, him with another cop, her in the back like she'd been freakin' arrested. I'm like, what now?"

"Did you talk to him?"

"He got out, came over, introduced himself. Seemed like a straight shooter." Riff caught himself. "As in, no bullshit."

"No, there's none of that in him."

"So you think he's okay?"

"Yeah. Serious for his age, but very solid."

"The shooting thing, you know?" Riff said.

I waited. He looked over at the bar.

"Like I said, I try to let her have her life."

"Right."

"But I had a feeling. My feelings are usually coming from something. You get a sixth sense when you're close to the end. It's true. You can read about it."

In the game, somebody hit a three. The guys at the bar said, "Oh, yeah." Riff looked back.

"She's been shopping for a gun. Online."

"Really."

"Cabela's, some other places. Had a bunch of handguns bookmarked. Like I said, I never snoop, but . . ." He paused. "I tell her, Bird, you did right. Give the asshole the money. It's not yours. They'll make it back in a friggin' day."

"Not worth dying over," I said.

We both sipped our coffee, Riff putting his mug back down with a wooden knock.

"You think Zombie would hit the same place twice?" he said.

I thought about it, then thought about what to say, with Sparrow, who could have a gun under her uniform shirt, Riff, lying awake worrying.

"Probably not," I said. "Now that the owner's carrying a gun on his hip."

Inside, I was thinking I wouldn't put it past Zombie. Rob a place twice, just to show he can.

"One thing I sure as shit don't want to do," Riff said.

"What's that?"

"Outlive her. She's my baby, you know?"

His eyes moistened and he lifted his cup as cover. I looked at him—gaunt, his sagging skin orange-yellow like a bad spray tan.

"I don't think you have to worry," I said.

Riff gave me a fist bump in the parking lot, shuffled in his black boots back to the house. I watched as he pulled himself up the steps, pausing on the stoop to catch his breath. Then, with a last push, he heaved the storm door open and went into the house. I wondered if Sparrow knew he'd broken out.

I sat in the truck, scribbled notes of the conversation. *One thing I sure as shit don't want to do is outlive her.*

So Sparrow was carrying, maybe. I could understand it. Why should she take one for the team with a dying dad to take care of? And it didn't matter how many task force patrols were circling the streets—they wouldn't be there in the time it took to pull the trigger. I wondered if Blake was helping her shop for a gun.

I put the notebook down, started the motor. It was almost two thirty, which meant home around four. If Sophie stayed for play rehearsal, Roxanne would pick her up at quarter past, be back by four forty-five. Which meant I had another hour to squeeze from the day.

My phone was on the seat. I picked it up, typed a text:

WOULD YOU BE AROUND IF I STOPPED BY IN AN HOUR?

I waited, phone on my lap.

A car pulled in and parked in front of the bar. Three women got out, laughing boisterously like they'd warmed up somewhere. Let the party begin.

The real life of Clarkston. A woman wearing rosary beads like jewelry, meth sores around her mouth. Raymond dead, Germaine terrorized. Only Father Ancesh seemed to think all was well.

My phone buzzed. Blake.

—YEAH. CHANDLER'S WHARF, *BAY WITCH*. FIRST POWERBOAT ON THE LEFT. JUST PAST THE BIG KETCH.

I was there in fifty-five minutes, running down the turnpike at eighty-five miles an hour.

I swung off Commercial Street, the sidewalks always filled with people looking to eat, drink, buy shiny things. Our three primordial urges.

The wharf was a jumble of shipping containers, fishermen's pickups, wooden pallets. I found half of a space, put the truck in four-wheel, and rammed it halfway up a snowbank. I gathered my notebook and phone, got out and slid down.

There was a shoveled path to the edge of the wharf on the north side, and I followed it, peered over the edge. A big sailboat, a trawler, and then *Bay Witch*: live-aboards, all of them wrapped in clear plastic. There was woodsmoke coming from a metal chimney that poked through the plastic on the cruiser.

I walked out on the wharf until I could see BAY WITCH, SOUTH PORTLAND, MAINE on the varnished transom of the cruiser. There was a ramp down to the float and I slid down that, too, holding to both railings. I walked down the float, stopped by *Bay Witch* and texted again.

Waited. In a minute, Blake appeared, a dim shape moving under the plastic. He pushed a small wooden door open and said, "Come aboard."

"No pipes?" I said.

"I could whistle," Blake said.

I climbed aboard and bent low to follow him inside.

It was warm inside the bubble, warmer still as we crossed the back deck, where chunked wood was stacked, and bent down again to go below. Four steps led to the main cabin, where flames showed in a small stove. The place was all varnished wood, built-in desk and table, bookshelves filled. History. A bunch of David McCullough. Blake's uniform shirt and trousers hung drying on a rack by the stove. His boots were side by side below the rack. A cat was curled up on a shelf near the stove. The cat was black and white, like a cruiser. The door to the bow berth was closed.

"Welcome," he said.

"Nice," I said.

Blake shrugged. "You either love it or you hate it."

He was wearing North Face running pants, a lined flannel shirt, and L.L.Bean slippers. He looked thinner without body armor. Taking a seat on a settee built into the hull, he motioned me to a canvas deck chair.

"A wooden boat," I said.

"You either love or hate that, too. For me she's family. Like a dog."

"Or the cat."

"Yeah," Blake said. "That's Siren. You can't resist her call."

"Coincidence that she's black and white?"

"Had to wait for one to come up at the shelter."

I grinned.

"Coffee?" he said. "I don't have any tea."

I thought of the street reporter's creed: Don't turn down a drink, a meal, or a cigarette.

"Sure. I may be up all night, but that's okay."

"I'll be up all night either way," he said, reaching for a pot off the stove and pouring some coffee into a mug.

He handed me the mug and I sipped. The coffee was better than the Red Hen's.

Blake waited. Not much for small talk.

"I talked to the person who gave Raymond the statue."

I told him about Germaine, the little house, that she'd been beaten up. Blake waited.

"Black eye, split lip, fingermarks on both sides of her face."

"Punched and slapped?" he said.

"A few times. Enough to scare the crap out of her."

"That would scare most people."

"She claims she fell in the bathroom. Said she gave the statue to Raymond and that's all she could say. When I pushed her on it, she told me I had to go, dragged me to the door, and locked it behind me."

"Didn't say who rented the storage unit?" Blake said.

"Never got that far."

"Homicide should talk to her."

"She won't crack easily," I said. "She's terrified."

"They can get through that if they want to. Throws a wrench in the theory that it was a hookup gone wrong."

"You think Sanitas would listen to an entirely new angle?"

"Doubt it."

"But we have Raymond's place wrecked in what might have been a fit of rage," I said.

"And Twinsey's a tweaker with rosary beads."

"And a fistful of cash."

"I'll talk to them," Blake said.

"Will they come down on you for going off on your own murder investigation rather than sticking to Zombie?"

"I've been come down on for less than that," he said.

He sipped. The cat jumped off the shelf, crossed the cabin, and hopped on his lap. It circled once and curled up.

"Or maybe we need more," Blake said.

"Germaine said she sells some of the abandoned stuff on Facebook."

"Marketplace."

"I wonder if there's anything identifiable on there, something that would be a trail to whoever left the stuff."

"Worth checking," Blake said. "I can do it. Go back two weeks before the murder, all the Clarkston listings."

"I'll talk to the dealers who sell the statues. See if it could have been valuable or something. And I met the priest. I'll go back to him, see what connection that Twinsey has with the church."

We paused. The cat stretched its paws out and purred. Blake scratched it under the chin.

"Sparrow," I said.

He glanced toward the bow, the berth, the bed. Just his eyes. When the boat's rocking . . .

"She's sleeping."

I hesitated. Got up and walked up and out of the cabin, stood under the plastic at the stern.

The cat jumped down and Blake followed me out, coffee in hand.

"She's shopping for a gun," I said.

Blake paused his mug halfway to his mouth.

"Where'd you hear that?"

"Riff. He snooped on her laptop, saw her search history. Handguns. Cabela's, other places."

He took a breath.

"Don't want to make trouble," I said.

"No trouble. I'm just surprised. She says she hates guns. But then again, maybe she feels helpless, working nights, Zombie out there."

"Isn't there some stat that store clerks with guns usually get shot?"

"Yeah. I saw some study that said in stores that allow guns, employees are seven times as likely to be shot. It's not that easy. Takes you two or three seconds to get the gun out and up, and a millisecond for the bad guy to pull the trigger."

He was quiet. A wake rocked the boat gently.

"When was she searching?"

I thought.

"He didn't say. I figured sometime after she was robbed."

We were quiet again. Somewhere a bilge pump switched on and I heard water splashing.

"She's pretty upset about Raymond," Blake said. "I mean, first there was the pandemic. If her dad got it, he was gone. The worst of it is over now, but Riff's getting sicker, and she feels responsible, like it's up to her to save him, manage his meds—all of it. She has a folder on her computer, logs every call, the details of every conversation with the State, insurance companies."

"A lot for one person."

"She puts it all totally on herself. I told her, some things you can't control. I had no dad. Bolted as soon as he heard my mom was pregnant. She died when I was two, on a sailboat with drug smugglers."

"Sorry."

"Whatever. My grandmother was a bad alcoholic, drunk by lunch every single day. It's the same with Riff, Sparrow's mother. They made their choices, you know?"

The pump clicked off and the water stopped running. The cabin seemed very small and still.

"If anything happened to her, he'd be on his own," I said.

"Made his own bed," Blake said. "Doesn't have to hold her down."

"You think he does?"

"What kind of life is it? Working overnights, being nurse and housekeeper and accountant during the day. He's an entertaining character and all that. But when it comes down to it, it's all about Riff."

A nerve.

"You like her a lot."

He hesitated. "Yeah. Totally different from any woman I've been with. My ex went to Colby College, writes fiction. She'd put Sparrow in a novel, or some patronizing version of her, but she wouldn't be caught dead at the QuikStop at three a.m. Sparrow—I mean, there's this urgency about her or something. Like, life is serious business."

That, in the end, was what they had in common, I thought. Plus the physical attraction. Goth and cop.

After a beat I said, "Is she working tonight?"

"Eleven to seven. Owner is paying time and a half for those shifts now. Everybody's quitting."

"The store guy with the Sig," I said. "I met him. Very gung-ho. She shoots Zombie, she'll probably get a promotion."

"She does that, she won't be the same person," he said.

"She's not the same person now," I said.

20

The day turned to deep dusk as I drove north, dark clouds moving in from the west, driving snow squalls in front of them like sheep. With business hours almost over, I pulled over just off the highway in Augusta, took a recorder from the console, searched for religious statue dealers on my phone. There were two, one in Maryland and one in Belgium. I called the number in Maryland: Reliquary Inc. A man answered, his voice coming through the truck speakers. I pressed the button to record.

His name was Dave. I told him who I was and what I did for a living. He didn't hang up. He said we had a bad connection, but it was the road noise. I told him I could hear him just fine.

I said I was writing about a man who collected all sorts of religious items, mostly statues, and I needed background. I asked where he got his inventory.

"Gosh, from the sixties to the eighties, Vatican Two, nobody wanted the traditional stuff. Even the architecture. Beautiful pieces went to the dump. My dad just started saving it, really. Filled a warehouse, and then another."

"And then people started wanting it again."

"You don't know what you got 'til it's gone."

"Right," I said. "So who wants it now?"

He said people buy to donate to their own church, or maybe make a shrine in their home. There was a voice in the background. Away from the phone, Dave said he'd only be a minute. I picked up the pace.

"So are these statues valuable?"

"Depends on the quality," Dave said. "You have your Daprato, Mayer Munich. They're manufacturers. High quality and not made anymore. That drives the price up."

A truck passed me trailing a cloud of dry snow. I waited.

"Up to what? Thousands?"

"Sure. For the rarer items. A nice Recumbent Christ. Matching sets of high quality. Mary and Joseph and Jesus. Archangels, those are very sought after. Your more obscure saints."

"How 'bout St. Apollonius?"

"Funny you say that. I almost never see him, but I just sold one, a Mayer Munich. Came from a chapel in Brooklyn, and we sold it to a private collector."

I hesitated.

"Was the collector in Maine?"

Dave's turn to pause.

"We keep our buyers' information private."

"Was his name Raymond Jandreau?"

He didn't answer.

"Because if it was Raymond, that's the guy I'm writing about."

"And he knows that? I mean, it's with his permission?"

"Oh, yeah. We talked quite a bit. Very interesting fellow."

I left off the past tense.

"Been working with him for years. Very knowledgeable. We must be careful who we sell to, as you can imagine. You can end up putting a religious work in the wrong hands. I mean, some very sacrilegious purposes. Nightclubs, bars. Sex clubs, even. Sickos. Let them go online and buy reproduction junk."

"But you trusted Raymond."

"Oh, yeah. A minute into our first conversation, I knew his motives were good. He's making a sort of museum or shrine. He said he's going to finish it and open it up for people who missed the old church. We get them looking for items for home chapels."

That part Raymond hadn't shared.

Another truck. A cloud of snow and a hiss of air brakes.

"Are you driving?" Dave said.

"Yes. I have to make this time behind the wheel productive."

"Of course."

"So, St. Apollonius," I said. "Raymond told me he was excited about that one."

"It was on our standing list for him. You know, things to look out for. If we saw one and it was up to Raymond's standards, and ours, just acquire it. We didn't have to ask."

"So did he like it?"

"Oh, Raymond hasn't seen it. Apollonius hasn't shipped. It's all crated up, but Raymond hasn't sent his payment. Raymond always pays in advance. We'd bill him at this point, knowing him so well, but no, he says we have to have our money first. I'm sure he will. He's busy, as you know. I don't know when the man sleeps. He's in the retail business."

Yes, he was.

"So tell me, Dave," I said. "Would Raymond send cash for these things?"

"Well . . ."—a pause as he considered how to say it diplomatically— ". . . as you must know, Raymond has interesting ideas. I mean, as Catholic conservatives go, even. He probably told you he doesn't believe in banks. He says they're the usurers in the temple. He just puts cash in an envelope and mails it. I said, 'Raymond, at least send it registered mail.' He never did. He said the Lord Jesus would protect it along its journey."

"And Jesus did?"

"We never lost a payment."

"But this payment hasn't arrived."

"Not yet," Dave said.

Traffic whooshed past. I waited for quiet and said, "Dave, I don't like having to tell you this, but Raymond is dead."

I heard a puff of exhaled breath.

"No."

I waited.

"Was he sick?"

"No. I'm sorry to say, he was murdered."

"Oh, my dear God."

I could hear him breathing, like he was running uphill.

"So this is why you're writing about him?"

"I wasn't sure how to tell you. I was already writing about him and then this happened."

"How terrible. Oh, dear. I can't believe it. Oh, Lord Jesus in Heaven. Oh, I'll pray for his dear departed soul."

"That would be nice," I said.

"Not that he needs me," Dave said. "The man was a saint."

The voice again in the background, then muffled as he put his hand over the phone. And then he was back.

"What happened?" he said.

"Someone interrogated him, put a plastic bag over his head and killed him," I said.

"That's why you're asking about the money."

"Yes. The cash thing. May I ask you how much St. Apollonius was going for?"

Dave fumbled a bit, like he was ashamed of taking Raymond's money, now that he was dead.

"Well, this shouldn't be in the story."

"That's fine," I said, knowing there might not even be one.

"It was three thousand dollars. The piece was thirty-four inches high. Very good quality and condition. Early twentieth-century wood, hand-carved. Paint had this lovely patina."

"And Raymond had that kind of money?"

"I guess so. It was at the high end of his purchases from us, but he never seemed to have a problem with funds."

"Big bills?"

"For the higher-priced items, he'd send hundreds," Dave said. "That was my advice. I told him it would make it less obvious that the envelope contained cash. He said he got the money from his work. I pictured him bringing in the smaller bills and changing them."

We both sat there, lost in our thoughts.

"I still can't believe this," Dave said. "He was such a good, gentle man."

"Yes, he was," I said. "I'm sorry for your loss."

Which I was, but I was mostly thinking the circle of suspects had just gotten wider.

I turned off the recorder and pulled out, headed north toward Belfast, the scenario playing out.

The cashier at the supermarket tells his wife, "There's this guy, Raymond. He brings in thousands of dollars in tens and twenties, changes them for hundreds."

"What is he, a drug dealer?"

"No, he's an older guy. I think he might be religious or something."

"Huh. Weird."

His wife tells her sister. Her sister tells her boyfriend, who hurt his back—roofing, construction—and now is addicted to opiates. He's in deep to his dealer. The brother tells the dealer, who is behind to his supplier in Lawrence or Rochester for that last kilo of fentanyl.

For Raymond and St. Apollonius, the die is cast.

I picked up the phone, started to go to Blake's number. Another reason the sex angle was way off. And the phone buzzed. Roxanne.

"Hey," I said. "I'm coming through Augusta. Be home by—"

"Sorry to bother you," Roxanne said.

"No bother. I always want to hear from you."

"Tara and Tiffance are here," Roxanne said.

Her tone was stiff.

"Oh. Everything okay?"

"Sort of. I'm in the bathroom to talk."

I waited.

"She's leaving Jason. She told him the Patriot Legion had to go, and he said he couldn't give that order."

"So she's the one who leaves?"

"Until she can pry him out of there."

"One call to the ATF," I said.

"He knows that. He said if she ratted them out, it would be bad for her."

"Criminal threatening. Just the guy you want to climb into bed with at night."

"Yup."

"Probably scared to death she'll bring the FBI down on their heads. Federal charges, serious prison time."

"He tried begging, just called her. Drunk, says he loves her, he'll stand by her. She said no, he flipped a switch, said if she isn't home in an hour, he's coming to get her."

I looked at my watch. 4:18 p.m.

"Call the sheriff's office. Or the State Police," I said.

"She doesn't want me to. It's like that's the last resort, no going back, she tells police what they're arguing about. She hopes he'll just pass out. She says she can stay with a friend, go back tomorrow when he's sober."

"Like he'll be more reasonable with a hangover? I wouldn't go near the place without a tactical team."

"I know, Jack. I'm just trying to be supportive."

She ran the faucet, said away from the phone, "I'll be right there, honey."

"I'll be home in less than an hour."

"Okay."

"If she hears from him again, just call the cops. Hell with it."

"Right."

And then she was gone.

I hit the gas: Augusta, Vassalboro, South China, the towns ticking off as I passed slower cars, floored it up the hills where the traffic moved to the right, the truck motor roaring. Things opened up in Palermo, and I was doing eighty past the frozen white sheet of Lake St. George. Then the back roads to the northwest, black-trunked woods, snow-covered spruce. The truck skidded on a stretch of ice in Freedom, and I headed down the ridge into Prosperity, slid around the corner to the Dump Road. Came over the last rise.

Saw Jason's pickup in front of the house.

21

I pulled alongside. Jason was in the driver's seat, on the phone. I parked diagonally across the end of the driveway between the snowbanks and reached under the seat for the Glock. I took a magazine from the glove box, snapped it in, and put the gun in the back of my waistband as I got out.

When I came around the end of the truck, Jason was doing the same. He was wearing a T-shirt and jeans, no jacket, and his gun was in the front of his waistband, butt against his gut. It was a big revolver, probably a .45, a long barrel like something from the Wild West. That meant hard to pull out, much less aim and shoot.

Perfect.

I walked toward him, smiled.

"Hey, Jason. What's happening, buddy?"

I stopped when we were ten feet apart, both in the road. He stopped, too, hands on his hips, the big gun butt in front of him.

"Come to round up the old lady," Jason said.

Like she was cattle.

"Not a good idea. Not with the kids around."

"Fuck the kids. She made her point, okay? Time for her to come home."

He was slurring.

"Not today, Jason," I said.

"Outta my way, you piece of shit."

"See, that's the problem. You're all wound up. When you let your emotions take over, you make bad decisions. So how 'bout you go home, calm down, we sort it out tomorrow."

"How 'bout you fuck off."

His right hand shifted from his hip, rested on the gun butt. I slipped the Glock out, pointed it at his head.

"You even think of pulling that gun and you're dead," I said.

He grinned.

"Like you'd shoot me, you pussy."

"But I would," I said. "Really. I'm sick to death of people like you. Angry, stupid, filled with entitlement and self-pity. Always picking on somebody you think won't fight back. I've seen so many losers like you in my time, Jason. No more reasoning. No more taking the high ground. I'm done."

And somehow, inside, I knew I really was. So many years facing drunk, self-serving, abusive guys like Jason, armed narcissists, lying scumbags. Roxanne trying to help pick up the pieces of the lives they ruined. So what if there was one fewer?

He must have sensed I wasn't kidding. He tried to hold my attention with the smile.

"Hey, listen. Let's start again, dude. I mean, Sorry if I—"

I saw him slowly slip his hand down the gun butt.

I pulled the trigger on the Glock, fired a round just to the left of his right ear.

My left. His right.

The hand froze.

I moved the gun so it now aimed directly at the center of his face. His smile fell away.

"You're a dead man, asshole," he said.

"We all are, eventually. But at least for me it isn't a finger-squeeze away. And you won't even get that thing out. Might as well have a telephone pole in there. Makes me wonder what you're compensating for."

He swallowed, his eyes locked on mine. His hands stayed on his hips. I could feel him building toward something. Drop and roll, maybe. Time to set this joker straight.

"I have a friend. His name's Clair. Kind of a quiet guy, but a serious hard-ass. Ex–Special Forces, Force Recon Marine. A real soldier. You and your buddies don't know anything about that. Anyway, he says a warning shot usually just delays things, so why bother."

Jason's eyes narrowed.

"So go ahead and try it. But suicide by reporter? Kind of pathetic."

He stared, then softened, attempted a sort of drunken grin.

"I just want her home," he said, like the moment of crisis had passed. "So we can talk things out."

"You sure you aren't just afraid she'll bring in the cops?" I said. "Put your band of brothers in federal prison. Hands on top of your head."

He didn't move.

"I'll count to three. If they're still on your hips, within reach of that gun, I'll take it as a threat and defend myself. You are trespassing on my property with a gun; you think anyone would blink an eye if I shot you? One, two—"

His hands went up.

"Clasp your fingers together."

He did.

I took a step closer.

"Now put them on the back of your neck."

He hesitated, but only for a three-count.

I heard the door of the house open, footsteps in the snow crust. I didn't look, didn't lower the gun. Roxanne appeared in the road and moving past me, straight to Jason. She reached to the front of his jeans and took the gun, the big butt followed by the very long barrel. Dirty Harry. Roxanne turned and strode past me, gun in hand. I heard her steps going up the driveway. The door to the shed opened and closed.

"On your knees," I said.

Jason shook his head. "No fucking way."

"I think you might have another weapon. I still consider you an active threat."

He looked at me, eyes filled with loathing. Dropped to his knees, first one, then the other.

"Now on your belly," I said. "Hands still behind your neck."

"You are so dead," he said before he fell to the ground, face-first.

Jason still was prone on the snow when the deputy arrived. He came out of the car and trained his gun on me. Told me to drop the firearm and I did, the Glock thudding on the gravel. Told me to lean over the hood of my truck and I did.

The metal was ice-cold.

Jason started to move and the deputy shouted at him to stay still, keep his hands on his neck. His face was down and when he lifted it, one side was red from the snow.

"I want to press charges," Jason said. "He shot at me, tried to kill me."

"Don't you move a friggin' muscle," the deputy said.

He was doing pretty well for someone who looked like he was fourteen. After he'd patted me down, he shouted at Jason again. "Stay down."

It was then that the first state trooper pulled up, got out. Small but with a weight-room build, she went to Jason, bent to put the cuffs on.

"This is an illegal arrest," Jason said, swung his arm backwards and caught her under the chin.

Her head jerked as he jumped to his feet, swung at her again.

She staggered, grabbed his arm, yanked him toward her, twisted it behind him as the deputy came at them, taser out. The trooper slammed Jason back down, face-first into the snow. She leapt onto his back, still holding his arm, put an elbow on the back of his neck while she snapped one of the cuffs on an arm. The deputy holstered the taser, fell on Jason's legs. The trooper had the other arm back, cuffed it, and said through clenched teeth, "You're under arrest. You have the right to remain silent."

"Fuck you," Jason shouted into the snow, his voice muffled. "You have no jurisdiction over me." He was writhing, trying to kick them off. The deputy had the spray out again, but the trooper said "No," yanked Jason to his feet, ran him to her cruiser, and bent him over the hood.

"Anything you say can and will be used against you—"

"I'm gonna own you," Jason screamed, trying to kick her, but missing.

She pulled him back again, put him down again. He grunted, landed with a thud. For a moment, she stood over him like she'd landed a big fish, then she yanked him to his feet, led him to the back of her SUV, and put him in the backseat.

"Watch your head, sir," the trooper said.

Jason turned and spat on his own shoulder.

Oh for two.

Another deputy arrived, a game warden on his heels, then a state police sergeant named Rousseau, who I'd met in the past. What you get when the call says "Shots fired at McMorrow residence"—lots of blue lights.

"Never a dull moment with you, Mr. McMorrow," Rousseau said.

"Beautiful day in the neighborhood," I said.

The five of them huddled, Jason glowering in the back of the SUV.

"You sure it was just the one shot?" I heard the trooper say.

"If he says so," Rousseau said. "He can be a royal pain in the ass, but he's no liar."

Roxanne came out just then, holding Jason's revolver by the end of the long barrel like she had a dead animal by the tail. She gave the gun to the deputy and then they went up the driveway and talked. The deputy took notes, and Roxanne went back inside. The same deputy took my statement, and then Tiffanee came out and both the deputy and Rousseau talked with her. At the end of the conversation, the deputy handed Tiffanee his card, and she walked back to the house.

That left me and the four cops. They talked more in the huddle, then Rousseau walked over.

"Picked the wrong trooper. Even I wouldn't mess with Fernald."

"Charges?"

"Criminal threatening, resisting arrest, assaulting a police officer. Probably violation of conditions of probation, too."

"Probation for what?"

"Threatened somebody with a gun down in Massachusetts. Road rage thing."

"Some people never learn. Will he do more time?"

"Up to the DA, but I'd say that's a good guess."

"Plus the new charges."

"Right."

"Five years, maybe?" I said.

"You never know with judges," he said. "Could also turn him loose."

We stood there for a minute, waiting while the deputy took a call on his phone, turned away.

Rousseau said the deputy considered arresting me for reckless conduct with a firearm but changed his mind. He'd tell the assistant DA the warning shot was fired in self-defense.

"Because you just fired over his head, right?" he said.

"It was a deliberate miss," I said.

He gave me a long look.

"Close enough," he said.

The girls were in Sophie's room. I checked in, found them lying side by side on the bed, earbuds in, Sophie holding Tara's phone up to her iPad. I glanced down. Riff Calderone leaning into the mic.

Sophie pulled an earbud out and I heard Riff, a tinny version of "Jambalaya."

"We're screen recording it," she said. "It's all, like, two-second cuts."

"Fun," I said.

"Figured it might make him feel better, being so sick."

I gave her a quick smile. She nodded, turned back to the screen.

Tara hadn't looked up.

Roxanne had made coffee and tea and the three of us sat at the kitchen table and held our mugs in front of us. There was a moment of silence and then Tiffanee said, "I'm sorry."

"It's not your fault," Roxanne said.

"I shouldn't have dragged you into this."

"You have to get him out," Roxanne said. "This is the first step."

"I said I was giving him three days. If all the Patriot Legion crap wasn't gone, I was calling the cops."

We sipped. Tiffanee's wrists were scratched like she'd tried to pull out of someone's grip.

"I knew he'd be mad, but it was worse than that. He got all quiet and stared at me real hard. He said that would be a bad idea—that he didn't know if he could protect me. He said his friends, they don't tolerate informants."

"He was threatening you?" Roxanne said.

"It would be like I was the enemy, he said. And they're going to war. And if he knew I was gonna rat them out and he didn't stop me, it would be like he was a rat, too."

"So you have to keep your mouth shut to save him?" I said.

"He said I'd be putting both of us in danger."

We considered it.

"I'd tell them," Roxanne said.

"It might not put them in jail right away," I said. "Nothing illegal about shooting guns in a gravel pit. Do they have automatic weapons?"

Tiffanee looked at me.

"You know. Machine guns."

"I don't think so. I think they're just pulling the trigger fast."

"You'd have to hope there are some felons in the bunch. They'd have to catch them possessing the firearms."

"But they're gone. I don't even know their names."

"They could lean on Jason," I said.

"He won't talk. He's crazy when he talks about this stuff—the corrupt government dictatorship, his rights according to the Constitution. He'll tell them to pound sand."

We were all quiet for a moment.

"What if they come sneaking back in the middle of the night, house in the middle of freakin' nowhere?" Tiffanee said. "Burn the place down with us in it."

Her mind was racing.

"Tell them what really happened," I said.

"Sure, but what if I do that and Jason just gets out? During COVID, they let everybody go. He's out, and he knows I told on him."

"Unlikely with the probation violation," I said. "But you never know. Depends on the judge."

"And he'll have a condition of release that he not come near you," Roxanne said.

"BFD," Tiffanee said. "Guys break those all the time."

She was right.

"Do you have other family?" Roxanne said.

"Boston area. Chelsea, Revere. Two sisters and my mom. My dad, he died. Breathing in shit at the shipyard." Tiffanee sagged back in the chair. "God almighty, my life is shit. And it isn't just me, it's Tara. What was I thinking?"

"Not your fault," Roxanne said.

"Hope springs eternal from the human breast," I said.

Tiffanee looked at me.

"It's from a poem," I said.

"Sounds perverted," she said.

Tara stayed while Tiffanee went home to get some clothes. Roxanne checked on the girls and came back to the kitchen.

"How is she?" I said.

"Silent. Fixed to the screen."

"Sophie?"

"Trying to take care of her, I think."

"In her genes," I said.

She came over and stood beside me against the counter. She blew out a long breath.

"Yes. Thanks for keeping him out."

We stood holding hands like junior-high kids at the school dance.

"I came close, you know," I said.

Roxanne squeezed again.

"If he'd made any sort of move, I would've killed him. My finger was pressing the trigger already. I had his forehead sighted in. You're supposed to aim for the core, but I didn't want him to exist anymore."

"But it didn't happen."

"No," I said. "Dodged that bullet, so to speak. Both of us."

We were quiet for a moment, then a couple more. In the living room, a horse whinnied, the girls watching a movie.

"He had a gun. He might have killed her," Roxanne said. "He might have killed me. The girls. You stopped him, Jack."

I smiled.

"For the moment. Him, and not the hundreds of others. A grain of sand."

Another squeeze.

"You can only fight one of them at a time."

A pause.

"What kind of world is this?" I said.

"The one we've got. The one you volunteered for, Jack, a long time ago. And Clair, and then Louis."

"You were already on the front lines."

"Yeah. And then Sophie came along, and now she's in this, too."

"I'm sorry about that part."

"But not the rest."

"No," I said. "I don't know how to do it any other way. I just don't."

We stood there, the two of us, feeling very much alone.

"He might have killed you, Jack."

"Nah. He's just a drunken fool."

"With a gun."

22

The four of us had dinner: me, Roxanne, Sophie, and Tara. Sophie chatted—TikTok (up to 1,100 likes), the nature video, Mr. Ziggy—but Tara was quiet. She picked at her mac and cheese, looked at the grilled tofu with suspicion, and didn't touch her salad. We kept up small talk until her mom got back from cleaning up at the house. Tiffanee thanked us and asked Tara to do the same, which she did.

We all walked outside together.

Sophie turned for a last wave. "I hope they keep Jason in jail," she said.

"I think they will," I said.

"What if he gets out and comes back?" she said. "Will you go to Tara's and make him stop?"

"That's what the police are for," Roxanne said.

"But Dad always gets there first," Sophie said.

Jason and Raymond, Germaine and Twinsey.

"Sometimes," I said.

We finished watching the movie about a girl in New Mexico who tames a wild horse. The girl's parents are always bickering and the horse is her sanctuary, like Raymond and the Church. Unlike Raymond, the girl is able to get her parents to see the error in their ways, and at the end they promise to do better.

"Jason should've watched this movie," Sophie said.

And then it was after nine, and Sophie was yawning. I said I'd feed and water Pokey tonight, but she could do it with me in the morning.

Sophie went to bed, and Roxanne switched to a show about people fixing up houses. I put on my parka and boots and walked down the path through the dark woods to Clair's barn. Twice I stopped to listen, imagining I heard footsteps in the crusty snow. Twice I kept going.

Pokey was philosophical, as always, looking at me with his big brown pony eyes and saying, telepathically, This too shall pass. I put grain in the bin, water in the heated trough. I brushed out his mane, patted him for a few minutes after that. And then I closed the half-door to the stall and left, saw that the lights were still on in the kitchen.

I went to the back door and knocked.

Mary opened the door, said, "Just took pumpkin bread out of the oven."

"I have a sixth sense," I said.

I followed her through the mudroom, where some of Clair's boots were lined up like it was a firehouse. The woodstove was going in the kitchen and CBC news was playing on the laptop on the counter.

She sliced the end off of the loaf of pumpkin bread, put it on a plate, and slathered it with butter. I leaned against the counter and took a bite, said the bread was delicious.

"You can have a loaf for the girls," she said. "I thought they might have had a rough day."

Mary had seen the police cars. I told her the story, right down to my finger starting to pull the trigger.

"I'm glad you didn't shoot him," she said. "You'd be in court for a year. When Clair shot that man who was shooting at the both of you, I thought it would never end. Wore out the road to Belfast courthouse."

"I remember."

"But I didn't shed a tear for that heinous human being, and this jerk today—why are men so insecure?" she said.

"The patriarchy is crumbling."

"Like Jericho, Jack. The walls of that kingdom are falling down."

I smiled.

The announcer went to a break, said, "This is the Canadian Broadcasting Corporation."

"What's the word from up north?" I said. "Clair says it's challenging."

"If he says that, it must be close to impenetrable," she said. "All he told me is it's a gilded cage, like those Saudi princes who lock up their daughters."

"A biker gang can probably lock things up pretty tight," I said. "I think they're doing recon, figuring out who comes and goes."

"What Clair did for all those years. Hide in the jungle and watch the enemy. He'd write to me, say the government was paying him to lie around, get a tan in a tropical paradise."

"And you waited then. You're still waiting."

"I'm a Marine Corps wife. It's what you sign up for."

"Vietnam was a long time ago, Mary."

"You know how it goes, Jack. You boys will always find a fight."

I finished the bread. Mary cut another slice and put it on my plate.

"You're too thin," she said.

I spread the butter. She went to the woodstove, opened the door, and put in a log from the rack. I took a bite.

"Yum," I said, and then, "You sound worried about him."

"He's not getting any younger. A step or two slower. Eventually he's not going to be able to do this anymore."

"He has Louis."

"Yes, the knight errant. That makes me nervous, too. He's in love with that Marta woman, and that doesn't help one's judgment. Plus, I trust that woman as far as I can throw her. Little femme fatale, from what I can tell. I told Clair, 'She got herself into this mess, why do you have to get her out?' "

"Because it's Louis."

"Yes, a fellow Marine. I get it. They'll die for each other on the battlefield. What I don't get is that they think they need to do it now, in Montreal, Canada. Both came back from their wars a long time ago. When does it end?"

I ate the bread, waited.

"I've been patient," Mary said, taking another loaf of bread from a pan and putting it on a rack to cool. "The two of you getting into these scrapes all these years. You've always come home, thank God, but I'm worried this time, Jack."

"Roxanne has a feeling, too," I said.

"Can we still talk about women's intuition? Maybe not, but it's real."

I waited.

"You know, it was always other wives who got their husband back in a casket with a flag. Wouldn't that be a rotten joke? All these years later, to have him die in a foreign country, fighting somebody else's battle? Just like in all those places nobody even thinks about anymore. Long Binh and Quang Nam and Chu Lai, and the stupid hills and trails and people's husbands and sons all dead and forgotten."

She put the spatula down and turned to me, a trim woman with crinkled arms, soft white hair, big brown eyes. It was a silvery beauty that still explained why Clair Varney had been smitten fifty years before. Now her face was flushed with anger and worry.

"I know why he does this," Mary said.

"You do?"

"All the death and destruction he was part of—it was kill or be killed, I get it. And he says someone has to be part of the warrior class or there's just anarchy. And then he came home and things were eating at him and he needed to do some good, even things up."

"Could've volunteered at a soup kitchen," I said.

"But he met you."

"Sorry."

"Oh, it's good. You've helped a lot of people over the years. Life saved for a life lost."

"Same for Louis, I'm sure. Other side of his ledger is Fallujah."

"Or some other place now completely forgotten," Mary said. "But when are things truly evened up—when you lose your own life? And what are you trying to make up for, Jack McMorrow? Something, I know. Something deep down."

It stopped me. Roxanne's question, different words. What are you after, Jack?

I started to yammer, "I don't know. I just . . ."

Mary waited, arms folded.

"To make a mark," I said. "To get things down before they slip away." I grinned. "Not like a newspaper is permanent. Crumpled up to start a fire in the woodstove."

"But it's more than that, Jack. You could accomplish that writing cute stories about lost cats. Just read one. The cat got loose in a rest area in New Jersey. A year later, it turns up at home in Pennsylvania. Walked the whole way. But you and Clair, you don't do cute."

I took another bite of bread, thinking, chewing.

"It's a way to make sure there's an accounting," I said. "So there is some sort of order. I mean, I can't send people to jail, but I can make sure the truth is known. Who killed this guy Raymond in Clarkston? And why him? If I don't put a spotlight on it, we may never know. And it's not right to let a life go—I'm not sure of the word here—without a headline. And the lives I pick . . ."

I searched for the right description.

"They're the kind of people who are just easy to dismiss. Not important to most people. A weird guy with a bunch of religious junk. This small-town hooker on Craigslist, just running from herself. A street kid, with nothing and nobody. A woman who picks the wrong guy and dies for it. 'Hey, what was she doing with him anyway?' Turn the page. If I'm doing my job, you can't turn the page."

"You make sure they get some justice," Mary said.

"Maybe. At least some respect. My stories, I hope, make you stop and look at this person. Because they're real and they have dignity. They deserve that much."

I took the last bite of bread.

"More than you wanted, I'm sure."

"No," Mary said. "I appreciate it. I need to make both of you think about why you do what you do. Make sure you tell us—me and Roxanne."

I nodded.

"You're right. I know it hasn't been easy for her. Worse for you. I wasn't off at the war."

"You're not just going to the office, Jack. Don't minimize what Roxanne has to deal with. And Sophie."

That stopped me, and I looked away.

Mary attempted a smile, but it was tinged with sadness, regret. Her stoic Marine-wife expression. Then the smile fell away and her eyes filled.

"I've hung on this long, I can do it a few more years."

She shook her head, dabbed her eyes with a finger. I crossed the kitchen and put a hand on her shoulder, was about to say that Clair was very good at this, and so was Louis, and if anybody could pull it off it was—

But she turned away, slipped a loaf of pumpkin bread into a bag, tied it off, held it out to me.

"Tell darling Sophie to come visit me. We'll have hot chocolate and she can tell me all the latest news from school."

"She's growing up fast."

"She'll have to, the world she's stepping into. All this Instagram and whatnot. Anyway, didn't mean to give you the third degree," she said. "It's just that, I do worry. More and more. Me and Clair—don't want it to end like this, some scum killing my wonderful husband. It can't, right? No way. It would be worse than losing him in a war."

She stepped closer, gave me a hug and held on.

"So you tell him, Jack McMorrow," she muttered in my ear. "He'll listen to you. Tell him if it doesn't feel right, just walk away. What is it they used to say? Abort the mission."

She broke the embrace, wiped her eyes again, said, "Give Roxanne a hug from me. Tell her she's a wonderful mom. And she's raising a wonderful girl. All of this will work itself out."

And then we stood and I nodded. She gave me a little salute, her hand pink against her white hair. And then Mary Varney turned back to the counter and started cleaning up.

I let myself out, thinking sure, I could talk to Clair. Until I was blue in the face.

23

I texted the deputy at almost midnight. He texted right back. Jason was in Waldo County Jail. He wouldn't be arraigned for three or four days because the court was still all backed up after COVID. They'd decide bail then.

I set the alarm for five, but was awake at four, on the road at 5:10. I was wearing my parka and had also grabbed my peacoat from the closet. My note to Roxanne said I needed to catch people as they came off their shifts.

Which, driving the truck through the blackness at eighty, I did.

It was gray and damp, 24 degrees on the dash thermometer, with a metallic light spreading from the east. I pulled into the QuikStop, saw Mo through the front window at the register. I thought I'd missed Sparrow, but as I was parking, she came outside pushing a dolly loaded with jugs of blue windshield washer fluid. She had them almost all stacked by the door when I walked up.

"Hey," I said.

"McMorrow," she said, her back to me.

"They have you on outside duty?"

"We decided they were being sexist and racist, making Mo do all the manual labor. So we switched."

She set the last jug on the display, topped it with the sign that said $2.99 A GALLON. Put the empty cartons on the dolly and turned to me.

"Those meth heads," she said.

"Yeah."

"They came in the next morning. The girl bought cigarettes, told me her boyfriend thought our story was bullshit. He thought we were there to roll them. She said it was good he was so high he couldn't remember where he'd left his gun."

"Fortuitous," I said. "Did you tell her I'm a real reporter and I do know your dad?"

"You can't talk to tweakers," Sparrow said. "By the time they say something, in their head they've already moved on."

"You think they killed Raymond?"

She blew on her fingers, stamped her feet in their red Converse.

"Maybe. But if they were there, they were just doing what they were told. I don't think they could be that organized to plan it."

"Rosary beads. Did Raymond collect those, too?"

"Yeah. He collected anything old-timey and Catholic."

She took the vape pen out, then blew a cloud of steam into the cold morning air. It was like she was a factory and there was a smokestack that came out of her mouth.

"I talked to a guy who sold statues to Raymond. He's down in Pennsylvania. He said Raymond paid with envelopes of cash."

Sparrow blew another cloud. Through the window behind her, Mo was selling somebody scratch tickets.

"Yeah. Raymond didn't believe in checks or credit cards or any of that. I used to tell him, 'Ray, you're the last person on Earth who doesn't use plastic or Venmo.' All of freaking Africa pays for stuff with their phone."

"What would he say?"

"He said charging interest was a sin. I guess it's in the Bible somewhere."

"Do you know where he kept all this money? Did he carry it around? Could somebody have seen it?"

Sparrow hesitated.

"He did have this box with a lock. He said in church they kept the candles in it. The ones that were like leftovers, blessed or whatever."

"Consecrated," I said. "Where did he keep it?"

"In the cellar," Sparrow said. "There was this little room where they stored coal back in the day. It was under all this crap."

"Did you see it?"

"No, he just told me about it. He said he kept special things in it."

A bearded guy wearing sunglasses came out with a fistful of tickets, went to his truck and sat scratching them with the dome light on.

"So if he hid anything, that's where it might be," Sparrow said. "But who knows. The whole place is like hoarder central."

We stood. She smoked. The guy with the scratch tickets was tossing them out the window onto the ground, one by one.

"Hey," Sparrow called out. "You gonna pick those up?"

The guy put the truck in gear and pulled out, flipped her off on the way by.

"I don't care, I'm sick of these people," Sparrow said. "Brandon said some guy spit right in his face last night. Said he had TB. They figured he was full of shit, but they arrested the guy for assault and took Brandon to the hospital to be tested."

"Jeesh. He coming by?"

"Mandatory OT until ten."

"I'll drive you," I said. "We can stop at Raymond's on the way."

The police tape was still up.

We slipped under it and walked to the side door like we belonged there. The door was locked. Sparrow went straight to a wooden milk crate at the end of the porch, lifted it, and got a key. She opened the door and I followed her in.

The statues lay smashed on the floor, all decapitated necks and heads. Paintings were slashed and a wooden cabinet was lying on its side, figurines of Jesus and Mary jumbled together like they'd been bulldozed into a grave.

We didn't go upstairs. The door to the cellar was in the kitchen, and we walked through, our feet sticking to the floor from liquids dumped from the cupboards and the refrigerator. Sparrow opened the wooden door and leaned in to find the light switch. She flicked it on.

Nothing. She turned on the flashlight on her phone and we stared into the dimness through its hazy blue light.

She started down the stairs. I followed.

The basement was filled with more wreckage. Boxes turned over and emptied, clothes and photos trampled. Plastic bins overturned, lids flung aside. Old tools swept off a bench, scattered across the concrete floor.

Sparrow navigated the mess like a maze, turning sideways between mounds of junk. There was a pile of clothes on hangers, both women's and men's. A denim jumper, a purple shirt with a long pointy collar. Stuff from the seventies, lines of shoes, work boots and sneakers with racing stripes, pumps with big clunky heels.

"His parents' clothes," I said.

"I know. Creepy."

At the far end of the room, she paused and reached for a light cord, and this time a bare bulb came on. There was a mound of soiled bedspreads and blankets, the smell of cat feces and urine. The pile had been shifted to one side. I pulled more of it up and beetles scurried across the floor.

"He used to say, 'I give my money to the cats in the basement,' " Sparrow said. "I said, 'You don't have a cat, Raymond.' He said, 'They're strays, like you and me.' "

She kept digging through the bedclothes, the odor wafting upward And then there was a paint-spattered wooden crate. Sparrow lifted the lid, revealing stiffened brushes, jars of old thinner, congealed varnish. I leaned in and pushed the stuff around and one jar knocked over. The sound was like I'd tapped a drum. Hollow.

I emptied the crate, tapped again. Jammed a screwdriver into the side of the wooden bottom and pried. It creaked and scraped and then came loose. The crate had a false bottom.

Inside was a red cloth. I lifted it out. Nested inside was a flat wooden box, maybe six inches high and fifteen inches long. It was unvarnished, said church supply on the front, and 10-inch candles. There was a hasp and a small padlock screwed to the top. I lifted the box out and it was heavy, like it was filled with paper. Sparrow stuck her fingernails under the side and tried to pry it, but it didn't budge.

"Did he carry keys?" I said.

"No," Sparrow said. "He left the keys in the ignition in the van. Took the house key out from under the milk crate. I don't think he had another one. One time he misplaced it and he prayed to St. Anthony."

Patron saint of lost things.

I turned to the mess. It would seem this key would be nearby, if he kept the van key in the ignition, the house key by the door. The mounds of clothes. If they'd been on a rack before the ransacking . . .

"The pockets," I said.

We started in. Plaid trousers. A leather coat, long with big lapels. A woman's jacket with shoulder pads. Many pairs of jeans.

The pile of discards grew. And then Sparrow said, "Yes."

A skirt with a small pocket in the front, in the shape of a flower. The key was brass, strung on a piece of red string. Sparrow fit it into the lock and the hasp popped open.

The candle box was filled with neatly placed stacks of cash.

I reached in and took out a stack, thumbed through it. It was all twenties, a total of $440. I counted another and it was all twenties, too, about the same size. There were eleven stacks, which meant the box contained about $5,000. The money was used, like it had come from a store, not an ATM. The cash drawer in the supermarket.

"Raymond was saving up," Sparrow said.

"For his next purchase," I said. "St. Apollonius." I paused. "He never sent the money. The people in Pennsylvania had a statue all crated up, ready to go. Raymond wouldn't let them ship anything until he'd paid."

Sparrow was quiet, staring at the money.

"He knew I was scraping by, trying to get the meds for Riff. But he had all this money here?"

"I guess St. Apollonius was higher on his list."

"That's what I hate about religion. All these churches and buildings and the ministers on TV who make millions of dollars, fly around in private jets and ask for money. If they cared about what Jesus said, they'd spend it all on poor people and sick patients and people who can't afford rehab and kids who die because they can't get medicine."

"The Vatican has rooms full of gold."

"The world is so messed up," Sparrow said. "Sometimes I feel like I just can't take it."

My mind flashed to an image of Jason, his forehead in my sights.

She lowered the candle box back into the crate, closed the lid.

"So if they said, 'Give us all your money or we'll kill you,' why would Raymond not turn this over?" she said.

"Maybe they never asked that question. Maybe it was another question altogether," I said.

Sparrow smoothed the last blanket.

"Like what?" she said.

"Like the same one they asked Germaine, the lady with the storage units. Beat her up because she couldn't or wouldn't answer. Until she did."

And then the same crew came to Raymond and asked the question again.

We left the house and I drove Sparrow home. She was silent on the ride until I pulled up in front of the house. It was spitting snow and the lights were on in the dark gloom.

"He was holding out on me," Sparrow said, one hand on the door handle.

"You knew he did this, the collecting."

"I thought he just traded them around. Not paid for them with all this cash. He knew about Riff. Couldn't he have one less statue and help me out? I mean, you couldn't go in there without tripping over a saint or Mary or Jesus."

"I know."

"And for what? Because it reminded him of his freakin' childhood? Hanging out in the church and chanting bullshit? If that's what floats your boat, fine, but Riff is dying. Real-world dead, not some hocus-pocus bullshit and a house full of statues of people who've been gone for a thousand years and are probably all made up anyway."

Sparrow shook her head as she swung out of the truck. "Fuckin' A," she said.

Alone in the truck again, I sat back, took a deep breath. Then grabbed my phone, searched for St. Apollonius, found a bit on Wikipedia excerpted from a book, *Lives of the Saints, Illustrated*. It was the reign of Marcus Aurelius's son, Commodus. Apollonius was a Christian scholar of some sort and, hauled before the authorities, refused to renounce his faith. "Yet if it were a delusion (as you assert)," he said, "which tells us that the soul is immortal, and that there is a judgment after death and a reward of virtue at the resurrection, and that God is the Judge, we would gladly be carried away by such a lie as that, which has taught us to lead good lives awaiting the hope of the future even while suffering adversities."

It was a good speech. When he was done, they lopped off his head.

I pictured Raymond remembering this as he was being tied to the bed. Beaten bloody, the plastic bag coming down on his face. A good life. Adversities. Reward for his virtue waiting at the Resurrection. A defender of the faith. His face blue, the blood-smeared plastic sucked into his swollen mouth, thinking it was all working out.

He didn't deserve that.

I texted Blake and then drove downtown. I swung into the Dunkin', thinking I'd see him, but there were no police vehicles in the lot or the drive-through line. I parked, showing some small bit of respect for the planet, and went inside.

The faces all looked familiar now, but I was thinking it could be my imagination—that maybe there were only so many variations of humanity in Clarkston, Maine.

And then the van pulled in and parked. It was the cleaning crew from the post-release program, probably through with the overnight shift and headed back.

Snow led the way in, the big guy Mumbo behind him. They got in line behind me, and Snow said, "Hey, newsman."

I turned, said, "Hey, Snow."

He was rocking on his feet, hands tucked in the pockets of his black hoodie. Mumbo was behind him, looking back out of the shop at the parking lot.

"Still writing those stories, dude?"

"No choice," I said. "How I make my living."

"You should write about me," Snow said. "I got stories to tell. How an outlaw went straight. From a life of crime to star floor mopper. A success story." He grinned.

"Good for you," I said. "How's that going?"

"Clean and sober, dude. Nine months and five days. Two more weeks and I go home. Hug my kid, my fiancée. Life is good."

"Gonna stay in the cleaning business?"

"Hey, why not? Home during the day, working while everyone else is partying. Not that I miss it. You know how much time I wasted? Now I—"

Mumbo had his phone out, tapped Snow's shoulder, said something, and turned and walked out of the shop, back to the van. The line moved forward.

Snow continued. "Patience, dude. That's what the program tells you. Shit doesn't have to happen as soon as you want it to. I can stand in this line for an hour. Just chillin'. The old Snowman would have been jumpy as hell."

I looked over his shoulder, saw the van back out of the space. I wondered if Mumbo was leaving Snow behind, but then he pulled into another space at the far end of the lot. Snow was still talking, how the Twelve Steps had saved him, how he'd started drinking when he was thirteen. The woman behind the counter looked at him with no reaction, like she'd heard his evangelizing before.

"Black tea," I said. "Just milk."

I paid and went to the pickup counter. Snow had turned to the guy behind him, was asking him if he was having a good day. I nodded as I passed him and he gave me a fist bump.

I walked to the truck, the snow more an icy sleet now, climbed in. Opened the tea and sipped. Checked my phone, saw a text from Blake.

He said he could meet me in the usual place at nine thirty. I texted okay, put the phone down. Looked up.

The cleaners' van was behind me, motor running, the hell with the climate. I sipped, saw a woman cross in the mirror, stop at the driver's door. She was talking, but Mumbo didn't have her get in. I adjusted the mirror, looked more closely.

For an instant she was just familiar. An instant after that I recognized her. It was Twinsey of rosary beads fame, the hood of her sweatshirt thrown back. She was talking, gesturing, both hands up, palms spread, as in "What do you want me to do?"

I watched as they kept talking. Mumbo was doing the talking now, Twinsey interjecting, then just listening. He seemed calm and resolute. Like, this is the way it's going to be. She nodded at something he said, and then turned and walked away and out of the lot.

I started the motor, pulled out to the street, looked right, and saw her get into a car parked at the curb just down the block. It was black and small, a Honda or a Hyundai. It pulled away.

It was 9:20. I headed for the mill, thinking, what was their connection? If she had money, and the rosary beads, what did that have to do with Mumbo? Had she been in prison with him? What were they talking about, him looking like he'd given her some sort of instruction? Bible study?

The religious drug dealer who wouldn't flip, model inmate, now rehabilitated? Model prisoner. But what was his story, really?

The pigeons were still flying. I turned the heat up in the truck and watched them swoop and dive, land and take off, like it was all choreographed. A director pigeon up there somewhere saying, "No. Still not right. Do it again."

Blake pulled in at 9:38, wheeled up to my truck, buzzed his window down. Salley was in the passenger seat. He leaned forward, said, "That story ain't done yet? What, *New York Times* comes out once a month?" He grinned but it had an edge, like in a different time he would have run me out of town just because he could.

I grinned back. Their motor idled, filling an awkward silence. Then Salley's phone rang, some bit of a heavy-metal guitar solo. Riff could ID it, no doubt. Salley started talking, then got out of the SUV and started walking.

"Cash escort assignment," Blake said. "This is his rolling office. He told me he made more money in three runs last week than he makes at the PD in a month. Big bucks running through that business."

"And he gets his cut," I said. "Pay him by the job?"

"Flat rate, with a monthly bonus based on the amount of cash moved."

"And he just drives?"

"Inconspicuous, just some guy in a car."

"If Zombie were smart, he'd forget the QuikStops and start knocking these guys off. Two jobs and you'd be sitting on a beach somewhere."

Salley was walking in small circles, still talking. "No, I can do a couple more a week."

Another head shake from Blake, a long sigh. "Like we don't have anything else going on."

"Twinsey knows Mumbo," I said. "Saw them talking this morning in the parking lot at Dunkin'. Kind of animated, at least on her side. He seemed to be giving marching orders."

"Huh," Blake said. "Both from the drug world, I guess. But he would have been inside since before she started getting in trouble."

"Maybe they have prison mixers, dances in the gym."

No smile from Blake. Interesting guy, but not a barrel of laughs. What shooting people did to you.

"Raymond also collected rosary beads."

"I know. Sparrow told me."

"Of course, you can also get them in pawn shops and yard sales," I said. "Town full of dying old Catholics."

"I can't picture her finding Jesus," Blake said.

Salley was saying, "All good, as long as everybody on your end keeps their mouths shut . . ."

The pigeons swooped through and lighted on the parapet above us.

"Mumbo and the boys clean the church," I said.

"Thinking they picked them up off the floor?"

"I'll talk to the priest. See if he knows her. Maybe Twinsey was in the Young Ladies' Sodality."

Blake looked at me.

"My grandmother's era. When Catholic girls were about fourteen, they joined up and learned about purity and virtue and how to interact with the opposite sex."

"I don't think she learned that at church," Blake said.

"Sometimes people surprise you," I said.

We sat, Blake waiting for Salley to finish. He looked over and said, "So, what's the matter?"

I hesitated, a first step with him beyond official business.

"One of my daughter's friends. Her mother's boyfriend is part of some militia, running around in the woods with guns, getting ready for war against the government or taking over the statehouse, who knows. She doesn't want them training on her land anymore and he won't kick them out. Yesterday she left him and came to our house, and he came looking for her, afraid she'd rat them out."

Blake waited. I told him about Jason and his big gun, me getting off the first shot, Jason in jail.

"Jesus, McMorrow," he said.

"I didn't have time to think about it."

"Sometimes you don't," Blake said. "Plenty of time to think about it later."

We sat a moment, me waiting.

"What would you have done with the second shot?" Blake said.

"Put him down," I said. "If he'd drawn his gun, I would have had no choice."

"He's dead, but you're never quite the same."

"Better than the other way around," I said.

"I guess."

A kid with a paintball gun the exception?

I lost him for a second, and then he was back.

"Mr. Six-Shooter is in jail—" he said.

"For now."

"But what about the rest of them? What if they get the idea this girlfriend could be an informant?"

Salley was winding up his call, walking back.

"I guess I'd need reinforcements," I said.

"You'd need an army."

I had a small one, I thought. But it was 250 miles away.

24

The same woman, Theresa, answered the door at the rectory. I asked for Father Aneesh, didn't bother with the smile. She looked at me and swung the door wide, led me in.

I sat in the same chair, looked at the same pictures of bishops, the same painting of Jesus. His expression told me he had my back. I hoped so. Roxanne's and Sophie's, too.

There was a soft padding of footsteps on carpet and then Father Aneesh walked in and over. I stood and shook his hand, and he sat in the chair next to mine, his black shoes planted side by side on the floor.

I looked at them. They were very expensive priest shoes, the leather gleaming.

"Custom?" I said.

"Ah, you know good shoes?"

He'd brightened.

"Yes, when I lived in New York, there was a great cobbler on Mulberry, between Spring and Prince. He made shoes for my father."

"These are Italian. There's a place in Rome, a wonderful master cobbler. He keeps a form of your feet."

"Cool," I said, and looked up from his shoes, at that moment in his good graces. "Gayle Dupuis. On the street she's known as Twinsey."

"I don't know a Twinsey, but I do know Gayle," he said. "She helped us out here a while back."

"Was this part of some probation thing?"

He smiled.

ROBBED BLIND • 229

"Something like that. We try to support people when they need it most."

"I see. What did she do here?"

"Housekeeping. She's been helping while Mrs. Thibodeau's out with her knee replacement."

"Is she Catholic?"

"Mrs. Thibodeau? Christened right here in the cathedral."

"No, Gayle Dupuis."

He hesitated.

"I don't think so. But it wasn't a requirement for the work. Like I said, we see it as Christian charity to help people at difficult times in their lives. The men who clean the churches in the city as part of their post-release program, they need the structure that work gives them."

"Good of you all," I said.

"The Lord Savior is all about forgiveness and redemption. But you're Catholic. You know that."

"Yes, but I'm also Irish. I sometimes have trouble with the forgiveness part."

Father Aneesh smiled. His hands remained folded neatly on his lap. Not much fazed him.

"Jesus turned the other cheek at a time when that was a radical notion," he said

"Yes."

"It's the only way to break the cycle of violence," he said.

I thought of Jason, guns in the woods.

"There's also the rule of law—that there are supposed to be consequences when you break it."

"How's that working for us?" Father Aneesh said, with a smug grin, like he'd just maneuvered me into checkmate.

"Sometimes it works just fine," I said.

There was a moment, him looking at me with an expression that blended pity with annoyance.

"Ms. Dupuis," I said.

"Yes."

"Did you give her a set of rosary beads—as a token of appreciation or something?"

He shook his head.

"The Church takes the mysteries of the rosary very seriously. We don't hand out rosary beads like party favors."

"Right. But Gayle's wearing rosary beads, like a necklace."

"A rosary is a sacred object," Aneesh said. "It's not jewelry."

"Like a rapper with a cross?"

"Yes. What does this have to do with your story about Raymond's death, Mr. McMorrow?"

"I don't know. I just met her, and she had the beads on, and I wondered if she was part of the parish community, like Raymond."

"You could have asked her," Father Aneesh said.

"It was a brief conversation and then she had to go."

"Ah."

"Did you talk to her about Raymond, Father? I mean, maybe among yourselves here in the rectory? Maybe she was just in the room, doing the cleaning or something?"

Father Aneesh looked wary, just a glimmer, and then regained his calm confidence.

"I don't know. We talk about a lot of things. She may have been there. Why?"

"I wondered if she knew about Raymond. Maybe I could get her reaction to his death? For the story, I mean."

He thought, held up his folded hands like he was praying for the right answer.

"Maybe Mrs. Thibodeau might know something. She's still out with complications following her surgery. We pray for her."

"I see. I hope she recovers."

He nodded. "It's in God's hands."

And those of her surgical team.

I waited. He looked at me and I waited some more. He caved.

"She worked with Ms. Dupuis for a week or so, showed her how we do things," he said. "There's a method to the way we clean the premises here. We have the men from the post-release program do things like the community hall, but in here, it's not like you just pick up a mop."

I glanced at the immaculate sterility of the place. Cleanliness and godliness.

"I'm sure," I said. "Mrs. Thibodeau and Raymond were close?"

"Oh, she thought the world of him. She may have brought him up in conversation. These ladies, they chatter away while they're working."

He smiled patronizingly. Women.

"Was Gayle working here when Germaine called about the statue of Jesus, the one in the storage unit?"

The priest hesitated, like I'd broken out of a check and this was a new gambit.

"I don't know. I mean, maybe. Probably."

"Who did Germaine call? Did she call you?"

He gave a little laugh.

"Oh, no. That sort of thing . . ."

Was beneath him.

"So Germaine knows Mrs. Thibodeau."

"For fifty years or maybe more. They were young women in the parish together."

"Right. So she might have called Mrs. Thibodeau, just to see if it made sense to give the statue to the church. And Mrs. Thibodeau would have said—"

"We aren't taking more reliquary. We're closing churches, unfortunately, but it's God's will. We have more than we can handle."

"But Raymond might have been a good option," I said. "And Mrs. Thibodeau would have known that."

"Yes, she would have."

"Because he collected this sort of thing."

"Yes."

"And when they were cleaning, talking about the proper way to dust or vacuum or whatever, they might have chatted about that."

Father Aneesh capitulated.

"I don't know if the two of them were here when it was being discussed. If I remember correctly, they chatted away most of the time. Once I had to ask them to quiet down. I was preparing a homily."

We sat for a minute, and then I stood. Father Aneesh did, too.

"Thanks," I said. "You've been helpful."

We started for the exit. He slowed.

"All of this seems a bit removed from the story about Raymond."

"It's the significant detail that you look for when you're reporting, Father," I said. "It's what really brings the person to life."

A beat.

"So to speak."

I sat in the truck, scribbled notes of the conversation. I paused, looked up at the rectory, the curtains precisely raised, the walk neatly shoveled, the Father's car tucked away in the adjacent garage. If part of the job of the newspaper was to afflict the comfortable, I'd come to the right place. Amid the mayhem, there was the Church floating above it all like God. And there was Father Aneesh—self-assured, detached, clearly not shedding any tears for the devout man who'd been tied up, beaten, and suffocated with a plastic bag.

Like taking calls from old ladies—it was beneath him.

I went through the key parts of the interview: that Dupuis/Twinsey could have been there if Germaine called Mrs. Thibodeau. That Father Aneesh employed people just out of jail, including Mumbo and Snow. That Twinsey knew Mumbo. That Twinsey didn't get her rosary beads from Father Aneesh, but maybe from Mrs. Thibodeau—a thank-you for vacuuming well done?

The phone buzzed.

A text.

The podcaster, Dunne.

—Got a good one for you—Zombie and the robberies. Exclusive, but I'll share!!

I considered it, wondered what the price would be. Picked up the phone, texted that I'd be glad to talk.

—Where r u?
In town.
—Awesome! Parking garage beside bank. I'm white Dodge SUV. In 10?
That's good.
—Fourth level, mill side.

The garage was empty after level two, the building thought up by some economic optimist. I wound my way up to four, swung off, headed for the mill side. The white SUV was the only vehicle in sight.

I parked beside it, looked over. Dunne was texting, didn't look up. I waited for ten seconds, got out, and went to the passenger side and got in. I sat. She texted. I looked around. Dunne was in jeans, knee-high black leather boots, matching jacket. The jacket was unzipped halfway, the sweater underneath about the same. A pendant with a red stone hung in the gap.

I looked away: beige leather, lots of buttons and screens. Fancy.

She finished, tucked the phone underneath her right thigh.

"Jack," she said, like it was a long-awaited reunion.

"Nice ride, Ms. Dunne," I said.

"Steph."

"Right. Steph. Podcast business must be treating you well."

"Ah, my ex, I put him through law school. When we split, I got a good lawyer. She got me a cut of everything he makes. But the alimony times out in a few months."

"I see."

"Enough about me, Jack. It's so good to see you."

She turned to me, the jacket and sweater open, as though to make sure I felt the same way.

"This is like that old movie, the one about the reporters and Nixon," she said. "I'm your Deep Throat."

"*All the President's Men.* True story."

She opened her eyes in mock wonder. "Really? That's amazing. Thanks for mansplaining."

I smiled.

She tapped my thigh. "Just kidding."

"Right," I said. "So, what'd you want to tell me?"

"Well, first of all I want to thank you and give you an update. Tagging you and the *New York Times* in the social promo was a freaking gold mine. I mean, in terms of advertisers, this is a whole different ball game. Click-throughs on Twitter were up over three hundred percent. Subscriptions just went crazy. Checked the metrics, and we're at six thousand subscribers and climbing by the minute. We were at, like, forty-eight twenty."

We.

She leaned toward me like the numbers called for a hug. I stayed in my seat.

"My person at Apple is connecting me with a production company. Still early, but looking good, baby."

"Glad to help. And you said you had something?"

"I do," Dunne said. "I also want to invite you to be my co-host on the next episode. We explore the Jandreau case, your pledge to bring the killers to justice."

"I didn't know I'd made one."

"You're here, aren't you?"

"Yeah."

She paused. Kept her eyes locked on mine as she toyed with the red stone. Her nails matched. I glanced down, then back up. She was attractive in a chiseled sort of way—like a blonde bird of prey.

"I know this is more than a story for you. You want revenge."

"I only knew Raymond for two days," I said.

"But in that short time, you grew to respect him. You connected. You liked and respected him. Maybe your own Catholic upbringing. Am I wrong, Jack?"

There was something relentless about her, like she was always maneuvering you into a corner.

"I suppose not."

"So will you do it?"

"I don't talk about myself. Or the stories. I just write them."

She turned and leaned again. The stone dangled in her cleavage like a hypnotist's charm.

"But you're part of your stories. I read a whole bunch of them last night. You clearly don't give up until you discover the truth."

"That's what journalism is. Accountability."

"Not always—not like the way you do it. Your stories get to the bottom of things. The real truths. I mean, what you do is so pure. It's like a reminder of why we get into this business."

We again.

I looked out the window at the roofs of the mills. Pigeons were swooping. I wondered if they were the same ones I'd seen earlier.

"Well?"

"I don't know. It's not my thing."

"Multimedia is the future. You can write your wonderful stories, but tell them through multiple channels. It's the way to reach today's audience. The news doesn't come from the paperboy anymore, Jack."

"Right."

"There's a huge audience that would eat up your stuff. Instagram, Twitter—invites them into the podcast."

"Uh-huh."

"Facebook, of course. And LinkedIn, too. That's a huge untapped market."

Maybe I'd need one, if Carlisle couldn't carry the day in New York.

"You can't be passive anymore in this business."

She leaned closer. Mascara and perfume and gloss with tiny spar-kles, on the edge of her lower lip. "You just have to go for it, Jack. If you want something, you just reach out"—Dunne hovered, her lips parted—"and take it."

I took a quick breath. "So, whatcha got?" I said.

She fell back, her jacket scrunching against the leather seat. "The check-cashing shop robbery."

"Right."

"The guy he tied up."

"LaPlante."

"Right. So Zombie puts a gun on him, marches him into the back room, ties him up. Never says a word."

"That's what the victim said, anyway."

"I thought about that," Dunne said. "That's a lot of interaction without talking. I mean, I can't stand next to a street sign without saying something."

"You're not robbing somebody."

"But what about the threats? What about 'Gimme the money or I'll blow you away' and all that?"

"He said the robber was silent."

"Bullshit. That's what I thought when I heard that. So I went to my sources."

"Cops?"

"His husband wouldn't talk. But his mom, this sweet old lady, I mean the white hair and everything. I brought her coffee and pastries. She says she can't talk because of the investigation, so we just chat about the city, how it's changed, how she likes the Somalis because they work the way she did in the towel mill when she was young. I'm like, 'You go, old white lady!' "

"Huh."

"And then I say, 'I'm glad the robber didn't threaten your son, try to scare him.' "

Dunne paused for effect, looked over at me to make sure I was really listening.

"Mrs. LaPlante says, 'He didn't make threats. He insulted what my son does.' I say, 'Meaning what'?" She says, 'The robber called him a usurer.' "

I looked at her.

"I know. I had to look it up. It's somebody who charges interest. And that's not all. She goes, 'He told Reginald that Jesus kicked scum like him out of the temple.' "

"The money changers," I said. "In the Bible."

"Looked that up, too. I'd forgotten Jesus could be kind of a hard-ass. Pretty weird, huh? Zombie some sort of Holy Roller? Maybe he's robbing the stores 'cause they sell condoms and alcohol."

"LaPlante must have told the police."

"And they're holding it back, like when they don't tell exactly how somebody was killed."

"You go to the cops with this?"

"Not yet. I'll put it out there first. Their response is a whole other episode. Gotta milk good content, Jack."

We sat.

"Jandreau," Dunne said. "He was super-religious."

"Yes."

"You think he could've—?"

"Nah. There are a lot of religious extremists out there. Besides, he's the wrong body type. Zombie is lithe and light. Can jump a counter. Raymond was a chubby guy. He'd have had to put his gun down and climb over the counter on his hands and knees."

I looked out over the rooftops. It was snowing in wet squalls, flakes that melted when they hit the asphalt.

"You're not going to try to connect him to this, are you?" I said.

"How 'bout I interview you and bring it up. You say why that's not possible. And then we talk about the murder, the city, the robberies. Sort of an overview of the city under siege."

"I'll let you know," I said.

"When?"

"Today. I have to make a phone call first."

Dunne smiled. I sat back in the seat.

"We could start recording it tomorrow," Dunne said.

"I'll call you."

"Great. This could be the next Serial, but in real time, you know? Everybody is doing true crime, but it's all these cold cases. This one, the crime is totally fresh. I mean, talk about dramatic tension."

"Right," I said.

Dunne high-fived me, like some mission had been accomplished, then clasped my hand and held on.

"Jack," she said.

"Yes."

"You're married, right?"

"Yup."

"Happily?"

"Very."

"That's nice. I was happily married too, for about six months."

She hesitated.

"I like to be direct. I don't have time to screw around."

"Time is click-throughs, I'm sure."

I waited. She still had my hand in hers, held awkwardly, fingers up.

"If you're ever not—happily married, that is—I'd be interested."

I didn't reply.

"Hey, no commitment, but maybe it could turn into something. I think we're a lot alike, Jack. We go for what we want, you know? We don't take no for an answer. We use—what do they call it?—extraordinary measures. There aren't a lot of people like us around here. And I find you very attractive. I think that feeling is maybe a little mutual."

I looked away, didn't reply. She let go of my hand.

We sat not speaking for what seemed like a minute but probably was less. Dunne looked content, like the silence was some sort of intimacy.

Across the way, the snow was starting to accumulate on the roof of the mill. The pigeons had stopped swooping, or moved on. The city looked still from up here, but down below it was a moving, writhing mass of colliding humanity. People who prayed. People who lied. People who killed.

"Usurers," I said.

She looked at me.

"You'll call me?" Dunne said.

"Yes," I said. "Either way."

25

Dunne drove off, didn't look back. I sat in the truck on the empty floor of the garage, all of it whirling around in my head. Her propositions. Her hot tip—that Zombie had called LaPlante a usurer. I looked it up, too: someone who lends money at exorbitant interest. Certainly, a check-cashing pay-day loan shop could qualify. In New York, I'd known places that charged more than twenty percent, taking $100 or more off the top of a $500 paycheck, mostly from illegals who didn't have a bank account. Interest on the loans could hit eighty percent.

So could Zombie really be some sort of religious vigilante? If he'd called store clerks panderers and pimps for selling condoms, I hadn't heard it. Sparrow had said he threatened to shoot her, but nothing else. Why no threats at the stores?

I turned on the motor and the heat, looked out over the rooftops. Sat and mulled, the answers staying just of reach. Mumbo knew Twinsey. They both worked at the church, where everybody knew of Raymond. Both Mumbo and Twinsey were criminals of some sort. Germaine was connected to the church as well. Both Germaine and Raymond had been assaulted. Germaine and Raymond were connected to the statue of Jesus, whereabouts unknown.

And Dunne was awaiting an answer. Would I go on her podcast? Would I join her in the sack? One was a maybe.

I picked up the phone, fired off two texts, waited. Roxanne didn't reply. Blake did.

I pulled out, started down the garage ramp, driving round and round, like the stuff swirling in my head.

It was five minutes to the Dunkin'. I drove along the frozen mill canal, the ice thin and treacherous and deadly as a tar pit. The whole city was like that, drab and dreary in a way that disguised the danger just beneath the surface. A robber with a gun, knocking off stores like some people visited national parks. Proprietors locked and loaded. Drug dealers on the streets and in the tenements, stone-cold killers on the loose, cops escorting bundles of weed profits. Immigrants working three jobs. A rock star dying, his pierced-up daughter tending him like a nurse. Old folks praying for who knows what, the priest who ministered to this battered town buying custom-made Italian shoes.

I pulled into the Dunkin' and parked with the front of the truck climbing a snowbank. Texted Roxanne again.

How are you doing?

Texted the deputy again.
Please let me know if Jason goes to court early.

Got out of the truck as Blake pulled in. Salley was with him, in the passenger seat on the phone. I went to the door and waited.

"How are you doing?" Blake said as we stepped inside.

"Just ducky," I said.

We got coffee and tea, sat in a booth.

"Salley took the OT?" I said.

"He's working his side job the whole time, scheduling runs, pickup points. They keep them random, store the cash in some back room in an industrial building. I asked if he was going to quit the force to do weed runs and he said why should he, when he can do both."

"Somebody's tax dollars at work. How's Sparrow?"

He hesitated, looked down at his coffee, like he was still new to the question.

"Okay. A little distracted, maybe. Nervous about working, getting shot and her dad being alone. But she got a raise and they need the money."

"Anyone taking a closer look at Raymond's murder?" I said.

"Only if it says Zombie did it."

"What if Raymond and Zombie were on the same side?"

I told Blake about Dunne and her tip, Mumbo and Twinsey, Father Aneesh. He listened, said, "I knew they were holding something back. Didn't know what it was. Task force will be pissed when it leaks."

"I'm sure. She wants me in the conversation."

"Riding your coattails."

"Not sure who's riding who," I said. "So what do you think? Zombie, the robber with religion."

"Seems like he would have picked a different character. A Templar knight or something."

"Crusader with a handgun."

"Except the Knights Templar became like a global bank," Blake said. "Only a small percentage were warriors, and that was for a relatively short time during the Crusades. Once the Holy Land was lost, they lost their appeal. In France, King Philip had them tortured and burned at the stake. That was in about 1300."

I looked at him.

"I read a lot," Blake said.

He drank more coffee. Looked out at the SUV. Salley was off the phone.

"Gotta go,"

"When are you off?" I said.

"Noon."

"I want to talk to Germaine again. I get that it might land you in hot water, but I've done it alone myself already. Might be better this time as a two-person job."

He was sliding out of the booth, turned back to me.

"I think it might be three," he said. "We'll meet you there."

Blake backed out, Salley pointing the way like he had a driver. Maybe Blake would rather be fired than chauffeur that cop around. I went back and ordered an egg-and-cheese bagel and a bottle of water, took them to the booth, and got my notebook out.

Sat back and thought.

Telling Blake something was the same as telling Sparrow. When it came to Raymond and the robberies, I doubted they had many secrets. Or did they?

I ate and scrawled. The conversation with Dunne, minus the second proposition. Reread my notes from the interview with Father Aneesh. Finished the bagel and started to clean up the papers and cup. And looked up.

It was Mumbo, but he was wearing jeans and a blue parka and new-looking tan work boots, not the janitor uniform. It also was midday, and I understood the post-release inmates were only allowed out of the halfway house when they were working.

I got up, tossed the trash, looked out at the street. No cleaning-service van, just an old Nissan sedan, black with a dent in the passenger door, plastic taped on where the glass had been. The driver was turned away, rummaging in the backseat. Turned back.

Twinsey.

Mumbo must have been released and gone directly to a meth-head friend. So much for staying straight.

I crossed the shop, stopped behind him at the end of the line. I leaned close, said, "Hi there."

He turned with a start, left forearm raising, fist clenched.

"Jack McMorrow," I said. "The reporter. I've met up with your buddy Snow a couple of times when you guys were in here."

Mumbo dropped his arm.

"How you doing, sir?" he said.

"Good. Not working?"

"Graduated. Looking for a real job."

"Maybe the church is hiring," I said.

It startled him, but he recovered in an instant, said, "Maybe so."

"Father Aneesh told me how he hired your crew to do the community halls. Said Gayle there"—I nodded toward the car—"cleaned for them, too."

"The foreign priest."

"Right," I said. "Nice guy."

He didn't comment on Father Aneesh.

I smiled. Time to shake the tree.

"I was talking to him about this guy Raymond. The one who was murdered."

Mumbo nodded, didn't flinch. The line moved up, and we moved with it.

"Yeah, I'm writing a story and Raymond was in it. Then he was murdered. He's still in the story, just in a different way."

Mumbo was looking up intently at the Dunkin' menu on the wall behind the counter, like it would suddenly list a new item.

"Heard somebody got killed. That's unfortunate."

"It is. Interesting guy, collected religious stuff. Cops think it was some sex thing, but I don't."

He stayed fixed to the sign, said, "That right?"

"He had something that somebody wanted. That's my theory. Wouldn't give it up, and they tortured him and finally killed him."

He stepped up to the counter and ordered. Two large coffees, one black, one with four sugars and extra cream. Twinsey the addict, her brain needing a sugar jolt.

We moved to the pickup line. I stayed close.

"I don't know what he'd have had that would be worth killing for," I said. "Bunch of old statues and pictures. Things taken from Catholic churches that closed."

Mumbo wasn't looking at me, but he said, "I'm sure there's value in spiritual things. To somebody who knows their real worth."

"But most religious-statue people aren't murderers," I said.

Mumbo turned, coffees in hand, started for the door. Stopped beside me.

"Just because somebody talks about God doesn't mean they aren't evil inside."

And then we were out the door.

Twinsey was watching from the car, smoking a cigarette, and I gave her a smile and a wave. She nodded, pulled her hood up like she was headed for a perp walk.

"I met Twinsey," I said. "At the apartment on Pine Street."

He looked at me, a slight perk, then feigned disinterest. The disdain I'd seen at Tiffanee's farm.

"That right?" Mumbo said.

"Small world, this town," I said.

No response.

"You look familiar. Ever been up to Waldo County?"

"Nah. I'm from Mass. This is far enough north."

I grinned.

He put one coffee on the car roof and opened the door. A puff of smoke billowed out, and he grabbed the coffee.

I moved closer, said, *"Pax vobiscum."*

That got a hard stare. With "Go in peace," I'd broken through.

We were parked around the block from Germaine's house. Sparrow had her hair covering the scabbed-over cut, her hood down, and had taken the rings out of her eyebrows and lips. Blake was wearing jeans and a black Carhartt jacket. I'd traded my parka for the peacoat. We were fit to meet someone's grandmother.

Blake drove to the house, and we parked in the street and got out. It was snowing still, and the driveway hadn't been shoveled. There were no tire tracks, no footprints going to or from the door. If she was home, Germaine was holed up.

Sparrow led the way, rang the bell as we stood behind her. We all smiled, like we were handing out religious pamphlets. After a minute there was movement in the curtain to our left. Sparrow rang the bell again. We beamed.

The door rattled and shuddered, then opened a foot and Germaine peered out. Her bruises had faded slightly and she looked pale and thinner, like she hadn't been eating.

"Yes," she said.

She looked to me.

"Hi, Germaine," I said. "It's Jack McMorrow again. This is Sparrow and Brandon. They're good friends of Raymond's. Can we talk?"

She peered at us, undecided.

"Brandon is a police officer," I said. "He's helping figure out what happened to Raymond, and we thought—"

Germaine looked panicky, like she might slam the door. Instead, she looked over our shoulders up and down the street.

"Get in here then," she said, opening the door wide. "Hurry up."

We sat in the living room, Germaine and I on overstuffed chairs, Sparrow and Blake on the matching couch. Her late husband stared down stonily from the wall above their heads.

"You doing okay, Germaine?" I said. "No more falls?"

She looked puzzled, then said, "Oh, no. Being very careful."

A pause, and then Sparrow stepped in, told about how Raymond had offered her a ride one subzero morning, and then every morning after that. How they became friends, talking about his collections and Sparrow's dad, and Raymond sharing about his life as a kid in a house full of anger.

"I spoke to Father Aneesh," I said. "He had lots of good things to say about Raymond."

"Oh, yes. A very good Catholic, the way we all used to be."

"Yes," Blake said. "So that's why what happened to him is so wrong. I know they'll be judged by God after they die, but if they're judged here first, it will tell other evil people that they can't get away with doing things like that."

"Well, they shouldn't," Germaine said.

"If they're sent to jail, it'll save someone else," Blake said. "You don't want to cause anybody to suffer."

"No," she said, one hand moving to the scrape on her arm.

"So in order to do that, we need to know how you really got hurt, Germaine," I said.

She looked away, eyes moving to her husband's photo. We waited. She took three or four short breaths, rocked with her hands on her knees, knobby through the fabric of her slacks.

"I don't want my name in there," Germaine said. "Don't tell anyone my name until you catch him."

Blake said. "We can do that."

A deeper breath, then a long sigh.

"You can do this, Germaine," Sparrow said. 'You're a strong woman."

Germaine clenched her hands together, turned her wedding ring around and around like she was unscrewing a bottle top. Looked at the photo again. Ludger must have given her the green light.

"He wanted what was in the unit," she said.

"Who wanted it?" Blake said.

"I don't know. He had a thing over his head. Like you wear in the winter."

"A balaclava?" I said. "Just the mouth and the eyes cut out?"

"Yes."

"Whose unit was it?"

"It belonged to someone named Scanlon," Germaine said. "That's what his license said, but I don't think that was his real name. He didn't look like the picture." She paused, took a breath. "He was bigger than you. And he was bald. At least, I think so. He had a baseball cap on. You know those guys who shave their heads but leave a goatee thing?"

I did. Mumbo, for one.

Germaine's knees were shaking.

"He paid a year up front. Hundred-dollar bills—boom, boom, boom. And then I never heard from him again. After the year was up, I gave him the usual sixty days. I called the number he wrote down, but it didn't work. I wrote to the address but it came back as no such place."

"The man who came here the other day—he wanted all of the contents, or just a particular item?" I said.

Germaine hesitated and then, in a small voice, said, "I told him all the stuff was gone. Auctioned off. There really hadn't been much stuff in there. Odds and ends, like from a house. And the statue of Jesus."

"Which you gave to Raymond?"

"Yes. I didn't even unwrap it all the way. I saw Jesus and the heart and I called the church, told them what I had. They said Raymond would find it a good home."

"Did you tell the man in the mask this?" I said.

"I said I gave it to the auction, that I didn't know what they did with it. I didn't want him to know about Raymond. I had a bad feeling."

"What did he say?" Blake said.

"He said I was lying.'"

"And then what?" I said.

She started to break down, tears streaming, lips trembling.

"Then he hit me. Right on the face, really hard. He called me awful names. I couldn't talk, I was so scared, and he hit me again. He said he'd hurt me more. He said, 'Let's go in the kitchen, you—' "

She was sobbing now.

"He grabbed my arm and picked me up out of the chair and pulled me into the kitchen and turned on the burner on my gas stove. He took my hand and started to put it into the fire, and I said—"

She paused, twisting the ring, and said, "I told him I gave it to Raymond."

Germaine wiped her eyes with a forefinger.

"He took my hand and put it through the flame. He said, 'Just a taste. If you're not telling the truth. And then he said—he said that if I told anyone, he'd come back with his friends and they'd force themselves on my daughter and make my grandson watch. They'd . . .'"

She trailed off.

"You can't tell him I told you. You have to promise."

We did. Germaine started to sob harder and Sparrow got up and crouched by her chair, rubbed her shoulder. We waited until the sobs subsided, and then Blake said, "And after that he left?"

"Yes."

"Did he ask where Raymond lived?"

"Yes, but I didn't know. I just knew that Raymond Jandreau lived in town, that he'd come to pick up the statue in an old van."

"What was this man wearing?" Blake said. "Other than the mask?"

"Black clothes. Everything was black."

"Tattoos? Jewelry?"

"He was all covered up. He had gloves on."

"Anything else?"

Germaine thought.

"He smelled nice," she said. "He was a horrible man, but he smelled like soap."

26

We were sitting in Blake's truck outside Sparrow's house, me in the back. They agreed it was most likely cocaine in the statue, the price of heroin and fentanyl and meth depressed because of oversupply. I assumed Blake knew this because he was a cop, Sparrow because she worked with one ear on the street.

"He could have been part of the tall guy's crew," Blake said.

"And maybe he killed that guy, too," Sparrow said.

"If he didn't get it, he's still looking," I said.

"He had the names of her daughter and grandson," Blake said.

"People-finder on the Internet," Sparrow said. "Family members, names, ages."

"Or he followed her to church and sat and listened to the ladies chatting," I said.

"Or he's from here and he knew somebody at the church," Sparrow said. "You think now they'll believe it wasn't a hookup?"

"They want Zombie," Blake said. "Everything else is a distraction."

Blake said he'd do his best with Sanitas and the others, tell them he got the information from an informant rather than putting Germaine out there yet. We agreed that was all we could do until he spoke with them, and he said he'd call Sanitas on the way back to South Portland. He had to get a little sleep and a shower before he came in for the overnight shift.

There was a holler from the house.

"Yo. Get your sorry asses in here."

It was Riff, standing in the doorway, the storm door open. He beckoned us to follow him and went back inside.

"Sorry," Sparrow said. "He's been alone a lot."

"I really have to go," Blake said.

"I'll come in," I said.

"For a reporter, you're a softie," Sparrow said.

"Our secret," I said.

Riff had made coffee, put out a plate of Oreos. He was sitting at the kitchen table eating one when we came in, said, "Where's Five-O?"

"He had to go back to the boat and get some sleep," Sparrow said. "He worked all night and OT this morning."

"Get used to it," Riff said. "Being married to a cop is just one step above being married to a musician."

"We're not planning on getting married," Sparrow said.

"That's what we said. Next thing we know, we had you and a minivan. Car seat stuck in there with the amps and guitars."

He held out the plate of cookies. I took one and Sparrow handed me a mug of coffee. She poured him one, too, added milk, handed it over.

"You know what they said about caffeine."

"Right. Caffeine, booze, cigarettes, reefer, sugar, sex. Might as well put me in the ground now." He looked at her. "Don't worry, Bird. It's decaf." Then, to me, "Gotta get a few more miles out of these kidneys. Or not. Maybe it's time to check outta the old Hotel California."

"Cut that crap," Sparrow said.

"Ever tell you about how I partied with Joe Walsh, before he was an Eagle? It was the early eighties, we were playing this thing called the Electric Cowboy Fest in Tennessee. Punkabilly stole the show. But anyway, whole buncha bands—Cheap Trick, Molly Hatchet, Joanie Jett—and we'd all have this sort of revolving party. Good times, let me tell ya. If you'd've told me Joe Freakin' Walsh would be signing on with Henley, I woulda said you were—"

"Riff," Sparrow said. "Did DHHS call?"

"Nobody called who was a real human."

"They said they'd get back to you."

"They say a lot of things, most of which is bullshit. Where you been, anyway?"

Sparrow looked at me.

"I'm still reporting my story," I said. "Sparrow's helping."

"You got Bird here doing some research?"

"She's a big help."

"She's a hell of a writer, too."

I smiled, drank some coffee.

"Did I tell you that my daughter put out a Riff Calderone clip on TikTok?" I said, changing the topic.

"No shit," Riff said.

I took out my phone and opened TikTok, searched for #punkabilly. And there he was.

I held it up for him and he watched intently. "Jambalaya" in snippets, Riff fingerpicking, Riff hitting the first big chord, Riff the whirling dervish, the sound reverberating.

"Hey," he said. "Did I put on a good show or what?"

"Riff, did you take your Zofran?" Sparrow said, holding up the medication container, each day filled with pills.

"Thank your daughter, for me. Tell her she has to get down here, meet the man himself."

"I'll do that," I said.

"Riff," Sparrow said. "The Zofran."

"It makes me dizzy," Riff said. "Don't want to spend my last days with my head in the clouds. Been there, done that. Tell your daughter to never do drugs."

She took a pill out of the container, went to the sink, and filled a glass with water. Held the pill out and Riff took it from her.

"In the mouth."

"Jesus. What am I? A two-year-old?"

"Sometimes," Sparrow said.

He drank and swallowed. She walked over to the counter, picked up an envelope and tore it open. Her eyes narrowed as she read the letter inside, eyebrow stud twitching.

"Goddamn them."

"No dice?" Riff said.

Sparrow closed her eyes, took a deep breath, opened her eyes, and looked at the letter again.

"You gave it a try, Bird," Riff said, then to me: "She was still trying to get a subsidy for the miracle drug nobody can afford."

"I was on the phone with this guy last week for an hour. The appeals person. He said he'd look into it further."

"I guess he did," Riff said.

"Son of a bitch," Sparrow said. "He let me go on and on, already made up his mind."

"This is the stuff that costs thousands of dollars?" I said.

"Yeah," Riff said. "They got billions for fighting wars all over the freakin' world, but they don't have a few measly grand to save a musician's life."

"So that's it," Sparrow said, flinging the letter onto the counter, then shouting at the piece of paper. "No more fucking around with these assholes. Friggin' rules, this form and that form. No more begging. They can kiss my ass. It's game on, you fuckers."

She stormed out of the room, slammed a door behind her deeper in the house. There were more shouts, muffled, something crashing to the floor.

"She's upset," I said.

"Yeah, well, this was sort of the last resort. I think she'd put all her eggs in that basket."

"Sorry."

Riff shrugged, lifted his mug. His fingernails were yellow. He sipped again, put the mug down. "Hey, it is what it is."

"How much money do you need?"

"To get started? Like, fifty-nine grand. And change. Hey, any money in this TikTok thing?"

"I don't know. Maybe," I said. "I'll ask my daughter."

A beat.

"So will Sparrow give up?"

"Bird? Hell, no. One thing I raised her to be is a fighter. She'll go down swinging. I remember one time we're hanging out after a show and Bird's there and this roadie—not one of ours—starts hitting on her. She goes 'I'm thirteen, you perv.' "

Thirteen. A year older than Sophie.

"He says, 'That's okay. I'll be gentle.' Me and my drummer at the time, Kiko, we're off the couch, gonna pound the crap outta the guy, but Bird, like in this flash, hits him. Crack. His nose starts gushing blood—it was broke—and he jumps up, holding his shirt on his face, cursing his head off. Bird, all hundred pounds of her, she winds up and boots him in the crotch. Like Karate Kid. Dude goes down, moaning and groaning, blood everywhere."

He grinned.

"So no, Bird don't give up. She'll fight for what she thinks is right."

"And that includes keeping you around for as long as possible."

"I guess."

"You worry about her, working the overnight?" I said.

"Sure, but old Zombie, he's come and gone at her store."

"Store robbers sometimes hit the same place more than once. Seems safer. Or it could be a copycat."

"The city's crawling with cops. Hell, she's dating one. They'll catch this dirtbag, lock his sorry ass up."

I looked around the kitchen. A couple of faded, signed concert posters for the Riff Calderone Band. An ad for Fender guitars, torn from an old magazine. Riff holding a Strat. He'd signed that, too.

I felt a sour epiphany, that the house was a shrine to his past, and his daughter's role was to keep food on the table and his ego burnished. And maybe get shot.

I said nothing.

I left him at the table, maybe thinking about what I'd said, maybe thinking talking to me was a bad idea, even if he did get in the *New York Times*.

I took a last look at the house, nothing on the outside hinting at the tensions within. I pulled out, turned around in a driveway, drove to the other side of the tavern and pulled back in. Shut the motor off and picked up my phone, texted Carlisle at the *Times*.

ARE WE A GO FOR THE JANDREAU ROBBERY STORY?

I waited, scrawled some notes from my conversation with Riff, some more from Germaine.

The robberies were just the entry point. The story led from Sparrow to Raymond to Riff and Blake. The priest and Germaine, Mumbo and Twinsey. It was like going into a cave, each chamber opening into another, the whole thing shrouded in darkness.

I picked up the phone. Started to text Roxanne, see how she was doing. It buzzed. Carlisle calling.

"Hey," I said.

"Jack. How goes it up there?"

"Good. The story's getting complicated."

"Why am I not surprised?" Carlisle said.

"No, really. The robberies, the murder, the church. This statue of Jesus that seems to run through it."

"Like the bird in *The Maltese Falcon*?"

"Right," I said.

"Sounds interesting, Jack. No surprise there."

Something in her tone.

"You're passing on it."

She hesitated. In the background, I could hear a reporter on the phone saying "Have a minute? I'd love to talk to you . . ."

Carlisle was moving. I heard the glass door of a conference room slide open, then shut. The newsroom hum was snuffed.

"Okay. Here's the deal. You carrying a gun, you finding the man's body. I mean, for the risk folks upstairs, it was off the charts."

"They should get out into the real world, stop counting beans."

"I know, Jack. You always push the envelope. And then some. But this time—I mean, with the national dialogue on gun violence? I tried, Jack. I gave it my best shot."

"I'm sure."

"And it's not like we're cutting you loose. We're just going to have to pass on this one. And then go a little slow. Give us something softer, maybe. I told them you always have more ideas in the pipeline."

"But I need to write this story," I said.

"I know. But even the way you say that, it seems like you're way too involved. Even for you. Definitely for them. And I have to say, this time, maybe for me."

I didn't reply.

"Are you okay, Jack?"

"No problem. I'll sell it somewhere else."

"I mean, apart from the story."

I scowled. Was everybody a shrink these days?

"I'm fine. It's just that . . ." I hesitated. "The fellow, Raymond—he was a good person. Quirky as hell, but he was doing what he thought was the right thing based on his religious faith. He got that as a kid, and he held on to it. Who does that? It was like this sort of innocence, and then these scumbags came along and killed him in this awful way. And nobody here—the police, I mean—seems to really care. They just want to catch the robber so they get the public and the city off their back. It's all bullshit."

I paused for a breath.

"You don't seem so fine, Jack."

"And we got mixed up in this weird thing—one of Sophie's friends, her mom and her boyfriend, a total dirtbag running around in the woods with guns. They were fighting and she came to Roxanne and he followed her. I had to—"

Put a nine-millimeter round past his head.

"—intervene," I said.

"I'm sorry," Carlisle said. "I'm sure it's all stressful."

"Yeah."

"But this story. There's something going on here with you, Jack."
Another pause. One beat, two.

"I know. I guess, in a weird way, Raymond is some other version of
me. I was raised in the same Church, believed a lot of the same things.
There was a time when it was, I don't know, a framework for my life.
My parents' life, their parents, back for generations. And then it just
slowly eroded. For him it went the other direction, but I get him. I get
how he was thinking—Jesus, Mary, and Joseph, and the saints and all
the rituals. He was hanging on to all of it. And he didn't deserve this."

"So it isn't just a story," Carlisle said.

"It's both," I said.

"I know how you work, Jack. But things are different here now.
Everything is so vetted. I'm running stories by Legal more than ever.
And the internet—I mean, one little misstep and somebody is on Twitter
saying, 'Why is the *New York Times* using armed reporters?' What if
this story runs same day as the next mass shooting?"

"It's not like I'm carrying an AR-15 and a manifesto."

"It's all mixed up now. A different world from when we started."

"Don't we stand up for what's right?"

"Sure we do. You do, I know. But it's a matter of where you draw
the line."

"They beat him and put a plastic bag over his head. Tortured him
and eventually let him suffocate. That's where I draw the line."

Carlisle didn't reply. We sat in silence until I said, "Sorry. I know
you tried. And you've always been in my corner."

"I still am, Jack. We'll get something else going soon."

"Right."

"Talk to you soon," Carlisle said.

"Yeah," I said. "We'll do that."

And she was gone, along with my career as I'd known it.

I flipped to my contacts. Scrolled. Called.

"Jack," Dunne said.

"I'm in," I said.

"Awesome. When?"

"I can talk right now."

"Fantastic. I'm home. It's downtown, 130 Porto. It's a condo. I have this little studio."

"Be there in ten," I said. "Let's poke some bears."

27

The condo was in a renovated downtown block, all brick and big windows. Lawyers were on the ground floor and a state district court was across the street. I parked out front, texted Roxanne.

You doing okay? I'll be home before dinner. Let's make stir-fry. I'll chop.

I waited. She replied.

—All quiet here. See you soon.

I got out of the truck, put the phone on silent, and slipped it into my pocket. It had started to snow again, like an on-and-off-again drizzle. When I looked up, Dunne was in the big window on the third floor. She waved, held up one finger. I went to the door and it buzzed, I pushed through to a small lobby with a plastic pine tree and an elevator. The display showed it was on three, then two, then one.

The door opened. Dunne stepped out, wearing boots and leggings and a bright red tunic sort of thing. She gave me a long, tight hug.

"Oh, Jack," she said as we parted. "This is gonna be so good."

"Yes," I said.

We rode up, Dunne standing close like I might get away. The doors rolled open and she led me in by the arm like we were newlyweds crossing the threshold. It was one big open room, with wide pine floors, high ceilings, and exposed beams. The front was the big windows you could see from the street, a view of seagulls and pigeons huddled on the snow-patched roof across the street.

Her lawyer ex must have been doing okay.

Furniture was minimal—black leather couch, bar on a rolling cart, a futon in the corner. The studio was in another corner: a phone in a tripod on the table. Two chairs that matched the couch.

"So what's the plan?" I said, shaking loose.

"Let's just talk. Like an exploratory thing. I'll record it just for notes. Record for real in a couple of days for the pilot. I thought we could start with you finding the body, what that felt like. Just walk us through it, set the scene. Then it's all background on Raymond. I'll prompt you with questions about the investigation, about how you feel the investigation took a wrong turn. We'll cut there. I'm seeing that as Episode One."

She went to the dining area, in the fourth corner of the room, and took two seltzers out of a refrigerator, a legal pad from the table. We went to the chairs and I took off my parka and hung it on one. I sat.

"Some podcasters like to script every word, you know. I like spontaneous. Just turn us on and off we go." She gave me a smile, patted my shoulder.

"How many listeners?" I said.

"With you? A lot," Dunne said.

She sat, crossed her legs. Primped at her hair, like subscribers would sense if it were out of place. Put the legal pad on her lap. It was filled with notes.

"Ready?" she said.

I nodded. She hit record and turned to me.

"Hello, everyone. I'd like to welcome you to 'Double-Crossed,' a new true-crime episode from Who Dunne It. We're gonna take part in an ongoing murder investigation in my fair city. It's a story of dark trysts, religious icons, and sadistic killers. And here with me to help kick things off is my new partner in crime, Jack McMorrow, freelance investigative journalist and storyteller extraordinaire whose amazing work appears frequently in the *New York Times*."

I said hello.

"Jack, you're not only reporting on this story, but you're part of it. In fact, it was you who found the body of Raymond Jandreau. My God, it must have been horrible. I mean, can you tell us what that was like?"

"It was disturbing, Steph, as you can imagine. I'd known Raymond for only a couple of days, but I'd really grown to like him."

"And now he's gone, murdered in a most grisly way. And the perpetrators still at large. What was Raymond like, Jack? Take us back to the beginning."

I recounted how we'd met, that he'd invited me in to look at his collection.

"Religious stuff?" Dunne said. "Like you'd see in an old church?"

I described the statues and paintings and tabernacles, where Raymond found his items, how people sometimes came to him.

"Just recently, a statue came to him from someone in the city who knew he'd give it a good home," I said.

"Like someone bringing a stray cat to the local cat lady?" Dunne said.

I winced inwardly, said yes.

"So you came back a couple of days later to talk to Raymond?"

I said that was right.

"And what happened? Take us through it."

"Well, the door was open," I said. "When I looked in, I could see that the place had been wrecked, statues smashed and paintings torn up."

"My God," Dunne said. "So what did you do?"

"I didn't know if the perpetrators were still inside, so I went back to my truck and got a gun," I said.

"To shoot them?"

"To protect myself. I didn't know what had happened."

"So let me picture this. You're walking in, very slowly, right? You've got your gun out. And you keep going and you're stepping over all the mess, and then you see . . ."

"Raymond was dead."

"How was he killed? Had he been shot?"

"I can't say, but it was clear he'd been killed."

"Were the killers in the house?"

"No. They were gone. But I didn't know that."

"What did you do?"

"I went through the house. And then I called 911."

"Did the police come?"

"Yes."

"What did they think?"

I hesitated.

"There was an item at the scene that indicated this might be something of a sexual nature. They decided this was something sexual that had gone wrong."

"Something consensual," Dunne said.

"Yes."

"But you don't buy that, right?"

I said I didn't.

"What do you think happened?"

"I think Raymond was killed because he wouldn't give up something the killer—or killers—wanted."

"Like what? Money?"

"I don't think it was just money. I think it had something to do with the collection."

"But wait," Dunne said, leaning toward me. "If the collection was there, all these religious things, why didn't they just take it?"

"I don't know."

"But you have a theory, right, Jack?"

"I have lots of theories," I said.

"Well, tell us just one."

"I think Raymond may have had something but had gotten rid of it. Or had hidden it. And they couldn't find it, so they tried to make him tell them where it was."

"But he wouldn't."

"Apparently not."

"Or maybe he told them and they killed him anyway."

"That's also possible, Steph," I said.

"But you're not giving up in finding the answer. Why you? I mean, don't journalists just write stories? Why not leave it to the police, Jack?"

"Because I don't think they're working very hard on it. I think they've fastened on to this sex angle, and they don't want to look beyond that. They're busy with the Zombie robberies, and this is just a distraction."

"But it's a man's life, right? How can that not be important?"

"It is to me," I said. "He was a good person, and he deserves justice."

"Which you will make happen?"

"I'm doing my best."

"Shaking the trees. Because the killer is out there."

"Yes."

"Do you think he, or she, knows you're on their trail?"

I smiled. "If they listen to this they will."

"And you're not afraid? I mean, these must be some nasty characters."

"They killed a defenseless man," I said.

"And you're not defenseless?"

"No," I said. "And there's an old saying: Right makes might. So if that's true, I should be able to take whatever they dish out."

Dunne paused.

"I have to say something, Jack. I mean, I've known a lot of journalists, but I've never met one quite like you."

"I just go where the story takes me, Steph," I said.

"I get that feeling. And good for the *New York Times* for sticking with you. Most mainstream media has been gutted, everyone so afraid of being sued or losing advertisers or whatever."

"Yes," I said. "Good for them."

Dunne smiled, said, "So that's where we're headed, folks. Down a dark and dangerous path. Remember, this is a fresh, unsolved, brutal and cold-blooded homicide. Unsolved, as in the perp is still out there. And I expect they will soon know they have turned from being the hunter to the hunted. Until next time, I'm Steph, and we're finding out 'WhoDunneIt'."

She leaned back in her chair and ended the recording. Turned to me and smiled.

"Fantastic, Jack McMorrow," Dunne said. "We're off and running. I'll get to editing, but for now, how 'bout I get you a drink. You're a beer kind of guy, right?"

Before I could answer, she was crossing the room to the fridge, taking out two cans of Baxter IPA. Good taste. She cracked one and handed it to me, opened the other, and led the way to the couch. Sat and then patted the black leather beside her.

"Don't worry," Dunne said. "I put my cards on the table. Next move is up to you."

She held up her ale and leaned toward me, her arm brushing mine. Our eyes locked and we clinked cans, drank. I didn't bite and she sat back.

"This will go live?" I said.

"Up on SoundCloud, the feed goes out, social media follows."

"Great."

"You're very good, Jack. Maybe time to switch media."

I smiled.

"Surprised the *Times* hasn't put you out there on its podcasts. Do you think we could get them to share this? At least a retweet? Or maybe they'd do a story?"

"I kind of doubt it."

"I'll tag them," Dunne said. "DM a few of their writers, see if we can get them to send it out to their followers. I mean, we ought to get into five figures, easy. You people have huge audiences."

"Yes," I said. "Some of us do. But I want this heard locally. Can you tag Maine newspapers? Local TV news? It needs to be everywhere, so they can't miss it."

"Who?" Dunne said.

"The killers," I said.

She smiled.

"So it's more than the cops you want to shake out."

"I want to push the murderer in my direction. I want to flush them out. Next time I'll hint at where the reporting is taking me, possible clues that would point to them."

She looked at me more closely.

"Christ," she said.

"That's part of it."

"You do push the envelope, McMorrow."

"The alternative is unacceptable," I said. "If you're not comfortable with it . . ."

"You know me, Jack."

I really didn't.

"I'll do whatever it takes. It's a war out there in podcasts. I mean, people have so many choices, you have to hit them in the gut. That's why I like this raw commando feel. I can't afford paid promotion yet, so everything's gotta be organic. Word-of-mouth, key influencers."

Dunne was flushed with excitement, her cheeks matching her nails.

I drank, a long swallow of ale.

"I just want it to ignite with a couple of people," I said. "Maybe three."

She looked at me hard, smiled.

"This is gold," she said.

"Only if it works," I said, and I finished the ale. I stood and Dunne did too. She leaned in and kissed me on the cheek, her lips lingering for a two-count, her face hovering close to mine. I left the can on the counter on my way out.

28

It was three thirty and time to head for home if I were to help Roxanne make stir-fry. I wanted to make good on that promise, at least, joining my family for dinner maybe offsetting the fact that there was no story, and we'd be short three grand.

That I'd decided to put myself out there as bait to murderers.

When I left Dunne's building, it was still snowing, wet, floating flakes that slid down the windshield. I pulled out, tires sliding in the slush, and glanced up, saw Dunne back in the big window. She waved at her meal ticket. I drove on.

I circled the block, drove north between the tenements on the back streets. Somali women walked back up the hill from the downtown halal markets, shopping bags in hand, hijabs showing their virtue and shielding them from the snow. I thought of their religion and Raymond's, their lives guided by stories a thousand years old. Through wars and famines and epidemics, generation after generation passing on the spiritual baton. In a time when nothing—from cell phones to the news cycle—seemed to have any shelf life, it was remarkable.

As I got on the highway, I was still contemplating: me and Raymond connecting over this shared ancient history. How maybe he'd martyred himself to be part of that tradition. Tell us where it is or we'll put the bag on again. Come on, Ray. Just tell us and we'll stop.

But of course they wouldn't, couldn't. Unless they were masked. Like robbers.

I picked up my phone, flicked to Blake's number. It rang. He answered, road noise in the background, the chirp of a police radio.

"Hey," I said.

"McMorrow," he said. "Where are you?"

"Leaving Clarkston, headed home. You?"

"Leaving for work."

"You cops and your OT," I said.

"It's all about the time and a half. That, and the doughnuts."

"Listen, I had an idea."

I told him about picturing Raymond's killers wearing masks, like the Zombie robber.

"Copycat?" he said.

"Or maybe the same guy, with a helper. Or maybe alone. Maybe he heard Raymond had a box of money. Why risk getting shot by a store owner when you can make ten times as much knocking over this religious guy?"

"If it's about the money," Blake said.

"Right. If you rob somebody and nobody knows."

"The falling tree in the forest."

I was thinking that killing Raymond was no public thrill crime, so even a copycat wouldn't benefit from putting the blame on Zombie.

"Something else," I said.

"I figured."

I told him about Dunne, the podcast. Waited.

"Really," Blake said. "The *New York Times* okay with that? Aren't you kind of scooping yourself?"

I told him they were passing, their reasons.

"What are you supposed to carry?"

"A notebook," I said.

"Like that will protect you from a bullet?"

A pause, Blake processing.

"So you're putting it all out there? The rosary? The money? That statue, and Germaine getting beat up?"

"Maybe. No names."

"There'll be a shit storm at the PD."

"I hope so."

"Makes you a target."

"Makes them a target, too," I said. "I'll make the rounds in the city, see who pops up."

"You'll need backup."

"Yes."

"I'm in, when I'm not working. Got anybody else?"

"They're in Canada on an assignment."

Another pause. I heard the sound of Blake's truck accelerating.

"I can see why the newspaper fired you," he said.

"They didn't fire me. They want me to write something softer."

"What are the chances of that happening?"

"Right now? Below zero."

A semi-trailer passed and showered the truck with grime. I hit the wipers, drove through the momentary blindness. I heard Blake's radio, a change in tone.

"Holy shit," he said.

"What?"

"Zombie came back to the QuikStop. Shots fired."

"Sparrow?" I said.

"She's there, working with Bob and Mo."

29

The last thing I heard was Blake's truck accelerating. I took the next exit, circled, jumped back on southbound. My heart was pounding. My stomach felt sick.

I passed two exits, took the third. On Porto Street, an unmarked SUV passed me, grill lights flashing. Then a K-9 unit, dog against the window, barking noiselessly behind the glass.

The store was surrounded by police, rescue, fire, all the lights blipping at once, red and blue. They were getting two dogs ready, one Clarkston and one state. The handlers snapped them on long leashes, bounded after the dogs toward the front door.

I pulled the truck to the curb, got out. Saw Blake's pickup in close, him not in sight. They were cordoning off the lot, pushing people back. I stood and watched as an ambulance arrived and a cop cleared the way for it to back in near the door. The paramedics jumped out, one going into the store, the other yanking the doors open, pulling a stretcher out. He got it to the ground and dashed behind it to the door, where a city EMT held the door open.

They all disappeared inside. I waited. Police SUVs zoomed past, turned onto side streets. A black SUV swept in, patrol cops on foot giving it a wide berth. A white-haired guy in a suit got out. The chief. One of the commanders from the check-cashing place scene came out and they huddled.

I waited. Thought of Riff at home. Pictured him taking in the news—that his daughter had been shot. Maybe he should have pushed back when she said she'd work the store job so she could be home during the day.

A TV news car sped toward me, flashers on—like anybody cared. It pulled over in front of my truck, back end of the car sticking out into the street. A guy and a woman got out, the woman holding a notebook. The guy started unloading a camera from the back of the car, snapped pieces into place and whirled around. As he trotted toward the store, he started filming.

I looked around, the traffic backed up, cops everywhere.

How could this guy get away? Where would he go? If he had a minute or two, how far could he have gotten—and where was he hiding now?

I waited. Pictured Blake, standing over his new girlfriend, paramedics hooking up IVs. I hoped.

Sparrow paying for being the dutiful daughter. Cut down before she could be anything else.

One of the dogs and its handler trotted across the lot, then turned abruptly to the right and went behind the store. The other K-9 team started down the street, sticking to the gutter, stopping at parked cars and sniffing like the dog was looking for drugs. Looking for the scent in a car, the robber hiding.

I glanced back at the lot, noticed a black Tahoe parked close to the building. No lights, no aerials. Bob's truck. Had he been working? Maybe it was the robber who'd been shot. Maybe there were two, and one got away?

The doors were pushed open, police holding them for the paramedics, who were guiding a stretcher.

First thing I saw was legs. Boots. An IV bag. An oxygen mask.

She was in the parking lot smoking when he did his walk-by. No jacket, leggings and combat boots under the QuikStop shirt. A good look when she turned to go back into the store. Tough little bitch, that whack on the head not slowing her down. He liked them feisty—or at least he would if he ever had the chance—but not too feisty. At some

*point, they had to know who was boss. If she didn't get it,
he'd give her another lesson.*

*He went around the block, stood at the bus stop, took
his phone out to check the time. That was in case anyone
was watching, him looking like some guy going to work,
pissed the bus wasn't showing up. He shook his head, part
of the act, headed back toward the store.*

*He could see her behind the counter, nobody else in
sight. He was thinking this time, after he had the money,
he'd make her get on her knees in front of him, beg for her
life. He'd move close, like he was gonna make her go down
on him, press the gun barrel against her forehead.*

*His line was pretty good: "Zombie gonna have to take
a rain check on that, bitch. Gotta run."*

*Then he'd shove her over backwards, like he didn't
want it anyway.*

*He smiled as he crossed the lot, stepped into the shadows.
Put on the mask, got the gun out and ready. Crossed the front
of the store, pulled the door open. Two steps to the counter,
gun up, saying, "Hey, baby. You know what Zombie wants."*

*She froze, eyes went left. He looked, saw a guy behind the
lottery tickets, black leather jacket like from an old Charles
Bronson movie, reaching for a gun from a shoulder holster,
shouting, "Freeze, motherfucker." The gun was still half in
the holster when Zombie fired, boom, a black dot in the
guy's white T-shirt. The guy wide-eyed, dropping the gun
as he fell backwards onto the floor. He turned his gun to
the chick, felt his trigger finger tighten.*

30

I waited. Listened for new sirens, a second ambulance on the way. An ambulance in a hurry meant somebody was still alive, treatable. Heard police radios. Traffic. And then—God, no—a siren in the distance. It was a rapid *whoop-whoop*, then a longer one. A klaxon horn. What had the first ambulance sounded like? It had already been on the scene when I arrived.

The TV reporter was live, standing in front of the camera with the store behind her. Another TV crew arrived in a van. Then a newspaper photographer, bailing out of a VW, cameras around his neck, running for the store until a big cop stopped him.

The siren was closer. Then lights in the distance down the street. They were blue, and in fifteen seconds, the crime-scene van pulled in. What did you need when one of the victims had died? No second ambulance, just a hearse to take the body to the ME.

I walked slowly toward the store. A detective came out with a Black man in a store uniform shirt. Mo. Where was Sparrow?

"Oh, God," I said. "Please, no."

I was at the edge of the lot when I saw Salley and a couple of other patrol cops on the sidewalk conferring with a sergeant. As I walked toward them, the sergeant said, "Now go." They turned back toward their vehicles, Salley seeing me, scowling and hurrying my way.

"Out," he said.

"Is there someone else shot?" I said.

"Back in your vehicle."

"I saw the owner. Is there another victim? Did Sparrow get shot? Off the record. I just need to know."

"No comment. You're in a crime scene. We got dogs working here. Get outta here before I arrest your ass."

"She's Blake's friend," I said.

"They'll tell you when they're ready to tell you. I'm gonna count to three and if you're not gone, I'm gonna cuff you and take you downtown."

I looked at him.

"Bullshit. They need you to be on the street searching, not harassing reporters."

"This ain't harassing. You'll know it if I'm harassing you," Salley said.

"Is she—"

Out of the corner of my eye, I saw the doors opening.

A detective, a woman, held one side open.

Sparrow walked through.

31

"I was at the counter," Sparrow said. "Bob was doing lottery tickets. Mo was in the restroom."

We waited. Blake at the wheel of his truck, Sparrow in the middle. Me on the other side of her. We were parked at the edge of the lot. The detective had asked Sparrow to hang around for a few minutes in case anyone else needed to speak with her.

"This isn't for a story, McMorrow," she said. "They said I can't talk to the press. It would jeopardize the investigation."

"Agreed," I said.

She took a long breath. Rubbed her hands together, said, "I'm freezing."

Blake turned up the fan and the heat.

"He said, 'You know what I want,' like he knew me from last time. Bob yells, 'Freeze, motherfucker,' like it was something he'd seen in a movie. And then Zombie shot him. I mean, like a second after he said it. Boom. Bob looks totally surprised, looks down at this hole in his shirt, like right here."

She touched the left side of her chest.

"And he falls down. Zombie looks at me and says I set him up. I didn't. I mean, how would I know he was coming back? But it was like in his head we were a thing. Like I'd cheated on him."

"He's been thinking about you," Blake said.

"Who knows what his delusion is?" I said.

"Then he stopped at the door, pointed the gun at me. And then Mo came running out of the bathroom."

"And Zombie ran," I said.

"Yeah, but first he said—" She paused.

"Said what?" Blake said.

"He said, 'Bitch, you are so dead.' And then he left."

"We'll get him," Blake said. "Don't worry."

"He could watch the store. He could follow me home. He probably killed Raymond. I mean, he could kill Riff."

There was a pause, the three of us running that scene.

"Poor Bob," Sparrow said.

"He's got a good chance," Blake said. "Word is it went through without hitting the heart."

"No. I mean this was his big moment, and he blew it."

"Yeah, but if he'd shot him," Blake said, "he'd have had to live with that—"

He didn't need to finish the thought, the gun in his fatal shooting a paintball replica, Blake living with the seed of doubt.

"They'll catch him this time," I said. "Don't you think?"

They looked at me.

32

It was almost nine o'clock when I crossed the Prosperity line, the woods black and cold, the sky crowded with stars, the smear of the Milky Way.

Now I was saying I'd hang out with Sophie before she went to bed. She could tell me about the Naomi Klein book, we could talk about climate stuff. Or Tara. Or how school was going. Or Pokey, how he was handling the winter. She could read to me.

After she went to bed, Roxanne and I could to talk. Our usual catch-up. Who'd been killed. Who'd been beaten. Who'd been shot.

I rattled onto the Dump Road, swerved around the frozen potholes, slowed to turn into the driveway. There was a beater Jeep parked by Roxanne's Subaru.

"Damn," I said.

I went inside, took my jacket off, hung it in the back closet, started to put my gun back on the top shelf. There were two sets of wet boots on the mat, one a child's, neither of them ours. I put my jacket back on, gun back in my waistband. Walked into the kitchen.

"Hi," Roxanne said.

Tiffanee looked at me, said, "Sorry."

They were sitting at the table with glasses of white wine. I grabbed a Ballantine from the refrigerator, opened it, and leaned against the counter. I could hear the girls talking in the den.

"It's Jason," Roxanne said. "He's out."

A moment to process.

"Did he escape?"

Roxanne looked to Tiffanee.

"He said he was having a heart attack," she said. "They took him to the hospital and they did tests. Now they say he's got all these heart problems."

"Since he got locked up?" I said.

"No. He used to do tons of coke when he was on the road working construction, and he's got wicked high blood pressure 'cause everything he eats is fried. The doctors said his aorta is all clogged up and some valve isn't working right."

"Good," I said.

"They said he needs surgery," Tiffanee said. "But he has to see other doctors, and that will take a while. They said they'd do the operation in Portland."

"And the jail would have to pay for it if he stays in custody," Roxanne said.

"So they let him go?"

They nodded.

"For God's sake. He's a violent felon with a probation hold for criminal threatening with a firearm. He's a time bomb."

"I know. I couldn't believe it. The victim person called me and she was like, 'I'm so sorry. But it could be a hundred-thousand-dollar medical bill for the County.' I said, 'What is my life worth? Tara's?'"

She looked away, took a deep breath.

"They gave him an ankle thingy," Tiffanee said.

"Like that means anything," I said. "Where did he go?"

"His cousin in Winterport. At least, that's what the lady said."

"What sort of person is this cousin?"

"Cleta's a drinker. Got all this money from a car accident, busted up her back. Chronic pain and lots of cash. Just what an alcoholic needs. Had lung cancer before the accident 'cause she smoked like a chimney. They took out one lung. Now she just sits in her new double-wide, breathing from a tank and watching Netflix."

Jason's adult supervision. I sipped the ale. Roxanne gave me a taut smile, looked to Tiffanee.

"I told Roxanne, I said, 'Hey, I'm so sorry to bother you again.' But I got off the phone and I couldn't just sit there, like, waiting for Jason to show up."

"Did he make more threats from jail?"

"No," Tiffanee said. "The advocate lady said he was a model prisoner."

I'm sure, I thought. Needs to get out to tie up this loose end.

"Has he called?"

"No. That's almost worse."

I locked eyes with Roxanne, who, with her DHHS experience, knew that for somebody like Jason, release conditions weren't worth the paper they were printed on. And even if he didn't cut off the bracelet, he could just call one of the other Patriots, somebody he met in jail. We also knew Tiffanee, the potential rat, wasn't the only likely target. I'd put a round past his head, made him kneel in front of me. People have killed for much less.

We looked to Tiffanee. She raised the glass and drained an inch of wine.

"I just needed to talk it out, you know?"

"It's okay," Roxanne said.

"You can't stay here," I said.

Roxanne nodded.

"It's the second place he'll look," she said. "What about your relatives in Boston?"

"Maybe. I'd have to see. They do hate his guts, which is good. But it's not like we're close."

"Friends?"

"The only one I could ask—Jason knows her, too."

She took another hurried swallow of wine. Roxanne held her glass in front of her. She nodded to me and got up and I followed her to the back door. We stepped out, huddled in the woodshed in the cold.

"What if I took her to the hotel in Portland?" Roxanne said. "The Oaks, with the pool."

Her safe-house for more than one abuse victim when she was at DHHS. I considered it.

"Sophie and Tara will have a good time in the pool," Roxanne said. "But they'd miss their video shoots."

"Mr. Ziggy can work around it. He is God's gift to education, after all. What about you?"

She shrugged. "It's no big deal. Like going back to work. And I don't want her to stay here."

"Rumor is Clair and Louis might be back as soon as next week. That would give us more than enough backup. Clair could handle Jason in his sleep. Might need Louis for the whole battalion of Patriots."

"So we leave, nobody knows where we are except us. I take her phone. We buy some time."

I said I could talk to the ADA in Belfast, make sure they alerted patrol deputies.

"But I was thinking of going back to Clarkston tomorrow."

She looked at me. "Your story?"

I told her about the robbery, Bob at the store getting shot, Zombie getting away again, Sparrow worried he was coming after her.

"God almighty," Roxanne said. "Is there no place that's not messed up?"

"You begin to wonder. But you can't give up."

"I'm not. This isn't exactly a vacation."

"I know. You're going above and beyond," I said.

A pause.

"The story," I said.

"Yeah?"

"The *Times* is passing on it. Someone posted that I was armed when I found Raymond. The legal folks freaked. Mass shootings, public opinion on guns."

She processed that.

"So you're not going back there for the story."

"Not for a story I'll write for them."

"Then for what?"

"Closure," I said.

She looked at me, frowned.

"Usually you have Clair or Louis for the closure part."

"I'll be fine."

"There's at least two of them and one of you."

"I have Blake."

"And there's Jason and his crew."

"He's a dolt. They are little boys pretending to be men."

She turned and moved close, gave me an unexpected hug, a long embrace that felt like a farewell. I thought of Mary, afraid that Clair would survive a war and die in a skirmish. Thinking eventually his luck would run out.

Roxanne eased out of the embrace, looked at me.

"I have a bad feeling."

"Nothing to worry about, baby," I said.

"Oh, but there is, Jack," she said. "This time, there's a lot."

They left like they were heading off on vacation, the girls chattering in an iPad glow in the backseat, Roxanne and Tiffanee cradling coffees in the front.

I went back in the house. Called Clair.

"*Bonjour, mon ami,*" he said.

"How goes it up there?" I said.

"About to pull the trigger. On the operation, I mean."

"Coming home?"

"One way or the other," Clair said.

I hesitated. A stark assessment.

"Just so it isn't in a pine box," I said.

He ignored me.

"Seventeen-thirty. I think we've got everything covered."

"You're sure it's worth it?"

"The alternative is unacceptable. Don't leave a Marine behind. Marta's an extension of him."

In the background, the sound of a clip snapping in.

"Besides," Clair said, "these are very bad people. Feeding her heroin and fentanyl. I look forward to ruining their day."

Rattling and a clunk. A weapon going into a case.

"How's the typing business?" Clair said.

"Been better. *Times* bailed on the story. Got fidgety about their writer carrying."

"Sometimes you need more than a pencil."

"And I misjudged somebody when I should have known better."

"What else?"

I told him. Jason loose, Tara the potential leaker. Roxanne and Sophie gone.

"Stake out your own house," Clair said. "Lights on, fire going. You're in the woods, north side, close to the road. Long gun."

"It's cold out there."

"If it were easy, everybody would be doing it."

I smiled. Put another log in the stove.

"How's Mary doing?" he said.

"Good. A true Marine Corps wife. Not sure what she sees in you, but whatever. She said to tell you that if anything seemed hinky, abort the mission."

"Huh."

"She's got a bad vibe. That you'll survive the war and get taken out by some dirtbag."

"Not my first one," Clair said. "Or yours."

"I know. I'm just telling you."

"Roger that."

Message passed, I closed the stove door. Fastened it shut. The flames licked the new log.

"How do we get into these situations?" I said.

"Sometimes by design. Sometimes dumb luck," Clair said.

"Most people would walk away."

"If everyone walked away, the world would be a pretty sorry place."

"I know, but it would be nice if somebody else stepped up once in a while."

"No, it wouldn't," Clair said. "They'd screw it up."

In the background, the sound of a gun case snapping shut.

"Mission set for Monday, zero-eight-hundred hours."

"Good luck."

"Hoping not to need any, good or otherwise," Clair said.

And he was gone.

I stood in front of the stove for a moment, phone in hand. Then went to the closet and reached up high for the key to the gun locker behind the coats. I unlocked it, took out a box of nine-millimeter rounds from the shelf, reached the twelve-gauge Remington from the rack.

Bringing the stuff to the kitchen table, I slipped the magazine from the Glock and fed in one round to replace the one that had gone past Jason's ear. I kept another loaded magazine out, then slid five shells, double-aught buckshot, into the shotgun.

My phone buzzed. I put the gun down, answered.

"Yeah."

"Jack."

Dunne.

"Yes."

"It's working."

"What?"

"The series. I put out the promo on social and it's taking off. More than nine hundred click-throughs to the site, more than half subscribed. Almost a hundred shares. And that's not even the episode."

"Nice," I said.

"But that's not it."

"What is it then?"

"DM on Instagram."

I waited.

"Somebody said if I didn't pull it back, I could get hurt."

"Okay. You sure you're up for this? I mean, these people—"

"Up for it? Are you kidding? We've hit the jackpot."

"Tell me exactly what they said."

"I'll send you a screenshot."

I waited. She did. @YerMuther69 had written:

—In over your head on this one, @WhoDunneIt, u and ur boyfriend. No joke. Drop it now.

"You see it?" Dunne said.

"Yeah."

"I'm gonna use it for another promo. I mean, this could totally take off for us."

"Or you could end up like St. Apollonius."

"Who's that?"

I told her.

"So he wouldn't back down, either," Dunne said.

"And they cut off his head."

"Hey, this isn't a Roman emperor we're dealing with. It's some local dirtbag."

"Who put a bag over Raymond's head until he suffocated. His face was blue and his eyes were bulging out of his skull. Also, this probably was done to him several times until they left it on. Just so you know."

Dunne didn't reply, and I thought maybe she was getting it, that this was about more than clicks.

Then Dunne said, "Whoa."

"What?"

"Another DM. Instagram."

I waited. "What does it say?"

My phone beeped. I opened the text.

—Yr parents: Tony + Holly Dunne, 24 West St., Topsham, Maine.

—Yr lil sis Maddie Dunne, works @ Punch's Pizza, Westbrook.

—Hot party pix, btw. May have to put her in the van and take her out into the country.

—Think before u post, bitch. Won't be the only one hurt.

"Getting serious," I said.

"How many times have you been threatened over a story?" Dunne said.

"Too many to count."

"You're still here."

"I've had serious backup."

"And most of it's just talk. So don't be a wuss, Jack. We want this guy, right?"

There was a pause.

"Six-hundred sixty-seven new subscribers. Six sixty-eight. Hey, Channel 6 News out of Portland. Holy crap. Daily Beast. McMorrow, we are off and running. And that was just a promo, not even a trailer."

She went quiet. I pictured her flipping through her phone.

"Gotta run," Dunne said. "Talk later."

And she was gone.

I put the phone down, listened to the house. It creaked and cracked in the cold. The woodstove ticked. I picked the phone back up, texted Clair.

"Still on schedule? Confirm when you're coming back. You and Louis."

33

I waited until almost five to text Blake in the morning, figuring nobody slept late on a boat. I was in the truck, on a black stretch of Route 3 in Augusta, when he called back ten minutes later. I told him about Jason being released, then Dunne—the podcast, the threats.

"Didn't I tell you she's poison?" Blake said.

"I guess I chose mine."

"Brass is gonna be pissed. Still pounding the pavement for Zombie, and now this."

"I smoke this guy out, they can cross one homicide off their list, keep chasing their shooter. Store manager still hanging in?"

"On a ventilator. Turns out the slug did miss his heart, but took a big chunk out of his lung and liver, clipped the artery leading to his kidneys. Where are you?"

"On my way to Dunkin'."

"And you want some backup?"

"Not that they can see," I said.

"I can do that. I'm back on at nine. Riding solo. Salley called in sick."

"What's his illness?"

"Bad sushi," Blake said, "aka, a weed cash run."

"What if somebody from the PD sees him?"

"It's Salley. He thinks he can talk his way out of anything. Besides, sometimes I think they're glad to have him out of the way. He's such a pain in the ass when he's around."

A pair of red eyes glimmered at the side of the road. I slowed. A deer bolted across, a flash of bounding shadow, then another and another. I hit the brakes, threaded between them. Wondered when my luck would run out.

"Anyway, this is what I'm thinking," I said, outlining it.

"That's not much of a plan," Blake said. He offered an alternative.

"You sure that's better?" I said.

"In terms of keeping you alive, yeah."

"Thanks."

"I said better, not guaranteed," Blake said. "For that, you'd have to stay home."

"Not an option," I said.

"No," he said.

I rolled into Dunkin' at ten past six, cars huffing exhaust in the drive-through line, a handful of people at the counter. I parked out front, sat with lights on and motor running. I picked up my phone to call Blake, saw a text pop up.

Dunne.

—DOING MORNING RADIO 0700. LONNIE AND LORRAINE. BIG AUDIENCE.

—ALSO, PRESS HERALD HOT ON DOING STORY ON US. I'LL STAY ON MESSAGE.

—CITIZEN MURDER INVESTIGATION WHERE COPS WON'T DO THEIR JOB. AND WE ARE CLOSING IN.

—DUNNE AND MCMORROW TO COLD-BLOODED KILLER: YOU CAN RUN BUT YOU CAN'T HIDE. . . .

—RIDING THE WAVE, JACK!! XO

I held the phone, took a deep breath. We were all in.

I called Blake.

"See me?"

"Yes."

"Then here we go."

I watched the shop for another minute, then got out. Walked quickly inside, got in line. It was tradesmen, a scraggly couple in their seventies buying breakfast, a high school girl with streaks of white-blonde in her black hair. She bought a large iced coffee with four sugars. I got a medium black—needed the high-test—went to the counter in the front window and stood.

People came and went. Nobody I recognized. I checked my phone every minute or so, like I was waiting for a text or a call. Drank coffee, stared out the window at the headlights, the exhaust plumes in the cold. People glanced at me on their way in, a guy alone looking like he'd been stood up for sex or drugs.

After twenty minutes, I tossed the coffee cup in the rubbish bin, walked out. Stopped by my truck and waited.

Held the phone up and talked.

"Moving now," I said.

"Got you," Blake said.

I walked across the lot, started down the street toward the downtown. Phone at my ear, I kept a brisk pace, like I was late for an appointment. Every block I paused, turned, looked like I was trying to pick up a tail. At the edge of the downtown, I crossed the street, passed a bakery, then another street, and stopped again.

Hurried to the bridge over the mill canal. Took another look behind me, then crossed the bridge, glancing down at the blackness below. I had a vision from the distant past, a body floating in a canal like this in a town upriver, arms out, facedown.

I walked in the center of the single-lane alley, through the brick-walled canyon. There was a light ahead, a dim glow. At the corner, I turned left, into the courtyard where Blake and I had parked, broke into a run. I slowed at the rusty ladder, jumped. Fell back. Tried again. Got both hands around the icy metal, reached for the next rung. I climbed until I got a foot up, kept going to the first platform.

Crouched. Stayed still. Glanced quickly at my phone.

A text. Blake.

S OMEONE COMING IN.

I tensed, listened. Heard the scrunch of boots on the ice and gravel. Saw a figure come to the corner of the wall and stop. Look around. He walked toward me, a slow saunter. Stopped again and looked across the courtyard. Came still closer and paused. Turned to glance behind him, then turned back. Took another few steps until he was under me.

He started to look up and was hit by a flashlight beam, someone on foot.

Snow, the kid from the cleaning crew.

"Freeze right there," Blake said. "Hands above your head where I can see 'em."

We stood in the courtyard, bathed in yellow light. It had started to flurry and the flakes fluttered down like moths. Snow was wearing a Yankees baseball cap on backwards and when Blake turned him to frisk him, I could see snow collecting on the brim. Snow wasn't armed.

"Jesus, dude," Snow said to me. "Just wanted to grab you to talk to you and you just kept on going. What are you on, some sorta mission? I didn't know there were freakin' cops. I mean, what the hell? Are you even a real reporter? What, are you undercover?"

"What did you want to talk about?" Blake said.

"You know. His story, dude. I been thinking about it. I mean, I'm out now and I'm, like, victimized by Zombie too, even though I just did time. So now I'm on the side of law and order, like catch this asshole, will you? Before he kills somebody. It's like everybody in prison isn't a criminal, you know what I'm saying? Let's not be stereotyping all the time, right?"

"Where did you see me?" I said.

"The Dunkin'. I was coming in and you were standing by your truck. I'm like, 'Hey, the newspaper dude. I'll tell him what I've been thinking.' "

I looked at Blake. He gave me an almost imperceptible nod.

"I can talk now, seeing as I'm not an inmate. And Mumbo isn't running my life."

"Where is he?" I said.

"I have no fuckin' idea. He's out. I don't know what he's up to. Haven't even seen him. Guy's weird, to be honest. Like he's God, the only one who has the big picture, you know? Like the rest of us are chumps."

He looked at me.

"So do you want to put me in your story or not?"

"Gayle Dupuis," Blake said. "On the street she's Twinsey. You know her?"

Snow shook his head.

"Nope."

"Friend of Mumbo's," I said.

"Didn't think he had friends."

"She's a tweaker," Blake said.

"Hey, who isn't in this shithole."

"Is Mumbo?" I said.

Snow looked to Blake. "You know what he was in for. There's dealers who use, deal to get high. Then there's dealers who wouldn't touch it themselves. For Mumbo, it musta been money."

"Selling guns?" Blake said.

"You can buy an assault rifle here for nine hundred bucks. Turn it around on the street in Mass. for three grand."

"What does Mumbo do with the money?"

"I don't know," Snow said. "Ask those TV ministers with the private jets."

He seemed to be considering saying more. We waited.

"Don't let the religion thing fool you," Snow said. "He's a mean fucker. In jail, almost drowned a guy in a toilet. Just held him there until you woulda thought he was dead. All 'cause the guy said Jesus was just another dude."

I thought of the bag over Raymond's head.

"But he doesn't just go around torturing people, does he?" I said.

"Nah," Snow said. "There's always a situation. It ain't like he's a total psycho."

We stood for a couple of minutes in the courtyard, the red-black brick walls all around us like a prison, Snow smoking a cigarette. Then Blake told Snow he could go, to which Snow replied, "No shit. I ain't done nothin'." And then, to me, "Hey, you had your chance."

We watched him round the corner of the mill, stood for a moment in the courtyard. The pigeons circled and an icicle dripped, heat escaping from the building someplace. The drips froze into a puddle on the pavement around a crushed beer can. Natty Ice.

"Follow the money," I said. "It's from Watergate."

"I know," Blake said. "The statue is worth something."

"What's inside it," I said. "I just saw a story about four pounds of cocaine disguised as a birthday cake."

"Maybe we've got the Blessed Virgin packed full of coke. Five pounds of plaster and fifteen pounds of drugs."

"Mumbo's retirement account," I said.

"And Raymond gave it away," Blake said.

"And wouldn't cough up the name of the next owner," I said. "His chance to join St. Apollonius in Heaven."

"Maybe he had a stash of meth, too, but that was waiting for him. Keeps Twinsey coming back."

Blake's phone pinged and he dug it out of his jacket pocket. Peered at a text.

"What?" I said.

"Salley. He's moving money. Says he has a weird vibe. Wants me to come over, watch his back."

He started walking, out of the courtyard, across the bridge over the black ice water.

I followed, caught up.

The drop was in an industrial park just past the ramp to the turnpike. Metal building, security lights on inside, spotlight on the parking lot. Steel-reinforced door, front right side. A couple of sets of tire tracks showing in the snow the plow didn't scrape off.

Waiting at the edge of the woods for the car to pull in. A big Dodge pickup, right on time. The cop parking, on his phone. Texting, his face gray in the phone-screen light.

Still in the woods, snapped one branch. Another. The cop still texting. Another crack, louder, and he looked up and out. Buzzed the window down, shut off the motor, left the headlights on. Sat for maybe fifteen seconds. Come on, you lazy load. Get out here.

Another crack, running out of sticks. Yes. He eased out. Stood. Flicked a flashlight on, waggled the beam over the edge of the woods, close to the building. Stared into the darkness, then turned around toward the truck. A branch tossed into the woods this time, rattling down into the trees. The cop turned back, slipped his phone out, whispered a text. "Hey, Siri." The words, "Something hinky going on out here. If you got a minute . . ."

Put the phone back in his pocket. Flicked the light on, traced circles in the blackness. Turned toward the door, silhouetted against the lights. Running out of the black woods to the right, into the open. The cop spinning, reaching for his gun, but too late. Bare neck showing as he started to bring the gun around, then the zap and crackle, him staggering. Another zap, his legs buckling. On his knees on the pavement, trying to shout but nothing coming but a weird oscillating moan.

A third time to make sure, the cop falling to his big belly, arms and legs twitching.

Then back to the truck, the case. The passenger seat, nothing. The floor in front of it, nothing.

Slid out and tried the back door, but it was locked. Went to the inside of the front door, started pushing buttons. Locks jammed shut, open. Went to the back door, opened it. Nothing.

Friggin' A. Around to the rear, pulling at the bottom on the tailgate. Scrabbling around down there, banging on the edge of the door. And then hit it, a button under the license plate.

The tailgate groaned open slowly. Ducking under it, the case there. Grabbing it and running for the path through the scrub. Shit, where's the opening? Goddamn it.

A car coming fast down the access road, resisting the urge to turn on the headlamp. Ten feet left, ten feet right, a scramble, then the opening. Jump the fringe of bushes, plunge in, weaving between the sumac and poplar. The cop shouting something, then the sound of tires on the crust of the lot. Then just the snow crunching underfoot, the path showing pale gray in the darkness.

The bag felt heavy. Like money.

34

Low profile: a double-locked steel door, a safe inside. Salley told Blake he never saw anybody when he made the drop, just put the money in the safe, locked the door behind him. Somebody would come and pick it up. He didn't know who.

We pulled in a little after seven, threaded our way past the sheet-metal buildings. They'd hacked the park out of saplings and sumac, and the drop site—truck doors over a loading dock, an office entrance to the right, facing the drive—was nestled in the brush at the far end of the park. Blake, in his truck, didn't have side spots, so he put the windows down, shone a flashlight out at the woods as we approached.

Salley's Tahoe was in front of the door, lights on, motor running.

We swung past the truck. Looked over toward the door. Saw Salley on his hands and knees on the pavement.

Out of the truck, Blake, with his gun out as he ran.

Salley was trying to get up, then fell back to all fours.

"You hurt?" Blake said.

"Stun gun," Salley said.

"When?"

"A minute? Maybe less? I don't know."

"They got the—"

"Messenger bag, full. Like, seventy-five grand."

"You see them?" Blake said.

"Zombie," Salley said. "I hit him, but the fucker zapped me twice. Put me down and kept me there."

He got to his feet slowly, shuffled to his truck, leaned against the driver's door. Blake had his phone in one hand, the gun in the other. When he started to tap a number, Salley said, "No. This one stays internal. Last thing I need."

He closed his eyes, took a breath. "My brain is fried."

He opened his eyes, looked at me.

"What's he—"

"McMorrow was with me when I got your text."

"All off the record," Salley said. "Everything. I'm asking you. Give you any other story you want."

"But what about Zombie?" I said.

"Hell with Zombie," Salley said. "I just need that money back."

"Which way?" Blake said.

Salley nodded in the direction of the truck bays, the brush and woods beyond.

"Heard him running."

We left him by the truck, trotted toward the woods. Put phone flashlights on and coursed up and down at the edge of the pavement.

"Tracks," I said.

They led into the fringe of the woods, a grove of dense blackberries and sumac. One set of tracks, smallish feet. Blake went first, flashlight glow on the snow. He holstered his gun to free up a hand to push branches aside.

The tracks went east, away from the park, toward the turnpike ramp. The footprints were close together, Zombie moving carefully after he was away from the parking lot. Blake followed the tracks while I looked over him, into the brush. After fifty yards, he stopped.

"Two branches."

Zombie had backtracked, started a new path to the right. Then backtracked again, so the paths were identical. We had to choose.

"I'll go left," I said.

He looked at me.

"Not your fight."

"I can't just watch. If he's caught, I want to be there."

Blake didn't object.

"If we hear him, stop and text," he said. "Don't go in alone."

"If he's moving, there'll be crunching."

"He's gonna come out on the other side. Have a car waiting."

We started off, the snow a foot deep, the tracks dark holes smashed through the crust. I stepped in one, felt the snow give at the bottom, my boot going way deeper. That meant Zombie was considerably lighter than me, and I wondered why Sparrow hadn't said he was a small guy, or just very thin. Maybe hard to tell, under a parka.

I kept walking, stopping every ten steps to listen. I could hear Blake tromping to my right, see his flashlight glow through the bushes and saplings. The track continued, fifty yards, a hundred, a hundred and fifty. No time to backtrack that far, which meant this was the right path.

I stopped. Listened. Heard a blue jay, trucks on the turnpike. Looked into the brush ahead of me. And saw something move.

A black shape fifty yards in, shifting in and out of sight. I slipped my phone out, saw the figure disappear. Put the phone back and broke into a loping, lurching trot.

And then he was in sight again, closer, slowed by a tangle of vines and scrub. I tried to be quiet, staying in the softer snow off the track. Lost sight of him again.

Took my gun out. Looked down to see the tracks bending to the left. I followed, moving in a semicircle now. Was he doubling back? Trying to flank me? Get back to the parking lot?

I peered into the brush. I couldn't see him, couldn't hear him. Looked to my left, turned and peered back on the track behind him. Snow, brush, trees. I took my phone out, started to call Blake, heard a crunch behind me, whirled around, gun up.

Sparrow.

The satchel was over her shoulder. The zombie mask was in her right hand. The stun gun was in her left.

"Hey, Jack," she said.

35

"These things really work," Sparrow said, holding up the black box, two prongs showing. "I was kinda worried. I mean, it's not like you can practice."

I lowered my gun, slowly.

She smiled. I stepped closer, the gun at my side. There was a red patch on her forehead, just under where Zombie, the other one, had hit her.

"The check-cashing place, I had an Airsoft. Way too stressful, him with a real gun."

"Just the two," I said.

"No stores," Sparrow said. "Small money, and I'd feel like a traitor."

"Why Salley?"

"Check-cashing place only had, like, three thousand. Didn't get me to the goal."

"I guess usurers don't always make bank," I said.

She shrugged. "He ripped off Mo one time. I told Raymond. Was thinking of them when I said it."

"I get it. Big score this time?"

"Feels like it."

"How will you explain it to Riff?"

She shrugged. "I'll just tell him GoFundMe took off. He never looks at the computer."

A pause, the two of us looking at each other.

"You know Blake is out here, too."

She took a long breath.

"I figured when I saw you."

"He thinks he's chasing the real Zombie. He could shoot you by accident."

Another pause, the two of us figuring this out on the fly.

"It'll be a tough conversation."

"Didn't think I'd have to have it," Sparrow said. "I figured Jerkface there would be on his own."

"He noticed something moving. Texted for backup."

"Right. Smarter than he looks. He's a real asshole, you know. Cheats on his wife. Cheats on the women he's cheating with. I hate liars, and he's a lying sack of shit."

"I have to call Blake," I said.

She mustered a resigned smile.

"Go for it, McMorrow. Let's rip this Band-Aid right off."

I did, told Blake I was with Zombie, everything was okay.

He said he'd be right there, and I could hear him crashing through the snow before the call ended. And then he was in sight, running hard, staying low, gun out.

I smiled and waved as he approached, and he slowed as he closed, looked to the left.

His mouth fell open as he tried to speak. And then he just stared.

"Zombie Two," I said.

"Hey, Brandon," Sparrow said.

He didn't reply.

"Had to go for the big money," Sparrow said.

"Almost pulled it off," I said.

Sparrow looked at Blake, said, "Still might, right?"

We stood there in the snow, time standing still. The light was coming up, blue jays were still calling against the backdrop of the turnpike traffic hum.

Blake shifted on his feet, crunched through the snow. Sparrow still was holding the mask and the stun gun.

"How were you going to get out of here?" Blake said.

"Under the overpass, over to Porto Street, walk on the street the rest of the way. I picked up an hour at the store, don't want to be late."

"Have a good excuse," I said.

"Had to hold up a weed cash run?" she said.

"You didn't have to," Blake said.

Sparrow smiled, shrugged. "But I really did. Once I knew the money was there, how could I not take it? I mean, this started coming together before us, Brandon. I know we've got a good thing. Really good. Like, maybe I'm falling in love with you. But my dad's dying, you know? What kind of person would I be if I just let that happen?"

I stood there listening, my mind racing to the implications. Arrest her? But for what, if Salley wouldn't file a complaint? Let her go, say we found the satchel but not Zombie. Return the money to Salley. Case closed. Blake covers up a robbery, sort of. He violates his professional code of ethics, personal sense of right and wrong. Not small things. But would he trade that for Sparrow's future and maybe Riff's life?

I slipped my gun into my waistband. Shuffled my boots in the snow.

They looked at me like they were surprised I was still there, then back at each other.

Sparrow shifted the bag of cash on her shoulder. Blake looked at the satchel for a ten-count, then back at Sparrow. I watched her, too, the arresting dark eyes, the bruise on her forehead. She'd taken the bandage off, all the piercings, too. She looked younger without her ornaments.

Her gaze was fixed on Blake. No give, no apology, no regrets. In some ways, they were the same, just playing the game by different rules.

He turned to me, avoided Sparrow's gaze, said, "Let's go."

Salley was leaning against his truck when we came out of the brush and crossed the lot.

Me and Blake.

Salley hoisted himself up, said, "Don't fucking tell me you lost him."

"Came out on the other side, onto the street," Blake said. "Must have had a car parked."

"Goddamn it," Salley said. "Let's go after him."

"He'll be long gone," I said.

"And what do you have to go by?" Blake said. "I don't think he'll still be wearing the mask."

"That little bastard," Salley said. "I'll cut his balls off. His fingers, one by one. He'll give the money back."

"Salley," Blake said. "You got nothin'. Can't bring in the department. No real description anyway."

"I'll track the money," Salley said. "Hard to keep sixty grand a secret in this town. He goes to Vegas, invites all his friends to the party—I'll hear about it. He'll wish he was never born."

"What if they catch him?" I said. "Robbing another store. He spills his guts for a plea deal. Says, 'Oh, yeah. I did the weed courier, too. The cop.' "

Salley looked at me, scowled. "Not if I find him first."

It was all bluster and we could see him deflate, falling back against the truck.

"Shit," he said, and then, "Hey, the company, it's their fault. They had the leak. I didn't tell anybody I was doing a side job, just you, Blake. And this has to be somebody who knew Zombie. Or a copycat."

He smiled.

"That's it. An inside job. Anybody can buy a mask, a Taser. Amazon, at your house the next day. They knew when I was gonna leave, how much I was carrying. Friggin' set me up. I coulda been killed. Those fuckers, they owe me big-time. My head is, like, totally fogged, could be permanent. Disability. They don't settle, they got a lawsuit like they've never seen before."

He turned, opened the door to the pick-up. Got in and sat down heavily in the driver's seat. He had his phone out, tapped, and then started talking. He looked at us, pointed at the road to the exit. Mouthed the word, "Go."

36

We drove in silence, out of the park, under the turnpike and toward the downtown. It had begun to snow, heavy wet flakes falling leadenly from the gray sky, and bareheaded people with snow in their hair walking along the plowed sidewalk. Among them was Sparrow, striding along a quarter-mile past the overpass. The satchel was gone, replaced by a grocery bag with flowers printed on it. As we passed, she stopped and leaned down over a dirty snowbank, picked up an empty can.

Twisted Tea. She shook it out, dropped it in the bag.

"Seventy-five grand and change," I said.

Blake kept going, silent until he pulled into the Dunkin' lot. He parked next to my truck, shut off the motor. We sat staring at the windshield as the snowflakes landed and ran down the warm windshield like tears. Blake took a long, deep breath.

"Supposed to get six inches," he said. "Good if the weed people decide to check Salley's story."

"May be busy hunting for leakers."

"I'm the leak. I was griping about how Salley was working another cash run, said he liked that he never saw anybody at the place, just put the money in a safe and left."

"You told her where it was?"

"Close enough."

A long pause, and then he punched the steering wheel.

"Goddamn it."

"So you feel betrayed."

"Well, yeah. Mostly I feel like the game's changed and I'm playing by the old rules."

"The world's changed, for you and me both," I said. "The *Times* spiked my story because I was carrying a gun. My daughter dances in short-shorts on TikTok. She's twelve."

"I've got everything arranged: good guys and bad guys. Nothing in between."

"And you took a job to enforce the rules."

"Somebody has to do it. At least I used to think so."

"You still do," I said. "There's got to be right and wrong. Problem is, sometimes it's not so black-and-white."

"Like someone stealing pot money to save their father's life. Which is still robbery."

The quandary hung in the air.

"Yes. Exactly like that," I said.

We sat. The snowflakes had started to pile up at the bottom of the windshield.

"She's a good daughter," Blake said. "Sparrow, I mean."

"She is."

"Maybe not the best girlfriend for a cop."

I considered it, said, "No. But maybe the best girlfriend for a good person, somebody who tries to do the right thing."

"I'm a terrible liar," Blake said.

"Maybe this time you don't have to try. Some things are better left unsaid."

"A lie of omission?"

"I guess that's the gray part," I said.

We sat. He turned the wipers on for a few seconds, smeared the melting snow across the glass. We could see the Dunkin' entrance, people standing in line, all shapes and sizes.

"Sparrow's trying to do the right thing," I said.

"The stun gun."

"Right."

"And it's not like the weed store is going to need the money," he said.

"Make it back in a week."

The snow was coming down faster, covering the windshield again, closing us in. Two guys stuck with a dilemma.

"I once let a guy take a murder rap to save the real killer," I said.

"Why?"

"He was a dirtbag, an abuser who would have graduated to murderer eventually. She was a sweet little kid and it was an accident. Suffocated her mother with a plastic bag while she was passed out. The mom was vomiting. The girl thought she was helping."

"So you saddle her with that or let the bad guy take the rap."

"No-brainer. But I'd never done that before."

"You've lived with it," Blake said.

"Yeah," I said. "What about the truth?"

"Sometimes you just have to suck it up. Carry the baggage yourself." He took another deep breath. Frowned.

"Catch one robber, let another one go?"

"It's going to be complicated," I said.

"Very," Blake said.

A half-hour later the QuikStop was busy, cars at the pumps, people coming out with coffee, breakfast pizza in wedge-shaped boxes. I parked out front, got out, and went inside, where two women—new clerks?—were staring into a line of customers that went all the way to the coolers.

I walked over, said, "Sparrow here?"

"Gone," the closest clerk said, not looking up, her tattooed hand waving at the scanner.

"Walked?"

"Called an Uber. Her dad's wicked sick."

I walked back to the truck, wondering what passed for wicked sick in Riff's life. A coma?

It was a ten-minute drive. Longer because the snow was changing to rain, which meant slush in the road, a few drivers crawling. When I pulled up there were tire tracks in the driveway next to the house where a car—the Uber?—had pulled in and backed out.

I parked out front, saw multiple footprints headed up the steps. Paramedics? A doc who made house calls? I leaned down, took the Glock out from under the seat, and tucked it into the back of my waistband.

Got out and walked up to the house and pulled the storm door open. Knocked. Waited. There was music playing inside—Talking Heads, "Burning Down the House." Cheering Riff up? Distracting him from pain?

I knocked again, louder.

Nothing.

Then footsteps, slow and deliberate.

The door creaked open.

Sparrow, her face ashen. Had he died?

"Hey," I said. "They said at the store your dad was sick."

She looked at me, didn't reply for a beat, then said, "Come on in."

It was an odd monotone. Had they taken Riff away? A crash for Sparrow after the robbery?

I followed her down the hallway to the kitchen, was hit by an odd smell—cigarettes, body odor, fruity gum. Sparrow walked to the table and turned, David Byrne singing. The door slammed shut behind me.

"Hands out and up. Or I'll cut your throat."

A man's voice. A second to ID him.

Mumbo.

"Sorry, Jack," Sparrow said.

A hand clenched my hair. A cold knife blade pressed across the front of my neck. I raised my arms.

"Hands on top of your head. Spread your legs."

I clasped my hands on top of my head. From my right, someone started patting me down. Small hands. I glanced down, saw Twinsey crouched behind me, felt her hands running up the inside of my thigh. She moved in front of me, yanked the zipper of my parka down with a dirty fist. Black nails. Scrawled initials and RIP, like something etched with a ballpoint pen. The rosary swinging against her washboard chest.

She took the gun. Mumbo moved up and she handed it to him. He took it in his left hand, a butcher knife in his right.

"Boots," he said. "I don't trust this one."

Twinsey crouched, checked for knives, another gun. Stood up again. Shook her head.

Mumbo tucked the knife in his belt, pulled the slide back on the Glock, the round slipping into the chamber. Pointed the gun at me.

"Sit him down," he said.

Twinsey got behind me, shoved me toward the one empty chair. I turned and sat, looked at the two of them.

"Just because people talk religion," I said.

"Enough," Mumbo said.

He reached into the pocket of his jacket and took out a roll of duct tape. Said to Twinsey, "Him first." She ripped off a length of tape, pulled my right arm down, taped my wrist to the arm of the chair. Did the same with my right ankle, then did the left side.

"He says jump, you say how high?" I said.

"I said enough," Mumbo said.

"When's your next bowl, Twinsey?" I said.

Mumbo took two steps, raked my face with the barrel of my gun. I felt blood run down my forehead.

"Got a mean streak for a man of God," I said.

"Praise be to the Lord, my rock, who trains my hands for war, my fingers for battle."

I thought of the Catholic militants at Jason's trained ground.

"You're one of those modern-day crusaders," I said.

"Jesus rode a white horse, his robe spattered in blood," Mumbo said.

"What about turning the other cheek?"

"If you don't fight for your faith, it will be taken from you. As it has been for thousands of Christian warriors. We're saving thousands more from the fires of Hell."

"Was killing Raymond fighting for your faith?"

"Raymond was not of the true faith. He turned against us."

"Decided gun runners weren't true Christians?" I said.

"This is about more than nostalgia," Mumbo said.

I looked over at Sparrow, saw that she'd closed her eyes.

Twinsey taped her up next, then stood, looked to Mumbo.

"Their mouths?" she said.

"Not yet. Maybe not at all. Answer the question, my good people, and we leave. Nobody hurt."

Blood dripped off my jawbone.

"Like you left Raymond?" I said.

He moved fast, hit me with the gun again. My mouth this time, my lip split.

"This is a one-way conversation," Mumbo said. "Where's the statue?"

"You ever see *The Maltese Falcon*?" I said. "I'm having déjà vu."

He moved in again, this time a punch in the side of the head. Pain, beginning in my ear. I reoriented.

"I'd help you if I could. But I don't know. Never saw it, that I'm aware. All I know is it went from the storage unit to Germaine to Raymond, and he didn't want it so he traded it away or something. That's it."

Blood was running into my mouth. It hurt to talk.

"Okay," Mumbo said. "That's a start. Let's keep the conversation going."

He nodded to Twinsey and she ripped a piece of tape off, moved in and wrapped it around Sparrow's head, covering her eyes. The next one covered her mouth.

"I call this the process of elimination," Mumbo said. "First we see if you're forgetting anything. True believers withstood all earthly pain, but I don't think you will."

He moved closer to Sparrow, slipped a lighter from his pocket. It was blue. He flicked it and the flame wavered. Sparrow clenched her hands on the chair.

"That's all I know," I said. "I'd give you the damn thing. What do I care? What does she care?"

Mumbo held the lighter close to Sparrow's temple, moved the flame to a blue lock of hair. It hissed and melted. Sparrow screamed under the tape.

"Don't," I said. "We don't know where it is. We'd have to make it up."

He moved the lighter again, behind her ear. Hair sizzled, turned to ash. The room filled with an acrid odor.

"When we run out of hair, we do the ears," Mumbo said. "Where is it?"

Sparrow was shaking her head.

The lighter moved again and Sparrow jerked away, crying out under the tape.

"A little skin that time," Mumbo said. "Thousands of the true faithful have gladly died at the stake."

"This is getting you nowhere," I said. "We can't tell you what we don't know."

Another wave of the lighter, Sparrow gritting her teeth.

"You tell me, then," Mumbo said. "Or we make a martyr of you." He held the lighter close.

She nodded frantically, tears streaming down her cheeks. Mumbo ripped the tape off, leaned close.

"Talk."

"Raymond said the statue wasn't special enough for him. Kind of run-of-the-mill. But he was plugged into this network of church-stuff collectors. He said he gave it away. He didn't say who he gave it to. Wouldn't have meant anything to me anyway."

Mumbo moved the lighter again. Sparrow clenched her jaw.

"That's not what Raymond told me," Mumbo said. "He goes, 'It's gone. It flew away.' Like that was funny, him keeping the statue just out of reach. Then I hear he has a friend with a bird name. You think I'm stupid?"

"No," I said. "Twisted but not stupid."

"And then he just smiles and dies. Gotta say, he was weird, but he was kind of a stand-up guy."

He leaned close to Sparrow, grabbed the tape at the nape of her neck and ripped it off, hair coming with it. Then the tape on the eyes, Sparrow grimacing, swaths of red across her face.

Mumbo looked to Twinsey, standing behind Sparrow.

"Drag her," he said, "Polycarp of Smyrna was burned at the stake but he didn't die, so they stabbed him. I think it is time for a reenactment."

He moved to my chair, took it by the back, and pulled me across the floor, down the hall and into Riff's room. Riff was in his bed, tape across the sheet at his neck and ankles, him huddled helplessly under the covers. He looked small, like a withered child. He looked at Sparrow as Twinsey hauled her in, said, "Leave her alone."

Mumbo had the knife out.

"Okay," he said, turning to both of us. "Last chance before I send this sinner to his judgment."

He leaned over Riff, the knife against his neck. Droplets of blood along the blade.

"Where's the Jesus?"

"Right outside of Philadelphia," I said. "There's a big warehouse there, like a clearinghouse for Catholic stuff from shut-down churches. Raymond gave it to them for credit. You know, that he could apply when he bought something from them. They did a lot of business with him."

"He packed it up in a crate," Sparrow said. "I was with him."

Mumbo turned away from Riff, kept the knife off his throat.

"Why didn't you say that? Why didn't he say that?"

Sparrow hesitated, thinking, said, "Raymond said it was our secret. He said if somebody came looking for it, don't tell them. He said he could feel this statue had evil in it. He said it was the Devil's work."

"Raymond believed all of that," I said. "To him, you coming to kill him, you were the Devil. He died defending his faith, like St. Apollonius."

Mumbo looked at me. Then at Sparrow.

Twinsey said, "I think they're telling the truth now."

"Shut up," Mumbo said. He leaned down over Riff. "Let's find out. *Deus vult*—"

There was a hammering at the front door. We all turned, missed the moment when Riff thrust his hand up from under the sheet, a knife blade disappearing into Mumbo's chest.

A grunt from Riff, another from Mumbo. I turned back. Saw the knife moving in and out, over and over, like a needle on sewing machine, the white sheets turning red. Mumbo tried to back away but couldn't, gasped once, collapsed across Riff's chest.

A crash from the front of the house.

In an instant, Blake was coming through the door of the bedroom, crouched, gun drawn.

Twinsey threw up her hands, said, "He made me do it. He said he'd kill me. Like he killed Church Man."

Blake slammed her on the floor, facedown and still talking, then moved to the bed. Took the knife from Mumbo's hand and tossed it. Yanked him off of Riff and rolled him onto the floor. Mumbo lay there, gurgling, eyes open, the knife still in his chest. And then the gurgling stopped.

Riff looked over at us, Mumbo's blood thick on his hands, his arms, his chest. Blake pulled the tape off and Riff took short, wheezing breaths. He looked at us, rasped, "Nobody hurts . . . my little Bird. . . . Nobody."

37

The house was a crime scene, yellow tape and a cruiser parked outside, police, crime-scene techs, news crews everywhere, like it was a movie set.

I stood and leaned against a cruiser, told not to leave until I'd been interviewed. After an hour, Sanitas and Jolie came to get me. We sat in the mobile command center, like there was anything left to take command of.

"Coffee?" Jolie said.

"Sure," I said. Even without a story, a reporter doesn't turn it down.

They were on one side of the little table, me on the other, like we were in a Winnebago at our favorite campground. There was a whiteboard with assignments on it. They'd drawn the short straw and had gotten me.

Jolie positioned the recorder, poised with pen on legal pad. Sanitas sat with his own pen and paper, but the paper was blank, and I figured it would stay that way. Jolie reached for the recorder, hit the button.

"I told you so," I said.

For a moment, then two, they said nothing.

The DA put Riff and Sparrow up at the Comfort Inn by the interstate, somebody passing a hat and collecting enough cash for three nights and a cleaning service—not Mumbo's. Riff wanted to come home, though, and that was where I met them, two days after Mumbo was killed. The cleaners had been through and the place felt like death but smelled like disinfectant. Blake and I leaned against the counter. Riff and Sparrow sat at the kitchen table. She was quiet. He was back in form.

"Some people are just bad to the bone," Riff was saying, hand on his coffee mug. "Like the blues song. I ever tell you about opening for George Thorogood in Jersey? That was the encore. He has me step in, me on the Tele playing off his slide. We were sharp as a freakin' knife that night."

No irony.

"So you didn't go for the counseling?" Blake said.

"Hell, no," Riff said. "What do I need counseling for? Stepping on that cockroach? Dumb shit shoulda known I wouldn't lie there every night, no way to protect myself. In this town? Screw that. Figured I was sick and helpless. Dude figured wrong."

"Yes, he did," I said.

"I had to wait until he got close enough," Riff said. "Didn't want to just poke the bear. It's like recording live, man. Only one take on that number."

We sipped the coffee, listened. Riff was telling this story like all of his others. He was at the center. Rocking CBGB. Killing the guy who attacked his daughter.

"Forgot all about that photo they used on the news," he said. "Battery Park show. The Clash headlined but they were late and the other opener didn't show up. We played for, like, three hours without stopping. By the end we're doing Bo Diddley covers. Kids there didn't know him from—"

He turned to me.

"Hey, Jack. How's my numbers on TikTok?"

"Through the roof," I said. "Hashtag, punkrockersavesdaughter."

Riff smiled. "Maybe I should put a band together, ride this freakin' hero train. I got some ideas, new stuff I been—"

There was a knock on the front door. Sparrow went to answer it, Riff still talking. She came back lugging a heavy cardboard box, set it on the kitchen floor. It was addressed to her. The return address was the same. All of it was in a precise cursive, like you'd learn in a very strict Catholic grade school.

"Raymond," Sparrow said.

"But you saw him putting it in a crate," Riff said.

"I made that up," she said.

She turned to the counter but Blake already had a knife out. He handed it to her and she sliced through the brown packing tape, slowly and carefully, like she was opening an ancient tomb.

Flipping the flaps up, she peered in, then reached down. Pulled out layers of bubble wrap, dropping them to the floor. Then she leaned down, lifted a statue out of the box, put it on the table, and began cutting away the plastic swaddling.

Mary emerged, like a butterfly from a cocoon. Sparrow fell back and we all stared like the Wise Men around the manger.

She was wearing a hood that draped over her shoulders, a light blue robe over a white gown. The gown had a gold belt, and there was a gold hem at the bottom. She looked sweet and shy, a lock of blonde hair poking out like Princess Diana. There was a chip on her cheek, the underlayment pink like raw flesh. Her hands were turned palms forward and she was barefoot, standing on a snake.

The snake looked dead, its forked tongue hanging limp. Satan vanquished.

Sparrow took Mary by the shoulders and laid her on her back. The base of the statue was rough cement-colored plaster. Sparrow picked at it with the knife, then turned the knife in her fist and hammered. The plaster came off in chunks. After a few blows, the knife broke through and Sparrow fished out a bundle of bills.

"Cash money, homie," Riff said.

"Mumbo's cash," I said.

Sparrow began pulling bundles out of the statue, piling them on the table. She went to the kitchen drawer and pulled out a fork with a long wooden handle, like you'd use on a barbecue. She stuck it in and more bundles fell out.

"Somebody up there likes us, Bird," Riff said.

There were at least twenty bundles, the outside bills all hundreds. Sparrow didn't count it, leaving us looking at a pile of money.

"The meds, Riff," she said. "That had to be what Raymond was thinking. He'd know what a hollow Mary statue would feel like. He knew there was something inside, and when they came after it, he decided he wasn't going to give it up."

I pictured the bag over Raymond's head. Mumbo letting him suffocate. A slow death.

Sparrow's eyes filled and she looked at me and Blake. "He didn't have to die. I was finding the money."

And now she had it, times two. Another seventy-five grand sitting under her bed or somewhere. Her secret. All she had to do was turn it into different drugs—Riff's.

"Small deposits, spread out," I said, "multiple accounts. Use the deposits to get credit cards. Put the meds on the cards, pay the minimum, every three months throw in a few hundred more. Use cash for all of your other expenses—rent, food. Anyone asks, say you don't believe in banks."

They looked at me.

"I wrote about it," I said. "Somebody who found money in a wall."

We looked at the pile of bills again, except for Blake. He leaned in, picked up his knife, folded the blade shut, put it in the pocket of his jeans. He nodded to Riff, moved to Sparrow. Leaned forward and kissed her, like he was going on a long trip.

"When will I—" Sparrow said, but Blake was out of the kitchen, moving down the hallway. We heard the door shudder open, then close.

"I should go, too," I said. "Have to get home."

I put my mug on the counter, zipped my jacket. Riff reached for his coffee. Sparrow gave her eyes a quick wipe, set the statue upright. Mary stood there with her arms out like she was giving a blessing to the whole bloody, tangled mess.

38

The robbery thing was getting old, like one of those Netflix series that went on too long.

The surveillance video going viral was cool, but it wasn't like it had gotten him a girlfriend.

Until now.

There was something about the Blade Runner chick, the way she looked at him like she could see right through the mask. Then the bell went off. She had a thing for him, most def, trying to keep him there, Mr. Zombie and all that. Pretending she thought he was a jerk, but not really. That's how some babes played hard to get. Say one thing, mean the opposite. No means yes. You got rough with them and they went crazy. Happened all the time in the videos. Maybe they'd make one. He'd have to cut a mouth hole in the mask so he could kiss her

Follow her home from work, knock on the door. She'd be out of her uniform, leggings and a thong, maybe one of those shirts with only one shoulder. Those were hot. Probably a tat or two under there, with all those piercings. Back of her waist, maybe. Or her shoulder blade. Maybe a dragon. Or maybe a snake. Wouldn't it be cool if there was a Zombie, her secret crush.

She'd be surprised, of course, but he'd step inside, close the door, grab her and plant a juicy one on her mouth. Feel her pretend not to like it but then she'd give up. Just melt.

She'd say, "I didn't know Zombie delivered." Her knowing
what that meant, little flirt that she was. He'd say, "Baby,
hang on. Zombie's gonna take you for a ride."

A good feeling to have a new plan. He'd have to move
on those other guys who were sniffing around, the cop giving
her rides home. The other guy, the reporter, the two of
them having heart-to-hearts. That guy was old, no match
for Zombie. Cop could be tougher, but face it, he was no
superhero. Look what happened to the last guy who tried to
take on Zombie. One shot, went down like a bag of rocks.

I called Roxanne at the hotel, heard the girls in the background.
Tiffanee had gone to the spa.

"How's the story?" Roxanne said.

Staying away from news.

"Pretty much finished," I said. "I'll tell you more. How's Sophie?"

"Good. Kind of mothery with Tara. Lots of pool time. Pizza and a
movie. Rehearsing their scenes for school. They wanted to do a poolside
TikTok. I said no."

"Tiffanee?"

"Hanging in. She's tougher than she seems."

"And you?"

"Like riding a bicycle," Roxanne said.

"When are you coming home? You need to extract yourself."

"Tomorrow," Roxanne said. "I love you."

"Likewise. A lot."

I sat on the couch, in the dark with the phone and the gun. Reality
check: One psycho dead, another with an ankle bracelet and a heart
condition. Progress.

The wind rattled the windows, the fire crackled in the stove. The
wet snow of the afternoon was now frozen and crunchy, a natural alarm
system. Clouds had been scattering and the moon slipped into the open,

turning the crust a pale blue. I sipped an ale, felt my body relax. Plenty of time to regroup for the next round.

I picked up the phone. Texted Roxanne.

CAN YOU TALK?
—YES, came the reply.
I hit the button. Waited.
"Hey."
Her voice was soft, silky.
"I just needed to hear you again," I said.
"Same here."
"Soon."
"Very."
"The madness is winding down," I said.
"And we're winding up."
"Can't wait."
"Tomorrow you won't have to," Roxanne said.
We rang off. I smiled. Sipped. It had been this way for all those years. No matter what the chaos, the reunion—a melding of mouths and bodies and spirit—eclipsed it.

I got up, put another log in. Poked the fire. And my phone buzzed. Dunne.

—YOU'RE GHOSTING ME JACK. DON'T DO THIS. NOT NOW.
A pause, the three dots wavering.
—WE'VE GOT THE BIG CLIMAX. THOUSANDS OF LISTENERS PRIMED AND READY.
—AND IT'S THE FREAKIN' DYING PUNK ROCKER WHO OFFS THE MURDERER!! AND YOU WERE THERE!!
—WE ABSOLUTELY, POSITIVELY HAVE TO TELL THIS STORY!!!!

I hesitated. Tapped a reply.

TIED UP AT THE MOMENT, BUT WILL BE IN TOUCH.

I put the phone down again, picked up my notebook from the table, turned it to the first page. Notes from my interview with Sparrow when I hadn't known her at all.

> —*standing behind the counter, unpacking tins of Skoal*
> —*looked up, right there, gun pointed at her face*
> —*said, Give me all the fucking money or I swear to*
> *God I'll kill you*

I tore the page out of the notebook, crumpled it up. Got up and went to the stove, opened the door and tossed it in. Watched as the paper blackened, then burst into flame. The world would never know the story of Sparrow and Riff, Raymond and Germaine, Mumbo and Twinsey. Dunne could chase her click-throughs. Maybe I could track down Mumbo's fellow crusaders, but the reporter who'd spent his life telling stories was keeping this one to himself.

I sat back down. Sipped. The house creaked and the woodstove ticked. I replayed it in my head, Sparrow and her piles of money, my collusion and Blake's. No black-and-white here, but maybe there never was. I picked up the Glock from the table, eyed it, put it down. Saved my life a few times—and ended my career. Live by the gun, die by the—

A crash, breaking glass.

Back of the house.

I grabbed the gun and ran through. Flames on the other side of the door to the deck, smell of gasoline. Ran back to the kitchen, grabbed a fire extinguisher, started to loop around through the shed.

Out the side door, the realization I was being flushed out. Too late.

I dove sideways as the shotgun clapped. On my knees, I raised the Glock and fired at the muzzle flash. Felt the second shot hit, white-hot on my chest, my neck.

Went down on the snow, my gun lost in the darkness. No pain, but I could feel something hot and liquid spreading out across my shirt.

Blood.

Lay on my side, put a hand over my neck. Blood trickled through my fingers, flowed down the top of my left wrist and hand.

I got up onto my knees, heard footsteps in the woods.

Walking not running.

Coming closer.

I felt for my gun in the snow.

To be continued . . .

ABOUT THE AUTHOR

Gerry Boyle is the author of a dozen mystery novels, including the acclaimed Jack McMorrow series and the Brandon Blake series. A former newspaper reporter and columnist, Boyle lives with his wife, Mary, in a historic home in a small village on a lake. He also is working with his daughter, Emily Westbrooks, on a crime series set in her hometown, Dublin, Ireland. Whether it is Maine or Ireland, Boyle remains true to his pledge to send his characters only to places where he has gone before.

ACKNOWLEDGMENTS

Many people helped shape *Robbed Blind*, including crime novelist Bruce Coffin, who generously put his detective hat back on for our conversations about robbery investigations; Dr. Diane Brandt, who advised on Riff's diagnosis and prognosis; Mike at Used Church Items, an extraordinary business that Raymond would have loved; and podcast producer Abakar Adan, who patiently guided me through the metrics of his profession. Apologies to all of the aforementioned experts for the considerable liberties I've taken for the sake of the story.

As always, I'm grateful to my editor, Genevieve Morgan, who saw the forest in *Robbed Blind* when I was seeing only trees, and offered wise and creative counsel. Also (according to order of edits), a shout-out to copy editor Melissa Hayes, who put *Robbed Blind* through her wringer, which is a very good thing.

Lastly, thanks to my friend Pete, who, throughout the writing of *Robbed Blind*, served as a reminder to "keep it real, dude." Rest in peace, bro.